D1250481

THE
INVITATION

Dear Stella,

Thank you for partnering with Harvest Home and Our Fathers Farm in 2012! Your prayers and financial gifts have made a tremendous impact as we continue to build God's Dream together! We pray the Lord will richly bless all that you put your hands to in 2013!

Love ♡ in Christ,

Danny + Rhonda
and Team

THE
INVITATION

Rhonda Calhoun

HEART
PUBLISHING
Holden, Missouri

The Invitation
Copyright © 2011 by Rhonda Calhoun
All rights reserved.
This book or parts thereof may not be reproduced in any form, except
for brief quotations in reviews,
without written permission from the publisher.

Requests for information should be addressed to:
info@harvesthome.org

Cover design by Carrol Schwabauer and
copyright © 2011 Heart Publishing. All rights reserved.

All scripture quotations, unless otherwise indicated, are taken from the New
American Standard Bible.
Copyright © 1960, 1962, 1963, 1971, 1972, 1973, 1975, 1977, by the
Lockman Foundation.
Used by permission. (www.Lockman.org)

This book is a work of fiction. Names, characters, places, and incidents are
fictitious and a product of the author's consecrated imagination. Any
resemblance to actual people or events are entirely coincidental.

Printed in the United States of America

ISBN # 978-0-9817-656-2-4

Dedication

This book is dedicated to the One
who gave His life so that He could save mine.
You are the One and only Life-Giver.

Thank You for seeking me out.
Thank You for the invitation to be Your beloved!
I am and always will be eternally grateful.

Life-Giver, all that I am is Yours.
All that I ever will be is because of You.
You are everything that I want to be.

A Special Thank You

There are so many people who had a part to play in the completion of this book – my wonderful husband of 35 years; my beautiful daughters, Misty, Dana, Shea, Alicia; and some of the best friends this world has to offer, Bev, Pamela, Barb, Carrol, Denise, Connie and Kristi. You encouraged me when I wanted to quit and challenged me when I needed it.
Thank you for your honesty and loving support.

A very special thank you to Susan Simon for the countless hours you spent reading and re-reading the manuscript.
Your eye is sharp and your heart is beautiful. This book would not be what it is without your amazing insights and wonderful expertise.
Your labor of love is so greatly appreciated.

CHAPTER ONE

In a time when kings ruled with iron fists and peasants prayed to stay alive, three orphan sisters huddled together beneath tattered blankets. Snow, fine as dust, blew through the many cracks of their dilapidated shelter as the howling wind drowned out the sound of their chattering teeth.

Sixteen-year-old Hadassah buried her face, trying to escape not only the bone-chilling cold but also the painful memories of when her life was turned upside-down.

No! she screamed inside, *I won't remember!* But her willpower was not strong enough to stop the memories always lurking on the fringes of her mind. Hadassah bit the back of her hand, but her papa's face only grew more vivid. She saw herself standing beside her parents' sweat-soaked bed. Six-year-old Hadassah could not understand what was happening. Her parents had been sick for days with "the fever". Her world was falling apart, and no one was strong enough to stop it.

Martha, her ten-year-old sister, sat in a nearby corner mindlessly staring at the wall. Eight-year-old Rebekah had taken up residence between her parents days before.

Rocking back and forth, Hadassah prayed fervently. Tears flowed unhindered down her face as she squeezed her papa's hand. He tried to respond but did not have the strength. Turning his face toward her, he tried to smile but failed at that as well. Beads of sweat covered his forehead running down his face and neck. He shivered uncontrollably. Gathering what little strength he had, he whispered, "Papa loves . . . you . . . all."

"I love you, too," Hadassah said, looking into his kind but pain-filled eyes. His eyelids fluttered for just a moment and then, ever so quietly, her papa left for a better world.

A thousand thoughts flooded her mind as she fought to take a breath. Burying her face against her papa's bony chest, she clung to the arm that had held her close every day of her life. "Papa!" she sobbed over and over, refusing to let go.

Her next memory was that of Rebekah crying out. Hadassah looked up. Her sister's eyes were filled with fear as she stared at their mama. Hadassah quickly scrambled across her papa's body. Cradling her mama's face in her trembling hands, Hadassah said, "Mama, it's me, your little treasure from heaven."

"Dassah, she's gone," Rebekah sobbed.

"Where'd she go?"

Rebekah forced herself to answer. "Same place as Papa."

"Where's that?" Hadassah asked, stroking her mama's cheek.

"I can't say, 'cause I don't know for sure," Rebekah said, kissing her mama's hand.

Martha spoke for the first time in days. "Papa always said folks who love the King get to live with Him in His palace when they die."

"Mama and Papa are dead?" Hadassah asked.

"Yes, Dassah, they're dead," Martha answered.

"Like the baby rabbit down by the creek? Like the coon caught in Papa's trap last winter?" Hadassah asked.

"Yeah, like them."

"They won't ever come back?" Hadassah asked.

"No, Dassah, they won't ever come back," Martha answered softly.

Hadassah cried out, "I love you, Mama! I love you, Papa!"

Sandwiched between the two people she loved more than anything, Hadassah promised herself to one day find the King's palace. She cried herself to sleep. *And as she slept, the unseen King and His Son, Life-Giver, kept close watch over the three girls.*

When Hadassah awoke, she found Rebekah asleep at her feet. Martha slept in the corner still clutching her doll. Like a blast of icy wind, the awful truth assaulted her senses — her parents were dead! She threw herself onto the floor and wailed bitterly. Her sisters hurried to her side. The three orphans clung to each other as they cried uncontrollably.

***

In an effort to stop the heart-wrenching memory, Hadassah threw back the blankets and jumped to her feet. Her sisters protested loudly, but she didn't care.

Inside their pitiful shelter, snow dusted the dirt floor. Hadassah looked through one of the holes in the animal hide covering the doorway; the snow was falling fast and furiously. The ground was covered with what looked like at least a foot of snow. The evergreen trees bowed low under the weight of the ice and snow clinging to their branches. The scene was breathtakingly beautiful, but Hadassah did not notice because of the storm raging within her own heart and mind.

The bitter cold quickly overcame her need to escape, and Hadassah turned back to her sisters. A wave of hopelessness swept through her. They lived in an abandoned shelter, wore rags they dug out of the garbage dump, and ate almost anything they could find. Their future looked bleak. "I don't know why I'm worried about our future," she said, shivering uncontrollably. "I doubt we'll even make it through this godforsaken winter."

Hadassah pushed her way back between her sisters, taking advantage of what little body heat they offered.

In an effort to avoid more torment, Hadassah forced herself to focus on the few memories she had of her parents before they caught the fever. Tears quickly filled her eyes as images from the past filled her mind.

Her mama loved life as much as she loved people. Before her family moved to the wilderness, her mama's delightful, outgoing personality always made her the favorite of every gathering. Her mama loved to sing. Sad or glad, she would make up songs, singing them with all of her heart. Her voice was not the best, but no one ever complained because her heart was as good as gold.

Her papa was a gentle man, a praying man. Morning, noon and night and many times in between he would stop and talk to the Great King regardless of where he was or who was watching. Hadassah remembered sitting on his lap as he ran his hand through her long, golden hair. "My sweet Dassah, don't ever fret over what folks think of you. The only opinion that truly matters is the opinion of the King."

"What's so special about the King?" she asked.

"Oh, sweet treasure of mine, the King is special for many reasons. One of them is the fact that His love for folks is so deep and strong that it killed His only Son."

Hadassah did not understand how love could kill someone, much less someone as powerful as the son of the greatest king who ever lived, but she trusted her papa. He was never wrong.

Looking back on those early memories reminded her just how much her parents adored their three treasures from heaven, as they often called them. How happy and safe she felt then! But not now — now she was neither happy nor safe. Every day was a battle just to survive. And to make matters worse, if they could get any worse, Hadassah had neither the faith nor the desire to pray anymore. *Papa would be so disappointed in me if he could see me now*, she thought.

An evil spirit named Fear reared its ugly head. The foul spirit sensed her despondency. Fear knew Hadassah well, for it had been with her since her parents' funeral. Through the years it taught her how to be afraid of everything.

Hadassah felt herself sinking.

Fear wrapped its long, skinny fingers around her heart and squeezed while whispering dark, fearful thoughts in her ear, speaking as though they were her own thoughts.

We're alone with no one to help us. We'll never survive, she thought. With the thoughts came the familiar pressure on her chest, and Hadassah braced herself for what she was certain would follow.

Attracted by the foul scent of Fear, a spirit named Anxiety slid in through a crack in the wall and slithered undetected across the snow-covered floor, sniffing the air repeatedly. Locating the source of the odor, Anxiety discretely joined Fear and sighed deeply, licking its grotesque lips. Anxiety and Fear then sucked her down a long, black tunnel into the next cruel chapters of her life.

The room spun as Hadassah was swept back in time. Her uncle's face emerged out of the darkness. Like so many times in the past, Hadassah was unable to stop the avalanche of painful memories.

Her uncle reluctantly took the three orphans into his home after their only other relative, a great aunt, refused. He was a cold, hard man who made the girls work like slaves for six long years. As difficult as that was, it was nothing compared to what happened next.

Growing tired of wilderness life, their uncle decided to return to his former village. Not wanting the burden of three useless girls, as he called them, he decided to sell them. Sixteen-year-old Martha was bought by a kind-hearted farmer whose wife had died, leaving him with a newborn and three very young children. The uncle sold fourteen-year-old Rebekah to a disgusting man who owned a brothel in the next village. A few days later, a rich nobleman caught a glimpse of Hadassah as his entourage passed by. He fancied her long, golden hair and pretty face, so he purchased the twelve-year-old for two hens and a small basket of apples.

Hadassah was accustomed to hard work, that was not what she hated about her new life. What was unbearable was what the nobleman did to her at night while his wife and servants tended to the needs of their seven children.

Hadassah despised her life and the evil man who violated her for his selfish pleasure. Pleading, begging and fighting only resulted in more pain, so Hadassah soon stopped resisting. Instead, she focused all of her energy into devising a plan of escape.

That opportunity finally presented itself two years, three months and four days into her enslavement. A fellow servant told her that their master had left for a fortnight. Announcing that she was going to fetch potatoes, Hadassah raced down the stairs to the root cellar. Trembling, she crouched in a corner. Her mind raced. *I can't run away. What if he finds me? What if I can't remember the way back to my sisters?* she thought.

"Hadassah, stop it!" she nearly shouted.

Fear and Anxiety hung on tight. Hopelessness had stalked her for quite some time. Finding Hadassah in such turmoil, it crouched down ready to pounce. To its horror, Life-Giver suddenly appeared. The three creatures cowered before the fiery eyes of the King's Son. Having subdued His enemies with just a glance, Life-Giver then turned His gaze to Hadassah. *"With Me by your side, nothing is impossible."*

Hadassah did not hear Him, but her spirit did. Taking a deep breath, she sighed. *This is what I've been waiting for. I can't back out now. I must find my sisters,* she thought. "I can do this. I know I can! Now get up, Hadassah!" she said to herself.

Life-Giver smiled.

Hadassah formulated her plan as she climbed the rickety stairs carrying a small basket of potatoes. Hiding a few potatoes under her bed, she returned to her chores.

The day drug painfully by.

Hadassah waited until she was certain everyone was asleep. Trembling, she grabbed the woolen blankets from her cot, retrieved the potatoes and then quietly made her way to the kitchen. Wrapping bread, cheese, fruit and the potatoes in her blanket, she rehearsed her plan.

Unknown to her, Life-Giver and His angels stood guard.

Hadassah looked around one last time and then cursed her master. Grabbing a cloak, a hunting knife and two wineskins, she slipped out the door and never looked back.

Hadassah traveled all night, refusing to submit to her fatigue or fear. With the rising of the sun she finally gave herself permission to rest. Hidden underneath a large bush, she tried to eat, but exhaustion quickly overwhelmed her. Wrapping the cloak and blankets around her like a cocoon, she settled down for a good, long sleep.

Hadassah woke much too soon. She was still tired, bone-tired, but the ache in her heart to find her sisters and the fear breathing down her neck drove her onward. She traveled for days. When her food ran out, she ate whatever she could find — mushrooms, berries, roots, leaves and even bugs. She traveled slowly and carefully, for she was terrified of being discovered and returned to her prison.

After two months of painstaking effort she finally reached her uncle's abandoned cabin. Without stopping, she proceeded directly to the home of the man who bought Martha.

Like a thief, she hid in the forest behind the farmer's house, watching and waiting. *Whatever will I do if Martha's not here?* she wondered.

Two days later, Hadassah nearly fainted when Martha, followed by four little ones, came bounding out the door. Hadassah watched her sister play chase with them as tears filled her eyes. It was all she could do not to call out to her.

The following day the farmer hitched his horse to the wagon and rode off. Not entirely certain Martha was alone, Hadassah paced back and forth hoping her sister would come outside. Unable to wait, she decided to risk entering the house.

Taking a deep breath, she ran across the yard and pressed herself against the wall by the backdoor. Her heart pounded in her ears as sweat formed on her palms. Her mind raced. "What if I get caught?" she whispered to herself.

"If you get caught, they'll send you back!" Fear answered.

"Just walk away," Hopelessness said, still stalking her.

"It's not worth the risk," said Anxiety.

Hadassah felt herself weakening. *Fear and Anxiety tightened their holds.*

Life-Giver stepped in front of her and laid His hand on her shoulder, saying, "Hadassah, there is no fear in love."

Hadassah did not hear Him, but that did not matter. Life-Giver's words never failed to accomplish what they were sent to do. Taking a deep breath, she told herself to relax. As quietly as possible, she opened the door. Stepping just inside, she waited. Hearing only the sounds of children playing, she tiptoed down the hallway and into the large kitchen. Seeing her sister bent over a washboard, Hadassah's knees buckled and she fell to the floor. Startled, Martha spun around. Her face clearly reflected the progression of her emotions — fear, then recognition, then confusion and then utter delight!

Dropping the garment into the tub, Martha hurried to Hadassah's side, nearly squeezing the life out of her.

"How? What? Is it really you?" Martha stammered, holding Hadassah's dirty face in her wet hands.

"I escaped," Hadassah whispered, her voice trembling as much as her body.

"I didn't think I'd ever see you again," Martha sobbed.

"Nor I you! I've come to fetch you."

"I can't leave the master's children alone."

"You *must* come with me! We've got to find Bekah!" Hadassah exclaimed as tears spilled down her face.

"I want to go with you more than anything, but how can I leave the children alone? They're too young," Martha said. The battle going on inside of her was obvious.

"Isn't there someone who can help you?"

"Well, there is a neighbor — a young slave girl who's a dear friend."

The following day, with her master's permission, Martha took the children on a picnic. They walked through the woods, across the valley and over the next hill. Hadassah followed, careful to keep well out of sight.

Martha was overjoyed to find Esther, the young slave, in the pasture playing a game of hide-and-seek with her charges. Bypassing a formal greeting, Martha said, "Esther, I need your help! I need you to watch the children for me."

"But why?"

"Please don't ask. It'll be best if you know nothing."

Seeing the desperation on Martha's face, Esther nodded. "I'll take good care of them. Be careful, my friend, and go in peace."

With a quick hug, tears pooling in both of their eyes, Martha ran into the woods where Hadassah paced. Their plan worked perfectly. The two overjoyed sisters disappeared into the forest.

It took nearly a week for Hadassah and Martha to discover the exact whereabouts of Rebekah. What they learned made them physically ill.

CHAPTER TWO

$\mathcal{U}$nlike most of Hadassah's memories, her recall of Rebekah's rescue brought a smile to her face. Having learned that every Sunday morning the girls were escorted to a secluded pond on the outskirts of town, she and Martha devised a plan.

The following Sunday, before sunrise, they hid in the woods surrounding the pond and waited. The small group finally came into sight, their only escort a little old man with a toothless grin.

"Perfect," Hadassah whispered, smiling broadly. "This'll be so easy."

Without removing their clothing, Rebekah and her four companions hurried into the water. The old man stretched out under a tree. The moment he closed his eyes, Martha and Hadassah pounced on him. Martha straddled him as Hadassah quickly tied his wrists and ankles.

Recognizing her sisters, Rebekah scrambled out of the water. Throwing wet arms around them, she cried, "I didn't know if I'd ever see either of you again!"

The three sisters collapsed on the ground, laughing and crying at the same time.

"I always hoped . . ." Martha said, unable to finish her sentence.

"I had to believe I'd find you!" Hadassah exclaimed.

"I didn't know what happened to you. I always wondered —" Overwhelmed, Rebekah could not continue.

Wiping her eyes, Hadassah looked at her sister. She was thin, much too thin.

"We need to get out of here," Martha said, nervously looking around.

"Wait. I must do something first," Rebekah said, jumping to her feet.

To their utter surprise, Rebekah knelt beside the old man. With a hand on his shoulder, she whispered something neither sister could hear. The man slowly nodded, his face reflecting his amazement. She then began untying the vines.

"What are you doing?" Martha asked, grabbing her wrist.

"I'm letting him go," she answered, shaking her hand free.

"But he held you prisoner."

"This man was not my captor, dear sister. He's a slave and can only do what he's told. There's no condemnation for him, and neither should there be punishment. I have the opportunity to set him free, and that's exactly what I'm going to do."

Turning her attention back to the frightened man, Rebekah said, "I regret that I didn't know you better, kind sir. If I had, I would've told you about the One who can help you in more ways than I. His name is Life-Giver and He loves you. If you but reach out to Him now, He will set your soul free and fill you with unending love and perfect peace."

With eyes wide, the man stared at Rebekah, his mouth hanging open.

Hadassah wondered at her sister's lovingkindness while Martha anxiously paced.

"Life-Giver loves you more than you can imagine. I've come to know Him in ways I can't describe, but this I can say — He is all you need, and He'll help you if you'll allow Him to do so. Won't you accept His extravagant offer for true freedom?" Rebekah asked.

Life-Giver knelt before the man with His arms extended wide and an inviting smile on His face.

Feeling a love he could not explain, the old man nodded as tears pooled in his eyes. *His spirit received the free gift of eternal life being offered.*

"For all eternity, you'll be glad you accepted His love," she whispered, tenderly kissing his forehead.

"Thank you," he said, "for showing kindness to an old man."

Life-Giver held the man ever so closely as resurrection life flowed into His dead spirit.

Rebekah helped him to his feet and said, "You need not thank me. I am neither the source of your freedom nor the giver of life. Now, you must hurry on your way, kind sir, for our master will soon come looking for us."

"I shall remember your kindness forever," he said.

Rebekah laid her hand on his shoulder and said, "Hurry on now. Go in peace."

As the man hobbled off, Martha grabbed Rebekah's arm rather roughly and said, "What are you thinking? That old man will alert everyone in the village!"

"Look at him, Martha — he's walking in the opposite direction. We have nothing to fear from him. To go back to the brothel without us would mean punishment or perhaps death for him, and he knows that all too well. He will do us no harm now, for he has met Life-Giver."

Martha released her grip, but her displeasure was obvious.

Rebekah turned to her four brothel companions and said, "The Great King has answered our prayers. Hurry, grab your shoes, and let's be gone!"

Hadassah led the way. They ran a short distance into the woods and then stopped to catch their breath. For safety's sake, the three sisters decided to separate from Rebekah's four friends. Rebekah, ignoring Martha's protests, took the time to pray for them. Bidding them farewell, she kissed their cheeks and they parted ways.

The three sisters ran as fast as they could. They traveled all day and through most of the night. It wasn't until the sun was nearly overhead that they felt safe enough to sleep. Hidden beneath thick overgrowth, they slept for a long time. It was nearly noon the following day before they continued their arduous journey. Turning east, they discovered an overgrown path, which they decided to follow.

Nearly a week later, well before sun-up, they came to a wide and treacherous-looking river. Hadassah's heart sank as fear filled her. The three sisters stood on the bank staring down at the rushing water.

"There must be a waterfall around that bend," Hadassah shouted over the roaring water.

Retreating to the edge of the forest, Rebekah was the first to say what they were all thinking. "We can't go back."

"True, but that doesn't mean we have to cross that river. To try would be foolish. We could stay here," said Martha.

"To stay here is much too risky. I'd feel much safer living on the other side of the river," Hadassah said.

"If we cross by noon we'd be dry before nightfall," said Rebekah.

"Good point," Hadassah said.

"Is this how it's going to be — the two of you against me?" Martha asked, her hands on her hips.

"No decision has been made, dear sister," said Hadassah. "We're merely discussing what we should do. You're free to add your thoughts."

"I've already said what I think, but what good did that do? It appears you have decided otherwise," Martha said, afraid of what was behind her and what might lie before her.

"You don't need to be afraid — the Great King has sent Life-Giver to be with us," Rebekah responded.

"I'm not afraid," she said, ignoring the truth. "I just don't want to cross that river. And just who is Life-Giver?"

"He's the King's Son," Rebekah said.

"Well, it's difficult for me to believe he's with us having seen neither hide nor hair of him."

"Just because you can't see Him doesn't mean He's not here. You can't see the wind can you?"

"Of course not," Martha admitted reluctantly.

"Life-Giver's like that. You can't see Him, but you can certainly see what He does. He's —"

"Rebekah," Martha interrupted, "I love you, but I really don't want to hear anymore about Life-Giver. I just want to stop running. I want to rest — for more than a few hours at a time."

"Martha, I believe Life-Giver wants us to cross that river," said Rebekah gently.

Martha stared at her long and hard, her foot tapping furiously beneath the tattered hem of her dirty skirt. "Did you look at that river, sister? We have no idea how deep the water is or how strong the current. How do you propose we keep from being swept away? Did Life-Giver tell you that?"

"We can pray for His help," Rebekah answered.

"*You* can pray — I'm not interested," Martha said, turning her back.

Hadassah looked at her two sisters. Kind and gentle Rebekah had already begun praying, and hot-headed Martha was fuming.

Rebekah talks to the Great King like Papa did, and she's kind even when we're not. I wish I was like that, Hadassah thought.

The sun rose painting the horizon a glorious red. Exhausted and discouraged, they decided to rest beneath an enormous weeping willow tree growing not far from the riverbank.

Hadassah spread out her blankets and invited her sisters to join her. Stretching out, she said, "What do you say we decide what to do when we wake?"

Rebekah agreed while Martha merely grunted.

Martha was the first to wake. She slipped out quietly. Standing beside the roaring water, thoughts of her papa filled her mind. Biting her lip and swallowing back the tears, she reminded herself how much she hated to cry. Hurling a rock into the water, she shouted, "I just don't understand! It's not fair and it's not right! I hate life and I hate you — if you exist!"

"I have always existed, Martha, and always will whether you believe it or not," Life-Giver whispered.

Martha heard nothing but the roar of the river mingled with the roar of her fears.

"Papa and Mama loved and believed in you and look what happened to them. What good is there in believing? What point is there? Why bother? I can't and won't let myself believe!" She hurled another stone through the air as hard and as far as she could.

Unknown to Martha, at her parent's funeral an evil creature named Accusation befriended her. Once she was comfortable with its hypnotic, sing-song voice, it began to tell her she was to blame for her parents' death, because she was the first to catch the fever. As she listened to Accusation's lies, she soon lost sight of the truth. That was when Condemnation joined them. The creature filled her mind with its vile poison. With each passing day, Martha grew more convinced that she was worthless and deserved nothing but punishment.

The sun burned Martha's face, but the pain felt good. Secretly, she wanted to feel pain, for guilt was consuming her like a disease consumes its host.

I don't want to cross that river! We can't take the chance. If something were to happen —, she could not bear to finish the thought.

"I will be with you, child," Life-Giver said.

Without understanding why, Martha felt herself relax as perfect peace surrounded her.

"I am always with you just like the air is always around you. And I am stronger and more powerful than anything."

Martha took a deep breath.

Life-Giver laid His hand on her shoulder, and grace filled her.

Martha imagined herself crossing the river, and somehow it did not seem as frightening. The more she thought about it, the more it felt like the right thing to do.

How is this possible? she asked herself. *Just moments ago I was terrified, but now I find myself wanting to do the very thing I didn't want to do.*

"There is no fear in love."

"I don't understand this, but I think we're to cross that river," she said to herself.

Puzzled, Martha returned to her sisters. Waking them, she announced, "I've changed my mind. I think we should cross the river. If it's too deep or the current's too strong, we just turn back." She turned to leave but then stopped and said, "And don't ask me any questions, because I don't want to talk about it."

A shocked Hadassah and Rebekah looked at each other and shrugged. "I guess we have our answer," Rebekah said.

Hadassah tied a vine securely around each of their waists. Carefully climbing down the riverbank, she stepped into the water and gasped. "It's freezing," she shouted. Rebekah braced herself and Martha desperately hoped she made the right decision.

Slowly and very cautiously the three sisters felt their way along the rocky river bottom. To their great relief, the water only came as high as their waists and the current was not nearly as strong as it appeared.

Crawling up the steep bank on the other side, the three sisters collapsed from sheer relief. The sun beat down on them, which felt good because the water was quite cold.

As soon as their clothes were almost dry, they set out to explore the land. Martha complained incessantly, so much so that even Rebekah asked her to stop. But, alas, it did nothing but further agitate her.

"Martha, why do you complain so?" Hadassah asked.

"I'm not complaining, just stating facts — it's hot, I'm hungry, these dreadful bugs won't stop biting me and my feet hurt."

"Perhaps we could focus on other facts, like — we're safe, we're together and we're alive," said Hadassah.

"Any one of those things could change at any moment."

"Martha, what's happened to you? You didn't used to be like this. Why are you such a pessimist?" Hadassah asked, having lost all patience.

An evil spirit named Self-Pity patted Martha on the back, for it took great delight in being noticed.

Martha answered, "I'm not a pessimist, Dassah. I'm simply stating the facts. Let me give you a list of those facts. Let's start with mama and papa's death and then our uncle who sold us into slavery where the two of you suffered atrocities that no human should ever experience. And now we're on the run like common criminals. Need I go on?"

Rebekah said, "Martha, Life-Giver once told me that every difficulty is merely an opportunity in disguise and we —"

Martha held her hand up. "I don't want to hear this." She walked off.

***

Three days later, they came upon a tiny village made up of a dozen or so mud huts. Keeping well out of sight, they watched and listened as the villagers went about their daily chores. They soon learned the land on that side of the river was called the Land of Despair, and it was ruled by a prince who had a tightly closed fist and a heart as cold as a winter blizzard. He loved neither man nor beast and took great delight in causing the pain and suffering of both.

After eating only roots and bugs for days, Martha could not resist the temptation to acquire two loaves of bread which had been left to cool on a large rock. Successful in her acquisition, with a loaf tucked safely under each arm, she rejoined her sisters. Seeing the bread and asking no questions, they quickly followed Martha into the forest where they found a small cave. Martha presented the loaves. Rebekah bowed her head, thanking the King for His provision.

Martha rebuked her. "Why are you thanking *him*? He didn't provide this bread — I did!"

"You didn't provide it; you stole it," Hadassah said, defending Rebekah.

"It was forgotten and left on a rock. The birds would've gotten it if I hadn't."

"I'm not condemning you, dear sister. I was merely thanking the King," said Rebekah.

Hadassah pondered her sister's devotion to the Great King as she devoured the delicious bread. With their stomachs full, they collected leaves for a bed and slept soundly for the first time since crossing the river.

Afraid of being caught, they decided not to return to the village but continued on into the heart of the forest. After two days, they came upon a strange sight. Ancient trees, taller than the cedars of Lebanon, encircled a clearing of some sort. It was impossible to see what was in the clearing because of the thick overgrowth.

"Let's just go around it," Martha said.

"There must be something important in there. Why else would anyone go to all the trouble of planting trees around it?" Hadassah asked, trying to find the easiest point of entry.

"Hadassah, it's not worth it," Martha called after her, sitting beside Rebekah on a fallen log. Hadassah ignored her. She had already pulled out her knife and begun cutting vines to make a path.

Stepping into the clearing, she called out, "Martha, Rebekah, you've got to see this!"

Martha and Rebekah scrambled to their feet and joined Hadassah. The three sisters stared at an abandoned garbage heap.

"We should be able to find all kinds of helpful things here," said Hadassah.

"You don't really believe we'll find anything useful in this mountain of rubbish, do you?" Martha asked.

"Yes, I do."

Without waiting, Hadassah and Rebekah began digging through the debris while Martha pretended not to watch. Rebekah soon found a large animal hide, worn, but still quite useful. Encouraged, they dug deeper and found several other treasures: a worn-out shawl, a chipped pottery bowl and a long, thin leather cord.

"We should be going," Martha said, glancing at the horizon.

Hadassah looked up. "Bekah, she's right. We'll return at first light."

They reluctantly left. In an effort to find a safe place to sleep, they walked farther from the dumpsite than Hadassah had wanted. Just when she was thinking of turning around, Rebekah exclaimed, "Look over there!"

Tucked beneath thick overgrowth was what appeared to be an abandoned shack. Hadassah called out. No one answered. Nervous, they cautiously approached. Standing before the tiny structure, Hadassah called out once more, but the only response was the cooing of a dove. She stepped through the doorway while her sisters waited outside. As her eyes adjusted, she felt something run across her foot. Looking down, she saw numerous mice scampering about. She shrieked and hopped from foot to foot on her tiptoes. Turning, she ran into Martha, who was coming to her assistance. The two collided and fell to the ground.

"It was mice," Hadassah said.

"Mice?"

"Yeah, mice."

What started as a chuckle soon turned into a fit of uncontrollable laughter.

"I haven't ever seen you dance like that," Martha said, wiping her eyes on her sleeve.

"That's because I haven't ever had mice running across my feet," Hadassah said.

"It really was funny," said Rebekah.

"If you two can pull yourselves together," said Hadassah, brushing the leaves from her skirt, "I think we've found our new home."

The cedar walls were falling apart in places but overall they appeared to be sound. "Cedar never rots," Rebekah said, running her hand over the rough wood.

"We'll have to find something to cover those holes," Hadassah said, pointing at the ceiling.

"And what do you propose we do about the mice?" Martha asked.

"I guess we pray they don't return," Rebekah said.

Martha rolled her eyes and left to gather leaves. Hadassah and Rebekah fastened the animal hide over the doorway using the leather cord.

Once that was done, they spread out their blankets on a thick bed of leaves. Lying down, Rebekah whispered a prayer of gratitude while Martha complained about the mice she heard scurrying about.

***

Rebekah coughed violently, startling Hadassah out of the memories of her shattered childhood. It took her a few minutes to get her bearings. Rebekah coughed again. Fear filled Hadassah's mind. She pressed her body closer to Rebekah. "Are you all right?" she asked.

"Yeah," she mumbled.

Snow blew through the cracks of the shelter. Despite being tied down, the bottom edge of the hide covering the door flapped in the wind. Hadassah glanced at the stick she used to mark the passing days. *We've been here over a year,* she thought. *Last winter was nothing like this. I wonder if we'll survive.*

She had often imagined her death to be a bit more dramatic — like being attacked by a wild animal or poisoned by a disease-ridden morsel of food.

Anxiety tightened its grip on Hadassah's mind as it stroked her brow. Thick drool ran down its chin.

Hadassah felt the familiar sinking feeling in the pit of her stomach. She knew it well and dreaded the horrible memories that were sure to follow.

Rebekah coughed again, interrupting Hadassah's dark thoughts. "Rebekah, trade places with me," she said to her shivering sister.

There was no response.

Hadassah was tempted to remain where she was; after all, being sandwiched between her two sisters did offer a little protection from the cold. "My body may be frozen, but my heart doesn't have to follow," Hadassah said to herself as she once more offered Rebekah her place.

Unable to get a response, she shoved her sister into the middle. Her disturbance caused Martha to curse.

Hadassah's unselfish act caught Anxiety by surprise. The creature lost its grip and fell to the floor. Scrambling to regain its hold on Hadassah's mind, Anxiety grabbed her arm. To its horror, Hadassah was now covered with oil. The creature sniffed the air and recoiled in terror, for it recognized the stench all too well — it was the obnoxious odor of sacrificial love!

As Anxiety retreated to the corner, it announced to Fear, "The stench of the King's love covers the daughter of man."

Fear shrieked as it fought to maintain control, for it knew its greatest enemy was Perfect Love. The oil made it very difficult, but Fear's hold over Hadassah had grown deep. The evil spirit had become one with her.

Not willing to surrender, Anxiety crouched in the corner growling, waiting for an opportunity to pounce. Had the creature not been so arrogant, it would have realized it was already a defeated foe.

Not wanting to fall into the bottomless pit of painful memories again, Hadassah considered praying.

Fearing the King's love, Fear called for reinforcements.

Sweat beads formed on Hadassah's forehead as her heart raced. From the past came her Papa's voice, *"Dassah, if you're ever in trouble, call out to the Great King and He will send help."*

"Great King, are you there?" she whispered.

"You're wasting your breath," Martha said as she rolled over.

Hadassah ignored her. She waited and listened and hoped for an answer or a sign but heard nothing.

I feel really silly talking to someone I'm not sure even exists, she thought.

Loneliness swept over her like the north wind sweeping over the land. Her loneliness was soon joined by agonizing grief.

Hadassah was unaware that two very familiar creatures had answered Fear's call for help. Their names were Loneliness and Ungodly Grief. Neither was she aware that Life-Giver was about to change her life forever.

Unable to suppress the avalanche of pain, she silently cried out, *Why did our parents have to die? If they hadn't died none of this awful stuff would've ever happened.*

Hot tears cascaded down Hadassah's face.

Life-Giver's presence flooded the atmosphere with faith, hope and love. Loneliness and Ungodly Grief fled without a word being spoken. Anxiety was right behind them, letting out a high-pitched shriek as it left. But Fear buried itself deeper in her heart, trying to hide, but no one and nothing can hide from the all-knowing Giver of Life.

Pointing at the slimy creature, Life-Giver said, "Fear, you have her for a moment, but I have her for all eternity. There is a day coming when she will no longer give you a place in her life, and Perfect Love will drive you out. Your time is short."

Fear tucked its ugly head under its wing and wished it was anywhere else but there. But Hadassah held onto the creature, for she did not feel safe without Fear.

"I need help," Hadassah said.

Life-Giver stepped back as the Spirit of the King completely surrounded Hadassah. Holding her in His arms, Comforter quieted her with His love as He sang over her.

From deep within the recesses of Hadassah's heart came a familiar tune. Unable to remember the words, she hummed it. As she did, she was flooded with a feeling she had not felt in a very long time — the feeling of being safe and loved. To her surprise, Rebekah soon hummed along.

In her usual matter-of-fact manner, Martha stated, "Mama used to sing that song when she tucked us into bed."

"Martha, please tell me you remember the words!" Hadassah exclaimed, bolting upright.

"Well, of course I do," she answered, yanking the blankets back around her.

"Then sing it, sister, for I must know them too."

As Martha sang, Hadassah tried desperately to remember every facet of her mama's face. Ten painful years had erased much. Hot tears stung the eyes and hearts of all three sisters.

And so it was Life-Giver and Comforter stood watch over the three orphans as they sang a song long forgotten. A song which provided the only warmth they had felt in a very long time.

CHAPTER THREE

𝒢lorious sunlight poured through the numerous cracks of the shelter as Hadassah slowly opened her eyes. It was quiet — much too quiet. Her sisters lay huddled together motionless. Fearing the worst, she bolted upright. Frantic, she shoved one and kicked the other. Rebekah groaned, Martha cursed and Hadassah sighed deeply.

"Sorry," Hadassah said, tucking the blankets back around them, "I thought you were dead."

"We're not so lucky," Martha mumbled.

Hadassah laid back down and snuggled close to Rebekah. She listened to the stillness and marveled at the sunlight — it had been more than a week of nothing but dreary, snowy skies and howling wind. "Did the King answer my prayer?" she whispered.

Fear bolted to attention and shouted, "Of course he hasn't. Why would he answer your prayers? He never bothered to do so before."

Hadassah looked around their tiny shack. They had nothing except a couple of tattered blankets, the ragged clothes they dug out of the garbage and a dwindling supply of frozen fish, berries and roots.

"Great King, I don't think we have enough food to keep us until spring. I'm not sure why I'm telling you this because I don't know that you can or care to do anything about it."

Fear licked its lips.

Tottering on the edge of despair, she quietly prayed, "Great King, Papa said you talked to him. So why won't you speak to me?"

Life-Giver laid His hand on Hadassah's head. Fear shrieked, covering its eyes while fighting to maintain its hold on her.

"Perhaps it's because I've done something bad. Is that why you won't talk to me? If that's true, just tell me — at least then I'll know you're real. I'm tormented by not knowing."

Hadassah had very clear expectations as to how the King should speak and what he should say. Therefore, she did not hear Life-Giver's gentle answer. *"I am watching over you, child. I will take care of you, and I will deliver you."*

Neither was she able to see His hand reaching out to her or feel Him wiping away her tears.

"I love you, Hadassah. I am revealing Myself to you even now. Be still, My precious one, and know that I am the Giver of Life."

Accusation crept close, hissing in her ear, "The king doesn't care about you just like he didn't care about your dead parents."

"Did you care about my parents?" Hadassah asked. She wiped her hot tears on the corner of the dirty blanket.

With just a glance Life-Giver silenced the voice of Accusation.

"There are many things in this life that do not make sense, sweet child of Mine. Long ago, Adam and Eve introduced something to your world that I never purposed to be here and that something is called sin. Sin is the fruit of man's desire. It unleashed sorrow, suffering and all manner of diseases on this earth.

"The Tree of Life was My gift to mankind, but sadly, Adam and Eve chose to eat from the Tree of the Knowledge of Good and Evil. As a result, unredeemed man has the seed from that tree within their soul. But do not fear, Hadassah, for I am the Tree of Life. I am the Remedy, the Antidote and the only One who can set you free from the consequences of that dreadful day. And that is exactly what I am going to do."

Even though she could not hear Him, His words calmed her fearful, anxious heart and mind. Sighing deeply, Hadassah said, "I sure hope this love I feel is real and I hope it's evidence of your presence. I'm so worried and I don't have anyone to talk to about it. Rebekah's been devastated by evil men, but she still believes in you — she even loves you. I'm not sure why or how she's able to be so kind and loving. It's a mystery to me. Martha's really angry and denies that you even exist. As for me? I don't know what to believe. I think I want to believe you're real, but even that scares me. Because if you are, then why do you allow awful things to happen to innocent people? I don't want to believe . . . or maybe I do. Oh, I don't know what I want!"

Hadassah chewed on her jagged fingernail as she continued her monologue. "If I don't believe . . . and if you aren't real . . . then what hope is there? Who will help us? Absolutely no one, which means we're destined to spend the rest of our lives in this miserable place."

"My precious one, in the days to come I will restore to Rebekah all that has been stolen. Martha will come to believe I am not only real but her Savior and Friend. And as for you, My dear one, you will not only believe that I am real, but you will love Me more than you love your own life."

Life-Giver placed His hand on top of Hadassah's. She felt something she could not explain, and because she couldn't explain it, she quickly dismissed it as just her imagination.

"If you only knew the One who created that imagination you wouldn't be so quick to disregard it. I created your imagination, yet you use it for everything under the sun except for Me. All that I created has a purpose, child, and I have a purpose for even this."

Lightly touching her forehead, He continued, *"In every temple there is a place of encounter, a place called the Holy of Holies. Your imagination can be such a place, if you surrender it to Me. Allow Me to cleanse and fill it with My Holy Spirit that I might meet with you there."*

Hadassah did not hear His invitation. But her spirit did, and her spirit bowed low. As a result, Hadassah felt something . . . something wonderful and so inviting. *What is this strange sensation*, she asked herself.

She took a deep breath, afraid to move. Unspeakable joy surged through her spirit, soul and body as perfect longing and holy desire drew her.

"I offer you My life in exchange for yours," Life-Giver said, His hand extended to Hadassah's dead spirit.

Hadassah suddenly felt convicted which caused her to become very aware of her need for a Savior. Afraid her sisters would hear and think she had lost her mind, Hadassah silently confessed, *"I don't understand any of this, but I'm compelled by some strange sense of love to give my life to You. I'm too weak to resist the cords of pure longing that are drawing me. Actually, I have no desire to even try. I accept Your gift and Your life, and I offer You mine in return."*

Joy exploded from Life-Giver's heart. "How blessed are those who do not see and still believe!" He shouted for all of heaven to hear.

Overwhelmed with joy, Hadassah said, "I want to know You like my papa knew You. Is that even possible?"

Life-Giver answered, "Not only is it possible, but it is your destiny. The Spirit of the Great King is now resident within you, and He will lead you into all truth. He will teach you and prepare you for your eternal destiny. Have no fear, for He does all things well."

Life-Giver turned His eyes heavenward and shouted, "Oh, happy day! Oh, glorious moment! Look at her, Father — she has chosen Perfect Love! She has chosen Life! Our hands are no longer restrained. We are now free to transform her into Our image of glorious beauty and splendor!"

Hadassah's mind was only vaguely aware that something miraculous had just happened, but not so with her spirit. Her spirit had been dead, but now it was alive. It had been shrouded in darkness, but now it was filled with marvelous Light. And most joyful of all — her spirit was now one with its Creator.

Life-Giver took her small hand in His strong one and said, "My Spirit will lead you into the wilderness. In that place, I will speak kindly to you and will lead you to the valley of suffering. But have no fear, for you will sing as in the days of your youth. There you will come to know Me intimately — like a loving Husband. I will enter into covenant with you — in faithfulness, in righteousness, in justice, in lovingkindness and in compassion . . . forever!"

For the first time in a very long time, Hadassah allowed herself to relax. Taking a deep breath, she closed her eyes. It felt as though someone had wrapped her in a thick, warm blanket. Her belly felt full and her heart soared. "I think I might love You," she whispered. "Is that even allowed?"

"Not only is it allowed, but it is as it should be. Now, rest in My Perfect Love. Sleep, My dear child, and dream of better days."

And that is exactly what she did — Hadassah fell asleep safe in the arms of One she had yet to see.

***

Spring arrived in all of its glory — warm, sunny days, cool nights, daffodils pushing their way through the melting snow, and robins searching diligently for materials to build their nests. To Hadassah, it was the loveliest spring she had ever seen.

Each morning Hadassah went to her favorite spot to pray and watch the sunrise. Her time spent talking to Life-Giver was melting the protective shell surrounding her heart and infusing her with hope. She was beginning to feel again.

As usual, Hadassah woke before the sun and quietly slipped out. The moon was full and bright.

Sitting atop a large boulder, her cloak wrapped tightly around her, she hugged her knees close and relaxed. To her surprise, a white dove suddenly landed on the far side of the rock. Cocking its head to the side, the bird watched her while making soft cooing sounds. Hadassah marveled at its flawless beauty and gentle song. "Have you come for some purpose, my friend?" she asked.

The dove strutted toward her, head bobbing. "And what purpose would that be?" The bird appeared as if it was dancing. Hadassah chuckled. With a stretch of its wings, as quickly as it came, it left. Hadassah watched as it disappeared into the trees.

Hadassah's parents loved doves. The memory of their death flashed before Hadassah's mind, but she felt peace.

They loved so well, Hadassah thought. Taking a deep breath, she whispered, "Life-Giver, one day I'd like to experience true love."

"You don't really believe that, do you?" Martha asked.

"Ahhh! You scared me!"

"Sorry. I was just curious to see what you do out here every morning."

"Don't ever sneak up on me again," Hadassah said.

"I said I was sorry."

"I know. It's just that you scared me," Hadassah said. She patted the boulder inviting Martha to join her.

Martha snuggled close as her sister wrapped the cloak around her. "Do you really believe you'll find true love?" Martha asked.

"Most of the time I don't believe it, but right here, right now, I guess I do."

"Then you, little sister, are a fool. Look around you — you're homeless and eating out of a dump! You have no dowry, so marriage is impossible. In the very remote chance someone should overlook your extreme poverty, who do you think would ever marry someone like you — or me, for that matter?"

"I'm not talking about a husband, Martha. I'm talking about *true* love. I'm talking about a love that's greater than human love. I'm talking about a love that lays down its life for another without expecting anything in return. I hope and dream that one day I'll come to know and possess that kind of love. I've had a little taste of it — that's why I come here every morning — but something tells me there's more. And I want whatever that is — I've been looking for it ever since Mama and Papa died. I just didn't know it."

Martha stared hard at her little sister. "You can waste your life dreaming impossible dreams if you want to," she said, "but I'm content with life just the way it is."

"How can you be content to live like this?" Hadassah asked. "Your life's empty. You have nothing of any real value — no peace, no contentment, no joy — nothing. You're miserable, Martha, and you know it."

"I learned a long time ago that the circumstances of my life are beyond my control. I can't make anything happen, and neither can I stop it. Some force greater than all of us rolls the dice and then sits back to watch us suffer the consequences. We can accept what comes our way, or we can fight and kick and scream. Either way, nothing changes. As for me, I refuse to put my hope in ridiculous fairy tales that only disappoint."

"Oh, Martha, there's more to life than acceptance or rebellion — there's the Great King and Life-Giver and —"

Martha interrupted. "Hadassah, the king, if he's real, isn't interested in us. Have you forgotten who you are and where you've come from? We're worse than servants. We live in a shack, eat garbage and worse, and our garments are filthy rags. We have nothing to offer this king you lay claim to. As for him helping us, I won't even comment on that ridiculous idea."

"We may not have money or nice things, but, Martha, we do have a heart that's capable of loving."

"What good's a heart when tragedy after tragedy slaps you in the face? What good's a heart when evil people enslave and take advantage of innocent children? What good's a heart when all it knows is pain and suffering and sorrow? In a world like this, I'd rather not believe, and I'd rather not have a heart, thank you very much."

"I *must* believe, Martha! If I don't, hopelessness and fear attach themselves to me like ticks on a dog. I can't keep living like that — I must believe there's something or someone out there who'll love me enough to overlook my present state of affairs and save me from myself and the evil surrounding me."

"Hadassah, you're just setting yourself up for disappointment, for no one, not even the king, is that good or powerful! Everyone I've ever known has been selfish . . . except Mama and Papa, that is."

"Don't you remember the stories they told us, Martha? They said the King loves everyone, especially sinners and orphans. What if it's true? What if He cares about us? What if He's just waiting for us to look for Him, to acknowledge that He's real? What if He's here right now, but we just can't see Him? Martha, I have felt His presence . . . sometimes, I wonder if. . ."

"Hadassah, you've always had such a vivid imagination —"

"If this is my imagination, then so be it!" Hadassah exploded. "Why do you think we were created with an imagination? Perhaps our imagination is to be given back to its Creator, so He can fill it with images of Himself. Perhaps our imagination is like the Garden of Eden was for Adam — perhaps it's meant to be a place where we can walk and talk with Him."

"Hadassah, I won't even comment on that. And I don't believe this king is real, but if I'm wrong I can guarantee you he isn't interested in people like us. If it makes you feel better, dear sister, then go on imagining there's something better out there, that there is . . . what did you call it? *True love*?"

"Martha, there have been times when it felt like unseen powers were going to choke the very life out of me, and when I cried out to Life-Giver those things loosened their hold. I believe Life-Giver is with me. I know it's strange, but I feel like He's drawing me to follow Him. I don't know what that means exactly, but I often hear a whisper inviting me to leave this place in search of Him."

"Oh, little sister, you are indeed delusional! How can you believe the king, or Life-Giver or whatever you call him, talks to you? I love you dearly and don't want to hurt your feelings, but there's nothing about you that would attract a king. If he's real — and that's one great big if — but if he is, he certainly isn't interested in homeless wenches like you and me."

"But He is real and I want to live for Him! I just don't know exactly how to do that. Do you know, Martha? You're older than me and have heard more stories than I have. Did you ever hear anyone say how one serves a King who cannot be seen and is hard to find? Don't hold back, sister, tell all!" Hadassah pleaded.

"Hadassah, I've heard many things, most of which I don't remember. My advice to you would be to just accept your fate and stop trying to change it. It's hard enough to survive without holding onto some illusive dream you stumbled upon in your imagination."

"But what if He *is* real, Martha?"

"Then he'll have to find us."

"What if He already has and you're just not paying attention?"

At that precise moment, the sun kissed the horizon. Darkness fled in a million different directions until it was no more. Struck by the beauty of the moment, Hadassah fixed her gaze on the scene unfolding before her. She pondered the reality of what might be while Martha wondered how she had become so hardhearted and bitter.

And all the while, an unseen King and His Son watched over them, drawing them with cords of love.

CHAPTER FOUR

"*T*his is the last of our food," Rebekah announced as she ripped the hard, stale bread into thirds.

"How are we supposed to quiet our stomachs with this pitiful morsel?" Martha complained, snatching the bread from her hand.

"Dear sister, can't you just be grateful that some traveler left it behind and that we found it before the animals?"

Hadassah did not hear their conversation, for she was much too distracted. *You will go out with joy and be led forth with peace — is that even possible, could it ever happen?* she wondered.

"Rebekah, would you read it to me again?" Hadassah asked as she handed her the scroll she dug out of the garbage weeks before.

"I've read it to you so many times I'd think you'd have it memorized," Rebekah teased.

"I do, but I really like hearing you read it."

Carefully smoothing the old parchment, Rebekah began, "Seek the Great King while He may be found; call upon Him while He is near. You will go out with joy and be led forth with peace. Enter by the narrow gate; for the gate is wide and the way is broad that leads to destruction. The gate is small and the way is narrow leading to life, and few there are who find it."

"Why do kings speak in riddles?" Martha asked. "Why can't they just speak plainly?"

"There's no riddle here, sister. It seems to me the King's inviting the people, whether evil or good, to come to Him for help," Rebekah said.

"But the part about the gate being wide and the other narrow makes absolutely no sense," said Martha.

"I think He's saying that most people will choose to live without Him, but there are a few who will give up what they have in order to find life."

"Life's difficult enough without giving up what little you have," Martha said under her breath.

"But Martha —" Hadassah began.

"I know what you're going to say, Hadassah, and I don't want to hear it," Martha said as she headed out the door.

Hadassah tucked the parchment in the waistband of her skirt. Placing her skinny arm around Rebekah's frail shoulders, she said, "I suppose we should go with her."

"We should."

The two hurried after Martha. As they traveled the well-worn path to the dumpsite, Hadassah prayed.

"Why do you bother?" Martha asked.

"Bother what?" Hadassah responded.

"Why do you bother praying?"

"How'd you know I was praying?"

"I heard you."

"Oh . . . I didn't realize I was talking loud enough for you to hear."

"Perhaps you're trying to irritate me?"

"I don't pray so that I can irritate you, dear sister. I pray because I don't know what else to do."

"Well, pray if you must, but please do so in a way that I don't have to hear. I truly don't understand why you bother, for I haven't seen your king do anything other than ignore your petitions."

"Maybe He hasn't answered because it's not time yet," Rebekah interjected.

Martha spun around. "Not time yet!? Perhaps he's waiting until we starve to death? Or maybe he's just waiting for a snake to crawl through one of the many cracks in our shack and bury its poisonous fangs into our flesh? Or perhaps he's waiting for our cup of suffering to overflow, and then, in his great mercy, he will decide to relieve our pain and end it all?

"No, Rebekah, I can't accept your suggestion that it's not time to help us. What better time to send help than now — *before* we all starve to death or worse?"

"Dear sister, the Great King is good and kind and just . . . it's men who partner with evil," Rebekah responded.

"Oh, really?"

Rebekah continued, "Martha, I *know* He answers our prayers, but not necessarily when or how we want. And I believe *all* things, even difficult circumstances and painful events, are meant to lead us to Him."

"You're so naïve," Martha said, turning away.

Rebekah grabbed her sister's arm, saying, "If you'd give Him a chance, Martha, He'd show you just how kind He is."

"I gave him a chance," Martha exclaimed, jerking her arm free, "and he took our parents from us! And then, to make matters worse, this king you believe is kind sat by and watched as we were sold into slavery. I begged and begged him to help, but he did nothing!"

"We've suffered a lot," Rebekah agreed, "but not by the King's hand. I don't really understand why any of this has happened, but I know He didn't cause it. Martha, He has and will see us through. He'll turn this for our good in the end. I don't know how or when, but I believe He will. He's a good King, and He loves us more than we know."

Martha bit her lip. She hated arguing with the only two people she loved, but try as she might, she could not seem to control her temper or her tongue. Looking into her sister's gentle eyes, Martha took a deep breath. Reminding herself that Rebekah was not the enemy, she asked, "Where did you learn such mercy?"

"In the brothel."

"In the *brothel*?" Martha exclaimed, taking a step back.

"When I was first sold, the evil that was done to me caused me to withdraw into a mindless, emotionless existence. That didn't last long, for fits of rage soon replaced my apathy. My cruel master didn't allow my outbursts to go unpunished, and I suffered greatly at his hand. I came to believe my only hope was to escape, which I tried but failed. The beating I received nearly killed me.

"That's when I began to focus my hatred on the King, but the more I cursed Him, the more I sensed His love. Night after night He invaded my dreams and spoke of His infinite love for me. In my waking hours, He whispered my name and reassured me He was with me and would help me, but I refused to listen.

"The months turned into a year and then two. And all the while, I felt like a rabid animal trapped in a cage while onlookers poked and prodded me for their sadistic pleasure. Consumed by thoughts of throwing myself out of the three-story window or slicing my wrists with the broken glass I had hidden beneath my bed, I fell to my knees. Exhausted and utterly miserable, I finally surrendered. Lying face down on the floor, I offered the King the wretch I had become. Without rebuke or correction, without hesitation or repulsion, the perfect, all-powerful King knelt beside me. Filthy as I was, He scooped up my frail body and held me close. I heard the gentle thunder of His great heart as He tenderly rocked me. The comfort He poured into me helped ease my agony and brought a glimmer of hope to my soul.

"I poured out my bitterness, telling Him I hated myself and everyone else. I asked for forgiveness. Instead of rebuking me, He said that His Perfect Love covers my sins. He then turned to an angel and instructed him to dress me in His best robe — He called it His robe of righteousness. As instructed, the angel also put the King's signet ring on my finger granting me authority. He placed shoes on my feet establishing the fact that I was a daughter and not a servant. Then the King shouted for all of heaven to hear, 'This is My *beloved* daughter! She was lost, but now she is found! She was dead, but now she is alive!'

"I was overwhelmed, Martha. His response utterly shocked me. After all, I had hated and rejected Him. In the midst of my anger, He still had room in His heart for me and His greatest desire was to be with me. It was hard to believe, especially since I felt so worthless. Then He sang me a song."

"Will you sing it for us?" Hadassah asked.

"Certainly."

"I love you like a mother loves her precious child.
I love you like a father loves his beloved daughter.

I love you like the morning sun loves the earth.
I love you like the stars love the night sky.
I love you like the desert sands love the rain.
I will love you both now and forever."

"As He sang, I looked into the kindest eyes I'd ever seen, eyes even kinder than our papa's. He told me that He wanted me to meet His Son, Life-Giver."

"I turned around, and a Man with dark brown, shoulder-length hair stood in front of my door. He had His Father's eyes — eyes of endless love. I could tell by looking into those amazing crystal blue eyes that He loved me just the way I was.

"I trembled from head to toe as Life-Giver approached saying, 'I am the Way, the Truth and the Life.'

"I bowed. He asked if I would accept His gift of eternal life. He offered to trade my broken life for His perfect one. I felt quite unworthy of such a noble and perfect gift, but I was so desperate that I dared not refuse. Bowing low, I said, 'I accept Your gift and Your life and I offer You mine in return.'

"Martha, the King's relentless love rescued me from a pit of self-pity, bitterness and rebellion. His beloved Son poured His very own life into me. I, who deserved to be punished, was shown mercy of the severest kind — a mercy that refused to give up on me even though I had given up on Him. His touch cleansed, delivered and redeemed me from guilt and condemnation. This kind of mercy can't be earned or repaid. Neither can it be purchased, for it's given with no strings attached, no vow to be made or promises to be sworn. The King offered it to me as a free gift. His only requirement was that I accept it, which I did. And then the most marvelous of all things happened — the King filled me with His Spirit! And when He did, it felt as though I was alive for the very first time!

"As time passed, I came to understand the truth that the King and His Son love me because They are love, not because I somehow managed to be good enough. I also came to understand that They love me the same on my worst days as They do on my best days. Their love is constant; it doesn't waver or change. When I am weak and find myself in compromise, Their lovingkindness draws me close.

"I told the other girls how much the King loved them. Soon, they all came to believe in and accept His Perfect Love. And, to my complete surprise, two of my 'customers' came to believe — they paid my master for my services, but he never knew we spent the time talking about the Great King and His Son. One of those men even tried to help me escape, but his efforts failed because it was not what the King had planned — He knew you were coming for me.

"Martha, you grow increasingly angry at the King because of our suffering, but your anger is misplaced. One day I asked the King why there was so much suffering and pain in the world. He answered, 'Rebekah, that is the price I paid and continue to pay to give mankind a free will.'

"The King feels our pain. He relates to the sufferings of His children in ways we can't understand. He told me His very own Son suffered at the hands of evil men. He was falsely accused, rejected, beaten, spit upon, mocked and horribly mistreated, but He loved and forgave them all. I took great comfort in His words. Martha, my circumstances didn't change, but my perspective did. I can never forget, not for one moment, that I was a sinner whom the King picked up and crowned with His glorious love."

"What can I say?" Martha responded, her tone much softer. "I dare not negate your experience, and I wouldn't even if I could, not to someone as gentle as you, sister. But you have your experience, and I have mine. You have your perspective, and I have mine. Who can say which is true?"

"There's only One who has that right, and it's neither you nor I."

"Then we shall have to wait to find out who's —"

"Shhh — something's wrong," Hadassah interrupted.

Acting on instinct, they quickly ducked inside a thick tangle of bushes. In the distance, they heard the sound of voices. Martha motioned for them to turn around, but Hadassah signaled for them to continue on. Without waiting for a response, Hadassah slowly stood. Her bare feet hardly made a sound on the forest floor. Martha and Rebekah looked at each other. Rebekah mouthed, "I'm not letting her go alone."

The three had gone a short distance when the sound of men shouting, horses snorting and metal clanging validated their suspicions. Dropping to their knees, they slowly and very quietly crawled as close as they dared to the circle of trees surrounding the dump. Waiting for just the right moment, Hadassah motioned for her sisters to stay put while she ever so slowly inched forward. Lying flat on her belly, she pushed back the brush the tiniest bit. To her horror, she saw a hideous-looking man dressed in royal attire perched atop the mountain of garbage while three soldiers dug through the rubbish.

"Ho, there! Captain, what's that in your hand?" the man shouted, pointing his blade at the soldier.

"My prince, I don't know," the captain answered, not daring to look upon his majesty.

"You fool! Bring me that scroll — NOW!"

The captain scampered up the mountain of garbage, slipping and sliding all the way, creating an avalanche behind him. Before he could properly present the scroll, the prince jerked it from his hand with a snarl and a string of curse words.

"You're stupid beyond reason," the prince said, shoving his foot in the captain's face. The poor man tumbled down the rotting mass of debris.

"Surely this is the lost treasure map," the prince said, "for it bears the king's golden seal."

Since he was a young child, the prince had heard stories of a lost scroll rumored to lead the way to the greatest treasure ever known to man. He became obsessed with finding it. That torment soon led to him being possessed by an evil that would stop at nothing.

Trembling, he broke the seal and quickly unrolled it. Turning his back to his soldiers, he read, "I, the Ancient of Days, the King of all kings, Lord of all lords and Savior of the world grant permission to the bearer of this scroll to spend one day with the Great King."

Hadassah's heart leapt. *A day with the Great King,* she said to herself.

"What!" the prince exclaimed, cursing and spitting. "A stinking invitation to spend a day with the king! What vile thing is this?" Furious, he sent the scroll flying through the air and into the forest.

Hadassah was unable to see exactly where it landed.

Possessed by Satan himself, the prince stormed down the cascading debris. "Why would I, the prince of this world, want to spend a day with the king? He should be on his knees begging to spend a day with me! After all, I'm the ruler of this world. I'm entitled to this world and all that's in it, for Adam, the man-child, invited me here."

Looking heavenward he screamed, "Do you hear me? The sons and daughters of man chose me — not you! You want *my* kingdom, but that'll never happen. I control your pitiful, disgusting, little peasants. And whoever controls the people controls the kingdom!" Shaking his fist in the air, he continued, "They serve *me*! They love *me*! They want what only I can offer and that's the freedom to decide for themselves what's right and what's wrong, what's good and what's evil. They desire to live outside of your suffocating rules and laws and boundaries, and only I can give them that. Do you hear me? Are you listening? *I'm* their god — not you!"

Surrounding the dump was a host of evil creatures all salivating, growling and fighting amongst themselves. As always chaos reigned in the unseen world.

Trembling, Hadassah quietly returned to her sisters.

The prince was insane with rage. Understanding the peril they were in, his soldiers hid their faces while wishing they were anywhere but there.

"I want that cursed treasure map, and I want it now!" he screamed. His men cowered.

A large, black vulture startled all but the prince as it flew out of a nearby tree. It screeched loudly as it circled overhead. Rebekah and Hadassah prayed fervently while Martha stared at a tiny spider.

The demons were wild with anticipation. They had seen the prince in a rage many times before, and to their delight it always ended in a blood bath. The spirit of Murder pushed its fat, grotesque, slimy body to the front of the ranks followed closely by Rage and Insanity. They circled the prince while enticing him to fulfill his fleshly desires.

"Where is it!? Where's the cursed treasure map?" the prince screamed as he thrust his dagger into the captain's belly and twisted. He then turned his attention to the other soldiers. Terrified, they dared not move.

The demons went crazy.

None left the garbage heap alive that day save the prince of evil.

CHAPTER FIVE

"*D*are we come out?" Rebekah whispered.

"It wouldn't hurt to wait a little longer," whispered Martha.

"The prince is probably at his castle enjoying a feast by now," said Hadassah. "You two stay put while I have a look around."

Hadassah crawled forward. Slowly pushing back the brush, she nearly vomited. The vulture now feasted on the dead bodies. Taking a deep breath she fought to erase the awful image from her mind. "Life-Giver, please help me."

Life-Giver placed His hand on her shoulder and said, "My peace I give you and My peace I leave with you."

Hadassah relaxed.

"Find the scroll, Hadassah," Life-Giver said.

Regaining her composure, she returned to her very nervous sisters. "It is worse than I feared. The prince is gone and his soldiers are all dead."

Tears pooled in Rebekah's eyes. Martha stared at the dirt beneath her fingernails.

"We should bury them," said Rebekah.

"Are you mad?!" exclaimed Martha.

Ignoring her, Hadassah said, "I must warn you . . . it's a hideous scene. There's a vulture —"

"Then we must hurry," Rebekah said, jumping to her feet.

"Don't leave me here alone," Martha said, running after them.

As they stepped into the clearing, Rebekah and Hadassah pelted the vulture with rocks and sticks until it flew away. Seeing the bloody bodies, Martha was unable to speak and Rebekah vomited.

Hadassah prayed.

Rebekah said, "Let's bury them."

Tearing her eyes away from the hideous scene, Martha exclaimed, "When the prince returns he'll see that someone buried them, and then he'll come looking for that someone!"

"That may be true," Rebekah said, "but that shouldn't keep us from doing what's right."

"I agree. We should offer these men what little dignity we can," said Hadassah.

"And how do you suggest we dig a hole?" Martha asked.

"We'll bury them with the only thing we have -- rubbish," said Rebekah.

Rebekah and Hadassah piled garbage on top of the bodies. Overcome by the evidence of the prince's brutality, they tried to comfort themselves by singing their mama's song, but it brought no relief. Martha refused to help.

Rebekah laid two sticks on top of one of the graves forming a cross.

"Why does life have to be filled with so much pain?" Hadassah asked.

"I don't know, but I refuse to believe that our life has to be like this forever. I believe the King has plans for us, plans for good and not evil," Rebekah responded.

"There's nothing but more pain and sorrow ahead," Martha said.

"Why do you say that?" Rebekah asked.

"Because that's all we've ever known."

"That's not exactly true, dear sister. When Mama and Papa were alive we were surrounded with goodness and kindness and love," said Rebekah.

Staring into the distance, Martha responded, "Those days are gone and will never be again. We must accept that fact and, in the meantime, do whatever is necessary to survive."

"There's so much more to life than just surviving," Rebekah said.

"I don't believe that and I don't want to talk about it. What I do want to talk about is getting as far away from this place as possible," said Martha.

"Where do you think we should go?" Rebekah asked, looking at Martha.

"Don't look at me. Ask her — she seems to have all the answers," Martha said, nodding toward Hadassah.

Ignoring her sarcastic tone, Hadassah answered, "Before we plan on leaving, I need to find that scroll."

"What scroll?" Martha asked.

"The scroll the prince threw into the forest. It's an invitation to spend a day with the Great King,"

Rebekah laid her hand on Hadassah's arm. Her eyes were filled with wonder. "How do you know it's an invitation?"

"The prince read it out loud. He threw it in that direction over there," she said pointing beyond the garbage pile. "I couldn't see where it landed."

"I'll help you," Rebekah said.

"Are you two crazy?' Martha said.

"Maybe," Hadassah said. Grabbing Rebekah's hand, they walked off.

Martha followed at a distance.

"Martha, why are you so afraid to hope?" Hadassah asked.

"I'm not afraid of anything!" Martha exclaimed.

Self-Pity, ready for a fight, rose up and said, "That's right, Martha, you're not afraid; you're just stating the facts."

"I think you're afraid," Hadassah said as gently as possible. "I think you're afraid to believe, because you fear being disappointed. Is that not true, dear sister?"

"Enough! If we're going to look for your stupid scroll, then we'd better do it now because I'm not staying in this godforsaken place much longer," Martha said, stomping off.

"You're brave," Rebekah said, locking arms with her sister.

"Not brave, dear sister, merely desperate, for I can't bear the thought of Martha being miserable for the rest of her life."

Martha pretended to search but gave up quickly.

"Please keep looking," Hadassah pleaded.

"I'm tired and that scroll's of no importance, otherwise the prince would've kept it," Martha said, kicking a large mushroom. Rebekah retrieved the uprooted mushroom and placed it in the pocket of her skirt.

"My heart tells me otherwise!" Hadassah said.

"The prince threw it away, Hadassah," said Martha.

"Perhaps the prince didn't understand its value," Rebekah said.

"Rebekah, the prince would never be that stupid."

"You don't know that," said Hadassah.

"Martha, it's obvious that you aren't interested in finding this scroll. And that's your right, but please stop harassing us," Rebekah said.

The two sisters continued their search while Martha stretched out of a thick bed of leaves in a nearby clearing.

"It can't just disappear, can it?" Rebekah asked, pushing a strand of hair from her face.

"It could be anywhere," Martha shouted.

"Rebekah, I *must* find that scroll," Hadassah said, growing increasingly frustrated with Martha's attitude.

"I don't know why you bother," Martha shouted.

"Martha, if you aren't going to help then would you at least be quiet?" Hadassah asked.

A very short but extremely fat, hideous-looking creature suddenly popped its head out of a nearby tree stump. Sniffing the air, Apathy cautiously approached Martha while speaking in a sing-song voice. "You're right, Martha, why bother? Nothing will ever change. Life isn't worth living. Just sit back and relax. Don't worry about anything. There's no point in even trying. Just give up."

Bitterness and Self-Pity welcomed Apathy in like an old friend.

It was not long before Martha fell asleep. She slept, but it was anything but restful. She woke feeling even more agitated than before. Re-joining her sisters, she announced, "I'm headed back. If you're smart you'll come with me."

"Stay and help us look," Hadassah pleaded.

"Hadassah, wake up and smell the garbage. Like I said, if that scroll had any value, don't you think the prince would've kept it?"

"If he thought it had value he certainly would've kept it. But, Martha, he was looking for a treasure map. It's easy to overlook treasure if it doesn't look like what you expect," Hadassah said, looking under the leaves of a giant fern.

"Now that the prince has discovered this place, we won't be able to come back here for who knows how long, if ever. He may return tomorrow with more of his minions, and if he does, I don't want to be anywhere near this place," said Martha.

"Martha, I *must* find that scroll!"

Throwing her hands up, Martha spun around and said to Rebekah, "Are you coming?"

"I guess so," she said, looking at the ground.

"At least you haven't lost *your* mind," said Martha.

"I'm not coming with you because I don't believe Hadassah. I'm coming because I don't think it's a good idea for you to be alone right now," Rebekah said.

"So why's it fine for Hadassah to be alone and not me?" Martha asked, her hands on her hips.

Ignoring her, Rebekah turned to Hadassah and said, "I'll pray for you to find it."

"Bekah, I *must* find that scroll."

"I know, Hadassah. Trust Life-Giver, Hadassah. He will lead you to it."

Hadassah watched her two sisters disappear into the forest. Her heart sank.

A black, cat-like creature named Discouragement peeked out from under a nearby bush.

A cold chill ran down Hadassah's spine. Looking around, she saw nothing.

Discouragement rubbed against her ankles as it purred softly.

Hadassah plopped down in the clearing and scratched her ankle.

Discouragement hopped onto her lap and purred loudly.

"Why does life have to be so very hard?" she asked herself.

Self-Pity quickly joined Discouragement and said, "That's right, Hadassah. Life's hard and it's not fair and it's not worth living."

"Life-Giver, I can't find the scroll."

"If you ask Me for bread, I won't give you a stone," Life-Giver whispered. *"All you need to do is ask."*

"Is that You, Life-Giver? Are You here with me?" she asked, her heart pounding.

"I am always with you."

"It is You! I can hear You!" she cried out. "I need Your help!"

Self-Pity and Discouragement shrieked as glorious beams of light suddenly broke through the trees. The golden light fell on Hadassah. Both creatures covered their eyes, but the light penetrated their defenses. Desperate, they dug their claws in even deeper.

Hadassah felt the battle but did not understand it. Overwhelming feelings of discouragement, self-pity and hopelessness rose up from the depths of her soul. *I know what this is,* she thought. She dreaded what would certainly follow. "Life-Giver, help me," she cried out, "I don't want to fall into that bottomless pit again!"

Without hesitation, Life-Giver scooped her up and said, "No weapon formed against you shall prosper, dear one."

Like a child rescued from certain disaster, Hadassah's defenses gave way and she sobbed uncontrollably.

"I will keep you as the apple of My eye."

"Don't listen to him — listen to me!" Self-Pity shouted. "Life's not fair. Your parents are dead, and your sisters have abandoned you. You'll never be safe or loved or happy. Life will always be painful and awful!"

"Just quit, give up, walk away," Discouragement added. "It's not worth the effort."

"You won't ever be good enough," Self-Pity added.

Life-Giver whispered in her ear, "Do not quit and you win, child." He held her closer while allowing her to choose which voice she would listen to and which she would believe.

All Hadassah could hear was the sound of her pain. She buried her face in her hands and wept bitterly.

Self-Pity mocked the King's Son while digging its claws deeper into Hadassah's heart.

"Your days are numbered, evil spirit," Life-Giver said with fire in His eyes. Self-Pity shrieked in pain, for truth never ceased to pierce like a fiery arrow. The heavenly light increased. Life-Giver leaned down and kissed Hadassah's forehead.

All she felt was the cold, hard ground beneath her.

"The daughter of man chooses us," Self-Pity arrogantly mocked.

"Only for a moment," Life-Giver replied, "for My love never fails to accomplish what it is sent to do."

Life-Giver brushed the hair back from Hadassah's face and said, "My dear child, you were born for greatness. You were born to receive My love and give it away. Now rise up and take your rightful place — choose life, Hadassah!"

Hadassah did not hear Him and was only vaguely aware of His presence.

Life-Giver leaned closer and said, "Before you were born, I knew you and placed within your spirit all you would ever need to accomplish the plans I have for you. You lack no good thing. Because I am with you, you can do all things."

Hadassah, hearing Him, leaned forward.

"Like a stone dug out of a quarry, you are being chiseled and hammered and crushed and broken, for I am making you into My image. My sheep know My voice, and they won't follow another. There are four voices in this world: Mine, yours, others' and Satan's. Hadassah, whose voice are you listening to? If a voice is not life-giving, then it is not Mine. It is time to pay attention to those voices in your mind. No longer allow negative thoughts to run rampant. Do not allow them to take root . . . cast them out and then ask Me to fill your mind with words of life."

Hadassah was overwhelmed, for she could hear His every word. "Fill my mind with Your words of life," she said.

Life-Giver's glory permeated the dark cloud that was fighting to take control of Hadassah's heart and mind. Her tears suddenly stopped, and she exclaimed, "I can feel Your love for me!"

She jumped to her feet.

Discouragement lost its grip and fell to the ground, but Self-Pity held on tight.

"Life-Giver, please forgive me."

"My love is always greater than your weakness, child. You are forgiven and cleansed."

Self-Pity fought hard to regain control.

"I need Your help to find that scroll," Hadassah cried out.

"Those who seek will surely find."

Self-Pity called for reinforcements. Doubt and Unbelief instantly appeared. The evil spirits assaulted her mind and emotions with an avalanche of thoughts. "Life-Giver doesn't really care about you.

He's deceiving you. He's mocking you. It's all in your imagination. It's not real."

Hearing the accusations, Hadassah asked, "Life-Giver, is it true?"

"Hadassah, remember who I am."

She heard Him. Taking a deep breath, she shook off the doubt and unbelief and proclaimed, "I refuse to listen to any voice that is not life-giving."

Life-Giver turned His gaze on the ugly creatures. Without a word spoken, Self-Pity released her and quickly fled to the cover of a nearby tree. Doubt and Unbelief had already fled.

Hadassah felt as though a ton of weight had been lifted from her. "I'm free," she whispered. A gentle breeze swept through the clearing, causing the leaves to form a tiny whirlwind.

"Rise up, My fair one, and come with Me," Life-Giver said.

"May I never again wallow in self-pity or doubt, for I belong to You!"

Sticking its ugly head out from behind the tree, Self-Pity shrieked. Life-Giver turned and faced the creature. "She no longer wants your help. Now go," He commanded.

Tucking its tail, the creature quickly crawled into a hole in the ground.

At that very moment, Hadassah heard twigs breaking. Diving beneath a thick canopy of bushes, she prayed fervently.

Fear licked its lips.

She waited. All was silent. Taking a deep breath, she slowly parted the leaves and peeked out. Greatly relieved, she did not know whether to laugh or cry, for not more than a stone's throw away was a doe and her fawn. "So, you're the cause of my near heart failure," she said as she crawled out.

To her shock, the deer simply stared unflinchingly at the girl before them. "Aren't you afraid of me?" she asked.

Curious, she slowly approached, but still they did not move. They remained steadfast until she was within arm's reach. At that point, they gracefully bounded into the forest. "What mystery was that?"

Shrugging her shoulders, she turned to resume her search, but something captured her attention. There, hidden within the hollow of a fallen log, was the much-sought-after scroll. With trembling hands, she retrieved the treasured possession and held it close. "Thank You!" she whispered.

"It is My pleasure to give you the kingdom, My child. The path is narrow that leads to life, and few there are who find it."

CHAPTER SIX

*H*adassah ran into the shack, hair flying and arms waving wildly. "I found it! I found the scroll!" she shouted.

"I knew Life-Giver would help you," Rebekah said, throwing her arms around her sister's neck. Martha rolled her eyes and turned her back to them.

"Life-Giver sent a deer and her fawn to help me find it! Bekah, please read it to me!"

Martha muttered something under her breath. Ignoring her, Hadassah said, "If only I could read — I would've read it already! What does it say? Tell me, please!"

"I thought you heard the prince read it," Martha said.

"I did, but I don't know if he read all of it. And besides, I want to hear it again."

"Give me a moment, dear sister. The parchment is quite old, and the words are severely faded. Have no fear; I'm certain I can —"

Hadassah interrupted. "Bekah, the evil prince was able to read it. Surely you can, too!"

"I might be able to if you'd give me a moment," Rebekah said smiling.

Wringing her hands, Hadassah vowed to keep silent.

"I'm ready, Hadassah, but perhaps you should sit down lest you faint," Rebekah said, enjoying the excitement she saw in her sister's eyes.

"Oh, may it never be! Just read, sister, and if I faint . . . I faint!" Hadassah said as she paced.

Martha groaned loudly.

Ignoring her, Rebekah cleared her throat and read, "I, the Ancient of Days, the King of all kings, Lord of all lords and Savior of the world, grant permission to the bearer of this scroll to spend one day with the Great King."

"Is that all?" Hadassah asked.

"That's all," Rebekah answered, looking intently at her sister.

Hadassah collapsed on the well-worn log. Rebekah knelt in front of her on the dirt floor and took her hands. "Is that disappointment I see in your eyes?" she asked.

"Disappointment?" Hadassah responded. "How could I be disappointed? We've just been granted permission to spend a day with the King. Such an invitation is more than I can comprehend. No, dear sister, this is so much better than anything I could've ever dared hope for."

"What are you saying?" Martha interrupted. "Don't you realize this scroll is worthless? The king and his son are either a fairy tale or long since dead! It's time to stop this ridiculous talk, Hadassah."

"Martha, He's not a fairy tale! I've heard Life-Giver's voice and felt His presence!" Hadassah exclaimed.

"I've heard His voice, too," Rebekah added.

Martha, with her hands on her hips, said, "Life-Giver's dead. He was killed long ago, crucified they say."

"Martha, don't you remember the story Papa told us? He said that Life-Giver came back to life."

"You're mad! *If* he's alive and *if* you happen to find his castle, do you think for one minute the guards will grant you entrance just because you have that scroll? Look at yourself, Hadassah! You're a peasant, dressed in filthy rags. You're nothing but skin and bones. Just one look at you and the guards will banish you from the kingdom — forever!"

"I *must* find the King, Martha."

"You're mad!"

Gentle Rebekah laid her hand on Hadassah's shoulder and said, "I'll go with you."

"You're *both* crazy!" Martha said, stomping out.

"Take no notice of her, Hadassah; she's just scared."

"I know."

"When should we leave?"

"As soon as Martha's in agreement, hopefully first thing in the morning," Hadassah said, thinking about the likely return of the evil prince.

"We must pray for her heart to change," said Rebekah.

Hadassah stepped outside. Martha was nowhere to be seen. She hurried to her favorite rock, reciting the words from the first parchment: "Seek the Great King while He may be found; call upon Him while He is near. You shall go out with joy and be led forth with peace. Enter by the narrow gate; for the gate is wide and the way is broad that leads to destruction, and many are those who enter by it. The gate is small and the way is narrow that leads to life, and few are those who find it."

Perched atop the rock, Hadassah prayed, "Life-Giver, the only way we can go out with peace would be for Martha to come with us. I can't bear the thought of leaving her behind, but neither can I bear the thought of not being able to follow this voice within that beckons me."

Hadassah was unaware that Life-Giver sat beside her. The two of them prayed for hours.

With the setting of the sun, Hadassah whispered, "I am poured out like water at Your feet. There must be more to life than this. I want all there is. I long to feel Your touch and see Your smile. I want to know You!"

"The day will come when you will know Me intimately."

To Hadassah's great delight, she heard His still, small voice. Taking a deep breath, she marveled at the all-consuming peace she felt. "Life-Giver?"

"Yes, child?"

"Am I more than what these rags say?" she asked, running her rough hands over her tattered, filthy skirt.

"Oh, Hadassah, you are so much more than what you see and think and feel! What you see will one day pass away, but your beauty will live forever."

"I know that I'm not the same as when You found me, but I have so far to go."

"Never the same when loved by Life."

"You're everything that I want to be. You're the Light that drives out the darkness in my soul. You calm my storms and hide me under the shelter of Your wings."

"When you look at yourself, you see darkness, but I see light. You see ashes, but I see beauty. You see flaws, but I see a masterpiece in the making. You see weakness, but I see your desire to please Me. You see failure, but I see a child who is learning to love."

"You see beyond my faults, and I'm so glad. Oh, Life-Giver, Your mercy and grace overwhelm me! Take me into Your heart, surround me with Your love, for that's where I belong."

"I took you into My heart before you were ever born and that is where you will always be. The real question is will you take Me into your heart?"

"How do I do that?"

"By surrendering."

"Surrendering what?"

"Your entire existence — your past, your present and your future; your failures and your victories; your weaknesses and your strengths. As you do so, I gain complete access to your heart and soul. I never force anyone to do anything. Instead, I draw you with cords of lovingkindness. As you surrender to My all-consuming love you will be transformed into My image."

Hadassah pondered His words. *How does one surrender everything?*

The sound of footsteps interrupted her thoughts. Turning, she saw Martha approaching, head down and feet dragging.

"Life-Giver, what should I say?" Hadassah quickly prayed.

"Words are not necessary — just love her."

Hadassah greeted her sister, inviting her to join her on the rock. As Martha settled in beside her, she said, "I'm sorry, Dassah. I don't know why I'm so hateful. I don't want to be, and I certainly don't want to hurt you or Bekah."

"I forgive you, dear sister."

The two were quiet for a long time.

Martha finally broke the silence, saying, "I hate to admit it, but what you said is true — I am afraid. I'm afraid of a lot of things. I'm afraid to stay and I'm afraid to go. I'm afraid to laugh and I'm afraid to cry. I'm afraid to believe in the king and I'm afraid not to. Mostly, I think I'm afraid to hope. I can't bear any more disappointment or pain. Dassah, I don't know what to believe or what to do anymore!"

"I understand," said Hadassah as she drew her sister close. Martha rested her head on Hadassah's shoulder and, for the first time in a very long time, allowed herself to be comforted.

"Do not be afraid, for I am with you. I will go with you," Life-Giver *said as He held them both.*

"So," Martha said, "when are we leaving?"

"At first light."

"I'll be ready."

"And you shall go out with joy and be led forth with peace."

***

That night, Hadassah had a dream.

She was walking through a forest when she came upon an abandoned cottage. She pushed against the door, and it fell off its hinges. The cottage was empty except for a small table in the center of the room. Sitting on the table was an earthenware jar. Hadassah found the jar irresistible. Brushing away the cobwebs, she made her way toward it. Picking up the jar, she examined it closely. Its simple yet exquisite beauty held her captive.

A voice from behind said, "It is beautiful, is it not?"

"It is," she said, turning to face a Stranger. "Do I know you?"

"You do, but not as well as you will in the days to come," the Stranger answered.

"Are you the creator of this piece of art?" she asked, running her hand over its highly polished surface.

"I am."

"For what purpose was it made?"

"This vessel was made to contain life and love and joy and peace. But, alas, it sits here empty and alone, hidden from the eyes of mankind. But that was never its destiny. It is actually quite valuable because it is one of a kind and can never be duplicated," He answered, looking deep into her soul.

"Kind sir, do you speak of the jar or of me?"

"You are both one and the same."

Hadassah tore her gaze from the Man and studied the vessel. She had not noticed the hair-like cracks covering its surface. "Do you know that this vessel is flawed? No one would ever consider it valuable."

"The cracks, like scars, merely represent your history not your worth or beauty. I am quite scarred myself but still have infinite value."

"You are scarred?"

"I am." Pushing up His sleeve, He showed her His arm, which was covered with hideous-looking scars. "My back, chest and legs look the same."

Unable to bear what she saw, Hadassah turned away. Running her fingers over the surface of the jar, she said to herself, "At least my flaws aren't very noticeable." She carefully placed the jar back on the table.

"Scars are not flaws, child. Just because you've been hurt and broken doesn't mean that you are flawed, and neither does it mean that you aren't valuable."

At that precise moment a gust of wind blew against the house causing the shutters to slam shut. Startled, Hadassah spun around, knocking over the table. To her horror, the jar crashed to the floor shattering into a thousand pieces. Unable to move, she stared at the impossible scene before her.

"All is lost!" she exclaimed.

"Nothing is ever lost in My kingdom, child, for I am a Master at finding and restoring lost things."

"But look — it's broken beyond repair. Just like the nursery rhyme Mama used to tell me. No one — not the king's horses or the king's men — can put it back together again."

The Man knelt down, chose two pieces and held them up, saying, "You're right. All of the king's horses and all of the king's men can't put this back together." With a smile, He pressed the two pieces together making them one.

"How'd you do that?"

"I simply applied what is called Unconditional Love," He answered. "It is what holds all things together, and it never fails."

Piece by piece, Hadassah watched as He carefully selected just the right pieces and pressed them together.

When finished He held up the jar, saying, "I make everything beautiful in its time."

Examining the pottery, Hadassah said, "I can't tell that it was ever broken. It's more beautiful than before, if that's even possible."

"Hadassah, I don't 'fix' people. I make them brand new. Many things have happened in your life that left you devastated and feeling hopeless — you were broken and spilled out, but that is not the end of the story. My Father and I love you too much to leave you in that state. Therefore, We have come to collect the pieces of your life and love you back to wholeness."

"How's that possible?"

"Nothing is impossible for Me, child, absolutely nothing. Now come away with Me, for you are the bride of My dreams."

"I am to be Your bride?'

"Did you not ask to know true love?"

"I did."

Hadassah bolted upright, her heart pounding in her chest. She looked around for Life-Giver. *It was only a dream,* she told herself. Lying back down, Hadassah rehearsed her dream over and over until her eyes were so heavy she could not keep them open.

"Dreams always come true when they originate from Me," Life-Giver whispered.

"Dreams do come true . . ." Hadassah said to herself as she drifted off to sleep.

CHAPTER SEVEN

𝒯he following morning, the three sisters walked away from the familiar into the unknown.

With each new day, Hadassah's past grew dimmer and her faith grew stronger.

As for Rebekah, the eyes of her heart remained focused on Life-Giver. She talked to Him about everything.

Martha promised herself that she would not complain, but, alas, she failed miserably. It seemed the harder she tried to be nice the more agitated she felt. For the most part, her sisters ignored her cutting remarks, choosing instead to pray for her.

"Are we ever going to get out of this mosquito-infested marsh?" Martha asked, swatting and slapping wildly at the swarm of biting insects.

"Life-Giver will show us the way out," Hadassah answered for the tenth time that morning.

"And just exactly how do you think he'll do that?"

"I'm not sure, but I'm not worried. He led me to the scroll, didn't He?"

"Hadassah, you found that scroll because of a deer."

"Life-Giver sent that deer in answer to my prayers, Martha. He'll help us again; I'm sure of it."

Martha bit her tongue while fighting the urge to shake some common sense into her sister.

Apathy and Bitterness stood at attention. Bitterness whispered, "Martha, why do you allow your sisters to make all the decisions? You're the elder sister, aren't you? They don't really care about you. All they care about is that worthless scroll."

Martha rushed ahead, pushing her sisters aside. "Why did I ever agree to come with you anyway?" she muttered.

Bitterness whispered in her ear, "You weren't given a choice."

Martha shouted back over her shoulder, "Like I told you, this quest is impossible and it will fail. And when it does, where will we be? I'm sick and tired of being ignored and miserable!"

"Martha," Rebekah called out.

"Don't even bother," Martha said, increasing her pace. Her frustration and anger blinded her as she ranted and raved about the misery and injustice of her life.

"Be careful, Martha," Rebekah shouted, but it was too late.

At that very moment, Martha stepped into a mud pit. Instantly, she was knee deep in thick, clay-like mud. She fought to pull her legs out but only sank deeper. Her anger increased as she realized she needed help. Looking back at her sisters, they were already searching for something they could use to pull her out.

"Martha, don't worry. We'll be right there," Hadassah shouted as she hacked away at a vine.

"I'm not worried. As a matter of fact, I don't really care what happens," Martha said, now up to her thighs in the muck and mire.

Apathy chuckled. "That's right, Martha, just give up."

"I wonder why humans fight so hard to stay alive," Martha mused.

"Because life is a gift and it's precious," Rebekah answered.

"Bekah, I'm sorry, but I'm really not interested in your lofty insights. I just want this nightmare to end. I'm tired, really tired."

"Well, it's not time to quit just yet, sister," Hadassah said as she and Rebekah pulled on the vine with all of their might. The vine came loose sending the two sisters flying backwards. Wasting no time, they jumped to their feet and hurried to edge of the mud pit.

Tossing an end of the vine to Martha, Hadassah said, "Now wrap it around your arm and hold on."

Unmoving, Martha stared at the lifeline in front of her. Hadassah and Rebekah looked at each other.

Apathy stoked the old fires of bitterness and hopelessness long resident within Martha.

Martha mumbled something no one could hear. Hadassah encouraged her to hold onto the vine while Rebekah begged for Life-Giver's help.

"She does not want My help," Life-Giver responded.

"But can't You help her anyway?" Rebekah silently asked.

"My dear child, I cannot ever force anyone to do anything against their will. Mine is a kingdom built on voluntary love, not forced obedience. I am drawing her with My all-consuming love, but the choice to receive it is hers."

Rebekah prayed harder.

Martha's thoughts suddenly turned to her papa. Words long forgotten filled her mind, *"My dearest daughter, the King's lovingkindness never ceases. His compassions never fail, and they are new every morning. Great is His faithfulness. The King is good to those who wait for Him, to those who seek Him."*

Martha whispered, "Could it be true? Is the king good to those who look for him?"

Afraid, Apathy called out for Self-Murder's assistance. The ugly creature eagerly responded.

Martha's eyes filled with tears. Angry at herself and at the world, she hastily wiped her eyes, smearing mud across her face.

Rebekah saw her tears and prayed harder.

"Martha, come on, just grab the vine," Hadassah coaxed, the fear obvious in her voice.

Martha was now waist deep and still sinking. She looked at Hadassah and Rebekah as if in a daze.

"Martha," Hadassah begged, "please hold onto the vine."

Tears ran freely down Martha's face.

Self-Murder had attached itself to her like a leech, flooding her mind with lies.

Staring at her sisters but not seeing them Martha said, "I've known great trouble and know it still. I've been made to walk in darkness and not in light. Why has the king turned his back to us? Why did he leave us as orphans and slaves? He's caused my heart to waste away and has broken all of my bones. He's besieged and encompassed me with bitterness and hardship. He made me dwell in dark places. He has walled me in so that I cannot be free; he's made my burdens heavy. Surely if I call for help, he will shut out my voice. He's made me desolate. He's filled me with bitterness. My soul knows no peace; I've forgotten happiness. My strength has perished and so has my hope."

"Martha, whose voice are you listening to?" Rebekah shouted.

Martha stared far away.

A holy, righteous anger rose up in Rebekah. "In the name of the Great King and by His authority, I command every evil spirit tormenting my sister to be silent!"

The three creatures were instantly bound.

"Martha," Rebekah shouted.

Martha blinked, slowly lifting her eyes. Rebekah prayed.

Rebekah, fearing her sister would disconnect again, said, "Martha, reach out your hand and take the vine. That's right, dear. Now wrap it around your arm and hold on tight. That's right. Now don't let go."

The two sisters pulled with all their might. Martha's hands slipped. The vine burned so Martha let go.

Rebekah and Hadassah prayed diligently as they tossed the vine back out.

"Martha, let's try again," Rebekah said. "Wrap the vine around your arm and hold on as tight as you can."

"I can't do it," Martha said.

"Yes, you can! Life-Giver is here and He wants to help you! Nothing's impossible for Him. Now, let's try again. On the count of three — one, two, three! That's right, hold on, Martha!"

Life-Giver placed His hands beneath her arms and pulled.

Rebekah and Hadassah pulled with all their might.

Neither Rebekah nor Hadassah were aware that a very strong angel pulled with them.

"It's working, Martha, hang on! You're doing great!"

Martha gritted her teeth as the vine dug into her arms and hands.

Dragging her to safety, the two sisters embraced a very muddy Martha. "I'm sorry," Martha said.

"I couldn't bear the thought of losing you," Rebekah said, wiping the mud from her sister's face.

"Don't ever scare us like that again," said Hadassah.

"Believe me, it wasn't what I had planned," Martha said, leaning against Rebekah.

"You're quite a sight," Hadassah said.

"At least the mosquitoes aren't biting me."

Hadassah looked at Rebekah and then suddenly jumped to her feet. "Of course!" Hadassah exclaimed. Dropping to her knees, she crawled to the edge of the pit and plastered herself with mud. Rebekah did the same.

That night, for the first time since entering the marsh, they slept soundly. The following morning they plastered themselves again and continued on. Martha was unusually quiet. Rebekah and Hadassah were not sure what to think about her silence, and when they asked she chose not to answer.

After two more very long days and nights, they finally came to the end of the dreadful marsh. Stretched out before them was a beautiful meadow of wild flowers. Running as fast as they could, they headed for the stream on the far side. Lying on their bellies, they gulped the cool water. After bathing they again plastered their bodies with thick red clay to relieve the itching.

"We're quite a sight," Rebekah announced as they stretched out on the sweet-smelling grass.

"At least we're not itching," said Hadassah.

Martha looked at her two sisters and burst out laughing.

"What's so funny?" Hadassah asked, mud sliding down her face and into her ear.

Martha laughed so hard she could not answer. Her tears made tracks down her muddy face. Soon, all three were laughing uncontrollably. It felt good, really good. Exhausted, they fell fast asleep, basking in the warmth of the late afternoon sun.

Unbeknownst to them, Life-Giver and His angels kept close watch as they slept through the night.

***

With the rising of the sun, they set out once again. Rebekah and Hadassah prayed fervently for guidance, listening closely for that still, small voice. For two days they walked through lush meadows, crossing many streams. To their delight, they found quite a large selection of edible plants and roots. Martha was once again her old, complaining self, which caused Hadassah and Rebekah to have mixed feelings.

At noon on the third day, they stood on the crest of a rather large hill not wanting to believe what they saw. Martha plopped down on the grass and said, "Now what are we going to do? And don't either of you say pray!"

Hadassah looked at Rebekah, who said, "We certainly can't go back."

"Don't tell me you expect us to try and cross *that*!" Martha exclaimed, pointing to the endless ocean of hot, white sand.

Without saying a word, Hadassah retreated to a huge oak tree and sat down beneath its broad canopy. Leaning her head back against the trunk, Hadassah whispered, "Life-Giver, what are we to do now? There's no way we can cross a desert like that one — it's impossible."

"I specialize in the impossible, and I delight in asking you to do the same."

Hadassah was too distracted by fear to hear Him.

Smelling her fear, the cat-like creature called Discouragement suddenly poked its head out of the ground. Sniffing the air, it followed the scent. Alerted by Discouragement, numerous other creatures trailed behind. Defeat scampered up Martha's arm while Discouragement targeted Hadassah.

Fear and Unbelief repeatedly tried to gain access to Rebekah but were unsuccessful. Rebekah was lost in worship, thanking Life-Giver for the journey behind and the one that was before them. As a result, fragrant oil covered her, which kept the creatures from her.

Defeat stroked Martha's brow, saying, "There's no need to continue. You and I both know the king isn't real. His city was destroyed thousands of years ago, and his son is dead. Turn back and find rest for yourself, for your journey is in vain. You'd be a fool to continue, and doing so will bring you nothing but more pain and hardship."

A cold shiver ran through Martha's body. She wanted to run away, but she had nowhere to go. She moved closer to Hadassah, who did not notice, for she was consumed by her own battle.

Discouragement invited Guilt, Fear and Unbelief to join the attack. They wrapped themselves around Hadassah's head, whispering their vicious lies.

Hadassah found herself wondering if leaving the Land of Despair had been a mistake. *Guilt whispered, "You should've never talked your sisters into following you. Your decision nearly killed Martha. If she had died, it would've been your fault. And now you've led your sisters to a desert, which will result in their deaths for sure."*

Discouragement added, "Now what are you going to do?"

Hadassah ran her fingers along the frayed edges of the scrolls; she wondered if her journey was in vain.

"Hadassah, whose voice are you listening to?" Life-Giver asked, drawing close.

Hadassah did not hear Him, but her spirit did. She looked around. Her eyes saw nothing, but her spirit perceived much — all of which she did not understand or comprehend. All Hadassah knew was that she was being compelled by some inner force to abandon her pursuit, and she felt helpless to resist.

"Rebekah, it's time to fight!"

Rebekah, who had been lost in worship, suddenly sat up and looked around. "Something's very wrong," she said.

Hadassah responded, "I know."

"I don't know what it is, but I don't like it," said Rebekah.

Martha added, "I don't like it either."

Not knowing exactly what Life-Giver meant, Rebekah prayed. Hadassah soon joined her, fighting a battle they could not see and did not understand. Martha, secretly glad they were praying, felt a tiny glimmer of hope.

As the sisters prayed, the creatures grew weaker until, as quickly as they came, they left. The spiritual atmosphere changed instantly.

Hadassah and Rebekah looked at each other. "Your prayers must be really powerful," Hadassah said.

"On the contrary, Life-Giver must be really powerful."

Martha quickly stood to her feet. Attempting to smooth her ragged skirt, she announced, "I'm just glad that whatever that was is gone. Now let's go find something to eat."

"Any suggestions?" Hadassah asked.

"Well, I wouldn't suggest we look in that godforsaken desert," Martha answered.

"There is no place on earth that I have forsaken. You will come to understand that in the days ahead, Martha."

Rebekah saw it first. "I think that's an apple tree over there," she said, pointing behind Martha.

The three sisters raced to the tree. Hadassah quickly climbed up the gnarled trunk. Overjoyed, she tossed down a dozen large, red apples.

Sitting beneath its branches, biting into the delicious fruit, Hadassah said, "We walked right by this tree, so why didn't we see it?"

"We were too tired to notice," Martha answered.

"Maybe, but I don't know . . . a tree this large and so full of bright, red apples . . . we should've seen it," said Hadassah.

"Don't go making assumptions, little sister. I know what you're implying, and you can't prove it."

"Who says one has to prove everything? Why can't one just choose to believe . . . especially those things that can't be proven?" Hadassah asked.

"You can, but that kind of thinking will eventually prove to be a great source of disappointment."

"Then I choose to take the chance, for I'd rather be guilty of giving Life-Giver credit than miss an opportunity to do so. And besides, I believe He has His hand in everything that touches my life."

"That's a bold statement, little sister. If that's true, then that also applies to the death of our parents," Martha said, spreading her apron on the ground.

Rebekah joined the discussion. "Martha, I'm sure you remember our parents telling us that the King holds life and death in His hands. If that's true, then He alone determines a person's lifespan. The death of our parents was awful, but we can't blame the King. His ways are higher than ours, and who can understand them? Life-Giver once told me that the King never wastes anything and that He causes all things to work together for good for those who love and follow Him.

"We've been given a most amazing opportunity, Martha, an opportunity to spend one day with the King. That's an opportunity

I'm not willing to miss just because we've come up against an obstacle."

"Rebekah, you grow more beautiful with each passing day!" Life-Giver whispered.

"An obstacle?! This obstacle you speak about could mean our deaths! We aren't just talking about some little molehill, Rebekah; we're talking about crossing a hot, godforsaken desert!" Martha shouted.

"Life-Giver said that obstacles are merely opportunities in disguise," Rebekah said.

Martha stared at her in disbelief. "Have you lost your mind? All this talk of Life-Giver and hope and opportunity has made you mad! If we try to cross that desert, it will kill us!"

"If we die, we die," said Rebekah.

"To die is to live," Life-Giver said.

Rebekah continued, "Martha, stop and think. You were trapped in that mud pit. Who do you think helped us get you out? Surely, you know!"

"No, I don't know. All I know is that Life-Giver and his father, the so-called Great King, have done precious little to intervene in our lives. It appears to me that, if he is real — and the stories are true — then he is quite fickle. Helping one moment and then turning his back the next. How can I trust a king like that?"

"I know it appears that way, but Martha, we can't see the end from the beginning. We don't understand the *why*'s of the kingdom, and neither can we know the future. But the Great King and His Son do. Life is like a river — it has a beginning and an ending. We can only see the place we've come from and the place we presently are, but the King sees the entire river from above. He knows every twist and turn. He knows every detail that will ever affect us. And He promises to always be with us — in life and death. Surely we can trust someone like that."

"You *are* mad!" Martha exclaimed. Turning to face Hadassah, she asked, "You aren't thinking about crossing that desert, are you?"

"Actually, I am, Martha. If we're to find the King's castle, we must continue onward."

Martha angrily hurled her apple core through the air, saying, "Once again, it appears I have no say in this matter, and you're going to do what you want to do, whether I like it or not."

Neither sister responded. Martha turned her back to them. Complaining, she filled her apron with apples.

Hadassah turned to Rebekah and whispered, "It looks like the old Martha's here to stay."

"Not necessarily," Rebekah said. "Life-Giver can soften even the hardest of hearts."

Hadassah climbed the tree once more, tossing down enough apples to fill their two blankets and cloak. Tying the corners together, they each slung one over their shoulders. They walked back to a stream where they filled their wineskins.

Taking a deep breath and uttering a silent prayer, Hadassah led her sisters back toward the desert. Standing before the ocean of sand, she prayed they were doing the right thing.

They had traveled only a short distance when Martha asked, "Just how do you propose we keep from sweating to death?"

"Life-Giver will protect us," Hadassah said, desperately hoping and praying her words were true. She looked at Rebekah for encouragement, which was immediately given.

"I will protect you from the burning rays of the sun with My cloud by day, and I will keep you warm with My fire by night," Life-Giver promised.

Within a very short time, thick clouds rolled in from the north, shading them from the brutal rays of the sun. At nightfall, as they stretched out on their blankets, they watched as the clouds rolled away, allowing the moon to shine full and bright.

What they could not see was the pillar of fire burning just above them, which kept them warm through the cold desert nights. And neither did they see Life-Giver and His angelic army surrounding them.

Each day the clouds covered them, and each night the invisible fire warmed them. Hadassah and Rebekah rejoiced and thanked Life-Giver while Martha grumbled and complained about the sand, the heat, the sweat and the futile journey they were on.

CHAPTER EIGHT

*O*n the sixth day, having eaten the last of their apples and drunk the last of their water, they stood before a wall of sand that extended as far as they could see in both directions.

Martha, with her hands on her hips, said, "I told you this godforsaken desert would kill us."

Ignoring her, Hadassah turned to Rebekah, who was already praying, and said, "Please tell me Life-Giver's talking to you."

"Well, not exactly."

"I don't know that it would do any good if he did," Martha said. "What do you expect him to do — move this mountain, part this sea of sand?"

"Maybe so," Rebekah replied.

"Oh, you're driving me mad!" Martha exclaimed, walking off.

Turning her attention back to Hadassah, Rebekah said, "Maybe we could follow the ridge until we find a place that isn't so high?"

"We could, but who knows how far we'd have to walk. And remember, we have no water."

"We have no choice but to trust Life-Giver," Rebekah said.

Frustrated, Martha returned. The three sat in silence; two of them prayed.

Life-Giver answered, "Trials bring about endurance; and endurance, proven character; and proven character, hope and hope does not disappoint."

"What does that mean exactly?" Rebekah asked.

"Rebekah, I waste nothing. Everything in this life is meant to bring you closer to Me. The facts are never greater than Me. No mountain is too high and no valley is too low with Me by your side. Now is not the time to give up but to persevere, for you never know when you are on the brink of a miracle."

"But this really looks impossible," she said.

"Choose faith instead of fear, Rebekah. Approach all things with faith and perseverance."

Rebekah turned to her sisters and said, "I believe Life-Giver wants us to press on."

"Then that's exactly what we shall do," said Hadassah.

"You two are going to be the death of me yet," Martha muttered under her breath.

"No, Martha, they won't be the death of you, but I will be. Unless a kernel of wheat falls into the ground and dies it cannot bring forth fruit. I will bring you to the end of yourself that I might give you life."

Rebekah gently but firmly said, "Martha, if you wouldn't complain so much you might discover that life isn't as difficult as you think. You might even find out that complaining only makes things seem worse." Without giving her a chance to respond, Rebekah turned to Hadassah, who was already on her feet, and said, "Now, let's go do the impossible."

"I'm with you."

Martha followed, complaining all the way.

They made little progress. No matter how hard they tried the sand was an avalanche beneath their feet and hands. "In case you haven't noticed . . . this isn't working," Martha called out.

"I can see that," Hadassah answered. "Maybe you have a better idea?"

"We should go back."

"We can't, Martha. It would take six days to get back, and we don't have any food or water."

"Let's pray for rain," Rebekah said.

"Rain?" Martha asked.

"Yes, if it would rain, then maybe the sand would be easier to climb."

"That's a great idea," Hadassah said.

"Yeah, except for the fact that it doesn't rain in deserts," said Martha.

"The facts don't matter to Life-Giver," Rebekah said.

Without further discussion, Rebekah sat down and began to pray. Hadassah joined her. Martha dozed in and out of sleep. She sat straight up when a big, wet drop of water fell on her face. "Was that a raindrop?" she asked.

"It sure was," Hadassah answered.

Hadassah and Rebekah danced wildly as the raindrops quickly turned into a downpour.

Self-Pity and Bitterness whispered their lies to Martha.

Hadassah and Rebekah quickly dug numerous holes. It rained so hard and so long that they were able to satisfy their thirsts and fill their wineskins. Highly encouraged, as soon as the downpour stopped they began their ascent again. This time it was much easier.

Hadassah's breath caught in her throat as she stood at the top of the ridge. Stretched out before her was an immense valley. A broad, crystal clear river snaked its way through it.

Rebekah stared in sweet silence. When Martha topped the ridge her knees buckled. Wave after wave of sweet relief swept over her. That was when she realized just how worried and frightened she had been.

"Truly this must be the land of the Great King," Hadassah said.

"You don't know that for certain," Martha said.

"Have you ever seen anything as glorious as this?" Hadassah asked, laying her hand on Martha's shoulder.

"That doesn't mean . . ."

"Martha, look over there," Hadassah said, pointing to a stone wall that was so high they could not see beyond it.

"What are we waiting for?" Hadassah asked as she ran down the ridge. Rebekah was right behind her, but Martha remained where she was. She wanted to hope, to believe, but the war within her mind raged out of control. Martha felt hopeless to save herself.

Watching her sisters, Martha whispered, "Life-Giver, if you're real, would you help me? Would you silence these tormenting voices?"

"I would love to."

The evil spirits within her instantly grew still and quiet.

Martha felt the difference. Without acknowledging Life-Giver's intervention, she hurried after her sisters.

Life-Giver blessed her.

"Look!" Hadassah shouted, running toward a tree heavy laden with figs.

Plucking two, she tossed one to Rebekah and bit into the other. "Oh, I can't remember the last time I had a fig," she said.

Rebekah said, "The last time was from Papa's tree. Can you remember Papa's fig tree, Dassah?"

"Yes, I do and what sweet figs they were," she said.

Martha soon joined them, and Hadassah tossed her a couple figs.

"Oh, I so love figs!" Martha said, wiping the juice running down her chin.

Stretched out on the soft green grass, Rebekah thanked Life-Giver, which reminded Hadassah to do the same. Martha busily filled her apron.

"Martha, I don't think we need to worry about food," Hadassah said.

Appearing somewhat embarrassed, Martha said, "I'm not accustomed to having plenty—"

Hadassah interrupted, "I understand, Martha. It's been a long, hard journey. But have no fear; we're almost at our destination. Now come and rest with us, dear sister, and leave your fears behind."

Martha tried, but she allowed her thoughts to have free rein. It was not long before she was feeling quite sorry for herself again. *Smelling the stench, her demons returned.* Out of sheer frustration, she left her napping sisters to explore the land that appeared to hold so much promise. Afraid of losing her way, she kept the fig tree in sight as she filled her apron with raspberries, strawberries and purple grapes. Time passed quickly.

"Martha, where are you?" Hadassah shouted.

"Over here," she yelled, waving from the top of a large boulder. "And I found a piece of flint!"

Hadassah and Rebekah squealed as they raced to her.

Martha proudly displayed the rather large piece of flint. "You know what this means." Martha said.

"It means a hot supper tonight," said Hadassah.

Martha then showed them the small cave she had discovered, the three sleeping mats she had made out of bulrushes and the large collection of fruit. Tears filled Rebekah's eyes as she thanked Life-Giver for His extravagant provision.

While Martha gathered firewood, Hadassah and Rebekah carved two spears and then ran to the nearby river.

Standing knee-deep in the fast-flowing water, Hadassah asked, "How long's it been since we've had roasted fish?"

"Too long to remember, but with Life-Giver's help surely we will tonight," Rebekah said, thrusting her spear into the water. Smiling broadly, she held up a large, wiggling trout.

The two were amazed at how quickly they caught at least a dozen fish. "Do you suppose Life-Giver's standing on the bank commanding the fish to come our way?" Hadassah asked, stepping out of the river.

"It wouldn't surprise me."

Life-Giver, standing in the middle of the river, smiled broadly. "I am always with you," He said.

Hadassah and Rebekah scaled and gutted the fish, washing them in the water. Hurrying back to Martha, the girls displayed their catch, careful to give Life-Giver the credit.

As the sun slid behind the ridge, they sat in the mouth of the cave around a campfire, licking their fingers. Hadassah said, "I wish I had two stomachs."

"I ate like I have two stomachs," Martha said, rubbing her belly.

"So did I," said Rebekah.

After tossing the bones far from their camp, they stretched out on their pallets just inside the mouth of the cave. Rebekah stared into the fire and whispered, "Thank You for all that You've done this day, my wonderful Friend."

"Delight yourself in Me, and I will give you the desires of your heart."

"I have but one desire and that is to be with You where You are."

"And so you will ever be."

***

The following morning, Martha was out gathering fruit and nuts well before her sisters woke. Returning with her apron full, she announced, "Bekah, Dassah, the sun is up, the birds are singing and breakfast is served."

Surprised by their sister's cheery disposition, Hadassah and Rebekah stared at her. "Are you well?" Rebekah asked.

"I am very well, thank you."

"Why are you so . . . happy?" Hadassah asked.

"Dassah, Bekah, everything we need is here — the best shelter we've ever had, a river full of fish and every kind of fruit and nut imaginable. What more could we ask for?"

Not waiting for them to respond, Martha opened her apron and continued, "Look, Dassah, I found a date tree! I know they're your favorite."

Hadassah happily received Martha's overstuffed apron.

"Martha, it's good to see you so happy," Rebekah said, laying her hand on her sister's arm.

"I agree," Hadassah said, devouring her fourth date.

Martha stretched out on her pallet between her two sisters. "I want us to stay here."

Rebekah looked at Hadassah who looked at the ground.

"Please don't say no. For once, can we do what I want?" Martha asked.

"Martha, how can we stay here when we're so close to seeing our dream come true?" Hadassah asked.

Martha responded, "It's your dream, not mine. Won't you at least consider it?"

"We can certainly pray," said Rebekah.

"Pray if you must, but I already know what I want to do," Martha said, trying her best to restrain the anger she felt.

Hadassah and Rebekah grabbed their spears and headed back to the river. "What are we going to do?" Hadassah asked.

"We're going to ask Life-Giver."

"Bekah, I have to find the castle, for that's where I'll find the King." Hadassah stopped to pick up a rock.

"What's that for?' Rebekah asked.

"I'm going to dig a hole to put the fish in so they won't flop around on the ground like yesterday."

"Good idea," Rebekah said, eagerly joining her.

Once the hole was dug, they stepped into the water. "Oh! The water's so much colder than yesterday," Hadassah said.

"I agree," Rebekah said, shivering.

The two stood in silence waiting patiently for a fish to swim by. Rebekah asked, "Life-Giver, what should we do?"

"Always pursue Perfect Love."

Rebekah knew what they should do. "Hadassah, I know you're eager to get to the castle, but I think it would be good for Martha to stay here for a little while. She is more important than our mission. As a matter of fact, love is our mission, don't you agree?" Rebekah said, thrusting her spear through a fish. She tossed it onto the bank into the hole.

Hadassah knew she was right, but could not bring herself to say it.

***

Throughout the month, Hadassah and Rebekah spent long hours praying for their sister. Seeing her so happy was bitter sweet. They agonized over the fact that they knew the day would come when they would have to leave. To their utter surprise that moment never came, for late one night Martha announced, "I think we should leave."

"What?" Hadassah asked.

"You heard me."

"I thought you wanted to stay?"

"I do, but I know that you and Bekah really want to find the king and his castle. And it's the only way to know for sure if the king is a fairy tale or real. Shall we leave in the morning?"

"Thank you, Martha," said Rebekah.

Martha, tears streaming down her face, turned away from her sisters and dared to hope that just maybe they would find the king and that he would be all they believed him to be.

"I am yours and My desire is for you," Life-Giver whispered.

The next morning they followed the river, which led to the stone wall. Approaching the gate, Hadassah prayed fervently, for she feared rejection more than anything. As they knocked on the wooden gate, they were shocked to discover that it was unlocked. It took all of their strength to push it open. Stepping through they were even more shocked to discover that there were no guards or buildings or people.

"This looks more like the countryside than a city,' Martha said. "Where are all the people and houses?"

"Can't say that I know," said Hadassah.

"Why would anyone build a wall around nothing?" Martha asked.

"Let's just keep going," said Rebekah.

They stopped often to sample the various fruits and nuts growing in abundance, some of which they had never seen before.

"This is indeed a land flowing with milk and honey," Hadassah said as she dipped her finger in a honeycomb she discovered in the hollow of a tree.

"It's certainly a land filled with much promise," Rebekah agreed, noticing how quiet Martha was.

With the setting of the sun, they made a bed beneath the boughs of a large tree.

Life-Giver, ever present, whispered, "Sleep, for tomorrow will be a day of great sorrow." He then summoned one of His archangels.

"My King," Michael said.

"Surround My children," said Life-Giver.

With a blast from his ram's horn, a dozen angels stood before Michael.

Unbeknownst to the sisters, a venomous snake had hidden itself nearby in the crevices of a large rock. One glance from Life-Giver alerted the angelic guards that the serpent was not to be allowed access to the sleeping beauties. Five angels immediately surrounded the snake while seven took up their positions around the girls. The serpent reluctantly retreated into the deep recesses of the brush.

Rebekah awoke while it was still dark. Silently singing, she worshipped the One who loved her most. *Life-Giver relished every word, every movement of her heart, drinking deeply of her affection and devotion. "Your love may be quiet, but it runs ever so deep. You have loved Me well, My precious child."*

"I pray that my life might be acceptable in Your sight and in the sight of my King. I know I don't have much to offer. Actually, all I have to offer is a broken and contrite heart. I hope and pray it's enough for someone as grand and glorious as You."

"A broken and contrite heart I will not despise, for your voluntary love is all I require and all I desire."

"I sense Your sweet presence drawing me," Rebekah said. She ever so quietly walked a short distance away where she fell on her knees.

"You're my first love! You rescued me from an evil prison. You held me close and wouldn't let me go. You've loved me more than I deserved and honored me beyond any expectation. My greatest desire is to be with You forever. This world holds nothing for me. I desire You and You alone. Oh, grant this prayer of mine and free me from this earth and all its troubles!" Hot tears streamed down her young, weathered face.

"Rebekah, your prayers have been heard and your desire shall be granted."

"I feel Your love for me! Thank You for coming! Thank You for loving me!"

He laid His hands over her ears.

Rebekah ears were opened, and she fell on her face.

Life-Giver sang,

"My love is like a cloud in the midst of a desert.
My love is like a fire in the midst of a cold, winter night.
My love is like summer rain — it refreshes those who are thirsty.
My love is like an ocean. . ."

Rebekah sat up and sang, "And I'm overwhelmed by Your presence!"

"My love is like a room filled with jewels — shining and bright, beautiful and rare."

"Your love takes my breath away, causing me to forget the pain of my past and my fear of the future."

"And I am lost in your gaze, My beautiful, beautiful child."

"And I am lost in the love that I feel. I am lost in the joy of Your smile. The warmth of Your touch melts my heart like nothing else can. I'm overwhelmed by the fragrance of Your garments — myrrh, aloe and cassia — You smell delightful! I'm overpowered by a love that is strong enough to transform my cold, hard heart. I'm free and I'm running into Your marvelous light. . ."

"I am the One who is overwhelmed, child." He laid His hands on her eyes.

Her eyes were opened, and she saw Life-Giver standing before her with His hand extended. Without any hesitation she placed her hand in His.

"Rise up, My love, My fair one, and come away with Me."

Standing, she whispered, "I will follow You anywhere. I will run the race." The two stood face to face, heart to heart.

"There is nothing more stunning to Me than a heart in love."

"You are stunning, indeed," she said, unable to look in His eyes.

"I was speaking of you."

"You are the One who is stunning! You find me stunning?"

"Dear one, I am unlike anyone you have ever known. I do not just possess love, I am love — unselfish, unconditional, unending, sacrificial love, love in its purest form. And I always respond to you according to who I am, not according to who you are or what you do."

"Yours is an uncommon love for sure," Rebekah whispered, looking at the ground. She pondered His words for a very long time. And all the while, His gaze never left her.

"No one has ever loved me the way You do."

"And no one ever will."

Rebekah sighed deeply.

As the sun rose and painted the sky orange, she dared to look up. His eyes took her breath away, for they were filled with intense, fiery devotion — devotion for her!

"Why have I found favor in Your sight, my Lord?" she asked, her voice trembling.

"Because you have captured My heart."

"How did I do that?"

"With just one glance of your eyes."

"Your grace is amazing."

"Rebekah, you withheld nothing from Me — not even your sins. You made Me your Savior and your Friend."

"I had nowhere else to go and no one else who could save me. You're the only One who has eternal life."

"I not only have eternal life, but I am Eternal Life."

"Life-Giver, I give You my life such as it is."

"Rebekah, your life is like a stone dug out of a quarry. I allowed people and circumstances to chisel, sand and polish away your rough edges. A life of ease and pleasure cannot transform a stone into a masterpiece. You will soon be lifted out of this earthly quarry and taken through the Door to eternity where you will be fitted together with other stones to make a holy city, a bride. In that place, there is no hammer or chisel, for all the work must be done on earth."

"I don't understand."

"The day will come when you will."

Gazing into His eyes, she responded, *"So lift me into Your arms where I'm safe, for I'm lost in this love I see in Your eyes."*

Like a father holding a precious child, her Beloved Savior and Friend held Rebekah against His beating heart. *"Hold me close, never let me go,"* she said softly as she drew great comfort from the rhythm of His heartbeat. *"Is there anyone or anything stronger than You?"*

"Nothing and no one is stronger than Perfect Love."

"Nothing?"

"Not death, nor life, nor angels nor demons. Not anything present or anything to come — not your weaknesses or your propensity to sin, not powers or height or depth or any other created thing is stronger than My love for you."

"That means I'm safe."

"You are safe."

As He held her, close and long, she sighed deeply. Years of sorrow, disappointment and pain flowed out of the deep recesses of her soul. And still He held her.

"I will never let you go," He whispered.

Mind-numbing Fear and Self-Rejection were the next to leave as Perfect Love flooded her being.

"Perfect Love casts out all fear," He said. As a result, two other evil spirits tucked their dragon-like tails and fled as fast as they could.

"I never knew they were there," she said.

Ever so gently, a peace that was greater than her understanding flooded her. The peace was not anything like what the world offered, but it was an anchor. It was strong and as sure as the sun rising. Again, she sighed deeply and snuggled even closer to the One she loved.

"You are precious to Me, and I love you dearly."

And this time, she believed Him.

CHAPTER NINE

*W*hen Hadassah and Martha woke they were surprised to see Rebekah sleeping a stone's throw away. "Rebekah, wake up!" Martha shouted over her shoulder.

When Rebekah didn't respond, Hadassah called out, "Bekah, let's go fishing."

Again, no response. "That's unlike her," Hadassah said, dropping her spear and hurrying to her side.

Kneeling, Hadassah shook her sister. And when she did, a snake slithered out from under her skirt. Jumping back, Hadassah screamed.

Martha came running. Seeing the snake, she asked, "Did it bite her?"

Hadassah pulled back her skirt. Looking at the puncture marks, Martha said, "Please tell me it wasn't poisonous."

"I'm afraid it was," Hadassah said, tearing a strip from the hem of Rebekah's tattered skirt. Tying it just above her knee Hadassah cried out, "Life-Giver, don't let this happen! You can't — not to sweet Rebekah! This can't be happening — not again — not to her, not to us! Oh, Great King, take me, but please don't take her!"

Martha held Rebekah's cold, clammy hand. "She's not going to die," Martha said, the words nearly choking her as she gritted her teeth to keep from screaming.

"Life-Giver, please!" Hadassah shouted. "Please help!"

"Hadassah, he won't answer! He won't do anything!"

"How do you know?"

"I asked him to help when Mama and Papa were sick and dying. I asked him to help when we were sold into slavery. He didn't do anything then, and he won't do anything now," Martha said as hot tears streaked down her dirty face.

"Shut up, Martha! Just shut up! How can you know the plans of the King? You can't! Who knows but He might answer favorably. You can't know, and I refuse to turn my back on Him. I'll plead and beg for His help as long as Rebekah's alive. And should she die, I will shout at the top of my lungs that He's good. Now, pray for a miracle, for that's Rebekah's only hope."

"I will see you through this," Life-Giver said, laying His hands on their shoulders.

Martha wiped the sweat from Rebekah's face with her apron. "Bekah, can you hear me?"

A pale Rebekah groaned in response.

"You'll be fine," Martha said, but her shaky voice revealed what she really believed.

Rebekah slowly opened her eyes. "Don't worry," she said.

Her calf had already swollen larger than her thigh. An angry red streak ran up her leg toward her heart.

"Shhh, don't try to talk," said Hadassah, pushing the hair from Rebekah's forehead. Beads of sweat ran down her face.

"I want to go home," Rebekah said.

Martha and Hadassah looked at each other.

"Home?" Hadassah asked.

"I want to go . . ." Rebekah said, closing her eyes.

Unbeknownst to Hadassah and Martha, Life-Giver leaned down and kissed Rebekah's forehead.

Turning to Hadassah and Martha, He said, "I know you do not understand what is happening or why, but I ask that you trust Me."

He laid His hands gently over the hearts of the two girls. "You only have one life to live, and it is meant to produce in you a heart like Mine. This sorrow, this tragedy will purify your hearts that you both might come to trust Me wholeheartedly — even in the face of loss and severe pain."

Neither sister heard Him.

Hadassah rested her forehead against Rebekah's shoulder and fervently prayed.

Countless evil spirits suddenly surrounded the three sisters. Before they could utter a word or make a move, Life-Giver announced, "You are trespassing." Michael and his army descended on the foul-smelling creatures, driving them far from the girls.

Rebekah opened her eyes. Mustering all her strength she said, "Don't be sad."

Martha said, "Don't you dare give up, Rebekah!"

"I want to go home."

"Where's home?" Hadassah asked.

"Home. . . is with. . .Life-Giver." Her eyes stared far away as if she was looking beyond their world. Whatever she saw delighted her. Her face appeared to be shrouded in light, peace and even joy. Hadassah gasped, overcome by her sister's beauty. *Rebekah was looking into Life-Giver's eyes, and what she saw was irresistible.*

"I am the One you love. I am the One you have pursued. And I am Beautiful."

Rebekah's spirit bowed low. "Life-Giver, my body hurts."

"I know, sweet child of Mine. Rebekah, don't focus on the storm. Focus on My arms that hold you."

Martha cried out, "Oh, Life-Giver, please be real! Please care! And please heal my sister!"

"I am here, Martha. And I do care. And soon you will come to know just how real I am."

Turning to three angels, He waved His hand. They instantly left to do His bidding. In the blink of an eye they stood in the midst of a flock of sheep.

The sheep scattered in twenty different directions. "What's happening here?" David, the master shepherd, shouted as he jumped to his feet.

"I don't know. There's no reason for them to scatter that I can see," a shepherd boy answered.

An angel named Messenger tapped the master shepherd on his shoulder and said, "Life-Giver requires your assistance in the west."

"Caleb, you come with me," said David. "Nicodemus, you and the other shepherds gather the sheep."

Without hesitation, David jumped on his horse and headed west.

"Where are we going?" Caleb asked, bringing his horse alongside David.

"I don't know for certain."

"Do you know *why* we're going?"

"I only know that Life-Giver has summoned me."

As they rode hard and fast, Caleb marveled at David, for he had seen him respond this way on several occasions. And each time, great deeds had been accomplished and even lives saved. David was not only a wonderful shepherd, but he was also a very caring person. *What an honor it is to serve as an under-shepherd to David*, Caleb thought.

They had traveled a short distance when David reigned in his stallion. "Over there — what's that?" David asked. Without waiting for a response, he turned toward them.

Martha ran out to meet them. "Kind sirs, please help us! Our sister's been bitten by a poisonous viper."

David and Caleb rushed to Rebekah's side. David hurried to suck the poison out of the wound while Caleb held her steady. Satisfied he had removed as much of the poison as possible, he poured wine into the wound. Tearing a strip from the hem of his garment, he doused it with oil and wrapped her calf.

Gently lifting her head, David encouraged Rebekah to drink some wine. She opened her eyes for a moment. The faintest smile appeared and she said, "You're a follower of the King."

"Yes, I know Him well and love Him dearly. Now drink, for this will give you the strength you need for the journey ahead."

With much coaxing, she drank enough to ease her pain. She soon fell into a deep sleep.

Pulling David aside, Martha asked, "What's to become of this?"

"Only the King knows the answer to that question, dear lady. We will take her to my home. But we must travel now while the wine has eased her pain."

"Thank you," Martha said, laying her hand on the man's arm, a gesture that was certainly brazen and quite inappropriate for a woman. Seeing him look at her hand, she quickly removed it. "I meant no harm. Please forgive me . . . I . . ."

"Do not fret, dear lady; you have not offended me. I understand your expression of kindness and take it as such. Now, let's get your sister to a more comfortable place."

Caleb lifted Rebekah into David's arms. He tied his prayer shawl around their waists to help steady the unconscious girl.

"Here, take my horse," Caleb offered.

"But how will you get back?" Hadassah asked as she helped Martha in the saddle.

"I'll walk. It will give me time to pray for your sister."

Martha reached down and pulled her sister up. "Thank you," Martha said.

"May the King be with you," David said, turning his horse toward Jerusalem, the city of the Great King.

"And with all of you."

"Blessed are you both for your kind, faithful service," said Life-Giver.

***

The sun was nearly overhead when they rode into a small village. Mercifully, Rebekah had remained unconscious. David led the way through the narrow streets to a small cottage nestled beneath the shade of a dozen or so palm trees. A young shepherd ran out to meet them. "Have you returned so soon?"

"Samuel, I require your assistance," David said as he untied the fabric holding the girl.

David carefully handed Rebekah down to the young man. "May the King be merciful to her," Samuel said, his face clearly reflecting his concern.

Neither Hadassah nor Martha waited for assistance. Following David, they entered his humble abode. "We don't have much, but it's more than enough," said David.

"Compared to what we're accustomed to this is quite extravagant," Martha said.

The room contained a cot, two sleeping mats, a sheepskin rug, several oil lamps, numerous baskets and a table. A middle-aged woman sat at the roughly hewn table shelling peas. "Shalom," she said. Her eyes fell upon Rebekah and her smile faded as quickly as it had appeared. In her haste to come to her aid, she knocked over the stool she sat upon. Ignoring it, she wiped her hands on her apron, pointed to the corner and said, "Over there! Place the girl there."

Samuel carefully laid Rebekah on the cot, asking, "What more can I do?"

"You can fetch us a bucket of water and a bar of fuller's soap," David said.

"What has happened?" David's wife asked.

"A snake bite on her right calf," said David.

Rebekah groaned as the woman carefully unwrapped the bandage.

David introduced the girls to his wife. Naomi looked up and smiled. "Pardon me, but I must see to this wound. I shall formally greet you in a moment." She turned her attention back to Rebekah before either sister could respond. As they knelt by their sister, Naomi appeared to be praying, but in a language neither sister had ever heard.

Samuel returned with the bucket and soap. "Is there anything more I can do?" he asked.

"You can pray," said David.

"And so I shall."

Kneeling by Rebekah's cot, Naomi removed the bandages as gently as possible. Rebekah opened her eyes and whispered, "May the . . . King . . . bless you."

Naomi smiled and patted her hand.

As she scrubbed the wound with the soap, Hadassah held Rebekah's hand, praying fervently. Martha stared at the wall. On several occasions Rebekah cried out in pain, further breaking her sister's hearts.

Naomi hurried to the table. Dropping to her knees, she dragged a basket from beneath the table. Carefully selecting several dried plants, she placed them in a bowl and ground them with a smooth rock. Pouring some wine in a cup, she stirred in the herbs. "See if you can get her to drink this," Naomi said, handing Hadassah the cup.

"What is it?"

"Something that will dull the pain and help her rest."

Lifting Rebekah's head, Hadassah said, "Bekah, try and drink. That's right. Now swallow. It will help you feel better. Come on, just a little more. You're doing good. One more sip and it's all done. There, all finished. Now rest, sweet sister, rest."

Sitting back on her heels, Hadassah fought to control her emotions. She wanted to run far away, but had nowhere to run. She thought of her parents' death. Wave after wave of deep sorrow flooded her. *This can't be happening . . . not again,* she thought.

Naomi placed her hand on Hadassah's shoulder and asked, "Are you all right?"

"Sorry. I was just thinking about something. How can I help you?"

"There's a basket of herbs underneath the foot of the cot. Would you fetch it for me?"

"Of course."

Naomi dug through the basket obviously searching for a particular herb. Finding the pouch she was looking for, she sprinkled the powder onto the bite. Using her finger, she pressed the powder into the wound. Rebekah cried out.

Life-Giver, where are You? Rebekah asked.

"I'm right here. I haven't left your side."

"The pain is more than I can bear."

"I will help you."

Naomi dipped a fresh cloth into a bowl filled with wine and oil. She wrapped the wound with it. Having done all she could, she bowed her head and prayed. Everyone joined her, even Martha.

Naomi, pushing herself up, said, "Come, you must be hungry and thirsty."

Before the sisters could refuse, she escorted them to the table. Naomi filled two cups with water, adding a couple of drops of wine. "The wine will strengthen you," she said.

As they drank, she placed a bowl of fruit before them. Spreading goat cheese on a thick slice of bread, Naomi said, "I'm so sorry about your sister. We shall continue to pray for a miracle, for one never knows what the King will do. David and I have seen Him do miracles greater than the one Rebekah needs."

Her eyes are kind like David's, like Life-Giver's, Hadassah thought.

Placing the bread on a plate, Naomi said, "Please eat, for it will do your sister no good if you faint from hunger."

Hadassah felt nauseous. "Thank you, but I don't think I'm hungry."

"This bread will calm your stomach. You will need the strength, child," she said ever so kindly. Laying her hands on Hadassah and Martha's shoulders, she quietly prayed. *As she did, their unseen Friend whispered, "You do not have to carry this burden alone. I am here with you."*

Angels lined the cottage walls. With so many in attendance, one would have thought it was the home of an important dignitary, not the home of a humble shepherd. But that is the way of the kingdom — those who are the least are truly great.

"Your Majesty, shall we prepare for Rebekah's arrival?" Michael asked.

"Not yet." Looking at Martha and Hadassah, He said, "They still need more time."

Naomi once more encouraged them to eat. Out of respect, they forced themselves to take a bite. In doing so, they realized just how hungry they really were. After devouring every crumb, they returned to their sister's side. Thankfully, she was in a deep sleep.

Martha squeezed Hadassah's hand and whispered, "Please tell me this isn't happening. Tell me we'll wake up in the morning and Rebekah will be fine and we'll take our scroll and go to the castle, spend a day with the King and live happily ever after."

Tears spilled down their faces. "Oh, Martha, I wish I could promise you that, but you and I both know that life is unpredictable and impossible to understand. I don't know why this is happening, but I believe with my whole heart that the King and His Son are good. I believe whatever the outcome, Rebekah will be healed — either she'll be healed and remain on this earth, or she'll be healed and live forever with the King, Life-Giver and our parents."

"I wish I had your faith."

"Faith is a choice, dear sister. It's not something that comes as a result of proof. Faith believes before there's proof. Life-Giver once said to me, 'Blessed are those who do not see and still believe.' *After* I decided to follow Life-Giver, He became real to me and grows more so with each passing day."

"You said that Life-Giver talks to you. So why don't you ask him now if Bekah's going to live?"

Hadassah stared at her sister. "I don't think I want to know the answer."

"Fair enough," Martha said, resting her forehead against the cot.

Life-Giver nodded ever so slightly and the angels scattered — a dozen or so completely surrounded the three sisters while the others faced the door with swords raised high. Glorious, blinding light emanated from Life-Giver as He turned to face the back door. Michael stepped toward the dark figure crouched there.

Michael asked, "Your Majesty, may I have the pleasure of escorting this dark one out?"

Every angel in the room looked expectantly at Life-Giver. It was obvious they would all love to be chosen to bring the dark one to justice. Life-Giver raised His hand; Michael tipped his sword in submission.

Without looking at the foul creature, Life-Giver addressed it, saying, "Death, I did not call for you."

"Her rotting flesh called to me," the dark being said, green slime oozing from the corners of its twisted mouth.

"I did not call for you," Life-Giver repeated.

"Let me put her out of her misery," the dark creature said, daring to creep closer.

With an almost imperceivable nod from Life-Giver, every angel pointed his sword toward the hideous being. Death stopped in its tracks.

"She does not belong to you," Life-Giver said. "Therefore, you may not touch her."

Rising up on its haunches, the creature said, "She's a daughter of man and that makes her mine."

With just a glance from Life-Giver, the creature cowered before Him.

Life-Giver said, "Death, I defeated you two thousand years ago. You cannot claim what does not belong to you. She is a daughter of the King. Now leave this place!"

Death had no choice but to obey.

The angels remained at attention as Life-Giver moved to Rebekah's side. Kneeling, He said, "I am with you, My precious child."

He then laid His hands on Hadassah and Martha's shoulders, saying, "My peace I give you. My peace I leave with you."

The two fell fast asleep, their heads resting on Rebekah's cot. Naomi covered them with a blanket and then blew out the candle.

CHAPTER TEN

A rooster crowed in the distance. Afraid to open her eyes, Hadassah silently prayed that Rebekah would not be dead.

Taking a deep breath, she slowly opened her eyes. Naomi was wiping the sweat from Rebekah's forehead. David knelt nearby, his head bowed. Martha was curled up on a sheepskin rug sound asleep.

"Is she any better?" Hadassah whispered, reaching for Rebekah's limp hand. It was cold and her fingernails were an awful shade of blue.

"She's none the worse," Naomi said.

"Have you been here long?"

"I've been with her all night. I knew the two of you were exhausted and needed to sleep."

"Naomi, why would you care for a stranger with such diligence?"

"I was once a stranger, but that didn't keep the King from showing me kindness. He reached down into the pit I was in and pulled me out. As filthy as I was, He drew me right into His arms and loved me. Now I have the privilege of doing the same for everyone the King sends my way."

Naomi dipped a fresh cloth in the basin and handed it to Hadassah. "Thought you might like to wash your face, child."

Hadassah wiped the sleep from her eyes. "Rebekah's so pale, she looks awful and . . ." Her voice faltered. Turning away, she said, "When I was six years old I watched my mama and papa die. It hurt so much; it still does. Naomi, if Bekah dies, I don't know how I'll survive. I don't know how Martha will."

"You can't do it, child. No one can — no one on this earth that is. But there is One who can bear any pain, and He will help you, if you allow Him to do so."

"I know in my head what you say is true, but . . . we've suffered so much and now this and I can't help but wonder how the Great King can allow so much suffering if He's good and powerful. I don't dare talk about this to Martha. She already hates the King. She claims He's not real, but in her deepest heart I think she knows. If Bekah dies —" Hadassah could not go on.

"I know it doesn't seem like it right now, but the King is good, Hadassah. No one can understand His ways, for they stretch far beyond this earthly realm. How can a simple mortal understand those things that belong to a realm where a human lifespan appears as a mere breath, a moment in time? There's so much more to this life than our appointed time on earth.

"I've lived five decades on this earth, and there's one thing I've come to know — the King doesn't just give life, He is Life. He doesn't just love. He is Love. He doesn't just comfort. He is Comfort. I say this to say that He is greater and more powerful than anything that could ever come your way — even this," Naomi said, looking at Rebekah.

"Hadassah, the King's own Son suffered unjustly — the Innocent for the guilty. If the Great King allowed His own Son to suffer injustice, who are we to accuse Him when we suffer unjustly?" She wiped Rebekah's forehead, allowing Hadassah the time to contemplate what she said. "Every life lived comes with a cross, and that cross is meant to bring about your death, dear one. But never forget that with *every* cross there comes a resurrection."

"I never thought I'd ever doubt Life-Giver or the King."

"Then tell Him how you feel. Never be afraid to tell Him the truth, child."

"I think I'll step outside for a moment. Please call me if—" Hadassah bit her bottom lip.

"Go and don't worry. I'll be here."

Sitting on the stone wall surrounding the cottage, Hadassah said, "Life-Giver, I hate to admit that I don't trust You like I thought I did.

Please help me believe You're good . . . especially if Bekah should die. Oh, please don't let that happen! I don't know how I'd bear it." She buried her face in her hands, fighting back the tears.

"I am here, child."

"I heard you! I really heard you — I think."

"I am faithful to complete that which I have begun," Life-Giver whispered.

"What does that mean?"

"It means that you don't have anything to worry about."

Taking a deep breath, Hadassah said, "Can I just sit here with You for a while? Will You stay with me?"

"I will."

"Naomi said I should tell You how I feel. The truth is I'm not sure how I feel. For so long, I've tried not to feel, but this pain is too great to ignore. Life-Giver. . . ."

"Yes?"

"I'm afraid. I need You now more than ever. When You're with me, I feel safe. Life-Giver, be my shelter. Oh, step through the veil separating us and be my refuge, be the strength I need. Help me, help Martha and *please* heal Rebekah."

"I am your life, your strength, your all-in-all."

"Life-Giver, is there pain where You are? Is there suffering and sorrow in Your kingdom beyond the veil?"

"There is a day coming when all sorrow, pain and suffering will end, but it is not yet."

Sitting upright, Hadassah said, "Are You saying there's pain there?"

"Sin brings My Father and I great pain, child."

"Why?"

"Because of the damage and heartache it brings to Our children. Anything that hurts you hurts Us even more because Our capacity for emotion is endless."

"Rebekah said the Great King hated sin because it was evil."

"I hate sin because of what it does to you. Sin kills, steals and destroys all that it touches. It is contrary to life. My Father and I impart life to all We touch."

Taking a deep breath, Hadassah asked, "Is Rebekah going to die?"

"There are things you cannot understand on this earth, child, things that must be. When faced with things that you cannot comprehend, it is vital that you choose to trust Me."

Hadassah took another long, deep breath. "I do trust You. Well, sort of. I want to trust You, but I don't know if I can."

"Here is something that will help you." A tiny drop of golden oil fell from His fingertip and landed on Hadassah's head.

"What's this?" she asked, running her hand through her hair.

"Faith. It is a gift and cannot be earned. Just one drop can move mountains."

The oil dripped off her forehead and landed on her chest over her heart. "It's real. I can feel it, but I can't see anything," she said, looking at her fingertips.

"Faith is the substance of things hoped for, the evidence of things not seen."

As Hadassah pondered His words, the oil continued its inward journey. She sighed deeply. "I was so quick to tell Martha to have faith, and here I am realizing just how little faith I have. Forgive me, I pray. I receive Your gift of faith. I choose to believe that You do all things well."

Smiling, Life-Giver stepped through the veil into her realm.

Hadassah saw Him — she saw Life-Giver! "Are You real? I mean, I know You are, but. . ."

Life-Giver chuckled. "Come and see," He said, extending His hand.

Clinging to the One she was learning to trust, Hadassah sobbed and sobbed. "I can feel You. Oh, thank You for coming to me!"

"I am near to the brokenhearted." He kissed her forehead as He held her tight.

And then He was gone.

Hadassah found herself sitting on the ground. *How did I get here?* She ran her fingers through her hair, but the oil was gone. *Was that real? Did I just see Life-Giver? Did He hold me?*

A voice that sounded like herself answered, "Of course I didn't. That wasn't real."

Standing, Hadassah said, "I'm not going to allow Satan to steal this from me." Hadassah chose to believe.

Faith, hope and love. Hadassah had just experienced all three in the person of Life-Giver. And the greatest of these is always love.

***

When Hadassah went back inside, to Hadassah's relief, Rebekah appeared to be sleeping peacefully. Naomi and Martha were deep in conversation. Not wanting to disturb them, Hadassah joined David at the table.

"You should eat," David said as he passed a bowl of dates and a plate of bread her way. "Did you get any rest?"

"I did, actually," she said, biting into a date. "I beg your forgiveness, kind sir, but I don't believe I remembered to thank you for your hospitality."

"There's no need, Hadassah. It's my pleasure to be of assistance. I'm thankful to the Great King for allowing us to do so."

"You're an answer to our prayers. I didn't think anyone would find us. And if by chance they did, I didn't believe they'd help us."

"Why not?"

"Because we're strangers," said Hadassah.

"We are all strangers here, Hadassah. This world is not our home."

Hadassah wanted to ask what he meant, but she was too distracted by her experience with Life-Giver to delve any deeper. Rebekah groaned.

"Is she in great pain?"

"I don't think so."

"Isn't there anything more we can do?" Hadassah asked, tears stinging her eyes.

"We've done all that can be done, child. Now it's up to the King."

A knock on the door caused everyone to look up.

"Caleb," David said, throwing the door and his arms open wide.

"How does the lady fare?" Caleb asked as he embraced David.

"She's in the King's hands," David answered. "What brought you here?"

"I thought I'd bring you this." He handed David an old, worn-out bag.

David looked inside. "Is this the snake that bit the young one?"

"I'd say so. Just after you left, the evil thing struck at me from beneath a bush. Thankfully, it missed. I brought my staff down on its head."

"This viper will never harm another," David said, looking at Rebekah.

"If only this creature's death could right the wrong that has been done," said Caleb, tears in his eyes.

"Only the King Himself can right that kind of wrong."

Caleb's voice was thick with compassion as he said, "I've alerted the other shepherds, and they're fasting and praying."

"Well done, my friend."

Life-Giver put His arms around the two men's shoulders and said, "You have learned to love like your King."

Both men were instantly aware of His presence.

"Life-Giver's here," David whispered.

Numerous angels encircled the three human beings.

"Why are we whispering?" Caleb whispered.

"Because Life-Giver is here," David whispered.

"But what does whispering have to do with His presence?" Caleb inquired, sounding somewhat inebriated as the joy of his Lord filled him.

"I don't know. All I know is that Life-Giver is here, in this room, right now, with us," David whispered.

Caleb giggled like a young boy.

"Why are you laughing?" David whispered.

"The same reason you're whispering," Caleb said, laughing harder.

At that precise moment, Hadassah saw Life-Giver step through the veil. She gasped. "He's beautiful, is He not?" she said, falling on her knees.

"He is indeed," Martha said.

Hadassah turned with a start. Martha stood just behind her, her face streaked with tears, her nose red. Her chin quivered as she reached out a trembling hand to Life-Giver.

Martha's lips moved as she silently talked to the One who died to give her life. A smile appeared on her face. "I love You, too," she whispered.

Hadassah felt as though ten years and a host of worries fell off of her shoulders. *Martha will never be the same,* she thought, *and neither will I.*

Hadassah cried as Life-Giver held Martha like a mother holds a small child. He sang their mama's song — loud and clear He sang.

In a mystery beyond anything Hadassah could understand, Life-Giver then stood behind her, yet she could still see Him holding Martha. Before she could ask how that was possible, wave after wave of joy crashed over her. Relinquishing all control, she fell back into the arms of the One who loved her beyond reason and beyond all comprehension.

Looking up into His beautiful face, she said, whether aloud or silent she knew not, "Your love, like a summer rain, washes away the dust from my journey. Your love, like the sun on a cold, winter day, warms my aching heart. Your love, like bread fresh out of the oven, nourishes my soul. Your love overwhelms me, and I'm lost . . . forever lost to everything but You!"

"Hadassah, I see perfect Love in your eyes."

"Life-Giver, I see me in Your eyes."

"It is as it should be. I pledge to love you for all eternity, Hadassah. I will never break My covenant with you even if you should do so."

"Life-Giver, I come to You broken and undone, and You come to me perfect and holy. And yet You love and accept me just as I am." Life-Giver drew her close, looking into the depths of her soul. His eyes communicated His holy desires.

"What is this that You're asking of me?" she asked. "Will I promise to love You no matter what, in the good times and the bad, even if it should seem like You've abandoned me? How is this possible? How can anyone love like that?"

"Such is the nature of the cross, Hadassah. When it seemed as though My Father had forsaken Me, I remained true. I chose to trust Him, surrendering to the One I could not see or feel, to the One My senses accused of forsaking Me. I knew the truth. I knew He would never leave Me nor forsake Me. Such is the nature of the cross, for it accuses the innocent while bringing death to the things that should not be."

Hadassah was greatly impacted. "How can I not pay whatever price I'm asked to pay? Is this not what You did for me? How can I do any less? Therefore, I will take up my cross and fall at Your nail-scarred feet."

And that is precisely what she did. Lying prostrate, she said, "I will love and trust You no matter what happens to Bekah."

Life-Giver picked Hadassah up and held her tight.

"Life-Giver, would You look into my eyes and tell me what You see now."

"I see My face, Hadassah."

"All that I am, all that I will ever be is merely a reflection of You. You are everything that I'm not and everything that I want to be. Oh that I might decrease so that You will increase! I am the moon and You are the sun. No one could ever take Your place in my life! I'm consumed by the endless love I see in Your eyes. I now know that I'm the one You love. I'm the one You've pursued, and I'm beautiful to You."

CHAPTER ELEVEN

$\mathcal{H}$adassah opened her eyes. David and Caleb were on their knees, eyes closed, hands raised. Martha appeared to be asleep. Naomi's head rested on Rebekah's cot.

"Martha, are you all right?" Hadassah asked.

"My guess is she's better than all right," said David.

"I just had the most wonderful experience of my life," Martha said, eyes still closed and not moving.

"I know," said Hadassah.

"Life-Giver told me about His Father, the Great King. Dassah, I won't ever be the same." Martha attempted to raise her head but found it impossible. "It feels as though I'm floating on a cloud," she said, giggling.

Her joy was contagious. The four of them laughed so hard they cried.

Wiping her eyes, Martha pushed herself up. Leaning against Hadassah, she said, "Life-Giver loves *me*. He *really* loves me."

"I know."

"Dassah, I'm so sorry for —" Tears filled her eyes as conviction flooded her.

"I forgave you a long time ago," Hadassah said, kissing her sister's cheek.

"I must tell Bekah what happened before —"

Both sisters looked at Rebekah. Martha said, "I don't understand why this is happening, but I will trust Life-Giver."

Hadassah could not help but smile. "Who are you, and what did you do with my sister?" She pulled her close, and they held each other for a long time.

"We'll make it through even this," Martha said.

"I know we will, but I have a feeling it's going to hurt really badly."

"It already does."

Helping each other up, they returned to their sister's side. Naomi excused herself, inviting David and Caleb to join her outside.

Martha gently stroked her sister's limp, bony hand. Tears pooled in Martha's eyes as she said, "Bekah, I don't know if you can hear me, but in case you can, I want you to know that I just met Life-Giver. It's true — just like you said — He loves me, Bekah. He *really* loves me."

Rebekah was unresponsive, but Martha continued, "Please forgive me for all the times I was mean and argued with you about the King. You were right and I was wrong. I'm really glad you were right. I've decided to follow Him, Bekah. And, in time, I'm sure I'll come to love Him as you do."

Martha kissed her sister's hand and then pressed it against her cheek. With her eyes closed she said, "Sweet Bekah, please fight. Please stay with us. We need you."

Martha gently laid her hand down and turned away.

Hadassah wiped Rebekah's beautiful face with a cool cloth. Rebekah's skin had turned an awful gray color. She felt cold and clammy to the touch, but sweat trickled down her face and neck. Her lips were a deep blue color, and her breathing was barely perceivable.

She looks like Mama and Papa did right before they died, Hadassah thought.

Pushing away the memory, Hadassah stroked Rebekah's cheek, saying, "I love you, Bekah. Please don't give up." Hadassah did not even try to fight her tears.

Rebekah moaned.

A nearly imperceivable light fell across Rebekah's face. She sighed. Her furrowed brow relaxed as did her body.

Rebekah suddenly saw herself walking on a beach. No one was in sight except a lone Man walking toward her. The Man waved. "May I join you on your journey?" *He shouted.*

"Are You not Life-Giver?"

"I am."

"Then you need not ask permission, my Lord," *she humbly answered.*

"Just because one is given a position of prominence and authority does not give them the right to dishonor another. In My kingdom, those with authority have an even greater responsibility to love and honor those they serve."

I wish I had served more, *she thought.* "Life-Giver, here I am at the end of my life, and I have nothing of value to offer my King," *she said, feeling pain greater than anything she ever felt on earth.*

A tear trickled down her flawless cheek. Life-Giver captured it in a crystal bottle that appeared to be filled with miniature diamonds.

"What's this?" *she asked.*

"This bottle holds every tear you have ever shed."

"But they look like diamonds."

"They are more precious than diamonds."

"Why?"

Holding up the bottle, He said, "Because I died for them."

"You died for my tears?"

"I died for every part of you," *He said.* "Come, let us walk together." *He then turned her around and led her back from where she came.*

"Rebekah, tell Me what you see."

"I see nothing but sand and water and sky."

"Are you sure?"

"Well, I do see footprints, but nothing else."

"Those footprints represent your walk through life."

Her heart sank. "There wasn't much to my life."

"On the contrary, My precious child. You see nothing but sand; I see fertile soil rich with hidden treasure. My dear one, your life accomplished much more than you realize. Every step you took impacted not only those who knew you but also the One who walked this life with you. Now come and allow Me to show you the many treasures formed by Me and hidden during your time on earth."

With a nod from Life-Giver, a knee-high wave pushed well past its natural boundary and washed over the beach.

"It is washed away," He announced.

Rebekah cried out, "Rightfully you have washed it away, for there's nothing noteworthy about my life. You know — You were there. I can't point to one good thing, other than knowing You. I've nothing but shame and guilt to offer You, and for that I am so sorry."

"Is that so?" He asked.

Rebekah followed as He walked back in time. Scooping up a handful of sand, He smiled as though He knew a secret. As He looked deep in her eyes, a gentle wave washed over His lightly closed hand. When the wave receded, He opened His hand. To her surprise, He held a large diamond.

Smiling, He took a step and scooped up another handful, allowing the water to wash away the sand. This time He held a glorious pink pearl, an emerald, a sapphire, a ruby, a topaz — He continued uncovering the truths hidden in her past until Rebekah's apron was weighed down with precious stones.

"I don't understand. Where did these jewels come from?" Rebekah asked.

"From your life."

"How is that possible?'

"You assessed your life based on your performance and your deeds, never taking into account the power of My sacrifice on your behalf. You see, Rebekah, I view your life through My performance, not yours. And My blood makes all things new and beautiful. As a result of accepting My invitation, I taught you how to love and that has made you very rich."

"I was not aware that I learned how to love, my Lord."

"May I show you?"

"Of course," Rebekah said, laughing softly. She found it amazing that this all-knowing, all-powerful Man would ask her permission for anything.

Knowing her thoughts, He said, "I will never trod on your heart or force you to do anything — not now or ever. Now, allow Me to show you that you did indeed learn to love. You see this topaz?" He asked, picking it up from the pile of precious stones and holding it up to the light.

She nodded, in awe of its exquisite beauty.

"It was formed when you were six years old and your papa told you about Me. You knelt down by your cot and gave Me your heart. Do you remember that?"

"I do."

He then chose a large emerald and said, "This jewel was made when you became an orphan and turned to Me for comfort. This ruby was fashioned as you chose to love your uncle rather than hate him. This sapphire and black pearl and onyx and jasper were formed when you were sold into slavery and chose to trust Me even though you believed I had forsaken you."

"But I didn't trust You. I was angry and bitter. I rejected You."

"Rebekah, you underestimate what I did for you on the cross. Your anger, bitterness and lack of faith were redeemed — I turned them into treasures. I restored to you all that was lost, and when I restore something I make it better than it was before. Because you received My love, My blood did not just cover your sins — it washed them away so that they are remembered no more. My blood is always greater than your weakness."

"And so is Your love."

"They are both one and the same."

Rebekah felt great peace.

Life-Giver dug seven more stones out of the sand. Holding them out for her inspection, He said, "These jewels were formed when you chose to love the men who used and abused you — they are most precious to Me, for they represent sacrificial, unconditional love.

Retrieving another handful of sand, He held up a pearl saying, "This pearl represents the sacrifices you made for your sisters. And this diamond . . . well, it was just formed. It came into being as a result of your snake bite."

"How did something so beautiful come out of something I had no part in?"

"You had every opportunity to accuse Me, but you chose not to do so. No anger, no accusation, no rebellion. You fixed your eyes on Me and loved Me through it all." Tears of adoration flooded His eyes.

"I had no idea what You desired and valued most of all was love," Rebekah said.

"Faith, hope and love. The greatest of these is love."

Life-Giver placed the jewels in her apron. Stunned, Rebekah stared at the beautiful stones representing her life. She looked up at Life-Giver and said, "You took my worthless life and gave it value. You took a weak, frightened soul and gave her courage. You took someone consumed with shame, guilt and hopelessness and gave her freedom, hope and joy! No one can do what You do!"

"You are right — no one can do what I do. I turn all things into good — beauty for ashes — that is the way of My kingdom. You give Me a stone, I give you bread. You give Me a chunk of coal, I give you a diamond. You give Me a dead, cold heart; I give you a heart that is alive with love."

Rebekah had so many questions. Life-Giver chuckled and said, "You have all eternity to ask your questions. But there is one I will answer now. You are still wondering how I can love someone like you. Rebekah, I am your Redeemer. Redemption, like the ocean waves, continually washes away the ugly while depositing the beautiful.

"You believed that performance and good deeds were what determined your value, but that is never the truth in My kingdom. That is what Satan hoped you would believe. He wants you to be performance driven not Spirit led. He wants you to believe the King is a dictator who rewards good behavior and punishes bad.

"Let's look at your life again. When your heart condemned you, I defended you. When shame cried out for a covering, I spread My robe of righteousness over you. When fear shut you down, I raised you up. When bitterness threatened to choke the life out of you, I breathed My breath into you.

"You have always been hidden in Me, and you are made perfect through Me. As you walked with Me, I filled in the gaps and redeemed those things in your life that were less than what they were intended to be. Your life is and was all about Me. And that is why you stand before Me today perfect, complete and very rich."

Rebekah handed Him the apron. "And that is why these belong to You."

Life-Giver smiled and said, "I receive your gift and your life, and I offer you Mine in return."

***

Rebekah tried to open her eyes, to tell her sisters what she had just experienced, but could not.

"Bekah's lips are moving," Hadassah said.

"Are you trying to say something?" asked Martha.

"Can you hear me?" asked Hadassah.

Rebekah nodded ever so slightly.

"We're right here," Martha said.

Rebekah whispered, "It's . . . about . . . love. Don't be. . . sad."

"Always thinking of others," Martha said, wiping her face on her sleeve.

Martha and Hadassah looked at each other as their hearts broke into a thousand pieces.

"Bekah, you *must* fight," Martha said, her teeth clinched.

"Don't give up now," Hadassah said, swallowing her tears.

"I want . . . to go," Rebekah whispered.

Hadassah and Martha stared at each other. Neither wanted to let her go.

"Bekah, we need you," Martha said.

"I love . . . you," she said trying to smile.

Martha looked down at her sister's ashen face. "I don't want you to suffer."

"Neither do I," Hadassah said.

"I want . . . to go . . . please."

Hadassah stared at Martha who stared at the floor. Hadassah reached down and took Martha's hand and squeezed. "Martha, we have to let her go."

"I know. I know."

"This is the hardest thing I've ever had to do," Hadassah said, kissing Rebekah on the cheek. "Bekah, you can go with Life-Giver now. It's okay," Hadassah tears ran like a river.

"And Bekah . . . don't be afraid . . . to fly," Martha said gently rubbing her sister's hand.

Rebekah's eyes turned toward the window. Life-Giver stood by waiting, watching and smiling. "Don't be afraid to fly," He said, arms extended.

Like a gentle breeze in the middle of summer, Rebekah's spirit escaped from her thin, frail body as she took her last breath.

"Good-bye dear sister," Hadassah said. The two sisters fell into each other's arms, completely unaware that Rebekah's spirit hovered above them.

Rebekah was quite elated to find herself not dead but fully alive — more alive than she had ever been.

A glorious Presence that Rebekah had come to know and love surrounded her being, drawing her toward the Source of all Life. Falling on her knees before the beautiful Man, she exclaimed, "My Savior and my Friend!"

"My beloved," Life-Giver responded.

"I have stepped out of darkness into Your marvelous light."

"How beautiful you are."

"Begging Your pardon, but You are the One who is beautiful."

"Do you dare correct Me?" Life-Giver teased.

"My Lord and my Savior," she said, smiling as she bowed low.

Pure adoration, unmatched and unknown by those living on the earth, flooded Rebekah and Life-Giver's hearts. Fragrance sweeter than ten thousand flowers emanated from Rebekah's spirit, flooding Life-Giver's heightened senses. "With just one glance of your eyes, you have captured My heart, My sister, My bride."

Michael and a host of angels watched in amazement, for no matter how many times they witnessed the reunion between Life-Giver and a human spirit, they were awed by the depth, width, height and length of such love. Since the beginning of earth-time, they had struggled to comprehend such love, and after thousands of years they were no closer than they were in the beginning.

Rebekah, standing by Life-Giver's side, looked back at her earthly home and was surprised to find that she was able to see both realms. "How dark, how dull life appears from this side," she said.

"The world is a very dim reflection of the glories that await you, My love."

"I was such a plain-looking girl."

"That was merely the mobile home you occupied; it was not and is not who you are. Like a beautiful bird out of its cage, you are now free to be who you are without any hindrances or obstacles. You are, first and foremost, a spirit who had a temporary experience as a human."

"For most of my life, I lived as if I was a human having a temporary, spiritual experience. Who am I . . . really?"

"You have all eternity to find out the answer to that question."

Rebekah looked at her sisters and said, "Sweet sisters, do not cry, for I am not dead — I am alive forevermore!" She felt so alive that she was surprised they could not hear her or feel her hand resting on their shoulders. Turning to her Beloved, she asked, "Is there no comfort for them?"

"I am near to the brokenhearted."

"I do not see any comfort."

"Look closer, Rebekah."

Rebekah looked again. This time she noticed a golden Light completely surrounding them. "Will they be comforted then?"

"You are seeing the light of My Spirit who is Comfort. I am always near to the brokenhearted."

Life-Giver turned to His angels and said, "Put My ring on her finger, My robe of righteousness on her shoulders, a crown on her head, for My delight is in her!"

"I don't deserve this, my Lord," she said as they adorned her with a beauty that far surpassed anything her world had to offer.

"You deserve it because of what I did for you. I took your reproach and your sins so that I might adorn you with My glory. It is as it should be, for I will have an equally yoked bride."

Rebekah bowed low.

Life-Giver said, "My Father, the Great King, eagerly awaits your arrival."

"Good-bye, Hadassah. Good-bye, Martha. Remember love," she said.

Rebekah stepped through the veil and was enveloped by all-consuming Light and Love. Hesitating, she looked back and was surprised to find that she could still see her sisters.

CHAPTER TWELVE

$\mathscr{T}$he following week was a blur. Neither sister ate or slept very much. Naomi dressed Rebekah in her wedding garment, saying, "It's quite fitting, actually, because Rebekah's about to be a bride." David graciously allowed Rebekah to be buried in his family plot.

David and Naomi encouraged the two sisters to remain with them while their hearts mended, which was a great relief to them. The weeks turned into months, and the months quickly turned into a year. Life-Giver and Comforter stayed close by their sides. But their grief was so great that much of the time they were unaware of Their presence.

On the anniversary of Rebekah's death, for the first time since her death, Hadassah unrolled the two scrolls. She could hear Rebekah's voice reading them. Sitting beneath the shade of an olive tree, she closed her eyes. *So much loss and so much pain,* she thought as tears pooled in her eyes.

"I am with you," Comforter said.

Hadassah sighed deeply as she became aware of His presence. She was grateful and told Him so. Leaning her head against the tree trunk and closing her eyes, she sat in silence, allowing His love to comfort her aching heart.

After quite some time, she opened her eyes and was surprised to see that Martha had joined her. Hadassah took her sister's hand and said, "It's hard to believe it's been a year."

Martha squeezed her hand. "I miss her so much."

Hadassah drew her sister close. "Me too."

Comforter hovered over and around them.

"Martha, I think it's time for us to resume our journey."

Martha was quiet. Her encounter with Life-Giver had dramatically changed her — for the good.

"Well, what do you think?" Hadassah asked.

"I suppose we should, but . . . it's so wonderful here. Naomi and David are so kind, and I'm learning so much about the King from our studies each evening. And Caleb and the other shepherds make me laugh, which is a rare thing indeed. I'd really like to stay, at least for a while longer." Martha's gentle eyes pleaded with her sister.

Hadassah, still feeling quite fragile herself, did not have the heart to press the issue. She rolled up the scrolls and placed them back in her waistband saying, "We'll stay awhile longer."

"Thank you, Dassah."

"Martha, I must admit that I haven't been eager to find the castle. Do you suppose that's wrong?"

"I dare not say. But Papa always said that the King, His Son and His Spirit were Three in One. If that's true, then that means when we're with Life-Giver, we're with the King and His Spirit."

"Life-Giver once told me that if you've seen Him you've seen the King."

Martha rested her head against the tree trunk. "That is a great mystery." Closing her eyes, Martha softly sang. Hadassah loved the sound of Martha's voice. It reminded her of her mama.

Martha sang:

Life-Giver, You know me.

You know when I sit down and when I rise up.

You understand my thoughts when they are still far from me.

You closely inspect my path to make certain it's exactly right for me.

You observe my times of rest. You are intimately acquainted with all my ways.

Even before there's a word on my tongue, behold, You know it already.

You've enclosed me behind and before and laid Your kind hand
on me.
Such knowledge is too wonderful for me; it's too high. I can't
attain to it!

Where can I go from Your Spirit?
Or where can I flee from Your presence?
If I ascend to heaven, You're there.
If I make my bed in Sheol, behold, You are there.
If I take the wings of the dawn, if I dwell in the remotest part of
the sea,
Even there Your hand will lead me and Your right hand will lay
hold of me.
If I say, 'Surely the darkness will overwhelm me and the light
around me will be night.'
Even the darkness is not dark to You, and the night is as bright as
the day.
Darkness and light are the same to You.
Therefore, I have nothing to fear.

You formed me in my mother's womb.
I give thanks to You, for I am fearfully and wonderfully made.
Wonderful are Your works, and my soul knows it very well.
My frame was not hidden from You,
When I was made in secret, when I was skillfully fashioned.
Your eyes saw my unformed substance.
The days ordained for me were written in Your book even before I
was born.

How precious are Your thoughts about me!
How vast is the sum of them!
If I should count them, they would outnumber the sand.
When I awake, I'm still with You.
Search me, Life-Giver, and know my heart;
Try me and know my anxious thoughts;
And see if there's any hurtful way in me.
Lead me in the everlasting way!

Hadassah was speechless. The two sat in silence for quite some time.

Martha cleared her throat and said, "We should help Naomi prepare lunch."

"I suppose you're right, but I hate to leave." Martha pulled her to her feet. Arms intertwined, Hadassah said, "I so love to hear you worship."

"I can't think of anything I'd rather be doing. Life-Giver has transformed my life. For that I will be eternally grateful."

The two walked arm in arm to the cottage not saying much.

After lunch, Martha, Naomi and the shepherds listened as David told them a story about a Shepherd who left His ninety-nine sheep to search for one lost lamb.

Wanting to be alone, Hadassah went for a walk.

To her surprise, Hadassah suddenly found herself standing in front of Rebekah's grave. She did not know whether to turn and run or stay and cry. Tears filled her eyes as she fell to her knees. "I miss you," she said. Hadassah wept long and loud.

Life-Giver captured each tear as Comforter held her close.

When her tears subsided, she picked a handful of wildflowers and placed them on the grassy mound. "Bekah, I wish you weren't dead."

"She's not dead. She is alive," Life-Giver said.

"And I wish my heart didn't hurt." A white dove flew overhead and landed on the nearby fence.

"You won't always hurt, dear one. Sorrow lasts for a night, but joy does come in the morning. There is a day when you will see heaven's side of this story, and then you will understand."

Unable to hear Him, but sensing the peace that accompanied His presence, Hadassah continued, "David and Naomi have loved us well, and I'm grateful. But nothing can change the loss I feel. I wish I was with You, Life-Giver."

"Not now, child. There is a day coming when the King of heaven will welcome you into your eternal home, but it is not now."

Heavyhearted, Hadassah fell asleep draped across her sister's grave. *Life-Giver and Comforter watched over her.*

A very curious baby rabbit sniffed Hadassah's hand. She woke with a start and scrambled to her feet. The bunny fled. Realizing where she was, she sighed deeply. "I love you, Bekah."

She stood and noticed a single rose, red as blood, growing on the fence. "Strange that something so beautiful would be growing amongst weeds, little flower," she said, her heart reaching out in sympathy to the flower's plight. "I know how you feel, for I once lived among weeds. Actually it was a garbage dump, but I wasn't nearly as lovely."

Unable to resist its beauty, she walked over and knelt beside the lone flower. "You are even lovelier up close."

"I cannot take My eyes off of you, Hadassah," Life-Giver said.

"It seems to me that I have two choices. I can pick you and take you home where I could display you in full sight of everyone, but that would result in your life being cut short. Or I can leave you here among these obnoxious weeds where no one may ever see or appreciate your exquisite beauty. Your life would be a bit longer, but you'd spend your days in a graveyard. So tell me, little flower, which would you choose?"

"A seed must die if it is to live."

"Perhaps dying is really living," she thought aloud. "Perhaps this life is not the ultimate goal. Maybe the life that awaits us after death is glorious and wonderful and the real reason we exist."

"You cannot comprehend the infinite glories that await you there."

"There must be more to life than this," Hadassah said, looking around.

"There is so much more, My child," said Life-Giver.

"I will one day soon resume my pursuit of the King. Perhaps He can help me understand such mysteries."

"That's right, Hadassah, set your focus on the King, for that is where your help comes from."

"I shall let you live out your days, lovely flower. Though none see you, know that I've seen you, and that you've touched my heart in a special way," she said, breathing deeply of its intoxicating fragrance.

Walking away, she stopped, looked over her shoulder and said, "I only wish my sister had been able to live out her days. . ."

"Oh, but she did! She fulfilled her destiny and glorified her King."

***

"Martha, six months have passed since we talked of pursuing the Great King," Hadassah said, scrubbing the garment against the rocks. "I really believe it's time for us to start out again."

"Are you certain, Hadassah?"

"As certain as I can be considering all that has happened."

"I understand, but I must admit that I love it here."

"So do I, but we have this invitation to spend a day with the King. How can we not go?"

"Dassah, I want to find the King too, but I really like it here. Perhaps we could wait a little longer."

"Martha, it's been a year and a half. Please ask Life-Giver what He would have us do. Will you do that?"

"I don't need to. You're right, Dassah. I'm just being selfish. Let's tell David and Naomi tonight, after dinner," Martha said, wiping the sweat dripping off her forehead on her sleeve.

"They'll be sad to see us go."

"We'll all be sad to go, but we'll see them again. After all, the scroll says that we can only spend one day with the King. We should ask Naomi if we can come back. We would serve them well and be no bother," Martha said, the pain in her heart evident on her face.

"We shall see," Hadassah said, laying her hand on her sister's hand.

Martha squeezed her hand in response. "I've cried enough for two lifetimes. I don't want to cry anymore," she said as tears filled her eyes. Changing the subject, she said, "David says the castle is a three-day journey by foot. You still have the scroll, don't you?"

"Of course I do. It hasn't been out of my sight for a moment," she answered, patting the scroll. "Let's speak with Naomi and see if leaving tomorrow would be suitable. And, Martha, don't worry — everything's going to be just fine."

"I know."

"Life-Giver has been so faithful to us," Hadassah said.

"That I can't deny. He's been more than faithful. He's become a dear Friend to me, which is something I never imagined was possible."

Beckoning Michael, Life-Giver said, "Prepare My angelic host, for we will soon go to battle."

"As You wish, my King," the archangel responded, bowing low.

If Hadassah and Martha had been able to see the unseen realm, they would have been in awe of the way Life-Giver so intently watched over them.

The sisters divided the laundry into two baskets, which they carried on their hips. As they climbed the steep path, Martha and Hadassah recited their favorite poem:

Lift up your heads, O gates,
And be lifted up, O ancient doors,
That the King of glory might come in!

Who is this King of glory?
The Lord strong and mighty.
The Lord mighty in battle.

Lift up your heads, O gates,
And lift them up, O ancient doors,
That the King of glory might come in.

Who is this King of glory?
The Lord of hosts, He is the King of glory!

By the time they arrived at the cottage, Hadassah was more certain than ever that the time was right for them to resume their search for the Great King.

After their evening meal, David and Naomi received the news of their departure with troubled expressions.

"Why do you look so distraught?" Hadassah asked.

David leaned close and said, "There's something I must tell you, Martha. It seems Caleb has admired you from afar. He has prayed and believes Life-Giver has chosen you to be his wife. This very morning, he asked me to speak with you. Martha, he'd like to become betrothed to you."

Martha was clearly surprised. Hadassah's eyes immediately filled with tears.

David continued, "Caleb asked for my blessing, for he recognizes that I'm like a father to you."

Martha said nothing.

"Perhaps you'd like some time to pray before you respond?"

"I never believed anyone would ever —" Unable to continue, she jumped up from the table, knocking over her goblet. She burst into tears and ran outside. Hadassah excused herself and then ran after her.

Martha fell to her knees in the garden and wept bitterly. Hadassah sat close, her hand resting lightly on Martha's shoulder as she silently prayed.

Martha finally spoke. "Hadassah, how can this be happening?"

"I don't understand, dear sister. Are you happy or troubled?"

"I'm both. Caleb is a dream I never allowed myself to have. On one occasion, for just a moment, I imagined being his wife but quickly promised myself to never do that again, for I believed it to be impossible. Hadassah, you know I have no dowry, no land, nothing to bring to this marriage. As soon as he learns of this, being a man of honor, he'll withdraw his offer. Oh, this can't be happening! It's more painful than never having been asked!"

"Perhaps a dowry is not important to Caleb. Perhaps he'll accept you without one. If that's true, what would your answer be?"

"I'd still have to say no, because I'm not worthy of someone like him. I'm a poor orphan, a homeless wench with nothing to offer but a past filled with pain, poverty and heartache."

"Caleb knows all that. I believe he's offered this covenant to you understanding you have nothing to give except yourself."

"Which is exactly what I did for you," their Unseen Friend said.

Looking into Hadassah's eyes, Martha exclaimed, "But Hadassah, even if that were true and he still wanted to marry me — I can't leave you alone! I cannot and will not!" Martha sobbed uncontrollably, burying her face in her hands.

"Oh, dear sister, I won't be alone," Hadassah said, holding her close. "I have Life-Giver. He's my dearest Friend, and He won't allow me to ever be alone."

"How true your words are, My child."

"Hadassah, Life-Giver doesn't have skin. You can't touch Him or feel Him or see Him," Martha said.

"Dearest sister, you're not responsible for my care or my happiness. I appreciate your concern for me, but I now know I have another path in this life than the one you are called to walk. You'd like to marry him, wouldn't you?"

"I think so."

"Caleb's a man of integrity, a man of excellence. Any woman would be proud to be his wife. I rejoice for you. You should always pursue excellence. Is that not the way of our Savior? Did He not live this way? Always the highest, always the excellent way — even if it meant pain or separation or self-sacrifice."

"Your words are true, but they do nothing to ease the pain I feel concerning you. I dare not leave you. Whatever shall I do?"

"We have nothing to fear, for we belong to Life-Giver. Our lives are hidden in Him, are they not?"

"As usual, you're right. But I feel more like a piece of trash in the garbage dump than a woman worthy of marriage," Martha said, tears pouring down her face.

"Some of My greatest treasures I found in the garbage heap. You are a pearl of great price and ever so beautiful," Life-Giver whispered.

"You have tremendous value, dear sister. Look at you — you love Life-Giver, you grow more like Him every day and you're ever so beautiful. Your heart's as good as gold now that Life-Giver has taken up residence within you. You have so much to offer Caleb. You're like a pearl, Martha. And just like the pearl, which is formed as a result of great irritation, the King has used the tragedies of this life to make you more like Him."

Michael stole a glance at Life-Giver who nodded, smiling broadly. "She is learning well the ways of My kingdom."

"Martha, I won't try to persuade you to accept his offer, even though I believe it to be a gift from Life-Giver. But I shall encourage you to ask Life-Giver what He would have you do. Once you know what He wants then the only thing left to do is obey."

"You're right. I'll do exactly that. Thank you, Dassah," she said, hugging her tightly. "We should return to David and Naomi. I left rather abruptly, and I'm sure they're concerned."

Later that night, after everyone had retired, Hadassah slipped out to the garden. Sitting beneath the beautiful, star-filled sky, she poured out her heart to her dearest Friend. "I want what's best for Martha, but I must admit that I'm a bit afraid. I don't want to be alone — and I know that I'm not really alone, but sometimes it's difficult to remember that. I won't stand in her way, for that would be selfish."

"Oh, precious child of Mine, I hear your prayers and receive your sacrificial love as the gift that it is. Come to Me, and I will give you the grace you need," Life-Giver said, laying His hand on her heart.

"May I ask You a question?"

"Of course."

"Will I be alone, my Lord?"

"You will never be alone. I will be with you through every storm, through every tragedy, heartache and triumph. Everything is in My hands; it's going to be all right, Hadassah."

"Then it is enough."

Hadassah soon fell asleep under the stars. *And under the careful watch of Life-Giver, who spread His garment over her.*

The following morning, as Hadassah and Naomi prepared breakfast, Martha ran into the room and exclaimed, "I dreamed last night that the King beckoned me to His chambers and He told me Caleb was His gift to me! He said He healed my past so I could live in the present. The King then gave me His blessing and said I was His daughter and He was my Father."

Martha threw her arms around her sister. "Hadassah, I saw Mama and Papa and they hugged me! I didn't want to let them go, but they said I must. That was when they told me Rebekah was with them. They said she is very happy and she wants us to know that she is praying for us. Mama and Papa said to tell you they love you dearly and are so very proud of the choices you're making. They kissed me and then said they had to go.

"Hadassah, it was so real. It didn't seem at all like a dream — it felt like I was really with them. They were so perfectly happy. I wish you could've seen them!"

"Me too," Hadassah said, wiping her eyes on her apron. "I'll see them soon enough, dear sister,"

"I can't remember the last time I felt this happy," said Martha, her face reflecting the joy within.

"I suppose a meeting with Caleb might be in order?" David asked, his voice sounding hopeful.

"Tell him my answer is yes," Martha said, beaming.

"Oh, how happy he shall be!" Naomi exclaimed, clapping her hands together, flour flying through the air. "Oh my," she said, laughing.

Taking Martha's hand, she said, "There's no one any better for you on this earth than he. Life-Giver has chosen the best for the best. You two will be so happy together."

David excused himself to take the good news to his friend. Martha ran after him, saying, "David, make sure Caleb knows I don't have a dowry. Tell him that I can't give him anything except myself. Please tell him I'll understand should he choose to withdraw his offer."

"I will relay your message, but I don't believe you have anything to worry about. Caleb's not entering into this marriage with the intention of increasing his estate; rather, he's entering into covenant with you so that he might give you all that he has and all that he is."

"Just like Me."

"Such love is too marvelous for me! It is too high, I can't understand it," Martha said.

"'Tis the love of Life-Giver that fills Caleb, for he's learned well the ways of his King," said David.

"I have so much to learn."

"And you will have a willing teacher for a husband," David said. "But I must hurry to his side, for I know he anxiously awaits your answer."

"Go then and give him my greeting."

"This is a glorious day!" David exclaimed as he hurried down the path to the fields where Caleb waited.

CHAPTER THIRTEEN

$\mathcal{O}$n the first day of autumn, Caleb and Martha became husband and wife.

Hadassah kissed her sister's cheek and asked, "Do you remember the conversation we had on the rock in the Land of Despair?"

"Which one? There were so many," she answered, taking her sister's hand.

"The time when I spoke of true love."

"Yes, I remember that."

"You found it — or rather, true love found you, chose you and cherished you. And now, true love has found you a second time," she said, tossing her head in Caleb's direction.

"I never thought I'd ever experience a love like Life-Giver's or Caleb's. What a gift and what a miracle!" Squeezing her sister's hand, she continued, "Thank you for believing. Your faith changed my life."

"I had a tiny part to play, dear sister, but it was really Life-Giver who changed your life."

"Well said," Caleb responded as he walked up. "Are you ready, my love?"

"Take good care of her," said Hadassah, laying her hand on his arm.

"I most certainly will. And, Hadassah," he said, laying his hand on top of hers.

"Yes?"

"You always have a home with us."

"Thank you, Caleb. May the Great King bless you both."

With a final embrace, Martha and Hadassah bid each other farewell. "When will I see you again?" Martha asked.

"I will return — after I've spent a day with the King."

"Will you be traveling alone?"

"I'm not alone, Martha. Don't worry. I have the best Companion and Escort there is."

Martha looked deep in Hadassah's eyes.

"I'll see you again," Hadassah said.

"Then I shall not say good-bye." Martha kissed her sister's cheek and held her tight.

"I love you," said Hadassah.

"And I love you."

Caleb took his wife's hand and then swept her off her feet. As he carried her to his wagon, she looked back at Hadassah, tears streaming down her face. The guests showered them with kernels of wheat as they shouted out blessings, but Martha barely noticed or heard.

With a final wave, Hadassah wiped her eyes.

"You are not alone," her constant Companion whispered.

"Thank You for being here with me," Hadassah said. "I'm so happy for my sister; it's a good thing."

"Even good things can be painful."

"You know that very well, don't You?"

"For the joy set before Me, I endured the cross. Keep your eyes fixed on Me, for I am your joy."

Naomi, sensitive to the fact that Hadassah was now alone, hurried to her side. Placing her arm around her waist she said, "I was thinking of taking a walk. Would you care to join me?"

"I'd love to."

The two strolled through the tall grass without talking. Once they were out of the sight of the guests, Naomi asked, "So tell me, how are you really?"

"I feared this day would be unbearable, but I'm at peace. I'm very aware of Life-Giver's presence, and I'm truly happy for my sister."

"That is how it should be," Naomi said, gently squeezing Hadassah's hand. "What are your plans now, dear one?"

"I will begin my journey within the week. But I must admit I do feel a bit apprehensive, especially since I thought I'd be making this trip with my sisters."

"It's not wise for a young woman to travel alone. Perhaps you should wait until David can go with you?"

"That won't be until winter. I can't wait that long. Patience has never been one of my strong points, and besides, there's a burning in my heart that grows stronger with each passing day. If I should ignore it, I fear the fire would go out and it would be lost forever. I must trust my heart in this, dear Naomi, and follow its leading, for my heart belongs to Life-Giver. Should He desire a traveling companion for me then I'm certain one will appear."

Looking long and hard at Hadassah's tranquil face, Naomi sighed. "Your faith has grown strong, my child. You do well to follow the wind of the Spirit even in the presence of fear. David and I will stand with you in prayer. But for now, let us climb this hill, for there are sights to be seen that will further ignite your heart for the journey ahead."

Naomi led the way. Reaching the top, they stopped in their tracks. Hadassah had never seen anything so breathtakingly beautiful. Stretched as far as the eye could see was a land more glorious than pen can describe.

"Naomi, what . . . where is this?"

"This is a glimpse of heaven," she answered, completely awestruck herself.

Hadassah tried to memorize every detail, but each detail in and of itself was more than her mind could comprehend. Colors unlike anything she had ever seen, beauty beyond description, sounds that were alive and musical in every way, smells that intoxicated the soul while lifting it to a higher realm, the very air seemed to invite her spirit to encounter the One who is Life Eternal.

"How is it possible to see this?" Hadassah asked.

"We are seeing beyond the veil into the unseen realm."

"You have seen this before?"

"I have, but only once. Life-Giver appeared in my dream last night and told me to bring you here. He said it was time for you to have a glimpse of His realm."

The glorious scene stretched out before them seemed completely foreign to earth, yet — in some strange way — appeared to be a reflection of it.

Or perhaps earth is a mirror image of the unseen realm, Hadassah thought.

Never had Hadassah seen anything so perfect, so inviting. The crystal clear river sounded as though it were singing as it gently wound its way through the lush, green valley. Grand trees, colorful flowers, butterflies and birds filled the land stretched out before her. The valley was surrounded by green rolling hills and in the distance stood majestic, snowcapped mountains.

The very presence of Life-Giver filled her senses, overwhelming her. Hadassah's knees collapsed beneath her, and she fell on her face. She worshipped without words as her tears watered the ground.

Overwhelmed, she stretched out on the ground. Rolling onto her back in the softest grass she had ever felt, she saw a majestic eagle gliding effortlessly on the wind. The magnificent bird was soon joined by a female carrying a small stick in her talons. Flying higher than the male, she suddenly dropped the stick; he immediately dove after it. With no effort at all and before it had fallen any distance, he retrieved the stick. Soaring upward, he displayed his successful catch to his potential mate. She did not appear to be impressed.

Turning away from him, she flew toward the ground. With amazing grace and agility, her enormous talons snatched a larger branch from the ground. Clutching it, she flew straight toward the attentive male. Just before reaching him, she dropped the stick. He dove after it. In a seemingly effortless swoop, he retrieved the falling branch in his fierce-looking talons. He once more displayed his prize before the female, who appeared to ignore his victory.

In a third dive, she returned carrying a larger branch. Before reaching him, and even closer to the ground than before, she released it.

"He'll never make it," Hadassah whispered as the male eagle instantly dove after it. The branch quickly approached the treetops. Undaunted, like an arrow, the majestic creature dove straight for the trees. Hadassah sat up. The eagle exploded out of the leafy mass clutching the prize.

Like a victorious warrior returning from battle, with head held high, he flew straight toward the object of his desire. The female, who watched from the clouds, acknowledged his heroic efforts for the first time. Her shrieks filled the air as she flew toward him.

The two danced figure eight's around each other as they celebrated and painted a picture of sacrificial love in the sky.

"Self-sacrifice, fearless devotion, proven love and glorious triumph," they screeched, displaying their mating ritual for all of heaven and earth to see.

And all the while, Life-Giver watched closely as His angelic hosts stood by with swords drawn.

"Like Naomi, Hadassah sees," Michael said.

"Is it not wonderful, Michael?"

"I am always amazed when a son or daughter of the King is able to see."

"All are able, but few are willing to take the time or pay the price to do so."

Turning His attention to the two women, Life-Giver said to them, "The female eagle tested the heart of her future partner. She must know: is he willing to risk his life to save a falling eaglet? Can he see clearly enough to save her offspring? Can he fly faster than they can fall?

"Mankind wants to know the same thing about Me. Am I willing to die for them? Can I see clearly enough to save them from the dangers lurking ahead? Can I fly faster than they can fall?

"This is the great test of love, for love must be proven. I, like this eagle, was tested once and for all time. I saw My offspring falling and died to save them. I was strong enough and fast enough. Nothing is stronger than My love — not even faith or hope. I came, I saw and I gave My all. I will always fly faster than you can fall — never forget that."

Naomi and Hadassah heard but neither spoke, for His message transcended mere words. Naomi responded by singing, and Hadassah joined her worship.

Michael said, "Hadassah's voice has improved greatly . . ."

Life-giver raised His hand; Michael instantly responded to His unspoken rebuke with silence.

"I do not look at outward talents or gifts, for they come and go like the wind. I fix My gaze on the inward beauty, which reflects the state of the heart. Michael, this is the sound of pure love; it attracts Me like nothing else."

Michael strained to hear the sound. Alas, he was unable to hear such love, for it was higher than his angel life form could discern. Laying His hand on the angel's shoulder, Life-Giver smiled. "I understand this is a mystery beyond your capacity to experience. Be at peace, My angelic friend, and know that all is well."

For quite some time, the two handmaidens worshipped with words and without words.

Unknown to them, Life-Giver knelt before them. His gaze was fixed as He savored every word and every movement of their hearts while the angelic guards protected the sanctuary from intruders.

Hadassah laid her head against Naomi's shoulder and silently prayed, *Life-Giver, You have more than passed the test. I'll follow You anywhere.*

"Rightly said and rightly promised," her Beloved Friend replied as He stood. *"But never forget that it is not your commitment to Me that keeps you, but rather My commitment to you. You can do nothing without Me."*

With a wave of His hand, the angels gathered. "Summon reinforcements, for tomorrow is the beginning of a long journey and another battle."

"What battle is that, my Lord?" Michael asked.

"The battle for the highest life," He said, His eyes reflecting the fierce love He held for one so small and weak.

"May I ask, my Lord, what is so special about Hadassah that You would love her so?"

"Michael, within Hadassah's heart lives a seed, a seed that contains My life. This seed cannot fall to the ground without greater life springing up from it. Life is always valuable and always worth saving.

"Hadassah is destined for greatness. My Father chooses the foolish things of this world to shame the wise. He chooses the weak things of this world to shame the things which are strong. My Father

chooses the base and despised things of this world so that no one can boast before Him. She has been chosen to be My eternal partner."

"Chosen," Michael repeated, pondering the word. *"My Lord, Your angels were created not chosen."*

"That is true, Michael. Angels do not have the same privileges as My bride."

"Is she the only one, my King?"

"On the contrary, Michael. She is one of many who will one day be united — Jew and Gentile with one heart, one soul and one purpose — to be My bride. Oh, what a glorious day that will be!"

Suddenly, the ground beneath Hadassah and Naomi began to shake. The eagles shrieked as they sought cover in the cleft of a nearby rock. Naomi and Hadassah scrambled beneath nearby bushes, where they hid from what they did not know.

Every angel fell on his face as the Great King approached.

"To be chosen," the Great King said, "is the glory of man, for one cannot be Mine unless they are chosen. And if they are chosen, they are Mine . . . forever!"

"My glorious Father!" Life-Giver exclaimed.

"My beloved Son!"

As the two embraced, a third Being joined Their celebration. The sound of a mighty, rushing wind filled the hilltop where Hadassah and Naomi lay prostrate in holy fear.

"My Holy Spirit," the Great King announced.

"Living King, full of wonder! Beloved Son, full of grace!" the Spirit responded.

As the Three-in-One adored each other in a manner that resembled the eagles' dance, the angels cried over and over again, "Holy, holy, holy, Lord God Almighty, who is and was and is to come!"

It was a scene full of awe — a scene which Naomi and Hadassah were not allowed to witness but certainly perceived.

For a moment in time (earthly time, that is, for time is always present tense in the unseen realm), the unseen realm overlapped the visible on that hilltop. The Father of all creation looked backward and then forward through earth's history. With a nod and a smile He turned to His Son and said, "It is good; it is very good."

His Son nodded in agreement.

The Father continued, *"The time of earth is nearly complete; Your bride is being prepared to rule and reign. She is growing in grace and truth, is she not?"*

"She is indeed coming of age and growing in the glorious attributes that will adorn her throughout eternity. Every bride longs to be beautiful on her wedding day, and this bride is no exception," said the Spirit.

"And so she shall, for she grows more like Us each day," Life-Giver said.

"She is a willing student, for she grows lovesick," said the Spirit.

"It will take a lovesick heart for her to endure the shame and agony of the cross she will soon be called to carry."

"A lovesick heart she will have," the Spirit said, *"for this is her destiny."*

"To be chosen is the glory of man," Life-Giver repeated.

Naomi and Hadassah trembled. Had they known what was happening right before their eyes, they would have understood why the ground was making its wild contortions. The unseen realm had collided with earth, and the supernatural always supersedes dirt.

Once the earth returned to its calm state, Naomi and Hadassah cautiously crawled out from their hiding place.

"Was that an earthquake?" Hadassah asked.

"I don't know."

"I fear this place is the very gateway to heaven itself," Hadassah said.

"I don't know if it's the gateway, but surely the unseen realm invaded earth today," Naomi said as they began their descent.

Hadassah sighed.

"What is it?" Naomi asked.

"I have this ache in my heart that is consuming me. I must *know* Him. I must find Him."

"Your desire to know Him intimately is a gift, dear one, for He always answers the cry of a hungry heart. Of that, you can be sure."

"My hunger has gone beyond mere appetite and has become that of a desperate heart. I have kept my desperation a secret lest you and David think me mad," Hadassah said, stopping to see Naomi's response.

Naomi turned, giving Hadassah her full attention. "Hadassah, you have nothing to fear from me, for I'm in no position to judge your motives. And neither is anyone else. The King alone earned the right to be your judge, and He never judges spiritual hunger or insatiable desire as madness. His love more than qualifies for such titles. So you have nothing to worry about on earth or in heaven, my dear. Give your heart the freedom it needs to grow in love and maturity, and if it is judged to be madness, then so be it!"

An angelic ambassador stood in front of Hadassah and announced, "Life-Giver has summoned you."

Hadassah was suddenly aware of a holy Presence. She looked around. Her natural eyes were of no help, so she closed them, shutting out all distractions.

The angel touched her eyes.

There before her, in the unseen realm, was Life-Giver sitting on a white horse. His left hand held the scarlet reins while His right hand rested on the hilt of a golden sword. He looked directly at Hadassah and smiled. Her heart stopped, she was sure of it. She could not breathe or move or cry out. Like a stone statue, she stared at the most beautiful Man she had ever seen.

Chuckling, Life-Giver said, "Breathe, Hadassah. If you don't, you will be joining Me sooner than I planned."

She took a breath, and as she did grace filled her.

"Your eyes tell me how much You care," she whispered.

"I love you more than I loved life."

"No one loves me the way You love me."

"And no one ever will."

"Thank You."

"It is My pleasure to love you. Hadassah, I am going to teach you what it means for two hearts to beat as one. As your life is submitted to Me, I will live My life through you, loving the least and the lost. Follow Me, Hadassah, for narrow is the path that leads to life."

The vision ended, and Hadassah fell on the ground as if dead. When she opened her eyes again, her head was in Naomi's lap, who frantically fanned her with a large leaf.

"What happened?" Naomi asked.

"I saw Him! I saw Life-Giver!"

"And?"

"He told me to follow Him. He said we will love the least and the lost. He also said something that I don't fully understand. He told me that I am to learn how two hearts can beat as one — that is what my life on earth is all about. I don't see how I could ever achieve anything as lofty as that. But regardless, I shall go, Naomi. I shall leave in the morning. I dare not wait."

"What an amazing day this has been!" Naomi exclaimed as she helped Hadassah to her feet.

"What a day indeed!"

***

Early the following morning, David and Naomi escorted Hadassah through the streets of Jerusalem to a small, insignificant-looking gate. Hadassah looked at it and then turned to David, the question evident on her face. He answered, "There are few who find this gate, Hadassah, and even fewer who choose to walk through it."

"Have you gone through this gate and walked on its path?" she asked.

"We have."

"Then I have nothing to fear?"

"You have nothing to fear except fear itself," David said.

"I must go, for there is One who has beckoned me come," she said, taking a deep breath.

Hugging Hadassah tightly, Naomi bid her farewell. "Remember the dance of the eagles and Life-Giver's words to you, Hadassah."

"How could I ever forget?"

David hugged her close and whispered, "Choose Life . . . every time, Hadassah."

"I will. I will choose life," she said, not really understanding what he meant.

Naomi handed her an overstuffed pouch. "This will keep your stomach full and your thirst quenched."

"Thank you for everything."

David and Naomi watched as Hadassah tugged and pulled on the thick vines growing through, around and over the gate. She managed, in her own strength, to pull away enough of the vines to open the gate a little, but not enough to squeeze through it. She thought of climbing over it, but it was too tall. She couldn't go around it, because as far as she could see in both directions was a tall fence.

"No one comes to the Father except through Me. I am the Door, the Sheep-Gate and the only Way," Life-Giver said in a still, small voice.

"I desire to walk this narrow path. I want to know You and Your Father intimately. Life-Giver, will You lead me to the King?"

"That is one request I never fail to grant." With a wave of His hand, the vines suddenly fell away and the latch fell open.

Amazed, Hadassah walked through the gate.

CHAPTER FOURTEEN

*H*adassah set out on her journey feeling great joy and confidence, but both were soon replaced by frustration. "Not only has the path become almost imperceivable, but the forest is so thick that it is difficult to know whether it's day or night. How can I find my way if I can't see?"

"You are to walk by faith and not by sight, My beloved."

Hadassah did not hear Him.

Discouragement had secretly followed her since she stepped through the gate. It now rubbed against her ankles, purring. "It doesn't make any sense to keep going. You should turn around now while you can still find your way back," it said.

"Maybe I should go back," Hadassah said to herself. "Oh, I can't go back!" Her hand reached for the precious scrolls securely tucked in her waistband. Hadassah forced herself to keep walking.

Discouragement continued flooding her mind with lies. "Life is a series of circumstances and events, nothing more and nothing less. Why bother? The important thing to remember is that it's your life, and you should live it the way you choose."

Hadassah tried not to listen but found it impossible to drown out the nagging thoughts.

"Martha misses you terribly. After all, you did abandon her and so soon after your sister's tragic death."

I wonder if Martha blames me for leaving, Hadassah thought.

Her chest began to ache. *Anxiety pushed against her. The evil creature rarely missed an opportunity to harass those with minds given to worry.*

Trying to distract herself, Hadassah focused on her surroundings, but that did nothing but cause her more distress. By sheer willpower, she kept going until she was too exhausted to take another step. Crawling beneath tent-like foliage, she thanked Life-Giver for her food and asked Him to be with her sister. She soon fell asleep.

The following day, after walking for what seemed like forever, she came upon a small clearing. Relieved to finally see the sun, she collapsed on the tall grass. Leaning against a fallen log, she basked in the warmth, the light and the fresh air.

Hadassah looked around. Just ahead, the path divided to the right and to the left. The path to the right was much like the one she had just been on — narrow, dark and frightening —, but the path to the left was wide, full of light and inviting. A dozen or so blue birds pecked at the ground on the wide path while baby bunnies played nearby under the leaves of a big fern.

"Which way should I go?" she asked aloud.

Discouragement answered, "It's obvious which path you should take. Choose the path of least resistance, the one most traveled, the one clearly marked . . . or you can always go back to your sister whom you abandoned."

Hadassah felt confused and discouraged and even angry.

"Hadassah," Life-Giver said.

"Yes?"

"Why has your countenance fallen?"

"Because what I thought would be easy is turning out to be very difficult. I have no idea which way to go. I left Martha alone. Well, she's not really alone, but I'm her sister and I should —"

"Hadassah."

"Yes?"

"Whose voice are you listening to?"

"I don't know."

"Sin is crouching at the door. And its desire is for you, but you must master it."

"I'm afraid."

"Then run to Perfect Love . . . where there is no fear."

Anxiety pressed with all its might against her chest. "You aren't safe here. You don't know where you're going or how to get there. There are wild animals lurking in the forest, just waiting to devour you."

Discouragement added, "This is no place for a girl, especially one as frail as you. You should go back and wait until you have a proper escort. After all, you don't even know which path to take."

"Hadassah," Life-Giver said.

Hadassah was so busy listening to the voices in her head that she did not hear Him call her name again.

"That's right, Hadassah, think about all the ways you could get hurt, about how difficult it is, about all the reasons why this is foolish and why you should return to Martha," Discouragement said.

Hadassah spread out her blanket. Wrapping her cloak around her, she snuggled down for the night. It took quite awhile for her to go to sleep. *Fear, Anxiety and Discouragement kept flooding her mind with their dark thoughts.* Life-Giver seemed nowhere to be found.

Michael looked at Life-Giver who remained by her side.

Hadassah woke, ate, worried, fretted, paced and slept some more. She repeated this routine several times over the next two days. Afraid of making the wrong decision, she made no decision at all.

And all the while, her Unseen Friend waited patiently for her to glance His way and inquire of Him.

"*My Lord,*" *Michael asked,* "*why do You not intervene?*"

"*There is a time and a season for everything. To not give her the time she needs to mature in this matter would dishonor her. I am not in any hurry, My angelic friend.*"

The angel bowed low and said, "*It appears she grows faint of heart, my Lord.*"

"*That is not necessarily a bad thing. It is vital for Hadassah to realize how weak she really is. When she does, I will be able to help her, and she will remember the lesson learned. Michael, I am more interested in her becoming like Me than I am with rescuing her from discomfort, especially when that discomfort will help transform her into My image.*"

"*Why does she not realize she needs You?*"

"*Because fear and worry blind the human heart and cause it to become introspective and self-protective.*"

"Is there hope for her then?"

"There is always hope, for I am Hope. That is why I am pouring out My love on her even now."

"But, my Lord, I do not see Your love."

"Love has many faces, Michael. In this case, My love patiently waits for her to lay aside her self-reliance and independence so that she will look to Me. For Me to rescue her before she has willingly laid that aside would hinder her growth, and that would not be life-giving to her. My love never fails to accomplish that which it is sent out to do. Watch and see."

Michael kept watching, but nothing changed.

As a matter of fact, Hadassah only grew more confused and despondent as she began to agree with the voices in her head.

Three days passed before Hadassah decided to get a closer look. Walking a short distance down the wide and pleasant-looking path, she stumbled over a rock and fell flat on her face.

Michael looked at his Master, for he knew Life-Giver had just given permission for a dark creature named Stumbling Block to place that rock in the path.

Life-Giver responded to Michael's unspoken thoughts. "What you are seeing is My mercy, Michael."

"Your mercy?"

"She has grown comfortable even in this place of struggle and uncertainty. In her discouragement, she decided to take the easy path. I love her too much to allow her to go her own way. Should she choose to, I won't stop her, but I will certainly make it difficult."

Hadassah did not rise. She remained face down on the ground, unmoving.

"Hadassah, nothing can separate you from My love. . . not even your mistakes."

Hadassah pushed herself up. Using the hem of her skirt, she wiped the blood from her chin and mouth. "Life-Giver, where are You?"

"I am right where I have always been — both within you and surrounding you."

"I need You; I can't do this alone. I thought I could, but I can't. Will You help me?"

Pressing the fabric tightly against the wound, she rocked back and forth. The words written on the first scroll came to her mind. "Seek the Great King while He may be found; call upon Him while He is near. You shall go out with joy and be led forth with peace. Enter by the narrow gate; for the gate is wide and broad is the way that leads to destruction, and many are those who enter by it. The gate is small and the way is narrow that leads to life, and few are those who find it."

Feeling great conviction, Hadassah confessed, "I have made *me* the center of my life rather than You. It's a subtle difference, but one I now see so clearly. I understand my life's not about *me* — it's all about You! Keep me from self-focus, self-promotion and selfish living, I pray."

"You are forgiven, cleansed and loved."

For the briefest moment, she saw in the spirit. She caught a glimpse of Life-Giver and the Spirit of Truth, for they are one and the same. Like a child disposing of vile garbage, she cast aside her fear, worry and discouragement while grabbing the hand of the only One who could lead her through the darkness.

With renewed strength, she proclaimed, "Life-Giver, show me the way, I pray." Hadassah stood. There was only one way to go. Leaving behind her fears, she chose the narrow path.

Michael asked, "Will her journey be successful?"

"Her journey will bring her face to face with the reality of who she is in Me and who I am in her. She is on a path through the inner recesses of her soul. The day will come when she will eventually face the question every human must answer."

Michael waited; he was unsure if he was permitted to look closer into the affairs of mankind's heart. He knew Life-Giver well enough to know that if this was information he was to have, it would be revealed to him, for absolutely nothing escaped his Master.

"Michael, the question every human following the King must answer sooner or later is: Will they go the way of the cross?"

"This child will be asked that question?" Michael asked, looking at the frail, little thing who had been so easily deceived.

"She will."

"And what will she do?"

"That is not for you to know."

"The ways of humans are quite peculiar," Michael said.

"Indeed they are, but so are the ways of angels to humans," Life-Giver said, chuckling.

***

Hadassah followed the dark, narrow path for hours. Her heart was overjoyed when she saw beams of sunlight directly ahead of her. She ran as fast as she could. Like a bird escaping a cage, Hadassah flew out of the forest.

Stretched out before her was a lush meadow. Seeing a patch of wild blueberries, she thanked Life-Giver. Once she picked the bushes clean, she found a place under the branches of a tree and stretched out beneath the evening sky. Hadassah soon fell asleep.

With the rising of the sun, Hadassah looked around. Behind her was the forest and before her was an endless field of rolling hills. *Which way do I go?* she wondered.

"Life-Giver, I don't know which way to go. There's no path to follow or directions to be had. I really need You to show me the way." Taking a deep breath, Hadassah listened but heard nothing.

"Well, what do I do now?" she wondered aloud.

Scanning the grassy land stretched out before her, she noticed a narrow stream not too far away, running along the edge of the woods. *A lot like a path,* she thought.

"I'm going to follow that stream, Life-Giver. If it's not right, please let me know." She waited and listened but again heard nothing. "I sure hope I'm doing the right thing."

As she walked, she talked with Life-Giver. *Fear and Discouragement kept trying to interrupt.* But Hadassah resisted them by recalling the wondrous things Life-Giver had done in her life and thanking Him for them. She soon discovered that it was quite effective. *The creatures hated it. They squirmed and shrieked and spit and cussed. They hated it so much that they grew quiet.*

The stream soon merged with other streams becoming a fast-flowing river. Hadassah followed it for four days. On the morning of the fifth day, she woke with the strongest impression to stop following the river and head east. "I don't want to go the wrong way. Oh, whatever should I do, Life-Giver?"

"Follow the wind," He said.

"Did You just say, 'Follow the wind'?"

Hadassah looked at the blowing trees and grasses. The wind was blowing to the east. "Life-Giver, this journey sure would be easier if I had a map," she said as she headed east.

"Even with a map you would still need Me."

"You're right; I would."

Stopping for the night, Hadassah wrapped the blankets around herself. Huddled against a tree trunk, she bid Life-Giver goodnight, asking Him once again to watch over her sister.

"Goodnight, My beloved one."

The next day, with the sun directly overhead, Hadassah stood on the crest of yet another hill. To her surprise, in the valley below was another walled city. The city appeared to have no end. She dropped to her knees. "Please tell me that this is the city of the Great King."

"My Father and His kingdom are endless."

"But . . . where's His castle?"

"His home is within you. You are seeing in the spirit, child."

"I don't understand, but thank You, Life-Giver, for leading me here!" Hadassah exclaimed as she ran down the hill so fast that she fell flat on her face. Laughing, she quickly got up only to fall again. Forcing herself to slow down, she made it safely to the valley floor. Without stopping, she ran straight to the city gate, which was shut tight. Running her calloused hands over the rough wood, she whispered, "I'm here. I'm really here."

A splinter pierced her thumb, but she barely noticed.

"Such is the nature of true love — it endures all things," Life-Giver said.

"It's real! It's really real, and I'm really here!" Spinning and running and twirling, she shouted, "I'm here, I'm finally here!" Dizzy, she fell down.

When the world stopped spinning, she said, "Life-Giver, I know this scroll is quite old — how old I don't know — but I do hope the invitation is still valid. Surely it is. You wouldn't have brought me all this way for nothing, would You?" Not waiting for an answer, Hadassah continued, "I pray that You will grant me the desire of my heart."

"What is her desire, my Master, and shall we deliver it?" Michael asked.

"Her desire is not something that can be delivered but must be achieved, My angelic friend."

"May I ask what it is and how it can be attained?"

"You may. Her desire is actually the highest pursuit of the human heart, which makes it the most difficult to achieve. It goes against the very nature of humanity."

"My Lord, what is this high pursuit of the handmaiden?"

"The true desire of her heart is to die to herself and live for Me — she wants nothing more and will accept nothing less."

"My Lord, humans are so confusing, for each one reacts so differently from another. But this is a pursuit I have never seen You refuse."

"And you never will, for it is also one of My deepest, greatest desires. Is it not what I did? Was it not the cry of My heart in the garden of Gethsemane? You heard Me, Michael; you were there ready to fight for Me. You heard My cry to My Father, 'Not My will, but Your will be done!'"

"I was there and so were myriads of other angels ready to do Your bidding. We could not understand why we were not allowed to defend You, the Innocent One, or why we were not allowed to defeat Satan and his angels. Neither could we understand why You submitted to the wicked schemes of evil men. We could only obey, and we did so without understanding."

"All that I did, I did for love, Michael. I died and rose again that Hadassah and countless others might die and rise again."

Michael had been with the Lord since the beginning of creation. He had fought with and for Him in many battles. He had remained steadfast by His side through every event in human history. Never before had Michael seen the depth of love and devotion that he saw displayed before heaven and earth as the King's Son hung on that despised cross. Michael knew that it was Perfect Love that held Him to that brutal tree, but he did not understand the purpose of such a costly and divine sacrifice.

Michael looked at Life-Giver, who was gazing at Hadassah. Michael fell to his knees, for Life-Giver had the same look of love on His face now as He did on the cross. Bowing low, Michael worshipped, saying, "Life-Giver, the eternal Word, the Creator of all, Son of the Great King, the beloved of the Father, the Lamb of God, the First-born of the dead, the glorious Redeemer, the unconquerable Warrior, and soon-coming King has been conquered and overwhelmed by the simple yet genuine love of a little handmaiden! Perhaps this is the greatest mystery of all! Perhaps this is the reason for —"

Dare he think it, dare he speak it?

The Great King suddenly manifested His presence as His Holy Spirit descended upon Michael, giving him the words he dared not utter apart from the unction of God. Michael exclaimed, "Perhaps this is the reason for creation? Perhaps this is the reason for Your death? Perhaps this is the reason for the resurrection? Perhaps this is the reason for life and death and freedom and suffering and joy and sorrow? Perhaps this is the reason for it all?"

Life-Giver smiled a thousand smiles.

Michael asked, "This maiden — is she the reason You died?"

"She and many more are the reason," Life-Giver proclaimed.

The Godhead gathered around the little handmaiden. Unknown to her, They basked in the beauty and glory of her simple yet profound love.

"You are the sparkle in My eye," her Father the Great King whispered.

"You are the object of My affection," Life-Giver said.

"And you are chosen," said the Spirit.

The angels bowed low, amazed once again at the power and beauty of Perfect Love.

CHAPTER FIFTEEN

𝓗adassah spread her blanket in front of the city gate and then neatly arranged her few belongings. "I'm about to meet the Great King — I think . . . or I hope I am."

Trying to relax, Hadassah took a deep breath and snuggled beneath her cloak. With arms folded beneath her head, Hadassah looked heavenward. The night sky was filled with more stars than anyone could ever possibly count. The moon was a mere sliver of light, which caused the stars to appear even brighter.

Hadassah felt the familiar tug-of-war within. In an effort to keep the negative thoughts at bay, she talked aloud. "I have nothing to fear, for I'm safe in Your arms. I know that You can fly faster than I can fall. You've proven Your love to me. I choose life. I choose love. I choose You! With You by my side, I'll fight the good fight and stand against everything that's contrary to love. I'll love You, and I'll love others."

"What about yourself?"

"Me? What about me?"

"You cannot love others if you do not love yourself. It's impossible to do so. You cannot give what you do not possess."

"I think I'll need Your help with that."

"It means no more putting yourself down, no more self-condemnation in the name of humility and no more speaking or thinking negatively about yourself."

"Is that even possible?"

"Hadassah, nothing is impossible for Me. Two hearts learning to beat as one — remember?"

"Yes."

"It's not your responsibility to 'fix' you — you couldn't even if you tried."

"Okay then, come and live Your life through me. As You know, I did try, but I wasn't very good at it."

"I will do exactly that. And for the record, I don't 'fix' people — I kill them and then resurrect them."

"Oh, that sounds painful!"

"That all depends on whether you cooperate with the process or fight against it."

"I choose to cooperate, whatever that looks like."

"That is wise. Now rest, for tomorrow is a brand new day."

Surprisingly, Hadassah quickly fell asleep and slept peacefully the entire night.

The moment she woke, she jumped to her feet eager to see if the gate was open. It was not. She felt the familiar twinge of disappointment but quickly reminded herself that it was still early. Looking around for water, she walked along the wall, singing her mama's song.

"You wasted so much time in the forest. It's too late for you. The gate is closed for the winter," Discouragement said, *rubbing itself against her ankle.*

Hadassah's heart sank. "I did waste a lot of time wallowing in my self-pity."

Hadassah forgot to take every thought captive. *Discouragement purred as it slowly and ever so quietly began to wrap itself around her ankle.*

"I've already waited so long. It's been nearly three years since I found that scroll and started my journey," Hadassah said to herself as she continued on.

"Time is a big deal to humans," Michael said.

Life-Giver responded, "Michael, the day will come when time will be as valuable to humans as their possessions, for it is one of the few things they have no control over. Whatever they can't have or control they tend to lust after — remember the tree of the knowledge of good and evil? This need to be in control and have whatever they want is the fruit of eating from that tree."

"It would be impossible to forget that event."

"As the end of earth-time draws near, many humans will be driven by the desires of their flesh while silencing the voice of their spirit. The love of many will grow cold, for many will become offended with Us. My Father will not do things the way humans think He should, and for most people that will become a stumbling block. That is why I am preparing My bride now, for I have overcome the world."

"Indeed You have, for I witnessed Your resurrection with my very own eyes. And what a glorious day it was!"

"What a glorious day it still is and always will be!"

Hadassah walked a short distance into the trees. "Oh good!" she said, stepping into a stream of crystal clear water. After quenching her thirst, she washed away the dust and dirt from her journey in preparation for meeting the Great King. Seeing her reflection in the pool, her heart felt sick. *What if He finds me ugly and rejects me?* she thought. *What if He exposes me for who I really am — a tramp and a beggar?*

"Hadassah, those are not words of life — they edify no one," Life-Giver whispered.

"You're right. I'm sorry. Will You give me words of life, please? Speak *Your* truth to my heart, for that is the only truth that matters."

"Gladly. The truth is you are loved whether you feel like it or not. The very fact that you have been chosen is proof of that fact. You are safe and beautiful. Do not be concerned about your appearance, for the King looks beyond the outward and sees the inward. As for your inward parts — I dwell within you. I took your sins and gave you My righteousness in exchange. Because I did that, you now shine like the sun. When the King and I look at you, We see My beauty and glory and perfection, which overpowers any and every fault, weakness or imperfection that you have."

Hadassah let out a deep sigh. "Thank You, Life-Giver. It seems that my heart is prone to darkness."

"Your soul is prone to darkness, but that is not true of your spirit."

Hadassah had no idea that a spiritual battle raged all around her. All she knew was that her heart and mind were at odds. Her mind was telling her to go back to Martha while her heart was telling her to run to the Great King. By the sheer act of her will, she determined not to give up.

Powerful angels of light fought against dark, hideous creatures.

Afraid she might miss the opening of the gate, Hadassah hurried back. But the closer she got to the gate, the slower she walked.

The Fear within her heart was choking the life out of her. "You are a stupid, foolish girl. If you think for one minute that the great king will welcome you into his kingdom then you are insane! You should be afraid to go anywhere near him. He sees not only your deeds but also your heart. You don't stand a chance, little girl."

Michael looked at Life-Giver. "My Lord?" he asked, lowering his sword.

"She invited Fear in, Michael."

"My Lord?"

"Whatever is not of faith is sin and that includes fear. Go and strengthen her, but do not engage the enemy. This battle is hers to win." His gaze was steady and sure.

Michael stepped to her side. With a wave of his arm, he released the strength of the King around her.

It was up to Hadassah to accept it.

She slumped to the ground a few feet from the gate. "I don't understand what's happening. Why am I so afraid? I've dreamed about this day for so long. How can I even think of giving up? What's wrong with me?"

"Hadassah, remember love," the unseen angel whispered.

"Where are You? I can't find You, Life-Giver! I can't hear You!"

"Remember love, for Perfect Love casts out all fear," he repeated.

Fear wrapped its snake-like body around Hadassah's heart and squeezed. Michael stood ready for the Master's command while the other angels continued to fight the demonic hoards sent to prevent her entry into the King's courtyard.

"Life-Giver, where are You?" Hadassah screamed.

"I'm in you and I'm as close as the air all around you. Remember love, Hadassah. There is nothing greater than love."

"I'm alone and feel so afraid. My family's dead, except for Martha, and she's too far away to help me now. I need You to come and rescue me. I can't do this alone!"

"You are right, Hadassah. You cannot do My part, and I will not do your part. But have no fear, Hadassah, for I have overcome the world and redeemed you. I have called you by name; you are Mine! When you pass through the waters, I will be with you. When you pass through the rivers, they will not overflow you. When you walk through the fire, you will not be scorched, nor will the flame burn you. I am all you need."

Hadassah still could not hear Him. She took a deep breath and sighed. "I pray that the eyes and ears of my heart might be opened."

Michael smiled, for he knew the result of such a request. Life-Giver touched her eyes and ears and then asked, "What is the truth, Hadassah?"

Hadassah lifted her eyes; the delight was evident on her face. She whispered, "The truth is I've put my trust in You. I won't be afraid of what man can do to me, because love that has no end is greater than fear. You are the light and my salvation, of whom shall I be afraid? You are the strength of my life, so I will not be afraid."

"Good, Hadassah. Now rise up and face your fears. You are not alone. You know the Truth; you know that I will never leave you. Take My hand and get up — now!" He shouted.

Michael was surprised by the intensity of His voice, for he did not see what His Lord saw — a very large demon crawling out of the earth just behind her.

"Get up, Hadassah! Get up NOW!" her Deliverer shouted.

Sensing something she could not explain Hadassah jumped to her feet. Turning, she saw a horrible-looking creature poised to pounce. From the deep recesses of her spirit she shouted, "Life-Giver loves me! His Perfect Love covers me, therefore you can't touch me. You're powerless against me, because I've put my trust in Him. I will not be afraid. Life-Giver is my light and my salvation. He's the strength of my life. Now go where Life-Giver tells you to go."

The demon fled. Life-Giver nodded at Michael. The archangel gladly followed the creature and drove it into the hole it crawled out of.

Hadassah collapsed, shaking uncontrollably. "What was that? What did I just see? Was that a creature from this realm or another?" Hadassah — confused, frightened and relieved — curled into a fetal position and cried out for Life-Giver.

Like a mother hen, Life-Giver spread His "wings" over her. Turning to His angelic host, He commanded, "Drive the remaining demons from this place."

With great joy, Michael and the angels overcame the demonic creatures. Michael then approached and bowed low. Life-Giver pointed to a snake hiding beneath the bushes and said, "You missed one."

With one swipe of his sword, Michael cut the bush and snake in two pieces. Another angel quickly gathered the writhing creature and flew off with its remains.

Hadassah looked up, her eyes wide with fear.

"I am with you, Hadassah. You have nothing to fear," Life-Giver said, calming her frightened heart.

"You're here!" she sobbed.

"I am."

"Why didn't You help me when I first cried out?"

"I did. It just didn't look like what you expected. Hadassah, I do all things well. You can trust Me to always, in every instance, do what is best for you. Therein lies your security."

"There's no greater security than knowing that Your ways are higher and greater and better than mine — even when I don't think they are. Forgive me, Life-Giver. I have so much to learn."

"And what a glorious journey it shall be."

CHAPTER SIXTEEN

*H*adassah stood before the enormous gate hoping, waiting and praying. "What if they never open the gate? How will I ever find the Great King?" she asked herself.

Fear crept out of the dark, joined by a scrawny creature called Insecurity. The two creatures snuck up behind her. Insecurity said, "You'll never be good enough to enter that gate."

Fear added, "The king isn't really good or kind — that's what he wants people to think. The truth is he's unfair and unjust. He's demanding and unreasonable. And he'll never honor the invitation on that worthless scroll. If you're smart you'll go back to your sister."

Hadassah could not understand why all of a sudden her mind was being bombarded with thoughts of returning to Martha and Naomi.

"I've come too far to turn back now," she told herself. "I'm determined to face my fears rather than run from them — the fear of the unknown, the fear of failure and rejection and the fear of success and blessing."

"What if the scroll is worthless? Or worse yet, what if it's genuine, and I'm found to be unworthy of it? What if I'm rejected? Where will I go and what will I do?" Fear said, speaking as if the thoughts belonged to her.

Insecurity wrapped its long, skinny arms around Hadassah's shoulders and whispered in her ear. "I am a poor, ugly orphan who is alone and afraid. I have no one, and no one wants me. I won't ever know true love, for true love doesn't exist for people like me."

Fighting against what she believed were her own thoughts, Hadassah fervently prayed. Even though she did not fully believe what she was saying, she stated, "I know better than anyone that I'm not good enough to spend a day with the King. I understand very well that I don't deserve such a privilege or honor. If I should be allowed to enter Your gates, it will not be based on anything I've done or even who I am. The only reason I'll be allowed to enter will be because of Your mercy. I'd be a fool to refuse such lovingkindness just because I'm afraid or feel unworthy of such love."

Her devotion and faithfulness flooded the unseen realm with beauty and sweet fragrance. Life-Giver stepped toward her, filling her with His strength.

Unaware of her Helper, Hadassah said, "Life-Giver, I will trust You with my future. If I'm to enter that gate, then You will make a way because You are the Way. If I'm not, then so be it. Either way, I will still love You."

Her surrender and acceptance of the sovereignty of Life-Giver tormented Fear and Insecurity like nothing else could. The two demons trembled as they ran for the cover of darkness.

Hadassah took a deep breath. As she turned, she heard what sounded like a whimpering dog. Scanning her surroundings, she saw a pile of rags a short distance away. The sound grew louder. Curious, she walked toward it. She discovered that it was not rags but a child who appeared to be nothing but skin and bones — whether boy or girl she could not tell.

Where are this child's parents? she wondered, looking around.

At that moment, Hadassah heard voices coming from the other side of the wall. *They're about to open the gate,* she thought. She ran back and grabbed her few belongings while trying desperately to block out the sound of the child's pitiful cries.

Life-Giver watched as the Great King picked up the wee one and held her close to His heart. "I am a Father to the fatherless," He said, brushing the sweat-soaked hair from her face.

"*Little one,*" He said, "*You have been chosen. You are not alone. Look, child, with your spiritual eyes and see that We are here with you, and We call you beautiful.*"

"Me, beautiful?" she whispered ever so weakly, for the child was desperately ill.

"*You are indeed.*"

"I don't feel beautiful."

"*That is because of what men have done to you. But rest assured that you are not only beautiful, but you are a wonderful, delightful treasure,*" the King said.

"I been told you could help me, so I been tryin' to find you."

"*I can and will help you, child. Just trust Me.*"

The battle for the child's life raged for only a few minutes more.

Suddenly, all was silent in both realms. Neither creature nor angel moved. *In the distance, Death screeched to the high heavens. Michael, Gabriel and every other holy angel turned to face the One who held the keys of life and death in His hands. They knew Life-Giver alone had the power to give life and take it away.*

Hadassah stood before the gate hoping and praying that it would open. She did not hear the child take her last breath.

Neither did she see the tears falling from Life-Giver's face onto the tangled mass of brown curls adorning the child's head. Holding her close, He wept. The angels marveled at the depth and intensity of His love.

Hadassah simply stared at the gate even after it was obvious no one was going to open it. She finally turned back toward the child, who was unmoving. *She must be sleeping,* Hadassah told herself.

"*Is this child to be resurrected?*" Gabriel asked.

"*She shall,*" Life-Giver said.

"*Then why do You weep, my Lord?*"

"*I weep because of the atrocities done to this innocent child. I see every mark, every injustice and every wound.*" As He traced the scars on her horribly disfigured face with His finger, His tears fell like rain.

"*I have a gift for you, little one,*" He whispered, kissing her forehead. "*I have a place in My heart just for you. No one else can fit there. I will pursue you until I win your heart. Where I am is where you belong. I am yours, and one day soon you will be Mine.*"

Every angel eagerly looked at the Master of All and perceived that something glorious was about to happen.

Hadassah looked back at the gate. *At any moment that gate could open and my fate would be decided,* she thought.

Fear, desperate to control her, flooded her mind with its poison. The creature understood that whoever or whatever controlled her imagination could control her. Its strategy was to plant as many destructive seeds as possible in her mind so it could control her imagination. "The gate is closed for winter. I should turn back before it's too cold to travel," *it said.*

"Where did that come from?" Hadassah asked herself. "I refuse to believe that lie. The truth is Life-Giver brought me here, and I will not leave until He tells me to do so."

Life-Giver looked up at Hadassah.

Hadassah's natural eyes saw nothing, but her spirit saw Life-Giver holding the child.

Hadassah looked over her shoulder at the child dressed in rags. There was still no movement or sound. Concerned, she slowly drew near. Dropping to her knees beside the tiny bundle, she whispered, "Oh, sweet child. . . I've been watching you, and you no longer move or cry out. Do you live, or have you joined my parents and sister in the unseen kingdom?"

Her trembling hand touched the cold, lifeless form and she cried out, "Oh! It's as I feared!"

Sobbing, she scooped up the filthy child in her arms. "Oh, wretch that I am! I saw you here and heard your muffled cries, but turned my face from you. Oh, Life-Giver, do not look upon me now, for I'm truly unworthy and the most wretched of all beings! My heart is cold and distant and self-serving. I'm selfish beyond belief. There's no good thing within me — I know that now! This poor child died alone, without comfort, without kindness, without love. No one should ever die alone. Life-Giver, withhold Your gaze from me lest You consume me with Your fiery zeal!"

Hadassah could not stop rocking the child, even though she was well aware that it was too late to offer her any comfort.

"It is never too late to love, Hadassah."

Brushing the mass of curls from the girl's ashen face, she gasped. Repulsed, she almost threw her down. The child's face was quite disfigured, whether from birth, abuse or both she could not tell. Regardless of the reason, the result was the same. Her crooked nose appeared to have been broken in several places, her mouth was horribly twisted, a jagged scar ran across her right eyebrow, and another across her forehead while a deep scar ran down the right side of her face. Upon closer look, the scars appeared to be man-made, for they bore the resemblance of the letter "F".

Hadassah wanted to withdraw, to cast her aside and pretend she did not see her. But how could she? That was how she first responded to the child, and now she suffered the painful sting of her deed.

"Oh, dear child, forgive me! I saw but I didn't see, I heard but I didn't hear. If only I'd seen with the eyes of my heart, then perhaps I could've offered you a bit of comfort. Life I don't have and can't give, but there's One who is Life and gives life."

"It's pointless and futile to cry over this pitiful life. You're too late," a voice whispered in her ear.

Hadassah studied the child's face. "I don't believe that. I can't believe that to be true! My tears may not affect her, but perhaps they may render me more like the One I have come to love. Did He not weep when His dear friend Mary clung to His robe as she spoke of the death of her brother, Lazarus? No, I shall not believe you, for tears tenderize the human heart. And my cold, selfish heart is in great need of being softened."

Michael and Gabriel turned to Life-Giver, who watched as the script of history unfolded, the same history He witnessed before the foundation of the world. "It is as it should be," He responded to their questioning gazes.

"You are Life-Giver," the two archangels exclaimed, for they perceived what was about to happen.

"I AM that I AM," the Great King and the Holy Spirit and the Son of God proclaimed in unison.

All of the angels in attendance fell on their faces proclaiming, "Holy, holy, holy, Lord God Almighty, who was and is and is to come!"

The Three-in-One never took Their eyes from Hadassah or the child.

Hadassah was unaware of the glories surrounding her.

"Hadassah, choose life," the Spirit of God said.

Hadassah suddenly remembered David telling her to choose life every time.

"Choose life," she whispered to herself.

"It's too late for that now," Fear said.

"If only I'd remembered David's words when I first saw this child, then perhaps I could've chosen life by showing her kindness and giving her comfort."

"Choose life, Hadassah."

"I hear You, Life-Giver. But how can I choose life now? The child is dead. I feel You tugging on my heart, but I don't understand what You want me to do. Help me know what to do."

"Be still, Hadassah, and know that I AM God."

Hadassah took a deep breath and listened. "What do You want me to do?" she repeated.

"I am the Resurrection and the Life, Hadassah. If anyone comes to Me, I will give them life."

"The child's dead; she can't come to You. It's too late for that now!" Hadassah cried out.

"Bring the child to Me," He calmly but firmly commanded. Then He touched her spiritual eyes. She saw Life-Giver standing before her, more radiant than the noonday sun. Like a dead man, she fell at His feet. Michael and the entire angelic host wielded their swords as they formed a fiery circle around them. Hadassah felt as if she was falling through the stars in the night sky.

"I can fly faster than you can fall," her Creator sang.

Hadassah melted into what felt like perfect peace. *"I'm not lost, but found!"* she whispered, staring into the eyes of Eternity Himself.

"You are because I AM."

"I am because You are," she responded.

"You are a fast learner."

"And You are a good Teacher!"

"Hadassah, why do you call Me good? Tell Me, what is good?"

"I suppose it would be everything that's not bad."

"There is so much more to good than that, My beautiful child."

"Then tell me, my beautiful Lord, what is good?" she asked, still lost in the gaze of His glorious eyes.

"For something to be good, it must proceed from My Father, for He is the Source of all that is good. Every good and perfect gift comes from Him. Many mistake good for God — they are not necessarily one and the same. Just because something looks good does not necessarily mean that it is. Remember the Garden of Eden where I planted a tree called the tree of the knowledge of good and evil?"

"Yes, I know that story."

"The fruit that Adam and Eve ate was called knowledge — what kind of knowledge?"

"The knowledge of good and evil."

"You see, dear one, Adam and Eve wanted the power to decide for themselves what was good and what was evil. Up until that time, My Father was the One who instructed them as to what was good and what was not. They had intimate fellowship with Him, but that was not enough for them. They did not understand that the only Way to true freedom is through their Creator — everything else is bondage and ultimately brings death."

"Then please tell me what is good concerning this child lying dead in my arms, for I don't pretend to understand how this could be good," Hadassah said, still lost in the warmth of His smile.

"You have chosen rightly to ask Me and not assume that you know what is good concerning her destiny. Unless a seed falls into the ground and dies it cannot bring forth fruit, Hadassah. Out of death comes life for those who are Mine." Laying His hand on Hadassah's eyes, He said, *"Now look and see."*

The vision ended as abruptly as it began. Hadassah opened her eyes. Staring at the dead child, she shouted, "You've chosen to restore her life! You're going to raise her from the dead . . . aren't You?"

"I am."

Hadassah looked around. There were no angels, no beautiful Man, no glorious gaze. Everything seemed as it was, yet it was different.

"Your peace and love have filled me, and I am not the same. I'm lost in the truth of Your life. I'm captured by the warmth of Your smile. I now know what I'm to do, but don't know how to do it. Life-Giver, take me beyond myself to that place where You rule and reign over death."

The only sensation she felt was fear, her familiar friend. Choosing to resist the enemy of her soul, she took the child's cold, lifeless hand in hers. Hadassah whispered, "In the name of Life-Giver — live."

Nothing. No stirring, no warmth, no breath . . . nothing.

"Live — in the name of Life-Giver!" Hadassah repeated.

This time, to her utter shock and amazement, the limp child coughed. Hadassah was so startled that it was all she could do not to throw her on the ground. The two simply stared at each other, each just as frightened as the other. The child's eyes were the prettiest green Hadassah had ever seen.

Life-Giver laughed. So did Michael and Gabriel and the myriads of angels in attendance.

Hadassah came to her senses and asked, "Uh . . . hi . . . what's your name?"

"Forsaken," came her frightened reply.

"What kind of name is that?" Hadassah asked without thinking.

"It's the only name I got," she answered, struggling to break free of Hadassah's grip.

Hadassah was so astonished by her resurrection that she did not notice how tightly she held the child. Releasing her, she said, "I'm sorry. Did I hurt you?"

"Nobody can hurt me!" she answered, scrambling to her feet. With hands on her hips, she asked, "So . . . what's *your* name?"

"Hadassah."

"What kind of name is that?"

Hadassah tried not to laugh. "I suppose that makes us even?"

"Yeah, I s'pose so!" she answered as her hands slid off her hips.

"Where are your parents?"

"Don't know. Folks tell me they sold me when I was a babe. I don't even know their names. I'm what people call an 'Or Fan,' whatever that is."

"I know what that is because I'm one too. An orphan is someone who no longer has a mama or papa."

Forsaken thought long and hard before she responded. "I don't need no mama or papa. I can take care of myself."

"I know how you feel. Maybe we could be friends — you and me? I could sure use a friend."

Forsaken looked at Hadassah suspiciously. "I s'pose it'd be okay, but I gotta be free to come and go when I take a notion."

"Sure, but maybe we could be the kind of friends who let each other know if the other one is thinking of leaving? That way neither of us would be scared that the other one is going to sneak off in the middle of the night. What do you think about that?"

"Sounds like a good idea, 'cuz a body never knows when they should be headin' on down the road."

"I know what you mean. But I'm hungry. How about you?"

"Kinda," she said, trying to hide the desperate look in her eyes.

"I just happen to have some goat cheese and fruit," Hadassah said, hurrying to get her pouch. Opening it, she broke off a piece of cheese and handed it to the little girl who hungrily devoured every piece, even the crumbs that fell on the ground.

"You don't need to do that; I have more." Hadassah handed her a bigger chunk, which she eagerly received.

"How about we pick out a new name for you?"

"What's wrong with my old one?" Forsaken asked.

"Well, there are many names out there, and this is a special day for you and —"

"And what?"

"And your name is kind of a sad name," Hadassah said as gently as possible.

"Sad or not, it's the only thing I got, so I'm gonna keep it," Forsaken said. The cold, hard look in her eyes revealed a child who had learned to be tough in a harsh world.

"Fair enough. But if you ever decide you'd like a new one just let me know, and we'll have great fun finding one that's just right for you."

Even though she was still hungry, Forsaken refused Hadassah's offer of more cheese because she did not like to be indebted to anyone. Hadassah tried several times to talk to her about her death and resurrection, but Forsaken made it very clear that she did not want to talk about it. The two sat in silence, watching the gate while Hadassah prayed.

***

Michael said, *"If I might be so bold, my Lord."*

"Yes?"

"There is a mystery that I cannot resolve. Hadassah refused to help the child. She turned away from her. Is there to be no consequence, no correction or discipline?"

"I do discipline those I love and My Spirit does bring conviction when warranted. I took her punishment, Michael. Her heart has already felt the sting of her actions and it is enough," He said, giving Michael His full attention.

Michael knew all too well the price paid to redeem mankind. *"I stand corrected before Your Majesty,"* he said, bowing so low that his forehead touched the visible realm.

"You have seen My endless mercy throughout the history of man, Michael. My mercy never changes, it never ceases, and it never fails to give life. I did not come to judge the world but to save it."

Michael replied, *"Your unrelenting, all-consuming love is beyond my ability to comprehend, my Lord and King."*

"That is because you are not God, My angelic friend. Look at Hadassah, Michael. Do you see a servant? Or perhaps a disciple or a child? Do you see a soul searching, hoping and dreaming? Is she a mere mortal to you? Tell me, Michael, is that what you see?"

"She is all of those things, is she not?"

"She is and so much more. She is a part of Me. She is flesh of My flesh and bone of My bone. She has My Spirit living inside of her. My blood flows through her veins. Michael, she was made in My image . . . the image of God Himself! She was not made by My spoken Word as all other created things were made. No, she was made with My very hands.

"She is a masterpiece, a beautiful song, a majestic mountain, a lush valley, a breath-taking sunrise, a student, a friend, a daughter, a bride — all of these things she is and will be forever!

"The glory of My Father is to see her step into her true identity, for it is the glory of the King to create true beauty from ashes. And nothing is more beautiful to My Father than a surrendered heart, which she has."

"My Lord, You are the Truth and the Life and Your ways are perfect."

"Hadassah is forgiven and needs no punishment for her sins, for they are not."

"You do not even see them, do You?" Michael asked, amazed and perplexed.

"I see them, but they are not what I use to determine her worth. As you know, I am not limited to time as it exists in the visible realm. I travel here, there and everywhere any 'time' I wish. I am the past, the present and the future — the beginning and the end!

"I see Hadassah through the eyes of the past, present and future — I know the end of her story. Michael, I didn't just forgive her sins — I took them as My own, so they no longer belong to her but to Me. She is forgiven and cleansed and free. What Hadassah needs most right now is My love — not punishment, not harsh words, not even correction."

"Your ways are perfect, my Lord, and truly amazing is Your grace toward mankind."

CHAPTER SEVENTEEN

$\mathcal{A}$s the sun began its westward descent, Hadassah pounded on the gate while Forsaken pretended not to watch. "They ain't gonna open that gate," Forsaken said, braiding long blades of grass into a crown. "You oughta give up."

"They may not open it today, but they will certainly open it. And when they do, we will be the first to go through."

"There ain't nobody else here."

"Come help me collect branches," Hadassah said, ignoring her remark.

"Why we collectin' branches?"

"To make a shelter. I don't plan on spending another day or night in the open."

"I'm use to sleepin' under the stars," Forsaken mumbled.

"Well, tonight you're going to have something over your head, and tomorrow you'll have shade."

In no time at all, they collected enough branches to construct a shelter on the edge of the nearby woods, where they had a clear view of the gate.

Two days passed. Forsaken slept a lot and ate even more. It was obvious from her emaciated frame that the child had been severely neglected. Hadassah questioned Forsaken about her life, but with each question, she would say, "Can't say that I 'member." It was obvious that the child either did not know or did not want to talk about it. Hadassah finally gave up and shared a little of her journey through life instead.

Forsaken listened intently. When Hadassah finished, Forsaken asked, "Can I see your scrolls?"

"Sure," Hadassah said as she carefully pulled them out. As Forsaken ran her dirty hand over each one, Hadassah recited the words.

Handing them back, Forsaken shrugged her shoulders and said, "You sure did walk a long ways."

"I'd walk 1,000 miles just to spend a day with the King."

"Why?"

"Because Life-Giver told me that His Father loves me, so I'd like to meet Him that I might love Him too."

"I ain't ever met anybody that I'd ever want to love," said Forsaken, a piece of mushroom falling out of her mouth. Picking it up, she stuffed it in her already full mouth. "Do you trust them?"

"Yeah, I guess I do."

"Why?"

"Because Life-Giver can fly faster than I can fall."

"What?"

"One day you'll meet Life-Giver, and then you'll understand."

"When will I meet him?"

"You can meet Him any time you want. He's as close as the air all around you. He's waiting to meet you."

"I didn't say I *wanted* to meet him. I only asked *when* I'd meet him," she said looking around, her eyes wide with fear.

"It's okay. He understands you're afraid, and He won't ever force you to do anything."

"I ain't afraid. I just don't wanna meet him," she said, running off.

Hurrying after her, Hadassah said, "Why don't we pick some flowers. We can give them to the King."

"I ain't gonna pick no flowers."

"Then come keep me company."

"I s'pose I can do that."

Finding a patch of mums, Hadassah selected a handful of red, orange and yellow ones while Forsaken wandered from place to place. Arranging the flowers into a bouquet, Hadassah sang,

If I could live to be 100,
I'd spend every moment of every day
Picking flowers for You.
If I could write 1,000 songs
I'd give them all to You.
I seek neither fame nor fortune.
There's only one thing I seek,
One thing I desire,
And that's to spend a day with You.

"You're strange," Forsaken said as they headed back to their shelter.

"Then you'd better be careful, because I've heard it said you become like the people you spend time with."

"I won't ever be like you, 'cuz I got plans for my life. I ain't gonna write no songs for Life-Giver or pick him no flowers. I'm gonna be rich and famous!"

"Why do you want to be rich and famous?"

"'Cuz I don't ever want to be hungry again," Forsaken shouted over her shoulder as she ran ahead.

Life-Giver stayed close by the child.

"Even though she rejects You, You stay near," Michael said.

"Especially when they reject Me, for that is when they need Me the most. Those who are well do not need a Physician."

Hadassah ran after her.

True to their nature, within moments black, slimy creatures began crawling out of every hole and crack in the ground. Michael raised his fiery sword and gave the shout. The battle over the child's eternal destiny had escalated.

Neither Hadassah nor Forsaken were aware of what was happening in the unseen realm, which was as it should have been. It was not their battle to fight; it belonged to Life-Giver.

"Your mother and father have forsaken you, but I will take you up," Life-Giver whispered to the child.

Forsaken looked around. Shrugging her shoulders, she continued on.

Returning to the shade of their shelter, they stared at the gate. *All around them an unseen war raged.*

Late that afternoon, Hadassah heard shouts coming from behind the stone wall. Grabbing the flowers and her belongings in one hand and the child with the other, Hadassah hurried to the gate. By the time she got there, the enormous gate groaned as it swung on its hinges. Hadassah's heart raced as she whispered a silent prayer. She checked to make sure the scrolls were safely tucked in her waistband. All was well; they were there.

Hadassah told herself to relax while wondering what future two orphans might have in the courtyard of the Great King. Perhaps they could sweep the streets — she had heard rumors they were paved with gold. Or maybe they could clean up behind the horses or light the oil lamps or —

Her anxious thoughts were suddenly interrupted by a tug on her skirt. Forsaken was trembling violently. "What's wrong?" Hadassah asked.

"I'm afraid."

"Of what?" she asked, kneeling beside her.

"Of everything."

"Oh, Forsaken, don't be afraid. I'm with you. I won't ever leave you. I'll take care of you."

Life-Giver smiled broadly. "Hadassah is becoming more like Me every day."

"Like a mama?" she asked, her eyes revealing more than she wanted. She quickly looked away.

"Yes, Forsaken, I'll take care of you like a mama."

"But, Hadassah, what if the king hates Or Fans like everybody else? What if he thinks I'm ugly? What if —"

Hadassah gently placed her finger over the child's lips. "Shhh, child. We don't want to play on Satan's playground of 'What if's', now do we? I know it's difficult to trust someone you don't know, but will you try? Will you give Life-Giver and me a chance to prove to you that we won't hurt you, that we'll take care of you?"

Hadassah laid her hand on the child's bony shoulder. "I promise that we won't ever hurt you, not on purpose."

"Sometimes I'm hateful so folks won't know I'm scared," Forsaken confessed.

"What's wrong with letting people know you're scared?"

"When folks know I'm scared . . . they hurt me." A flood of tears ran down her cheeks.

"I'm so sorry people hurt you. I'm so very sorry," Hadassah said.

Forsaken looked at her. Not believing what she saw, she touched Hadassah's tears. "Why are *you* cryin'?" Forsaken asked.

"Because I care about you and love you."

"You don't even know me," she said, pushing her.

Hadassah fell back. Standing, she said, "In some ways I do know you, because I was much like you. You have so much beauty hidden beneath all that fear and anger, and I really do know how you feel."

Forsaken, showing no emotion, simply stared at her.

"Will you give me a chance?"

Without saying a word, she slipped her hand in Hadassah's. Hadassah smiled as Forsaken said, "S'pose we should go meet this king you keep talkin' about."

At that precise moment, Michael cut off the head of Bitterness, a large and powerful demon trying to gain access to the child's heart.

The heavy wooden gate was now fully open, and Hadassah felt as though her life was either coming to an end or beginning anew. She reminded herself that should she be denied entrance she would still trust Life-Giver. Should she be admitted . . . well, that thought was equally terrifying.

Taking a deep breath she stepped through the gate with the child hiding behind her skirt.

A kind-looking gatekeeper stopped the trembling pair. "Good day, fine lady! Good day, child! What brings you to the outer court of the Great King?"

Hadassah tried to speak but was unable. The words just would not come. Forsaken saved the day. With a confidence that was contrived, she announced, "We're here to spend a day with the Great King!"

Chuckling, the gatekeeper asked, "Little lady, would you please tell me why the two of you should be allowed to enter?"

Forsaken suddenly lost all confidence and ducked behind Hadassah. Like one who wakes from sleep, Hadassah stammered, "I, I found this scroll, and it grants me . . . uh . . . us the right to spend one day with Him."

The scroll shook like a leaf in the wind as she handed him her most prized possession.

"Thank you, my lady," he said. Unrolling the tattered object, he smiled even more broadly. "Where did you find this?"

"It was buried in a garbage heap," said Hadassah.

"Some of the King's greatest treasures are found in garbage heaps," the gatekeeper responded looking over the scroll at her.

"That's where He found me," Hadassah said with the gratefulness of one who has received an undeserved gift.

The gatekeeper smiled. "What you confess is true of all of the King's followers, but rarely do I hear one admit to it. You are a true follower, and you may enter His gates," he said, placing the scroll back in her hand.

Relief washed over her as joy flooded her soul. "It is to be! I'm to see the King face to face! Come, Forsaken, you're about to see for yourself that all I've told you is true!"

"Excuse me!" the gatekeeper said.

"Yes?" Hadassah asked.

"I said *you* may enter, but permission was not granted for the child to enter. She does not know Life-Giver. One must know Life-Giver if they are to spend a day with the King — there is no other way," the gatekeeper said.

"She hasn't met Life-Giver yet, but she will. Of that I'm sure."

"That may be, but she has chosen *not* to meet Him."

"Are you refusing her the opportunity to know the Great King? Should she meet Him, she'd surely choose Him," Hadassah stated, trying diligently to be kind.

"This matter is not for me to decide, for I am nothing more than a keeper of the gate. I am merely obeying the statutes and ordinances of the King. You must take up this matter with Him."

"Where is He that I might appeal to His good and kind nature?" she asked, frantically looking around.

The gatekeeper, in a tender yet firm voice, responded, "The Great King is not a man whom you can instruct in *your* ways. If He should desire for the child to enter, then He will certainly introduce her to Life-Giver — without your pleading or beseeching."

"But He invites us to beseech Him. He tells us to come boldly before His throne that we might find help in our time of need, does He not?"

"He does, my lady."

"Then I beseech you, kind guardian, to allow me the opportunity to present my case. This child has done nothing wrong and deserves to enter the courts of the King."

"On one point you are correct; on the other you are wrong. It is agreed that this child has done nothing wrong," he said, "but no one *deserves* to be here. There is nothing anyone could ever do that is 'good enough' to deserve the glory and majesty that the Great King freely bestows on those who are His children."

"You are correct, my lord; I'm mistaken and beg your forgiveness," Hadassah said, bowing before the one she believed held the destiny of the child in his hands.

"Do not bow before me, for I am merely a servant and messenger of the Great King, much like you. Because you have accepted and pursued His invitation, it is granted for *you* to spend one day with the King, but the child must remain outside the gate. You may enter, but she shall not."

Michael, ever watching, asked, "My Lord, You are testing her heart, are you not?"

"I am."

Hadassah spun around, grabbed Forsaken's hand and practically dragged her away.

"Where are you going?" the guard called after her.

"To spend the night with the child — outside the gate."

Forsaken fought to free herself, shouting, "You don't need to take care of me! I ain't no baby, and I don't belong to you — I don't belong to nobody! Let me go!" Secretly, she hoped Hadassah wasn't listening.

Hadassah released her grip, and the child ran into the woods. Hadassah ran after her praying fervently.

Forsaken did not stop until she came to the stream. Angry, she spun around and faced Hadassah shouting, "I don't need nobody! I don't need you or the king or Life-Giver!"

Kneeling in front of Forsaken and taking her hands in her own, Hadassah locked eyes with the frightened child. "There's something you need to know about Life-Giver. He doesn't just live behind those castle gates. He lives inside of me. He lives outside of me. He's here, right now, surrounding you and me. If you close your eyes and look with the eyes of your heart, you can feel Him, hear Him and sometimes even see Him."

"I don't care."

"Yes, you do. You're just afraid."

"I'm afraid you won't get to spend a day with the king 'cuz of me."

"I want to spend a day with the King, but not enough that I'm willing to abandon you." *I can't believe I just said that,* Hadassah thought.

Forsaken's chin quivered as she fought the tears threatening to expose her true feelings.

"Forsaken, I promise you — I'll never forsake you, because Life-Giver didn't forsake me. And remember the story I told you about the eagles?"

"Yeah."

"He can fly faster than you can fall."

"Why are you doin' this?" Forsaken asked.

"Doing what?"

"Bein' so nice to me!" Forsaken shouted.

"Because Life-Giver was nice to me when I didn't deserve it or believe it to be true."

Trembling, Forsaken stared into the eyes of uncommon love. The foundation of her insurmountable wall of self-protection began to shake.

"I love you and want to help you," Hadassah said.

"No," Forsaken cried, "I don't want you to love me or care about me! Just hit me, curse me, call me any name you want! Do anythin' to me — just don't love me!"

"Why?"

"'Cuz it hurts too much," Forsaken sobbed. "It just hurts too much!" She shoved Hadassah out of the way and ran off again.

Hadassah whispered a desperate prayer for help.

Michael and his army pushed against the raging hordes of hell that had been sent by Satan to prevent Forsaken's breakthrough.

"Why is the battle so great over this Forsaken one?" Michael shouted over the screams and shrieks of hundreds of demons.

"Because one day she will give her life to save Hadassah's," Life-Giver answered.

Michael looked back in time and saw the day when Life-Giver did the same thing. What a battle that day was!

"But the child is so weak and small," Michael mused.

"Michael, do not focus on what she presently is but on what she has the capacity for — this little one has a great capacity to love. My Father chooses the weak things of the world, those things that are not, those things that are foolish in the eyes of the world, that He might be glorified. Now watch and see the power of Perfect Love."

With a glance, Life-Giver delivered the final blow to the beam supporting Forsaken's wall of self-protection, and the barricade came tumbling down.

Forsaken stopped running and threw herself on the ground.

Life-Giver whispered in her ear, "Love is exactly what you need and want, little one."

Forsaken sobbed uncontrollably.

When Hadassah sat beside her, Forsaken fell into her outstretched arms. "It's going to be all right," Hadassah said, stroking her hair. Forsaken eventually cried herself to sleep as Hadassah rocked back and forth, singing her mama's song.

"The last shall become the first and the least the greatest, the most beautiful," Life-Giver said.

"My Lord," Michael said, "they do not know they are at war, do they?"

"They do not understand the ways of the unseen realm," He said, turning His attention for one brief moment to the battlefield. "There is not much time left, Michael. Call for reinforcements that this battle might be swiftly won."

"At Your word," Michael said. Pressing his shofar to his lips, Michael delivered three short blasts. Instantly, three legions of angels appeared before the Lord of hosts.

Seeing the reinforcements, Satan, the commander of demons, summoned a very ugly beast to his side and shouted, "Blow, you stupid creature!"

The beast blew his ram's horn and the earth vomited out hundreds of vile creatures.

Life-Giver turned to Gabriel and nodded. The angel responded to His unspoken command and took his place beside Michael. With swords lifted high, the two archangels shouted in unison, "Lift up your heads, O gates, and be lifted up, O ancient doors, that the King of glory may come in!"

Every demon on the battlefield froze, the terror evident in their eyes.

Michael added, "Who is this King of glory?"

Gabriel responded, "The Lord strong and mighty, the Lord mighty in battle — the Lord of hosts is His name!"

The ground shook beneath their feet as holy angels fought fallen angels over the destiny of a little child and a young maiden. And all the while, Life-Giver stood confident of the victory, for it had been secured before the creation of the world.

CHAPTER EIGHTEEN

*W*ith the rising of the sun, Hadassah opened her eyes. Forsaken's frail little body was curled so tightly against hers that Hadassah dare not move. Propping on her elbow, Hadassah studied her. Long, brown ringlets framed her disfigured face. *What a beautiful child she could've been*, Hadassah thought.

"You blew it," an uninvited voice whispered. *"You had your chance to go through the gate, but you refused. And why? Because the king that you think is so wonderful refused to allow this pitiful creature entrance."*

"Who are you?"

"I'm the one who stands before the king's throne."

"That isn't who you are but what you do. I repeat, in the name of Life-Giver, what's your name?"

"I'm Satan, the beautiful one, and I've come to offer you a gift you can't refuse."

"Life-Giver warned me about you and your trickery. I'm not interested."

"Oh, but you'll be interested in my offer. It's what you've been praying for, and I alone can make it happen."

Satan now had Hadassah's full attention, and he knew it. Taking a step back, he waited, for he knew she would give in to her desires soon enough. Hadassah looked at the castle gate and then back to the little one sleeping so peacefully against her. "What do you have that I want?"

Feeling quite smug, Satan waited to answer.

"Perhaps you did not hear. What is it that you have?"

"I have the key to that gate."

"You have no keys," Hadassah said.

"Oh, but I do," he said. "Listen and believe." Keys rattled in the distance.

"I can open the gate so that you and the little wench can go into the castle and see your precious king . . . but there's a small price. There's always a price in the world of humans, is there not?"

"What is it?"

"A simple price, really, one that won't cost you anything other than your pride."

"So, what's the price?"

"All I want is one song from your lips."

"A song? Why would you want a song?"

"Because I am the angel of worship, and I am to be worshipped. You desire to go through that gate with this pitiful child, and I desire your song. A simple trade will satisfy us both. You give me one song, and I will open the gate."

Hadassah pondered his offer.

Michael asked, "Shall we intervene, my Lord?"

"This battle is hers to fight. But I would have you go to her, for Satan plans to step beyond the boundary I have set. Go and stand against the wicked schemes of My enemy. Do not allow him to destroy either of them."

"It is my pleasure to do so," Michael said, eager to obey his Creator and defend the two innocent orphans.

Life-Giver summoned Gabriel, saying, "Satan's arrogance grows. Take him a message. Tell him his days grow short . . . the end of his reign is near."

"As You command, my Lord," Gabriel said, bowing low.

As Hadassah contemplated Satan's offer, Life-Giver said, "Choose life, Hadassah."

Gabriel returned and bowed before Life-Giver, who motioned for him to speak. "Satan sends you a message, but I dare not repeat it for fear of insulting my Lord and desecrating Your holy place."

"You do not need to repeat his words, my angelic friend, for I know all things. You have done well."

Life-Giver lifted His eyes and prayed. "I come to You, Holy Father, and ask You to keep Hadassah. She is not of this world, even as I am not of the world. I do not ask You to take her out of the world, but to keep her from the evil one. Sanctify her in the truth; Your word is truth. As You sent Me into the world, I also have sent her into the world. I pray that she will know that You love her, in the same way and the same measure as You have loved Me. Oh, Righteous Father, although the world has not known You, yet I have known You and I have made Your name known to her."

His prayer intoxicated and invigorated His Father even more than fine wine.

Hadassah took a deep breath as the grace sent from the King steadied her heart.

"Just one song," Satan said.

Michael stood nearby, his sword unsheathed and ready to intervene should Satan overstep the boundaries set for him.

Hadassah said, "I shall not sing for you, for all I am and what little I have belongs to Another, to One who is worthy of all my honor and praise. You I do not know and will not worship."

"Then you are a fool," Satan responded.

"It seems to me that you are the fool."

Intent on the maiden's destruction, Satan reached through the veil. Instantly, Michael stepped in front of him and said, "The Lord rebuke you!"

"You cannot stop me; she has given me permission!" he hissed.

"You are a liar and a thief! She has rejected your temptation. You cannot touch either of them in the name of the Lord of hosts!"

Satan drew back his hand. "I'll have my day, Michael. You will see not only this pitiful girl worship me but the entire earth."

"In the name of the Lord of hosts, you are a defeated foe. Be gone from her."

With his head held high, Satan left.

Forsaken woke to the sound of Hadassah singing. "You sing pretty," she said.

"Thank you."

"Will you teach me that song?"

"Sure."

Forsaken was a fast learner. The two sang at the top of their lungs while watching a gate that did not open.

Five days came and went. On the morning of sixth day, Forsaken asked, "Why do you s'pose I came back to life?"

"I don't know, but I'd love to hear about what it was like if you want to talk."

"It was like a dream, 'cept it was real. A kind man told me I was beautiful — nobody ever said that," Forsaken said as she looked away. "But that wasn't all."

"Will you tell me?" Hadassah asked.

"The man was holdin' me. He was cryin' for *me*! Nobody's ever cried for me — 'cept you." Forsaken wiped her eyes with the back of her hand. "The man held me. I ain't never felt anything that good — I don't never want to forget it either. I 'member him sayin' he had a gift for me, but I can't remember what it was. I wish I could. I keep tryin', but I can't."

"Do you know who the man was?" Hadassah asked.

"Nope."

"Forsaken, do you suppose he was Life-Giver?"

"Don't know. I wish I could 'member what he gave me."

"If it's important, you will when the time's right. Now, how about we go exploring? Who knows, we might find some berries or more mushrooms. I know you really like mushrooms."

"I'd really like an apple — a big, red, delicious apple."

"Then we shall pray and ask the King for some apples," Hadassah said as they started out.

"He don't answer my prayers."

"Sure He does. He answers everyone's prayers. He just may not answer them the way you want Him to — I learned that the hard way."

"Well, I prayed for help and nothin' happened," Forsaken said, kicking up a cloud of dust.

"It seems to me He did answer. Here you are and here I am. The Great King always answers our prayers — sometimes He says 'yes', sometimes 'no' and sometimes 'not yet' — but He always answers."

Seemingly ignoring her, Forsaken ran ahead. Hadassah whispered, "Life-Giver, if You've ever heard my prayers, please hear me now. Would You please give Forsaken an apple?"

Familiar with the kind ways of his Master, Michael looked at Him. As he suspected, the One who spoke creation into existence pointed through the veil and said, "Uproot an apple tree from My garden and plant it there near that pomegranate tree."

"You are extravagant as always, my Lord," Michael responded, smiling broadly. He nodded at the two angels who had already dug up a beautiful apple tree from the Garden of Eden. They stepped through the thin veil separating the two realms. In less time than it takes for a heart to beat, the tree was planted. Pouring water from the River of Life around its base, the angels completed their mission.

Forsaken stepped into the clearing just moments after the two angelic beings stepped back through the veil. Forsaken squealed louder and longer than one would think humanly possible.

Hadassah broke into a run.

"Hadassah," she shouted, "you're not gonna believe this!"

"What is it?"

Crashing through the thick brush into the clearing, she collided with Forsaken, toppling her to the ground. Apologizing, Hadassah dropped to her knees beside the girl. Forsaken exploded in laughter and Hadassah joined her. Tears ran down their faces as the anxiety of the last several days left.

Rolling onto their backs, they stared at a beautiful, full-grown apple tree heavy with delicious looking fruit. Forsaken said, "I s'pose I should pick some, since it's what I kinda asked for."

"What do you mean 'kind of'?" Hadassah asked, jumping to her feet. Reaching into the thick branches she chose a large, red apple and tossed it down to Forsaken. She picked another for herself.

Biting into its crisp, juicy flesh, Forsaken sat up and moaned deeply. "This is the best apple I ever ate! As a matter of fact, it's the *only* apple I ever ate!" she exclaimed as juice ran down her chin. "Can I have another?"

"You haven't finished that one."

"Just lettin' you know I'd like another. I ain't askin' you to fetch it for me. Don't mind climbin' up that tree to fetch it for myself."

"You can have all the apples your little heart desires."

The two ate until their bellies ached. Then Hadassah filled her cloak with as many as it would hold while Forsaken filled the pouch. Holding her stomach, Forsaken groaned all the way back to their shelter.

In an effort to ease her discomfort, Forsaken stretched out on the ground. Staring blindly at the gate, she asked, "Why's the king so mean?"

"Why do you think He's mean?"

"'Cuz he told the gatekeeper I couldn't come in."

"It seems the only people who can enter the courts of the King are those who have an invitation."

"How do I get an invitation?" she asked, looking away.

"Whosoever will . . . may come. My invitation is for everyone who has ears to hear," Life-Giver whispered.

"I'm not sure. I guess we should ask Life-Giver. He'll know, He knows everything."

"Don't bother yourself none. I was just wonderin'."

"You don't need to be afraid, Forsaken. Life-Giver and the King are very good and kind."

"If the king's so good, then why does he let so many people get hurt and be hungry?"

"I think the better question is: Why do *we* allow so many people to be hungry and do nothing? Why do *we* cause so much suffering, and why don't *we* do something to help relieve the burdens of others?"

Forsaken pondered her words, her forehead wrinkled.

Hadassah continued, "Life-Giver once told me that if I've seen Him, I've seen His Father because they are One and the same. So that means the King is good, compassionate, forgiving and ever so beautiful."

"Hearin' your story, it don't seem like he's done much for you," Forsaken said, secretly hoping Hadassah was right about the King.

"He's done more for me than I could ever deserve even if I live to be one hundred. He loved me before I knew Him. He forgave me before I ever asked to be forgiven. And He never gave up on me or my sisters.

"When it seemed like He wasn't with us — I found out He really was. When our circumstances screamed that He didn't care — He was working behind the scenes to deliver and redeem us. Life-Giver isn't trying to win a popularity contest. He does what He does because it's the greatest and highest thing to do."

"I just wish he didn't let folks get hurt," Forsaken said.

"Unfortunately, suffering's a part of this life. I don't suppose there's any chance we humans will ever escape it."

Forsaken stared off into the distance.

"Forsaken, you remind me of my sister, Martha."

"Will you tell me about her?"

"I'd love to."

This time Hadassah told her about being sold into slavery and how they escaped and reunited. Forsaken gently laid her hand on Hadassah's arm and said, "I know how you feel and I'm real sorry."

"Yeah, me too."

"Do you miss your family?"

"Yes, I do. Probably always will."

"Not always. 'Cuz one day you'll see the king. Ain't that where they are?"

"Yes," she said, twirling a strand of hair.

"Then you just gotta be patient and don't give up hope."

Hadassah was surprised by her response. "I hope you're listening to yourself right now."

"I stopped hopin' a long time ago. But it ain't too late for you."

"Forsaken, it's never too late for anyone. As long as you have Life-Giver in your life, you have hope."

"Well, I ain't got Life-Giver."

"You can get to know Him, if you so choose."

"I don't want to know no man."

"But —"

"I'm tired," she said. Turning her back to Hadassah, she wiped the tears from her eyes.

Hadassah soon fell asleep. But Forsaken was in agony of heart.

Life-Giver stood over her, protecting His child from the onslaught of her enemies.

She quietly prayed, *"Life-Giver, I'm scared of you, but I think I might need you. Do you need me? I sure hope not cuz folks hurt me when they need me."*

Life-Giver spread His robe over the child and answered, *"I love you with the purest of love. I would never hurt you."* He kissed her forehead.

Forsaken was surprised by the peace she felt. "Is that you?"

"There is none other."

"I could stay with You forever," she whispered.

"That is My plan, dear one."

The angels rejoiced.

The Great King, sitting on His glorious throne, summoned the angel named Gatekeeper. He arrived instantly, bowing low.

"Open the gate and allow them both to enter," the King said.

Gatekeeper, with a big smile on his face, excitedly left to do as he was commanded.

CHAPTER NINETEEN

*H*adassah's heart leapt within her. "Forsaken — wake up! It sounds like they're opening the gate!"

Nothing more needed to be said. Forsaken rubbed her eyes and scrambled to her feet. Hadassah slung the heavy pouch over her shoulder, picked up the blanket filled with apples and then grabbed the child's hand.

"I ain't gonna run away," Forsaken said, snatching her hand free. "And I ain't no baby!"

"I'm sorry. It's a habit — one that I developed with my sisters. Please forgive me. You don't have to come with me if you don't want to."

"I'm goin' with you, 'cuz you need me. Who's gonna take care of you if I don't?"

Hadassah smiled to herself. "Perhaps we should pray?" she asked.

"You want *me* to pray?"

"We can both pray."

"You can if you want to, but I'm still waitin' to see if Life-Giver's real."

"What about the apples?" Hadassah asked.

"It's gonna take a whole lot more than a few apples to make me believe," Forsaken said. "But I did decide to give Him a chance." The sparkle in her eyes said more than her words.

"Life-Giver isn't worried, and neither am I," Hadassah said, placing her hand gently on her shoulder. "Now, if you don't mind, I'd like to pray."

Forsaken turned away but bowed her head and closed her eyes.

"Why are you bowing?" Hadassah asked.

"'Cuz this is how folks do it."

"You can pray with your eyes open, you know."

"I s'pose that's good to know in case I ever wanted to pray."

"You are a special one," Hadassah said. Turning her attention to Life-Giver, she prayed, "We need help to get through that gate. We don't have anything to give You other than our devotion, and we sure don't have anything to impress You with. All we have is an invitation. Please allow Forsaken to enter Your gates. Thank You."

"Let's go," Forsaken said, feeling excited.

"Aren't you worried?" Hadassah asked.

"Nope."

"Why not?"

"'Cuz."

"'Cuz why?" Hadassah asked, stopping to look at the child.

"'Cuz I asked for Life-Giver's help last night," she said with a big grin on her face.

"You did?"

"Yep, I did," she said, skipping off.

Hadassah watched the little one march toward the gate, her head held high. "Thank You, Life-Giver."

"It is My pleasure to give you the kingdom."

The same gatekeeper greeted them, smiling the same warm smile.

"Good morning, kind sir," Hadassah said.

Forsaken suddenly grabbed Hadassah's hand and squeezed it so tightly that it hurt. Hadassah looked down into eyes filled with fear. *How strange*, Hadassah thought, *just a moment ago she seemed so confident and assured.*

"Don't give up," Hadassah said, leaning down. Laying her pouch on the ground, she lifted the child's chin just enough that she could see her eyes. She looked so small and frightened. "Forsaken, dare to believe because you just might be on the brink of a miracle."

"Excuse me, my lady," the gatekeeper said, "but I have news that might cheer the wee one up a bit."

Forsaken lifted her eyes slightly.

Smiling, he said, "The Great King has granted permission for *both* of you to enter His gate."

Overjoyed, Hadassah scooped up Forsaken and spun her around. "Oh, happy day," she shouted.

Forsaken tried to hide her excitement but was not very successful.

"No longer forsaken," Hadassah said.

"You're makin' me dizzy," Forsaken said, laughing. Hadassah put her down and the child staggered for a moment.

"Thank you, kind gatekeeper," Hadassah said, bowing slightly.

"Do not do that," the gatekeeper said. "I'm not worthy to receive your appreciation or your worship."

"You're right . . . again," Hadassah said. "I shall thank the Great King myself — in person — as soon as I see Him."

As they stepped through the gate, Forsaken suddenly let go of Hadassah's hand. Returning to the gatekeeper, she pulled two apples from her pockets and said, "These are for you."

When he hesitated, she added, "I didn't steal them. . . promise."

Chuckling, the gatekeeper said, "I never thought you did. Thank you, child, for your kindness. May the Great King bless you."

"Uh . . . sure," she said, turning on her heels with a wave.

"That was so thoughtful," Hadassah said.

"Just wanted to make sure he had somethin' to eat, 'cuz it's terrible awful to be hungry."

***

With great excitement, the two explored every street, building and garden in the Outer Court. As they walked, the two girls asked everyone they met where they could find the King, but, alas, no one knew. Everyone knew *about* Him and could tell them various stories, but they did not encounter one person who knew Him personally.

How can that be? Hadassah wondered. *How could anyone live in the Outer Court of the King and not seek Him out?*

Tired and discouraged, Forsaken plopped down on an old brass bench. "What happens now? We ain't seen Life-Giver or the King or His palace, and nobody knows nothin'."

"It appears the people are content with just knowing *about* the King rather than having a relationship with Him," Hadassah said more to herself than to Forsaken.

The two sat in silence watching the people hurrying here and there.

Biting into an apple, Forsaken said, "Nobody looks happy here."

"I noticed."

"I don't wanna stay here no more. Let's go back."

"We can't go back. We must find the King."

"I just don't understand why it's so important to find the King," Forsaken said, throwing the core into the nearby bushes.

"Because there's more to life than what these people have — I know it. I know it's difficult, but I believe it will be worth it."

"So we keep lookin' 'till we find Him," Forsaken said standing. "He's gotta be here somewhere."

At that moment, an elderly Man leaning heavily on his walking stick stopped directly in front of them. He stared so long and hard at the two orphans that Hadassah felt quite uncomfortable. When she stood to leave, He asked, "May this old Man rest His weary bones beside you?"

Hadassah sat back down.

Nodding, Hadassah pulled Forsaken closer. The Man plopped down on the bench. Resting His walking stick against His knee, He turned and said, "My name's Emmanuel and yours is?"

"I'm Hadassah and this is Forsaken."

"Forsaken but not forgotten," He said, tapping His stick on the ground three times.

"What's that s'pose to mean?"

"Your mama and papa may have forsaken you, but the Great King will take you up."

"How'd you know my —"

Hadassah interrupted, asking, "Do you know the Great King?"

"I do. Very well, actually."

"Oh, finally we've found someone who knows Him! We've been searching for Him and have traveled a long way, but we haven't been very successful — until now."

"Ah, yes. Everyone who comes to the Outer Court comes looking for the Great King. Some grow comfortable and stay, others return from whence they came, while others continue on to the Inner Court. A few even pay the price to continue on to the Holy of Holies."

"Hadassah and me wanna go wherever the King is," Forsaken said.

"Dear child, the King is everywhere, all of the time. Like the air surrounding you — you can't see Him and neither can you live without Him."

"But I have this invitation," Hadassah said, pulling out the scroll. "It grants me permission to spend a day with the King. Forsaken and I are searching for His palace, but we can't seem to find the way."

"There is only One way to the Father," Life-Giver said.

Turning toward Hadassah, Emmanuel smiled, laid His weathered hand on top of hers and said, "You will find Him when you search for Him with all of your heart."

Hadassah was offended. Pulling her hand from beneath His, she thought, *I've given up everything and gone through much hardship in order to find Him. How dare this man insinuate that I haven't searched hard enough.*

"Choose life, Hadassah," Life-Giver said.

Far away, a dark creature named Offense sniffed the air. Recognizing the foul scent of pride, it rubbed its gnarled hands together. Turning to its fellow tormentor named Arrogance, it said, "I smell another offended child of the King."

Before Hadassah could blink, both creatures were by her side with their octopus-like arms wrapped around her upper body.

Hadassah was not aware of the hideous-looking creatures, but Emmanuel was.

Offense whispered in her ear, "Just who does this old man think he is? You're right, you've given up everything to find the king, and he accuses you of being lazy."

In the other ear Arrogance said, "You've certainly paid a dear price to find the king. Look at all that you've left. Look at all that you've suffered. And what have you gained from it? You don't deserve to be treated this way."

"Hadassah, you're as close to the King as you choose to be," Life-Giver said.

Offense cleared its throat. "You've done everything, and what has the king done? He makes you do all the work while he sits on some throne waiting for you to come and grovel at his feet."

"Love is not easily offended," Life-Giver said.

Michael and her guardian angels watched and waited, but Life-Giver did not commission them to intervene.

"Hadassah, this is not who you are. Rise up and conquer the enemy of your soul!" Life-Giver said to her spirit.

Hadassah suddenly felt conviction flooding her being. *How quickly I succumb to these dark thoughts. Why must I be so self-focused?* she thought to herself.

Taking a deep breath she silently prayed, *Life-Giver, please forgive me. I will trust You.* Turning her attention to the dark voices, she commanded, *In the name of Life-Giver, be gone from me. I will not listen to your voices or your lies anymore.*

Life-Giver glanced at Michael and Hadassah's guardian angels. They drew their fiery swords. The creatures shrieked as they removed their tentacles from around her. Tucking their tails, they ran.

Emmanuel chuckled; His eyes sparkled with delight. "Life is a journey, child. It takes a lifetime to find the Great King."

"I hope I don't have to die to find Him," Hadassah said.

"One never arrives until one dies, because that is when you finally live the fullness of your destiny."

Hadassah looked closely at the wise, old man. His tan face was weathered and wrinkled. His crystal blue eyes were clear and bright, kind actually. His nearly shoulder-length hair and beard were white like fresh fallen snow. His mouth was soft and gentle.

"Who are you?" Forsaken asked, leaning forward.

"I am an old Man who has seen more than you could ever imagine."

"And you said that the Inner Court is where I can find the King?" Hadassah asked.

"Like I said, the Great King can be found everywhere. He is not limited to one place just as He is not limited to one realm or one event or one time in history. The King is beyond time, beyond this earth, beyond a human's ability to control or understand. But there is one thing that He is not beyond and that is your reach. He is never beyond your reach, dear children. And you will always be as close to the King as you choose to be."

"But, kind sir, we've searched every part of this courtyard, and He's not here. If He's everywhere, then why haven't we seen Him?" Hadassah asked.

"Because you have not looked with the eyes of your heart," the old Man answered. "You believe Him to be a certain way, so you often miss encounters with Him."

Hadassah and Forsaken looked at each other. "Are you what my papa called a prophet?" Hadassah asked.

"Some people have called Me that and some people have called Me worse," He answered, His eyes alive with excitement and mystery and life.

"There's something about you that's very different. And I don't mean because you're so old. I mean, uh — elderly," Hadassah said, embarrassed by her slip of tongue.

"Do not worry, child. You have not offended Me, for Love is not easily offended. I am indeed old, ancient actually, but that is a good thing. Now, I have a question for you two young ladies. Do you have a place to sleep? Do you have food to eat besides your apples and mushrooms?"

Forsaken and Hadassah looked at each other. "How'd he know that?" Forsaken mouthed.

Hadassah shrugged in response.

Clearing her throat and squaring her shoulders, Forsaken asked, "Sir, I don't mean to be stickin' my nose where it don't belong, but how'd you know what kinda food we got?"

Smiling, He answered, "I know a whole lot more about you than what kind of food you have. But, we will speak of that another day. Right now, we need to see that you have a warm place to sleep and some hot food to eat. Hey, that could be a poem . . . warm place to sleep and hot food to eat." The old Man laughed so hard the girls feared He might hurt Himself.

"I ain't never met anybody like you," Forsaken said once He stopped laughing.

"You are certainly right about that," He replied. "Without further ado, let us be off."

"What's *a do*?" Forsaken whispered to Hadassah.

"I'm not sure," Hadassah answered.

"How can they not know that Emmanuel is the Great King?" Michael asked.

"They do not know Him yet, but they will," the Spirit of God said.

"Why does He not tell them who He is?"

"Because they would not believe Him. They would reject Him because He does not look like or behave like what or how they think the King should."

Michael sighed. "Just like before."

"Yes, Michael, but there is a day coming . . ."

CHAPTER TWENTY

$\mathcal{H}$adassah and Forsaken could barely keep up with Emmanuel as He led the way. "How's he know everybody's name?" Forsaken asked, surprised that He greeted every person He met.

"I don't know."

"How come he's got a walkin' stick? He sure don't need it," Forsaken said.

"Don't know."

Hadassah and Forsaken were nearly out of breath when, to their relief, Emmanuel stopped before a beautiful house made of white stones.

Forsaken elbowed Hadassah and said, "I thought he was poor."

"Shhh — he might hear you."

Stepping through the white picket gate, Emmanuel called out, "I am with you!"

What a strange greeting, Hadassah thought.

The front door immediately opened and a Servant ran out. "Welcome home! All is ready, for we've been eagerly watching for Your arrival."

To Hadassah's amazement, Emmanuel heartily embraced His slave and even kissed both of His cheeks.

"Rapha, I've brought home two of the King's beautiful daughters," Emmanuel said.

Forsaken could not believe her ears. "He called me beautiful," she whispered.

"Welcome to the Father's House. I am Rapha, your humble Servant," He said, smiling and making eye contact.

"Nice to meet you," Hadassah said.

"Nice to meet you," Forsaken said, ducking behind Hadassah.

Rapha smiled and then excused Himself, hurrying across the yard to fetch a basin of water warming in the sun.

Emmanuel invited the two girls to join Him on a bench.

Rapha returned, setting the basin in front of Forsaken. He smiled broadly as He offered to wash her feet. She immediately looked at Hadassah, fear filling her eyes. Emmanuel took her hand and said, "You are safe here, child. No one will hurt you or use you. We want nothing from you and desire only to lavish Our devotion on you."

Forsaken wondered if it could be true. She looked in Emmanuel's eyes. "I won't ever hurt you, child — I promise," He said.

For some reason beyond her ability to understand, she believed Him.

With a nod from Emmanuel, Forsaken extended her foot and Rapha joyfully set about His task. The moment He poured water over it, she started giggling. And she giggled the entire time. As Rapha massaged her feet with fragrant oil, Forsaken fell against Hadassah hysterical with laughter. Tears ran down her dirty face. Emmanuel and Rapha laughed with her while Hadassah looked on in wonder.

"I am finished," Rapha said.

"It's a good thing you don't have more feet," Emmanuel said. "I don't think you could have taken much more."

Wiping her face on her dirty skirt, Forsaken said, "I ain't ever laughed so hard."

"I am glad I was able to bring you such joy, My lady," Rapha said.

Forsaken looked up. *He called me a lady,* she thought. Tears filled her eyes.

"You are not only a lady, but you are a beautiful lady," Rapha said, kissing her hand.

"Uh, thank you," she said, blushing profusely.

Rapha placed the basin before her. Hadassah was mortified by what she feared was about to happen. The kind Servant looked at her and said, "Oh, please don't hide your face, My lady. I, too, have had My feet washed. The journey through life is difficult and often defiles the human heart, I understand that. Please allow Me the honor of washing away your past with this living water which flowed from the very throne of the King."

Hadassah glanced at Emmanuel, who nodded and smiled. She looked back at Rapha. His countenance reflected His meek and gentle nature. He waited patiently, His hands folded in His lap. Whispering a silent prayer for courage, she slowly offered her foot. Unable to look at Rapha, Hadassah stared at the stone floor. With great gentleness, He washed her feet while quietly singing. Hadassah tried her best to relax but found herself growing more self-conscious with each passing moment.

After massaging her feet with the fragrant oil, He said, "Thank you for allowing Me to serve you."

"May I ask why it is that you find so much joy in such a menial task as washing someone's dirty feet?"

"I desire more than anything to make the King great. One way I can do that is to become the least."

Hadassah was not at all sure she understood what He meant. Just as she was about to ask, Emmanuel called Rapha. He quickly set the bowl aside and joined Him, sitting at His feet.

Unable to hold her tongue, Hadassah asked, "Excuse me, I don't mean to be bold, but aren't you going to wash your master's feet?"

Looking at Emmanuel, Rapha said, "He has no need of cleansing." Rapha immediately turned His attention back to the Object of His affection.

"My friend, tell Me about Your day," Emmanuel said.

Emmanuel listened closely as Rapha told of visiting orphans and widows, feeding the hungry and praying for the sick. When He was finished, Emmanuel reached down and hugged the Man.

Hadassah's mouth fell open. Turning to look at her, Emmanuel chuckled. "You might want to close your mouth lest a fly finds a home there."

"Sorry," Hadassah said. "It's just that I've never seen or heard of a master addressing or embracing his servant like that. And neither have I seen a servant who loved his master like Rapha does."

"I am no respecter of persons, Hadassah. I love everyone as much as I love Rapha. Shall we join the others?"

Emmanuel led the girls into a room as big as a ballroom where people of various ages and many different races were overjoyed to see their Master.

Embracing people as He went, Emmanuel led the two girls into the center of the room. When He raised His hand, the room instantly grew quiet. He announced, "Allow Me to introduce My new friends, Hadassah and Forsaken."

I'm your friend? Hadassah thought.

Forsaken ducked behind Hadassah and buried her disfigured face in her skirt. Hadassah reached back and held her hand, squeezing it tightly.

Emmanuel announced, "Come, let us eat and rejoice."

As He led them across the room, Hadassah asked, "Are all of these people your servants?"

"They are so much more than servants, Hadassah. They are bondservants."

"What's that?"

"When a man or woman's time of servitude is up and they are free to go, there are those who choose to remain in service to their master because of love — they are called bondservants. See the piercings in their ears? Those mark them as bondservants."

"I can't imagine *choosing* to be a servant."

"Me neither," Forsaken said.

Smiling broadly, Emmanuel held a chair for Forsaken and Hadassah. "You can't imagine it because My kingdom is unlike anything you know; it is an upside-down kingdom. But we will speak more of that in the future."

This old man has a kingdom? Hadassah thought. She was about to ask what He meant when Rapha announced that the table was ready. A simple yet delicious feast was set before them. Rapha took His place at Emmanuel's right hand. To Hadassah's shock, the entire household ate at the same table as their Master. And then, when dinner was over, Emmanuel and Rapha were the first to begin clearing the table. Hadassah was dumbfounded.

Hadassah and Forsaken offered to help, but Emmanuel said, "There will be plenty of time for serving in the days ahead. For now, just rest and enjoy yourselves."

Forsaken's face lit up. She ran to a nearby basket, which she had noticed moving during the meal. Kneeling, she removed the lid. Two adorable puppies stuck their heads up and licked her face. Forsaken squealed. Emmanuel laughed and responded to her unspoken request. "Of course you may take them out, child."

As she struggled to lift the first wiggly puppy out, the basket toppled over and two little bundles of joy pounced on top of her. Forsaken's laughter filled the air. Everyone, even Emmanuel, stopped to watch as the puppies chased her around the room.

Hadassah scanned the crowd. Everyone, without exception, looked so happy. Emmanuel and Rapha appeared to be the happiest of all. Hadassah still could not believe that He was washing the dishes. *What kind of master serves alongside his servants?* she wondered.

Hadassah suddenly noticed an elderly Man, sitting on the other side of the room. Their eyes met. The Man smiled, motioning for her to join Him. Hadassah sat on a stool at his feet. "Hello, Hadassah. I'm Joshua," He said.

"Hello."

"You asked what kind of master serves alongside his servants. The answer to that question is only found in true love."

"How'd you know I asked that question? And how'd you know about true love?" Hadassah asked, intrigued and perplexed.

"In this place, child, there isn't much that isn't known."

"Exactly where is this place?"

"You are on the outer fringes of the kingdom. Knowledge and law, rules and traditions are abundant here. But the further you journey into the kingdom the more you discover that mercy, compassion and unconditional love always triumph over judgment. At the very heart of this kingdom you will find true love, for the King is Love. But, alas, there are many who are afraid to make the journey into the center of His heart."

"Why would anyone be afraid of the King?"

"Many people are comfortable with their lives the way they are, and they do not want anyone, not even the Great King, to interfere. They want to live in His land and partake of His blessings but not fully surrender to His plans and His ways."

"Why does He allow them to stay? Why doesn't He send them away?"

"You are here, are you not?"

"I am, but I don't plan on staying. I'm looking for the King's palace."

Not so far away, Arrogance lifted its ugly head and sniffed the air.

"There is one thing that you must know about this King you seek — His love is *never* based on a human's performance or a lack thereof. His love is based on one thing and one thing only — *His* heart of mercy. He does not reject those who have yet to fully surrender, but He calls out to them even more, drawing them closer with cords of love."

"I've been told this before — several times, as a matter of fact."

Arrogance stood at attention.

"Perhaps you need to hear it — again," Joshua remarked.

"The King resists the arrogant but gives grace to the humble," Life-Giver said.

Hadassah was suddenly aware of her pride. "You're right, sir. I do need to hear it. Thank you for reminding me."

The Man smiled. "Your journey has produced in you an ear to hear."

"How do you know so much about me?"

"There isn't much I don't know, child," He said with a twinkle in His eye.

Hadassah looked around the room. Men, women and children, rich and poor, old and young were joyfully working together. Laughter filled the air. "Are these the people you speak of? Are these the ones who have chosen to stay in the Outer Court?"

"No, child, these are bondservants. They will never be free to do as they please — by choice. But, if the truth were known, they are the freest people alive."

"I have so much to learn," Hadassah said, feeling rather overwhelmed.

"Indeed, you do," Joshua replied. "But have no fear, for you are on the right path." He then rested His head back against the chair and said, "If you will excuse an old Man, I believe I need a nap."

"Of course," Hadassah said. "And thank you for sharing your wisdom with me."

"It is My pleasure," He said closing His eyes.

Hadassah searched the room for Forsaken. She was easy to find, because she was the only one rolling across the floor. Seeing Hadassah, Forsaken jumped to her feet, saying, "Hadassah, watch this."

Forsaken started running, and the puppies followed. "They like me, they really like me," she said. Spinning around, she lost her balance and fell against a table. A large vase toppled to the floor, shattering into pieces. Forsaken froze, a look of horror on her face. The puppies tucked their tails, running back to their basket.

Forsaken's eyes filled with tears. No one scolded or rebuked the child, but she cowered as though they had. "Don't worry," Hadassah said, wrapping her arms around her. "I'll help you clean it up."

Emmanuel knelt in front of her. Taking her hands in His, He said, "Forsaken, that vase can be replaced. The things of true value are those things that cannot be replaced. Do not worry yourself about this, for 100 years from now it will not be important."

Forsaken looked into His eyes. "Thank you, kind sir," she said. "I'll clean it up." She frantically picked up pieces, her hands shaking.

Emmanuel gently squeezed her hand and said, "Forsaken, you are going to cut yourself. This is not a job that you can do. Leave this to Me, dear one. There are some messes that only I can clean up."

"But I —"

"Allow Me to do this, precious child," He said. "If you want to do something, there are two scared puppies over there that really need your love and attention."

"Oh, I forgot about the puppies!" she exclaimed. Emmanuel picked her up and said, "Allow Me to carry you lest you cut your feet."

Setting her down, she scooped up the puppies and held them close, quickly forgetting the mess she had made.

Hadassah and several others helped Emmanuel collect the pieces. He said to Hadassah, "The child has been shattered by many, but she is not so broken that the Great King cannot heal her."

Hadassah stared at the Stranger, wondering just who He was and how He knew so much. "Folks here seem to know the secrets of people's hearts," she said.

"Is that a bad thing?" Emmanuel asked.

"I don't know, I guess it could be, especially if one is flawed."

"You need not fear anything or anyone, for Perfect Love abides outside of earthly fear," He said.

Hadassah pondered His words. "May I be so bold as to ask if you are rich? For you are the most joyful man I've ever seen."

"Riches and joy do not have anything in common. As for Me being rich, I have all that is important, which makes Me rich indeed. But do not be deceived, Hadassah; true riches are not what a man can accumulate or achieve. True riches only come from laying down one's life for the benefit of Another. And you, dear one, are well on your way to becoming quite wealthy."

"What!? Me?" Hadassah laughed at the thought.

"Yes, you. Just look at that child over there. Did you not lay aside your desire to spend a day with the King in order to stay with her?"

"How'd you know that?"

"Well, didn't you?"

She looked at her hands folded neatly in her lap and studied the dirt caked beneath her fingernails. Embarrassed, she sat on her hands. "I couldn't just leave her behind," she said, still wondering how He knew. *Perhaps he knows the gatekeeper.*

"I do know the gatekeeper, but that is not how I knew you sacrificed your desire for what was best for the child. I also know that your compassion coupled with Life-Giver's resurrection power gave her a new beginning and the opportunity to know the King personally."

"You truly are a prophet," Hadassah exclaimed, "and a scary one at that!"

"Hadassah, you have come here in search of the Great King. Your heart is pure and your motives are right, but secretly you fear you're not good enough. You believe the King and His kingdom are outside of your reach. Your fears will keep you from finding Him. The truth is," He said as He leaned toward her, "the One you so desperately seek is much closer than you know."

"You're right; I am afraid that I'm not good enough. If you knew my past and where I came from, you'd understand. You see, Emmanuel, I have nothing, I am nothing. All I have is this little flicker of love and devotion burning within. I wish I could do more, give more. I wish I could be great for Him. If I only knew what the King expects, then I could work on doing it, but no one seems to know what He demands. Do you know what the King expects? Do you know His laws?"

Emmanuel sat beside her and took her hand. "Where you came from means absolutely nothing to the King. He actually chooses the weak, the foolish and the simple to be His closest friends. There are many who want to do great things for the King, but there are few who want to make *Him* great."

Hadassah's eyes filled with tears.

"You asked if I know His laws. I know them very well. I also know that you cannot keep them, no matter how diligently you try. That is why His Son lived as a common Man and died an uncommon death. In doing so, He took every one of your sins with Him into the grave. Because of *His* actions, not yours, you are free from the law of sin and death! His gift makes you worthy. You asked what the King expects you to do — the most important law of all is the law of love. You are to love your King with all of your heart, soul, mind and strength and love your neighbor even as you love yourself."

"Is that even possible?" Hadassah asked.

"It is possible because Life-Giver is with you — everywhere, all of the time — and His Spirit resides within you," Emmanuel confided.

Hadassah's heart burned within her as she looked into His sparkling blue eyes. For a fleeting moment, she wondered if this old Man might be the King in disguise, but she instantly dismissed the idea as being absolutely ridiculous.

Gently taking her hand, He looked deep into her eyes and said, "Hadassah, the gate is small and the way is narrow that leads to life, and few are those who find it. Choose life every time."

Hadassah gasped. She mumbled something about needing air and quickly excused herself. Running outside, she pressed her back against the stone wall and took a deep breath. *The Great King would live in a castle and have thousands of servants. He would be powerful, strong and rich beyond reason. He would never be a servant. He would never be so friendly.*

"Oh, I'm so confused!" she cried out, sinking to her knees.

Forsaken, with puppies following, ran up to her. "Don't be confused," she said, kneeling beside her. "Be happy."

Hadassah studied the child's face. Even more obvious than her scars was her worry and distress. "I'll be all right, Forsaken. It's just that nothing is turning out like I thought it would. I'm just feeling a bit confused and overwhelmed right now."

"Hadassah, can we stay here?"

"Emmanuel said he'd give us a bed for the night."

"No. I mean can we stay here forever? Can this be our home, our family, our puppies?"

"Emmanuel hasn't asked us to stay forever."

Forsaken's countenance fell. "Hadassah, I don't wanna leave. I want a family. I want *this* family."

"I don't know what to say."

"Hadassah, there's somethin' here that I ain't ever felt before. Emmanuel said I was beautiful. He didn't hit me or curse me when I broke his vase. He let me eat at his table instead of under it, and I could have all I wanted. His servant friend washed my feet and made them smell good. I ain't never known kindness 'cept for you. I can't leave. I gotta live here forever."

"Forsaken, I don't want you to be disappointed, but I don't know that we can stay. I know it's good here, but I *must* find the King — that is truly where our home is."

"But what if He's the King?"

"He can't be the King."

"How do you know? Have you ever seen the King?"

"No, but I —"

"Then you don't know. I believe He is and I'm gonna ask Him if I can be His daughter and live with Him — forever." Forsaken turned and ran into the house, the puppies close on her heels.

"Gabriel, take this message to Satan: Tell him the child he calls Forsaken is My Beloved," Life-Giver commanded.

"There is no greater message I would rather carry, my Lord,"
Gabriel responded, bowing low.

As Gabriel delivered the message, a blood-curdling screech was
heard throughout the unseen realm. Satan clawed at the ground in a
rage. Spewing a string of insults toward Forsaken and Life-Giver, he
disappeared into the darkness. When the smoke cleared, Life-Giver
stood in the midst of the battlefield. With one breath, He turned the
ashes into beautiful, glorious light.

"The battle for your soul has been won, Forsaken. You are Mine
and I am yours — forever," He whispered. His words hovered above
His head. With the simple wave of His hand they took the form of a
beautiful, white dove. On the wings of the dove, Life-Giver sent His
Perfect Love through the veil and into the realm called Earth.

Just as Emmanuel picked up the last of the broken pieces,
Forsaken ran into the room. Dropping to her knees beside Him, she
said, "Thank you for not hating me."

"I could never hate you or anyone. As a matter of fact, orphans
are my favorite kind of people."

"I ain't never known anybody as kind as you," she said, gently
shoving a puppy away from her face.

Emmanuel laid His hand on her shoulder and said, "I am so sorry
your life has been so painful, dear child."

At that precise moment, a snow-white dove flew through the open
window. The bird circled the room. The puppies chased after it while
barking wildly. Hadassah entered the house just as the dove landed
on Forsaken's shoulder. Feeling both delighted and afraid, the little
girl did not move. Emmanuel and Rapha grabbed the puppies and
held them close. Every eye in the room was on Forsaken. The dove
bobbed up and down a few times softly pecking her cheek. It cooed
in her ear and then pecked her cheek again before it flew out the
window.

Forsaken ran out the door. Hadassah thought she was running
after the dove, but Emmanuel knew the truth. And so did Joshua.
And Rapha. They knew what was happening inside that little
orphan's heart.

When Forsaken didn't return right away, Hadassah went looking
for her. Finding her perched in a tree, she climbed up on the nearby

stone wall and waited. For what, she was not sure. She just knew she needed to wait.

Quite some time passed before Forsaken even acknowledged Hadassah's presence. "Hadassah, somethin' just happened that I can't explain."

"You need not explain it. Just share your experience, and it's enough."

"The dove . . ."

"Yes?"

"Well, the dove sang a song . . ."

"Yes. I heard it cooing," Hadassah said.

"Yes, but could you hear the words the dove sang?"

"Words?"

"I told you I can't explain it!" Forsaken exclaimed. "The bird was singin' to me, Hadassah! He knew my name and that I was an Or Fan. He also knew I secretly wish for a mama and papa — *nobody* knows that!"

Forsaken climbed down from the tree and joined Hadassah on the wall.

"Go on," Hadassah encouraged.

"The bird sang these words, 'Your mama and papa have forsaken you, but the Great King will take you up.' Hadassah, how'd that bird sing words, and how'd it know about *me*? And what does it mean for the King to take me up?"

"I don't know, but what I do know is that the King is everywhere, all the time. It seems everyone knows the secrets of our hearts in this place. Only Life-Giver and the King can make something like this happen . . . surely you believe that?"

"I do. I really do! I don't know how that bird did that, but I know what I heard and what I felt. I ain't never felt so . . . so loved! And the love was brought by a bird!" Forsaken said, giggling.

"This is the strangest place," Hadassah said thoughtfully.

"Hadassah, that wasn't all the bird said. Do you remember me tellin' you that when I died a beautiful man gave me somethin', but I couldn't 'member what it was?"

"How could I forget that?"

"Well, the bird told me — he told me what the gift was."

"And?" Hadassah asked, eager to hear.

"It was a new name, Hadassah! That beautiful Man was Life-Giver, and He gave me a new name! At the time I didn't want it, 'cuz I liked the one I had. But that ain't true anymore. Now I want it!"

"May I ask what your new name is?"

"My name's Beloved!" Forsaken exclaimed. "Can you believe it? Even I know what *that* name means!"

"Yes, I can believe it! You are Beloved!" Hadassah said, holding the little girl close as they both cried tears of joy.

"Hadassah, there's more."

"Yes?"

"The dove asked if I'd like to be part of the King's family. I said yes, and when I did, the dove kissed my cheek."

"Beloved, you're truly one special little girl!"

"I think I'm startin' to believe that."

"Your love is astonishing!" Michael exclaimed.

"There is nothing as powerful as My love — faith pales in comparison and so does hope, for the greatest of all is love!"

Michael bowed low before Life-Giver. And as he did, he wondered what further mysteries were hidden within the endless depths of Life-Giver's heart.

CHAPTER TWENTY-ONE

$\mathcal{B}$eloved could barely sleep. She tossed and turned, flipped and flopped, eager for the morning sun that she might explore the wonders of her new life and identity. When exhaustion finally overtook her excitement, she dreamed about a dove and puppies and having a beautiful, flawless face.

In the middle of the night, Beloved found herself wide awake. Tiptoeing across the room, she opened the shutters as quietly as possible. The night sky was alive with countless twinkling stars. The soft light of the full moon caressed every part of her face. Seeing her reflection in the glass, she touched the scars. "How will anyone ever love me?" she whispered.

"I love you," Life-Giver said.

She heard Him!

"Life-Giver?"

"The One and only."

"You love *me*?" she whispered.

"More than you can believe."

She thought about His words, not sure if she was going to believe them or not. "I ain't ever been loved the way I've been loved lately," she finally said.

"You've been loved this way since the day you came into being, child. You just didn't know it."

"How can Somebody like You love somebody as ugly as me?" she asked, staring at her reflection.

"You are My Beloved, and I love you just the way you are. Your outward appearance does not affect My love for you."

"I want to believe that, but it's hard 'cuz folks always told me I was too ugly to be loved. But I ain't gonna believe that no more. With the stars and moon as my witness, I think I've found love."

"On the contrary, Love found you. And I find you to be quite beautiful."

Tears of joy mixed with past hurt flowed unhindered over the despised flaws. Reaching up, she traced every misshapen feature. "I've been called a lot of names, but beautiful ain't one of them. I'm too scarred to ever be beautiful."

"I am scarred."

"You're scarred?"

"Yes."

"How'd You get scars?"

"Like you, I was wounded by men. I know how you feel."

"Oh. Does that mean You're ugly?"

"I am actually quite beautiful, and so are you. Beloved, your outward appearance will one day fade away as quickly as the flowers of the field, but your spirit lives forever. And the suffering you have experienced is creating for you an eternal weight of glory far beyond all comparison. You do not understand that now, but the day will come when you will see and will be glad." He put His arms around her, holding her close.

Beloved felt loved, and she liked it — a lot.

"You are no longer flawed, no longer alone, no longer forsaken."

"Is this really happenin'? Am I dreamin'?" she asked.

"It is really happening, child."

"Then how come I can't see You?"

"Happy are those who do not see but still believe."

"It's kinda hard to talk to somebody you can't see."

"But you can see Me, if you look with the eyes of your heart."

"How do I do that?"

"I gave you an imagination. The eyes that imagine all kinds of things are the same eyes that can see Me."

"Hmm. I gotta think on that for a while," she said.

"Beloved."

"Yes?"

"Being in My presence transforms you."

"What does that mean?"

"It means the more time you spend with Me the more you will look like Me."

"I want that."

"Good. Now rest and dream of better days."

Suddenly aware of her fatigue, Beloved returned to her bed. No sooner had she pulled the covers over her head than she drifted off.

She dreamed it was her wedding day, and she was marrying Life-Giver. As He escorted her down a golden street, a white dove landed on a looking glass nearby. Life-Giver escorted her to the mirror and asked, "May I lift your veil?"

She hesitated, not wanting Him to see her scars.

"I make all things beautiful in their time," He said.

"Go ahead," she said, holding her breath.

As He lifted the veil, she laughed and cried all at the same time, for her face was flawless. She was beautiful.

***

The morning sun brought with it a flurry of activity, for the farm animals were ready to be fed. Just outside Beloved's window a rooster crowed loud enough to wake her. Jumping out of bed, she shivered as she ran across the cold floor. Standing in front of the window, she giggled as she watched the two puppies chasing anything and everything that moved.

Beloved dressed quickly, eager to greet the day. To her surprise, she found Emmanuel in the kitchen bending over the fireplace, stirring a large pot of porridge. "Good morning, kind sir," she said cheerfully.

"A good morning to you. I trust you slept well?" He asked, glancing over His shoulder.

"Sure did. I dreamed 'bout Life-Giver and the dove."

"Dreams are the King's way of talking to you when you are too tired to interrupt Him. In a dream, the King can say whatever He wants, and you have to listen," He said, laughing heartily.

Not sure if He was kidding, Beloved shrugged. " I got a new name!"

"Oh, dear Beloved, do not hold Me in suspense any longer! Tell Me this new name!" Emmanuel said, laying down His wooden spoon.

"You're teasin' me. You just called me by my new name. How'd You know it?"

Ignoring her question, Emmanuel replied, "And what a fitting name it is! Have you looked closely at your new name?"

"What do You mean?"

"Well, every name has a meaning, and your name is quite obvious as to its meaning. *Be loved.* Life-Giver is saying that you are to be loved — that is why you were born: to be loved by the King and His people and to love them in return! It is a simple but powerful mission for sure."

"It's gonna take me some time to get use to it, 'cuz I've always been Forsaken."

"You are no longer Forsaken, child; that name is no longer true for you. Oh my! I rhymed again! Perhaps I should become a poet!"

Giggling, Beloved said, "A poet you ain't. But don't be sad, 'cuz you got lots of other wonderful traits."

"You are kind indeed," the old Man said. His countenance reflected His immense delight in the little girl.

"To go from Forsaken to Beloved is gonna be hard for somebody as little as me, but I think I can do it."

"I have no doubt that you will progress nicely with such a wonderful name."

Beloved climbed on a tall stool and said, "I dreamed I was marryin' Life-Giver. I saw the dove, and it landed on a lookin' glass. At first, I was scared to look, 'cuz folks told me my whole life how ugly I was. They said I was hideous, whatever that means. I figured it was worse than ugly. But I got brave and looked in that mirror, and I was beautiful — really beautiful. I only wish . . . I wish it wasn't a dream. I wish it could be true."

"Dreams do come true, child."

"Not this one."

"That's where you're wrong. One day you will be a beautiful bride."

"Are You sure? How do You know?"

"I know because I know everything about your life. I read the script of your life before you were born."

"How'd You see me before I was born?"

"You were born from above, child."

"What's that mean?"

"You were born again, born from above. That is what has happened to you — your old self died and you have been born again as a new creation. Life-Giver gave you life, which always brings with it a new identity. Your new identity is that of being a be-loved member of His family. No longer forsaken — but from now until forever you are His Beloved," Emmanuel explained as He returned to His kettle.

"Does that mean I get a new family?"

"That is exactly what it means, dear one. And not only a family but a new life. You'll never be the same again. You are brand new and loved immensely, child."

"Someone like *me* is loved — amensely — whatever that means. It's good, ain't it?"

He chuckled. "It is good."

"I got a family. So that means I'm no longer an Or Fan . . . right?"

"You are no longer and never will be an orphan again."

"If I ain't no Or Fan, then I must have a papa and a mama." Looking at the floor, her smile faded. "Emmanuel, who's my papa? Who's my mama?"

"The Great King is your mama, papa, brother, teacher, your best friend, your comforter and your constant companion. He will never —"

Holding her hand up, she interrupted. Her smile returned. "I know what You're gonna say — He'll never forsake me!"

Her smile lasted only for a moment. Looking quite serious, she asked, "Are *You* the King?"

"I am."

"I knew it! I told Hadassah, but she didn't believe me. What are You doin' here? Why ain't You at Your castle doin' king stuff?"

"I am doin' King stuff — I'm loving you." Arms outstretched, He said, "Come and allow your Papa to hold you close, for you deserve to *be loved*!"

"Because I was born from above!" she exclaimed, running into His open arms.

Emmanuel held His daughter close.

"Can I stay with You forever?"

"You can, child, you can and you will."

***

Hadassah entered the kitchen. She could not believe her eyes, for Beloved was peering intently into a looking glass. But that was not what shocked her. It was the fact that Beloved was smiling — broadly — that she could not believe.

Seeing Hadassah standing in the doorway, mouth hanging open, Beloved exclaimed, "I'm *beautiful* and *loved*, Hadassah! My heart's good — not ugly, not bad, not dark, but beautiful! Can you believe it? I almost can't, but I know it's. . . I *know* it's true! Oh, Hadassah, I've been re-borned! My heart feels as though it's gonna burst."

Jumping down from the stool, she ran to Hadassah and threw her arms around her waist. Beloved hugged her tightly, announcing, "I love you, Hadassah! I love You, Emmanuel! I love you, world!"

Releasing Hadassah, she spun wildly, crashing into the table and upsetting the candlesticks. Giggling, she announced, "I gotta tell the puppies the good news!" And out the back door she ran.

Hadassah was speechless. Emmanuel cheerfully hummed as He stirred the porridge.

"Thank you," she said.

"It is My pleasure to love the child."

"I can see that in your eyes. It appears to me that you delight in everyone whether old or young, rich or poor, smart or otherwise. How is it that you love like this?"

"Everyone is a delightful human being who deserves to be valued and cherished and loved. Hadassah, life is a journey into the heart of the Great King. Not everyone is at the same place along that path. Some are still searching while others have found the way. Kindness brings out the best in most people. I choose to always love, and I choose to always be kind — even to those who seemingly do not deserve it."

"I wish I had the ability to do the same."

"Oh, but you do because the Creator of the world lives inside of you! Imagine what that means. Nothing is impossible for Him, therefore nothing is impossible for you.

"The Great King is the center of everything in existence. Self-centered efforts and self-focused living will never impress a perfect King. Therefore, the wisest thing you can do is surrender and allow Him to live His life through you."

Hadassah pondered His words. It was not the first time she had heard that message. *Will I ever get it?* she wondered.

Beloved hurried in carrying a dozen or so eggs in the folds of her skirt. The two puppies followed close behind.

"I see you found the chickens," Emmanuel said as He shooed the puppies away from His feet.

"Yep, I did. I broke one. Sorry," she said, slightly cowering.

"I guess the puppies have had their breakfast then?"

"You're not mad?"

"Child, I'm not mad. Just look at all the eggs that aren't broken — there's more than enough. I do not get mad when you make a mistake. Mistakes foster growth."

"You're different from anybody I ever met," she said, placing the eggs in a basket. "It's gonna take some time to get used to You." With a smile, she raced off again with the puppies nipping at her heels.

Emmanuel looked at Hadassah. "Along the path of life eggs get broken, but good can come out of it." He filled a bowl with steaming porridge and set it before her. Placing the honey jar in front of her, He said, "And everything tastes better with a little honey."

"Thank you," she said.

"You are most welcome."

"I don't know what to do," Hadassah said, drizzling honey over the steaming bowl. "You're so kind and For— I mean, Beloved is so very happy. I've never seen her this happy, but . . ."

"But?"

"But there's more. I know there's more. The people in your home aren't like the people I saw on the streets yesterday. They love each other, and everyone helps each other. No one acts like they're more important than another. The people on the streets were polite and nice, but they all had a list of *do*'s and *don't*s that they pulled out of their pockets anytime I asked them a question. No one seemed to have much joy or love, and no one seemed interested in helping or serving. And nobody knew where to find the King, yet they said they were followers of Him."

"Your assessment is mostly correct. So what do you plan to do about it?"

"I don't know. I'm praying, and until I hear we shall remain here, if the child and I are welcome that is," Hadassah said, blushing at being so forward.

Emmanuel chuckled, "You are both a joy and a delight to have in My home. You are always welcome here."

"Thank you, kind sir," Hadassah said. "I shall find some way to repay you."

"It is impossible and unnecessary to repay a gift, for that negates the very nature of the gift, does it not?"

"I suppose so."

"You would insult Me should you even try. So rest in the truth that My home is your home for as long as you like — for all eternity should you so desire," He said, meeting her questioning gaze with a smile.

Beloved returned with the two puppies racing behind her. She was laughing so hard she could barely breathe.

"Hadassah! You gotta come see what I found!" she said, grabbing Hadassah's hand.

"Excuse me, Emmanuel; it seems my presence is required elsewhere," Hadassah said as she allowed Beloved to drag her across the room.

Emmanuel stood in the doorway and called after them, "Remember the One you seek is also within you!"

"What?" Hadassah asked, looking back over her shoulder. But the kind Gentleman was gone. "Where'd he go?" Hadassah asked.

"He's stirrin' His porridge," Beloved answered, tugging on her hand.

The puppies followed them across a pasture. "Look!" Beloved said, pointing to an orchard.

"Yes?"

"Don't you see it?" Beloved asked.

"I see a bunch of trees."

"Apple trees, Hadassah! They're apple trees!"

"So?"

"So . . . the apple tree outside the castle walls, remember?"

"I remember."

"I bet that apple tree came from here. Look over there — you can see where one was dug up. I bet Emmanuel had His servant dig that tree up and plant it outside the gate just for us!"

"That's impossible. First of all, he could never move it. And secondly, why would he? He didn't even know us then, and what you're suggesting is impossible."

"Hadassah, don't you see who He is? Didn't you look in His eyes? Emmanuel's not regular. You can see that, can't you? He's the Great King."

"Beloved, I certainly admit that he's not ordinary, but to say that he's —" Hadassah stopped, afraid to say the words.

"I can say it — 'cuz He told me!"

"He told you?"

"Yeah."

Hadassah plopped down on a log. "That can't be true. He can't be the King."

"He is so!"

"I never thought it would be so difficult to spend a day with the King. I thought I'd walk into the palace, hand a guard my scroll, and it would be done. Everything's so complicated, and I don't know what to think, Forsaken!"

"My name's Beloved. And you been sayin' you want to spend a day with the King, and you're gonna miss it! Just ask Him like I did."

Looking into her eyes and seeing nothing but childlike faith, Hadassah surrendered. Chuckling, she said, "Beloved, you just might be right. He might be. . . I doubt it, but maybe he is. Come on, let's go ask."

"Now you're gettin' your wits about you."

Hand in hand, they skipped back to the house. Stepping into the kitchen they stopped abruptly. It was empty — not one pot, bowl, basket or candlestick.

They hurried into the ballroom. It was empty. Running to their bedroom, they found nothing but their few belongings. The house was not only empty, but it appeared as if it had been abandoned for quite some time.

"I know we weren't dreaming," Hadassah said.

"The dove — it was real . . . wasn't it?" Beloved asked, a hint of fear evident in her voice.

"Yes, child, it was real. I saw it with my own eyes. You have nothing to fear, for all that happened here was real."

They stepped out the front door into the sunshine. Hadassah said, "I guess it's time to be moving on."

"We ain't goin' back, are we?"

"No, we won't go back. We'll continue our journey to the palace of the King. Isn't that why we came?"

"That's why *you* came here. I came lookin' for the King 'cuz I didn't wanna be alone," Beloved said, her chin quivering as her eyes filled with tears.

"Beloved, come here," Hadassah said, pulling her close. "You won't ever be alone again. I'm with you and so is Life-Giver. He'll never leave us or forsake us. And we'll search for the King with all of our hearts, for that's how we'll find Him."

"He found us. . .but we didn't know it cuz He was in disguise."

"I think you might be right."

"Then you believe me?"

"I think I believe you. How can I deny this great mystery?" she said looking around. "Since He left, then that must mean He wants us to follow. So what do you say we get our belongings and be on our way?"

"No point in stayin' here now."

As they gathered their few belongings, Beloved said, "I'm glad He didn't take our stuff."

"Emmanuel would never do anything like that."

"Oh, yeah. I forgot that He's different."

They made one more round through the house. Closing the front door, Beloved said, "Wait! We forgot about the puppies!"

"I'm certain Emmanuel has taken them with Him. He's kind and will not forsake man or beast."

"Can't we just look?"

Seeing the pain in her eyes, Hadassah could not refuse.

"My Lord?" Michael said in response to being summoned.

"*My children are on the move. Surround them with warriors, strong and mighty, but do not interfere with their choices. Neither shall you allow Satan or his minions to trespass the boundaries I have set for them. This journey is crucial to their growth and will soon deliver a final blow to the stronghold in Hadassah's heart.*"

"*Your will be done on earth as it is in heaven; Your kingdom come,*" the angel replied.

CHAPTER TWENTY-TWO

$\mathscr{H}$adassah and Beloved walked the streets for most of the day only to discover they were walking in a circle. Flopping down on a rickety bench, chin resting on the back of her hand, Hadassah sighed deeply. "I can't believe this is happening."

Beloved plopped down beside her. "Maybe *she* knows the way," Beloved said, pointing across the street to a girl dressed in rags and begging for coins.

"I don't think she —" Before Hadassah could finish her sentence, Beloved was on her feet and headed across the street.

"Beloved," she called, but the child ignored her. Hadassah hurried after her.

"Hi," Beloved said.

"Do you have a coin for me?"

"We don't got no coins. But we do got some apples. Would ya like one?"

The girl nodded energetically. Hadassah handed her two apples, saying, "Here's one for now and one for later."

Sitting on the curb, the girl took a huge bite. Bits of apple flew out of her mouth as she thanked Beloved. Beloved sat down by her.

Hadassah guessed the girl to be no more than thirteen. Her clothes were tattered and dirty. Her brown hair was nothing short of a rat's nest. Her shoes, if you could call them that, were merely pieces of fabric wrapped around her feet and secured with leather strings. Her face was dirty, but beneath the filth her features were quite striking. When the girl looked up, Hadassah gasped, for her big, green eyes were breathtaking. The girl smiled broadly exposing perfect, white teeth.

"Hi. I'm Hadassah and this is Beloved. What's your name?" she asked, sitting beside Beloved.

"I've been called many names," she answered, sitting up tall and straight, "but the name I like most is Sunshine. What do you think? Look closely, do you think I shine like the sun . . . maybe a little?" She turned her face to the side, nose elevated.

Hadassah chuckled. "You most certainly do. It's a pleasure to meet you, Sunshine."

"It's a pleasure to make your acquaintance."

"Where do you live?" Hadassah asked, suspecting she was homeless.

"I live any place I can find, but I was born in the palace of the Great King," she said with pride.

"You were born in the King's palace?" Hadassah asked.

"I sure was," she said, wiping her mouth on her filthy sleeve. "Not only was I born in the palace, but the King Himself named me."

"The King named you Sunshine?" Beloved asked.

"Well, actually He named me Bethany. But I liked Sunshine better, so that's what I go by."

"My name used to be Forsaken, but the King changed it to Beloved."

"I like your new name much better."

"Yeah, me too. And I like Bethany. If it ain't no bother, I'll call you Bethany, since that's the name the King gave you."

The girl shrugged. "Makes no difference to me what you call me."

"How long did you live in the palace?" Hadassah asked, hoping the girl could help them find the King.

"I left just after my thirteenth birthday. Been wandering the streets for just over a year now."

"Why would anyone want to leave the King?" Hadassah asked.

"I wanted to make my own decisions, and I wanted to find out for myself what love looks like," she said, tossing the apple core over her shoulder. Rubbing the second apple on her sleeve, she continued,

"But mostly, I wanted to have some fun. Not that I didn't have fun with the King and His people. But I wanted to have fun the way I wanted it to be. So I decided to leave, and the King let me go."

Apple juice ran down her dirty hands. She licked it off.

"So, did you find it?" Hadassah asked.

"Find what?"

"Love. You said you wanted to find out what love looks like. Did you?"

"Nope, I can't say that I did. I found what some folks called love, but I can tell you for a fact that it isn't anything like the King's love. He told me once that the only true love is unselfish love, but I didn't believe Him. Now I know better. I've learned a lot of lessons this past year, lessons I don't want to repeat."

"What are you gonna do now?" Beloved asked.

"Actually, I'm on my way back home, to the palace," she said, tossing what little was left of the second core behind her.

"Will the King let you?" Beloved asked.

"Oh, He always lets you come back! I've seen Him throw His arms around men and women who've done worse things than I've done. You got anymore apples?"

Beloved studied the girl as Hadassah handed her another apple.

"Thanks. I've always been an independent sort, I guess. So was my mama. She died about the same time I took my first breath. I don't even know who my papa is.

"The King said He found my mama walking the streets getting into things that would harm her, so He offered her true love. Knowing I was growing in her belly, she had sense enough to accept His offer. He brought her into His home and loved her like His very own daughter. He said she was beautiful and very kind. He also said my mama really loved me. I sure wish I could've known her." Bethany looked away, tears glistening on her eyelashes.

"I can rightly say I know how you feel," Beloved said, laying her hand on the girl's arm.

Wiping her eyes with the back of her hand, Bethany continued, "The King told me many times that I was His princess, but I never believed Him. I felt like anything but a princess. I used to ask Him how I could be a princess when I didn't even know who my papa was."

"What'd He say?" Beloved asked.

"He said that a princess is made not born. I never understood that, and I still don't — not really."

"The King sure sounds like someone I'd never want to leave," Hadassah said, thinking aloud.

"You say that, but people do it all the time. As for me, I felt sorry for myself because I was an orphan. I pretended like I didn't need anyone or anything. I was blind to the fact that the King really was all I needed.

"Thankfully He wastes nothing — not even our mistakes — and He will redeem everything I bring to Him. That's why I'm going back home. I've got a lot of garbage to give Him."

"May I be so bold," Hadassah said, taking a deep breath, "as to ask if we can come with you? We've been trying to find His palace, but we just discovered that we've been walking in circles."

"There's only one Way and only One Person who can lead you to the King, and it's not me."

"So you won't take us?" Hadassah asked, trying to hide her disappointment.

"I didn't say that. I was merely pointing out the truth that Life-Giver is the only way to the King."

"You know Life-Giver?"

"Of course I do. I lived with the King, remember?" she said. Hadassah detected what she perceived to be a hint of arrogance.

Hadassah answered, "I just didn't think that Life-Giver would . . . I didn't think that He lived . . . oh, I don't know what I was thinking."

"If you know Life-Giver, then you know that He's the King's Son. Like Father, like Son. Life-Giver is *exactly* like the Great King. He does nothing apart from His Father. Never have you seen a more obedient, selfless Son or a more caring, loving Father."

"I know very little about the King. What little I know I learned from Life-Giver. I long to know more, that's why we're searching for Him. We did meet a Man named Emmanuel who told Beloved that He's the King."

"You met Emmanuel?" Bethany asked, giving them her full attention.

"Yeah. You know Him?" asked Beloved.

"If you know the King, you know Emmanuel — They're one and the same."

"I told you!" Beloved exclaimed, playfully punching Hadassah's arm.

"You did tell me. I just find it so very hard to believe."

"Why?" Bethany asked.

"Because He didn't look like what I thought the King would look like."

"Was it His frayed and worn clothing? Or His meekness? Or friendliness? Or perhaps it was His common speech that made it difficult for you to believe He was the King?"

"It was probably all of those things."

"Hadassah, in this kingdom, in case you don't know this, it's never wise to judge by outward appearances — to do so will almost always prove you wrong. It's most important to see with the eyes of your heart, for that's the only way to know truth. And the truth is the Great King is meek and lowly of heart, a Servant to all," said Bethany.

"How'd you get so wise?" Hadassah asked, amazed by her insights, which were well beyond her years.

"I did grow up in the King's palace, you know," she said with a smug look.

Pride, a grotesque, snake-like creature, held tightly to Bethany's arm.

This girl thinks way too highly of herself, thought Hadassah.

Bethany looked up. Hadassah turned away.

"Jealousy is a dangerous friend," Bethany said.

Rolling her eyes, Hadassah turned her back to the two girls.

Bethany said, "Hadassah, ignoring the problem won't make it go away."

"Just who do you think you are?" Hadassah said, spinning on her heels. "You don't have the right to correct me!"

Jealousy laid its slimy arm around Hadassah's shoulder and pulled her close. The red-eyed creature grinned from ear to ear, green drool oozing out of its large mouth.

Hadassah reached down for Beloved's hand and said, "Come on, let's leave this girl to herself."

Beloved looked up with tears in her eyes. "But . . . we don't know the way."

Bethany stared at the two girls. "Well?" she asked.

"You talk as if you have conquered your weaknesses. Well, I've got news for you — you think you have all the answers, but *no one* has *all* the answers," Hadassah said.

"Well, actually you're wrong. There is Someone who —"

Hadassah interrupted. "There you go again."

"You're right, Hadassah. Trying to 'fix' people is one of my weaknesses. I'm working on it. Please forgive me."

Pride cringed.

Hadassah took a deep breath.

"Are we gonna stand round here talkin' all day?" Beloved asked, trying to diffuse the situation.

Bethany shrugged her shoulders. "I'm sorry, Hadassah. What do you say we start over? I don't mean to be so prideful. I'd be glad to lead the way and have your company."

Hadassah took another deep breath and forced herself to respond. "Sorry."

Beloved grabbed their hands and said, "What are we waitin' for?"

With Beloved in the middle, the trio set out. "Bethany?" Beloved asked.

"Yes?"

"Do you think the King'll let me in His palace?"

"Of course He will. It's your destiny," Bethany said.

"What's destiny?"

"Destiny is the King's plans for your life."

"How do you know it's my destiny?"

"Because the King wants everyone to be with Him. He wants to be close to you."

Hadassah interrupted. "An intimate relationship with the King? I have a fairly close relationship with Life-Giver, but I can't imagine having that with the Great King. The most I'm hoping for is to be able to spend one day with Him. I can't even imagine someone as powerful as the King taking the time to talk with me, much less having a relationship with Him."

"That's where you've judged Him wrongly. The Great King loves the least the most! And didn't you say you met Emmanuel?"

"Yes."

"Well, He's the King."

"He was easy to talk to because I didn't know who He was. He wore rags and acted like a servant and cooked porridge," Hadassah said.

"The Great King is a Servant at heart, so you have nothing to fear."

Hadassah slowed her pace. Beloved and Bethany were having such a great time talking they did not notice Hadassah lagging behind.

"Life-Giver, I sure hope it's true that Emmanuel's the King, because if that's true, then I don't have anything to worry about."

Life-Giver responded, "Throughout history My Father and I came to mankind in disguise so they could receive Our love."

"I'm sorry for wavering. Why's it so hard for me to believe You could love me like this?"

"It's difficult because you still do not believe you are worthy and because you do not truly know Me."

"How do I overcome my past? I can't change it or rewrite it. It is what it is."

"That is true. You can't change it. But you can change your perspective and your response to it."

"How do I do that?"

"Bring those memories to Me and allow Me to show you the truth. The memories are not the source of your pain. The source of your pain is what you believe to be true about those events. For example, you do not really believe that I was with you during your slavery. Allow Me to open your eyes to see where I was and what I was doing."

His words instantly brought an image of the nobleman to the forefront of her mind. Her heart raced as her palms grew sweaty.

Fear licked its lips and rubbed its hands together as it tightened its grip on her heart.

Hadassah only vaguely sensed the dark creature.

A large creature named Anxiety pressed against her chest.

"Hadassah, use the eyes of your heart, your imagination, and look around that memory and find Me; I was there with you."

Hadassah stopped walking and leaned against a post. Painful images of that time filled her mind. She felt the same sick feeling in the pit of her stomach that she felt when she was there.

"Look around the room, Hadassah. I was there," Life-Giver repeated.

To her surprise, she saw Him standing in the middle of the room, His arms outstretched. Hadassah saw herself run into them. As He held her tight, He said, "I know this is very painful, but I will see you through and deliver you. One day, I will make all things new — even this." He sang softly. As He did, Hadassah could feel the old, familiar pain, anguish and fear fade away.

As suddenly as the memory came, it left. Hadassah opened her eyes. She felt strange, really strange. It took her a few moments to get her bearings. And when she did, she realized that she felt as though a load of rocks had been lifted from her chest. She felt herself smiling. As she thought back to the memory of the nobleman, for the first time ever, she felt nothing but peace. "Thank You, Life-Giver," she said, tears streaming down her face.

"I have redeemed even this," He said.

Fear and Anxiety retreated, waiting for a more opportune time.

Hadassah looked up the street. Bethany and Beloved were almost out of sight. Wiping her face on her skirt, she set out after them.

Beloved turned and shouted, "Hurry, Hadassah! We've found the gate!"

Hadassah ran. She found the two of them standing in front of a gate that was even smaller and narrower than the first gate she went through. Bethany announced, "This is it."

"This is what?" Hadassah asked.

"The gate."

"This tiny gate leads to the palace?"

"Not exactly, but it's the entrance to the Inner Court. We must travel through the Inner Court and then to the Holy of Holies."

"Please tell me there's a shortcut."

"There's no shortcut. There's only one way to the King," Bethany answered.

Hadassah said, "I had hoped we were almost there."

"We are."

"Then the path through the Inner Court is short?"

"That remains to be seen."

"But you just said — what do you mean?"

"The path is different for everyone. And no matter how many times a person travels on it, it's always different. That's why I can't tell you how long our journey will take."

"This is sad news indeed," Hadassah said.

"It's good news, Hadassah. We're gettin' closer," Beloved said, taking her hand.

Bethany pushed open the squeaky gate. "Sounds like it's been awhile since anyone's opened it," she said.

"I sure hope you know where we're going," Hadassah said as she shut the gate behind her.

"Of course I know. Do you think I'm stupid or something?"

"I didn't say you were stupid," Hadassah snapped back.

Beloved quickly stepped in front of Bethany and asked, "Bethany, how many times did you run away?"

Bethany took a deep breath, stole a glance at Hadassah and then turned her attention to Beloved, saying, "The thing about this kingdom is that if you've thought it in your heart it's the same as actually doing it. I ran away too many times to count."

Hadassah was surprised by the sadness she saw in Bethany's eyes. Her heart softened. "Do you feel guilty?" she asked, trying to smooth over her bad attitude.

"I did until the King told me there was no room for guilt in His kingdom. He said guilt was a thief and no thieves were allowed in His land."

"What's that mean?" Beloved asked.

"He told me that guilt steals the things that really matter — like joy and peace and confidence. He said that anything that robs me of His nature is not to be allowed in my life."

"So how'd you get rid of it?" Hadassah asked.

"Once I knew the King hated it, I simply gave it to Life-Giver. And when I did, He gave me a blood-stained parchment decreeing my innocence. It felt so good to be free."

"I wish Life-Giver would just make all the changes needed in my heart with a snap of His fingers or a wave of His hand," Hadassah said, more to herself than to Bethany.

"You're not alone in wishing that, but that requires no relationship or trust. The King longs for an intimate relationship with His children," said Bethany, leading the way.

"Hadassah appears to still be distressed," Michael observed.

"She is afraid," the Spirit said.

"Afraid of what?"

"She is afraid of many things, but mostly she is afraid to discover that she is a woman of great destiny," the Spirit said, hovering in both realms.

"I would think she would be delighted to realize the truth of her greatness."

"Michael, humans often concern themselves with matters that angels never give thought to. For Hadassah to accept the truth that she is destined for greatness would mean she would have to walk in excellence, and that scares her more than anything. As long as she believes she is ordinary then she can remain as she is, which means she would never achieve the greatness destined for her."

"Excuse my ignorance, but it seems to me that humans become proud when the King bestows greatness on them."

"That can happen, but greatness does not have to result in pride — Life-Giver is a perfect example of that. Never was there One as great and never was there One so humble. The key to resisting pride is to remember the Source that enables the greatness and to respond with gratitude, which is exactly what Life-Giver did. He did nothing except what He saw His Father do and then He gave His Father the glory.

"True humility says, 'I am glorious because I belong to the One who is glorious, and my glory is merely reflected glory. I am who I am because of His grace.' Hadassah is afraid to discover that she is glorious, so she hides her light behind all manner of things."

Michael recited the words Life-Giver spoke while living on the earth, "'Let your light shine before men that they may see your good works and glorify your Father in heaven.' She does not know nor does she understand that she is like the moon reflecting the glory of the sun."

"She will, Michael. One day she will know, and she will shine brightly in the face of great darkness."

CHAPTER TWENTY-THREE

*B*ethany navigated the narrow path with a very excited Beloved close by her side. Neither noticed that Hadassah lagged behind. And neither did they perceive the two dark creatures that jumped on Hadassah's back the moment she stepped onto the path.

Coming to a pool of fresh water, they stopped for a drink. That was when they noticed Hadassah had fallen behind.

Beloved ran back to her. "Hadassah, you look sad," Beloved said.

"I'm fine," Hadassah said, looking away.

"No, you're not," Bethany said. "What's wrong?"

"I don't want to talk about it."

"Why not?"

"Because I don't."

The creatures rubbed their hands together.

Beloved, head down, walked the rest of the way in silence.

Hadassah knelt by the water and splashed her face.

One of the creatures whispered in her ear. "Hadassah, look at Bethany and Beloved. They have such pure hearts. Now take a good look at yourself. You're nothing special. As a matter of fact, you're extremely selfish. All you care about is getting to the palace of the King."

She dried her face on her skirt.

What am I thinking? she asked herself.

Hadassah was startled when the voice answered, *"You need me. You don't want to be disappointed again, do you? I will protect you from that."*

"Is this the voice of the King or me or something else?"

"I am Self-Protection."

"Uh . . . Life-Giver's my Protector," she said, struggling with the fact that she was conversing with someone she could not identify.

"Then where is he?"

"He's here," Hadassah said looking around. "I just can't see Him."

An obese creature named Guilt whispered, "He's not here because you're not worthy. Have you so quickly forgotten how you turned your back on that poor, defenseless, dying child? You're kidding yourself if you think the King will ever accept the likes of you."

Hadassah cringed. The creature knew her secret. Unable to come up with an excuse, she said nothing. *As a result, Guilt increased in size.* Hadassah felt its weight pressing against her shoulders and back.

"I've been forgiven for that," she said to herself.

"Are you sure? How do you know? You're guilty of so much," Guilt said.

Bethany was just talking to me about guilt, Hadassah thought. *What did she say? Something about the King not letting guilt in His kingdom.*

"The king's a judge who punishes the guilty. And you're a child-killer," the voice of Guilt said.

"I am not!" Hadassah said aloud.

"You're not what?" Bethany asked.

"Nothing."

"Who you talkin' to?" Beloved asked.

"Nobody."

Bethany studied her face. "I've learned from experience that the more I pursued the King the more voices I heard trying to discourage me. And the most common accusation was that I wasn't good enough."

"It's true," Hadassah said.

"What? That you're not good enough?"

"Yeah."

"How can anyone be good enough to deserve the amazing gift of unconditional love that the King offers?" Bethany asked.

"I've heard this before, but I just can't seem to overcome my —"

"Your lack of perfection?"

"I guess so."

"Who told you that you had to be perfect?"

"I don't know. I don't want to talk about this anymore," she said, sitting on a large rock by the water's edge. "I'm so frustrated that this journey's taking so long, and it's much more difficult than I ever dreamed. And I'm tired. I know this is stupid and I won't do it, but everything in me wants to turn around and return to my sister and friends."

Beloved wrapped her bony arm around Hadassah's thin shoulders and said, "You can't go back! Please don't leave me!"

Guilt squeezed Hadassah's chest, whispering in her ear, "This is the very child you let die without any comfort or ease. You don't deserve her affection."

Be quiet, Hadassah silently responded.

"If the pitiful wench knew what you're really like she certainly wouldn't be begging you to stay."

"Don't fret, child, I'm not going anywhere," Hadassah said, prying Beloved's arm from her.

Standing up, Hadassah walked away and sat down beneath a large oak tree. "Life-Giver, are You here?"

"Michael, Gabriel, guardian angels."

"Yes, Life-Giver," they said in unison.

"Look how beautiful Hadassah is!"

"I am confused, my Lord. At this moment, she does not appear very beautiful. She is filled with doubt and unbelief," Michael said.

Gabriel added, "And she is self-focused."

"She is growing like the dawn. She is learning to trust My saving grace, which is important, because she will not love One she does not trust."

"But she has nothing to fear, my Lord," Gabriel said.

"You and I know that, but she fears facing the truth about herself more than any other thing."

"Shall we deliver her from her accusers?" Michael asked, sword lifted high.

"No, My warrior, this is another one of those battles she must fight."

"Hadassah, you can't quit! Remember — you got that scroll," Beloved said standing in front of her, hands on her hips.

"Here — you can have it," Hadassah said, thrusting the scroll against Beloved's belly. "You deserve it more than me. After all, you're the one the dove came to. You're the one Life-Giver calls Beloved." Beloved allowed the scroll to fall to the ground.

Self-Protection and Guilt pressed with all their might against her mind and emotions in an effort to control her will.

"Hadassah, I didn't find this scroll, you did. It's yours. Now get up and fight," Beloved said, kicking the scroll toward her.

Guilt pressed harder.

"I'm too tired to care anymore," Hadassah said.

Not knowing what else to say, Beloved looked to Bethany for help.

Bethany stepped closer. "Life-Giver isn't the One accusing you. Hadassah, you're the one accusing yourself."

"What do you mean?"

"Did you and your sisters not leave your home fully expecting that the three of you would journey to the King's palace and spend a day with Him?"

"How'd you know that?"

Ignoring her question, Bethany continued, "And you encountered various troubles along the way and —"

"To put it mildly," she interrupted.

"And now you're wallowing in self-pity. It's really yourself you're disappointed with."

The two stared at each other. After a moment, tears formed in Hadassah's eyes. She looked away. *Life-Giver, please help me*, she silently whispered.

With a nod from Life-Giver, Michael cut off the head of Guilt.

Beloved threw her arms around Hadassah's waist and held her close. "Oh, Hadassah, please don't cry! It's gonna be okay, 'cuz Life-Giver keeps His eyes on the sparrows and in His presence is joy," Beloved cried.

Hadassah laid her hand on the child's arm. "What do you mean?"

"I don't know; I just heard Him say to tell you that."

Taking a deep breath, Hadassah closed her eyes and said, "Life-Giver, help me. I surrender. I can't fight this alone."

Life-Giver glanced at Michael and nodded. The archangel instantly grabbed Self-Protection by the neck, pulling the creature off of her. Then he threw it into a bottomless pit.

Life-Giver whispered, "Hadassah, the only way out is through." Then He dropped what appeared to be a tiny seed into Hadassah's heart, and faith took root. "Faith instead of fear," He said.

"Hadassah, please don't give up," said Beloved.

"Don't fret over me, dear child. Bethany has spoken the truth. I've secretly felt guilty, so I hid behind my self-righteous confidence. But the truth is I proved myself to be unworthy before I ever stepped through the stone gate. You see, little one, I haven't been able to forgive myself or others for so many things." Falling to her knees and covering her face with her hands, Hadassah sobbed uncontrollably.

"Hadassah, please don't cry," Beloved pleaded.

Bethany prayed while Beloved buried her face in Hadassah's skirt and cried with her.

Michael noticed Self-Condemnation lurking in the shadows. One glance from Life-Giver sealed the creature's fate. Michael shouted, "For the King and for His kingdom!" He drove his sword through the demon's heart. In response, numerous creatures stepped out of the darkness hissing and spitting and vomiting. Michael grabbed Self-Pity by the throat and broke its neck. Holy angels fought the hordes of hell, securing Hadassah's deliverance.

Life-Giver looked directly into the eyes of her Accuser. "Satan!" He said.

The evil one stepped out of the darkness. "Yes?"

"You are a liar and the father of all lies, and you are a defeated foe." Satan reluctantly bowed before His Maker.

Gabriel, who had been holding back a demon named Self-Focus, lifted his fiery sword over its head and delivered a swift blow to the grotesque creature. All around him, demons of every size and purpose fell to the ground like flies. Disappointment and Discouragement were among them.

Life-Giver turned His holy eyes of love back to Hadassah. He took her in His arms and whispered, "Hadassah, you are not and never have been a disappointment to Me. I knew what I was getting when I chose you. I do not expect you to be what you are not. You cannot be your own Savior, and neither are you perfect. I died to be those things for you."

Hadassah felt His presence and heard His words. *I sure feel like a disappointment.*

"Disappointment only comes if One has expectations that are different from reality. I always know what you will do; therefore My expectations are always based on reality not on hope, which means it is impossible to disappoint Me."

"That's good news."

"My precious handmaiden, does a mother and father not delight in their infant even though that babe has much to learn and much to overcome? I see the end from the beginning, so I see who you will be. I take great delight in every stage of your maturity. That means you can have confidence and be at peace in each stage of growth. Allow My Spirit to prepare you for eternity. That is not your job, child. You cannot and never will be My Spirit, so please stop trying to do His work. Instead, rest in His power to complete and perfect that which He has begun in you.

"I understand your desire to please Me, but striving is not the way to do so. You please Me most when you surrender, when you give up and say, 'I can't, but You can.' My precious child, you are and always will be a delight and a joy to Me — not because of your performance but because of who you are. I am not asking you to be great, but I am asking you to forget your unworthiness and define yourself as one loved by Me. That is your identity."

Hadassah sighed long and deep.

"Carry this truth in your heart and allow it to grow into a tree of life that it might bring forth much fruit."

"And so I shall . . . with Your Spirit's help, that is." Hadassah felt His presence slowly diminishing. "I love You and thank You."

"It is My pleasure to give you the kingdom."

Lifting her head, she wiped her eyes on the hem of her skirt. Beloved looked up at her. Hadassah smiled. Taking a deep breath, she turned toward Bethany and said, "You're right. I've been terribly disappointed with myself to the point I felt disqualified. Even though I was consumed with the desire to spend a day with the King, I felt so guilty that I secretly feared meeting Him. I was afraid He'd reject me or worse — expose me for the hypocrite I believed I was. But, as strange as this may sound, something just happened, something I can't explain and don't fully understand."

"What?" Beloved asked, her eyes displaying her eagerness to know.

"Life-Giver just set me free from my guilt, self-condemnation and much more. I no longer fear His rejection or displeasure. For the first time in my life I truly feel at peace with the fact that I'm not now nor will I ever be perfect . . . not on this earth, that is. So I announce to both heaven and earth that I'm not 'good enough.' I give up! From this day forward, I will focus on being 'His' and on the fact that I am loved!"

Lifting her eyes, she continued, "I'm the moon and You're the sun. The moon has no light of its own but is completely dependent upon the sun to do what it was created to do — simply reflect light. With Your help, I want to spend the rest of my days reflecting Your beauty and Your light! I want to show the world just how great You are!"

Hadassah stood to her feet. With a smile on her face, she said, "Shall we continue?"

"Let's go," Beloved said.

Hadassah took Bethany's hand and said, "Thanks."

"For what?"

"For speaking the truth."

"Sure."

Hadassah said, "When I lived near the garbage dump, I found two scrolls. One was an invitation to spend a day with the King and the other was a riddle. My dear sister read it to me until I memorized it. It read, 'Seek the Great King while He may be found; call upon Him while He is near. You shall go out with joy and be led forth with peace. Enter by the narrow gate; for the gate is wide and the way is broad that leads to destruction, and many are those who enter by it. The gate is small and the way is narrow that leads to life, and few are those who find it.' That's the path I want to walk on."

Beloved responded by clapping her hands together and jumping up and down. "Hadassah, we're walkin' on the path your scroll talked about!"

Hadassah said, "I believe we are, Beloved. I've gone through three gates. The first one was the gate David and Naomi led me to, which took me through the wilderness. The second was the gate to the Outer Court, where I met Emmanuel and both of you. The third has led us here. Each time, the gate and the path get narrower. I would guess we only have one more gate to go through. Is that right, Bethany?"

"You're right."

"Let's keep goin' then," Beloved said.

Smiling broadly, Hadassah said, "Let's keep goin'."

The three followed the narrow but well-worn path through the meadow. As they walked, Beloved asked Bethany, "Why'd you go from callin' yourself Bethany to callin' yourself Sunshine?"

"For as long as I can remember the King sang a song to me called, 'You Are My Sunshine.' When I was a child, I believed it was true. As I grew older, I became quite cynical and found myself doubting that I could be anyone's sunshine. Only recently have I come to believe that I might have a right to shine."

"I guess we all struggle with feeling like we're not good enough," Hadassah said.

"Yeah, I guess we do," said Bethany.

"I've always known I wasn't good enough for nothin' 'cept what folks decided they wanted to do to me," Beloved said.

"But you know better now, right?" Bethany asked.

"Yeah. Life-Giver told me I'm special and loved, but sometimes I still feel like a good-for-nothin'."

"The Great King will make sure you know the truth," Bethany said. "What exactly do you two know about the King?"

"Not much," Hadassah answered.

"I know He don't yell at folks when they break His things," Beloved added.

Both girls laughed.

"Well, He don't," Beloved said.

"You're right, Beloved," Hadassah said, laying her hand on the child's shoulder.

Turning to face Bethany, Beloved said, "That's why we're headed to the palace. We wanna know Him, not just hear about Him."

Bethany said, "This journey will bring us face to face with truth. And part of that truth is that no one has the right to tell you who you are except the One who created you."

Beloved exclaimed, "I ain't ever known who I was or exactly where I came from. I'm sure the King'll be nice in His describin' me, 'cuz He's kind to Or Fans. Oops, I forgot — Emmanuel said I ain't no Or Fan anymore."

Hadassah thought long and hard about what Bethany said. On one hand, she felt excited to find out who she really was, but on the other hand she was afraid. She pondered the question for the rest of the day. *What if I'm even worse than I think I am? Stop it, Hadassah. Don't embrace that old way of thinking. Life-Giver said it is His responsibility to make me beautiful.*

Hadassah looked at Bethany. She appeared to be at perfect peace — she was in no hurry, appeared to have no agenda or ulterior motives. Neither was she striving to be something she was not. "You seem so mature," Hadassah said, "to be so young."

"I've seen and experienced much in my short life, which has a way of causing one to grow up fast," Bethany answered. "In many ways, I'm just like you. It isn't important who I am. What is most important is Who I know."

"Michael, summon the angels, for Satan is relentless in his pursuit," Life-Giver ordered.

"As You command, my Lord," Michael said.

"And Michael."

"Yes?"

"In the end, perfect Love wins."

CHAPTER TWENTY-FOUR

$\mathcal{T}$he path through the meadow led directly into a dark forest. The light was so dim that it was nearly impossible to see more than a few steps ahead.

"Now I understand why people in the Outer Court are content to stay there," Hadassah said, fighting her way through a large spider web.

"I told you to stay behind me," Bethany said, laughing softly.

"I know, but I got distracted."

"Distractions are one of Satan's tools."

"Tell me, truthfully, will we find the King in the Inner Court, or will I have to wait until we get to the Holy of Holies?" Hadassah asked, removing the web from her hair.

"He's everywhere, Hadassah," Beloved said. "And when we find Him, I'm gonna sit on His lap."

"What if He doesn't let little girls sit on His lap?" Hadassah teased. "He is a King, you know."

"He's gotta like little girls sittin' on His lap, 'cuz He's a good Papa — that's what Life-Giver told me."

"Life-Giver's right. He's *always* right. The King is the best Papa there is, and He *loves* little girls with the purest of love. You don't have anything to worry about," said Bethany.

"And He *never* hurts little girls," Beloved said.

"It's impossible for Him to do so," said Bethany, pushing through a thick wall of vines. She came to an abrupt halt, for she stood on the edge of a great precipice. To her right, the path led up a steep slope, and to her left the path went straight down.

"Be careful," she shouted over her shoulder, "we're on the edge of a high mountain."

"How'd we get on a mountain?" Beloved asked.

"Sometimes the journey is so gradual that you don't realize you're climbing," Bethany said. "But have no fear; we'll just follow the well-worn path of those who've gone before us."

"Sometimes you don't seem real," Hadassah said.

"What do you mean?"

"Well, you always know what to do and you always have the answers."

"I guess I learned more from living with the King than I realized."

"I'm afraid," Beloved said, clutching Hadassah's skirt.

"It's okay. Just don't look down," Hadassah said.

"We'll go slow," said Bethany.

With every step they took, the three prayed. With their backs against the mountainside, they inched their way along the narrow ledge. Hadassah said, "In case you haven't noticed the sun's going to set soon, and we won't be able to see."

"Yeah, I noticed," Bethany said.

"And for once you don't have a solution or an answer?"

"Hadassah, that wasn't very kind," Beloved said.

"You're right, Beloved. Please forgive me, Bethany. I'm just scared."

"I understand and forgive you. And you're right — I don't have an answer. We can't continue on this path in the dark. And we can't sleep here; there's barely enough room to walk. Now would be a good time to pray."

"We already are," Hadassah said.

"I delight in doing the impossible," Life-Giver said.

"Oh my!" Bethany said.

"What?" Hadassah asked, holding her breath.

"I think our prayers have been heard."

Having stepped around the bend, Bethany could see that the footpath led into a forest. "Thank You," Hadassah whispered.

"You are most welcome," Life-Giver answered.

Just as the sun slid over the treetops, the three entered the forest. Collapsing on the leaf-covered ground, Hadassah took a deep breath and realized just how frightened she had been. She silently prayed, *Life-Giver, I want to be strong and trust You, but I find myself faltering every time something difficult comes my way. Why do I get discouraged and fearful so quickly?*

"Just don't give up, just don't give in and you will win," He said.

Suddenly the hair on Hadassah's neck stood straight up as a cold chill ran down her spine. A dark and foreboding presence hovered over her. Grabbing Bethany's hand, Hadassah whispered, "What evil lurks in this forest?"

"I don't wanna know," Beloved answered, clutching her arm.

"One must know their enemy if they're to win the battle," Bethany said.

"But I don't wanna fight," Beloved whispered.

"Who goes there?" Bethany shouted.

Deep, dark silence shouted back.

"I'm really scared," Beloved whispered.

"So am I," said Hadassah.

If Hadassah and Beloved had looked with the eyes of their heart, they would have seen that an army of powerful angels surrounded them. But, alas, Bethany was the only one who saw them.

"Let's go back," Hadassah whispered, tugging on Bethany's sleeve.

"We can't go back. There's no way we could navigate that path in the dark. And the King has sent His angels to be with us," said Bethany. "You don't really want to go back, do you?"

"Maybe," Hadassah answered. "Something's out there, Bethany. I can feel it. It's really evil and I don't like it!"

"Hadassah," Beloved said, squeezing her arm, "I'm scared too, but we can't go back."

"Your past cannot hurt you, because I am there. Your present is secure, because I am here. Your future is nothing to be feared, because I have already been there. Trust Me."

A fierce wind suddenly descended on the forest assaulting everything in its path. Trees groaned as their limbs bent and cracked from the intensity of the storm. Streaks of lightning raced across the sky as thunder shook the ground. "We really should go back," Hadassah shouted.

"I've learned to never run from my fears," Bethany shouted back.

Fear fought desperately to control Hadassah's emotions.

"Life-Giver, we need Your help!" Beloved shouted, her tiny voice lost to all, save One.

"Gabriel, spread your wings over them," Life-Giver commanded.

"It is done, my Lord."

"Michael, drive Satan from this place," He ordered.

Michael took a stand in front of Satan and ordered him to leave.

"On whose authority?" he asked.

"The Lord rebuke you, Satan!" Michael responded.

His words caused Satan to recoil. Hissing and spitting, he reluctantly withdrew, disappearing into the darkness.

With the crash of a lightning bolt, Bethany spotted a hollow tree trunk. "Follow me," she shouted, grabbing Beloved's hand.

There was only room for two inside the trunk. All three tried to be the one left out. Beloved won, for she wiggled her way out of Bethany's grip and quickly scampered beneath the shelter of a nearby bush.

The Great King stood before Beloved.

"I know this feelin'," Beloved said to herself. She thought back to the day she died — the beautiful Man, the beings of light, the complete absence of fear and the overwhelming sense of being loved. "I know what this is . . . well, I sorta know what it is," she said to herself.

Beloved's spiritual eyes were opened, and she looked up into the eyes of a beautiful, white-haired Man. "Emmanuel," she said as she ran out from under the bush. She was shocked to find that the rain had stopped and she was bathed in beautiful light.

"Emmanuel?" she repeated.

"What is it, child?"

"You're the Great King, ain't You?"

"I am."

"And You're my Papa, ain't You?"

"I am."

"And You're here with me?"

"I am always with you."

"Always?"

"Yes, always."

"Even when I'm bad?"

"You are never bad, child, for all that I made is good. You have made a few bad choices, but that does not make you bad."

"But sometimes I feel like I'm bad."

"Just because you feel bad does not make it true. When you find yourself feeling less than who I say you are, do not ignore those thoughts or try to talk yourself out of them, but rather give them to Me."

"What will You do with them?"

"I will throw them into the deepest ocean never to be seen again."

"Papa?"

"Yes, My precious child?"

"Why'd You pick me to be Your Beloved?"

"I saw you, therefore I loved you."

"You loved me just 'cuz You saw me?"

"Exactly."

Tears pooled in her eyes as she thought back over her short, pain-filled life. *"Most folks make fun of me when they see me. I ain't never had anybody love me just 'cuz they saw me."*

"I am so sorry that you were not loved the way you deserved to be."

"Thank You for lovin' me even though I'm not pretty."

"You are better than pretty — you are beautiful!"

Beloved paused.

"I am?" she asked.

"You are."

"It's hard to feel beautiful when you got scars all over your face."

"Scars cannot take away your beauty, because true beauty comes from the heart. One day those scars will be gone forever."

"I'll be glad when that happens."

"I look forward to that day, too, My precious child."

"Papa?"

"Yes, child?"

"Are you tired of my questions?"

Chuckling, He answered, *"No, never."*

"Why not?"

"Because I am the Answer."

"Hmmm. I gotta think about that for awhile," she said, tilting her head sideways and smiled. "Okay, I'm done thinkin' about it. . . Papa?"

"Yes, dear child of Mine?"

"I love You."

"I love you, too, child, more than you will ever know while on this earth."

Emmanuel opened His arms, and she ran into them. He held her close, closer than she could have ever imagined. And for the first time, she felt completely satisfied through and through.

The vision ended and Beloved heard someone calling her name. Hadassah grabbed her, shouting, "Beloved, what are you doing?"

"I was just —" Beloved looked up. "Look! Hadassah, Bethany! Don't you see them?"

"See what?" Hadassah asked, looking around.

"The beings of light! They're everywhere and so many — too many to count! And they have swords and they're —"

"They're what?" Hadassah asked, feeling a bit frustrated that she couldn't see whatever Beloved was seeing.

"They're cuttin' off the heads of dark, ugly creatures," Beloved whispered.

"I wish you hadn't told me that," Hadassah said.

"I wish I hadn't seen that."

"Come on, let's get out of this rain," Hadassah said, grabbing her hand and dragging her back toward the tree. Beloved yanked her hand free and ducked beneath the bush.

Hadassah snuggled close to Bethany, who asked, "Like I said, how will you win this battle if you don't know and can't see your enemy?"

"What battle?" Hadassah asked.

"The battle you entered the day you accepted Life-Giver's offer to be part of His family. Until you understand we're at war, not much in this life will make sense."

"What are you talking about?" Hadassah asked.

"When you see a starving child, dressed in rags — do you accuse the King of not taking care of her? Or when death takes a loved one or your dreams lie in a heap at your feet, do you blame the King?

When people do evil things to the innocent, do you recognize that man was given a free will? The King never forces anyone to do the right thing."

"Right."

Bethany continued, "Hadassah, this world's at war and innocent people get hurt and even die, but that doesn't make it the King's fault, now does it? Whose fault is it?"

When Hadassah did not respond, Bethany went on, "Satan hates you because the King loves you, and his goal is to destroy as many humans as possible. He makes grand promises and then devours those who are naïve, gullible, greedy or lazy enough to believe him. He tempts and deceives people to do terrible things to the innocent. The truth is the war has already been won, but the battle continues."

"Where did you acquire such knowledge?" Hadassah asked.

"A very old King shared it with me," Bethany said smiling.

Hadassah stared out at the darkness. The wind picked up as the lightning continued to split the sky. Hadassah felt increasingly anxious, but Beloved was at peace because she had seen Emmanuel. He loved her and promised to always be with her. Closing her eyes, she prayed, "Papa, I love You so much. Thank You for thinkin' I'm beautiful."

"Do you trust Me?" the King asked Beloved.

"Yeah."

"There is no greater love than to die so another can live."

"Just like Life-Giver?"

"Yes, dear one, just like He did. He was born to die and so were you. Will you give Me your life?"

"I already did."

"In a general sense you did, but will you lay your life down so another can live?"

"If I do, will that mean I get to be with You?"

"Yes, My dear one, you will get to be with Me forever."

"There's nothin' I'd rather have than that. So I'll do it, but I don't know what it is I'm s'posed to do."

"All of you for all of Me," the King said. *"All I ever wanted was to love you."*

Beloved looked around. The King's voice was so clear that she was certain He was present. But He was nowhere in sight. "Papa?"

"Yes, child," the Great King answered.

"Just checkin' to see if You're still here."

The King chuckled. "Beloved, I won't ever leave you."

Eager to share what had just happened, Beloved climbed out from under the bush. Stinging rain pelted her face, but she barely noticed. "Hadassah," she shouted.

Hadassah looked up. Before Beloved could say anything a dark figure crept out of the thick brush. Hadassah did not see it, but Beloved did. The drooling animal fixed its red eyes on Hadassah. In one swift move, Beloved threw herself between the creature and her dearest friend.

At that exact moment, a flash of blinding light accompanied by the largest clap of thunder any of them had ever heard filled the air. Eerie silence followed.

"Papa?"

"Yes, child?"

"Just checkin' to see if You're still here."

"I am not going anywhere, child, for I am everywhere — all of the time."

"What does that mean exactly?"

"I am everywhere, so where can I go that I am not?"

"Will You stay with me?"

"I will, child."

"Will You hold me?"

"I am."

"Will You hold me tighter?"

"I would love to," the Great King said.

Michael, Gabriel and a host of angels watched in awe.

Life-Giver and the Holy Spirit joined the Great King. The Three-in-One said, "There is no greater love than this."

Beloved's life-blood soaked into the ground.

***

An obnoxious smell assaulted Hadassah senses. She could not see, for she was enveloped in a thick shroud of darkness. Her ears rang with the sound of a dozen bells. She called out but to no avail, for she could not hear if there was any response. "Life-Giver, what's happened?"

"Nothing is greater than love," He answered, laying His hand on her shoulder.

Hadassah did not hear Him.

"My King?" Michael inquired.

"It is by permission," the Great King replied.

"Shall we anoint the child or shall You resurrect her?" Gabriel asked.

"You shall anoint her, for she has run her race well and has accomplished what was given to her — she has laid down her life for another. Her life is now swallowed up in victory. Bring My Beloved home," the Great King said.

Angels hurried to Beloved who stood looking back and forth between the two realms.

"I am dead then?" she asked.

"You are dead to the world but more alive than ever," the largest of the angels answered.

Another angel arrived holding the King's royal robe of righteousness. Beloved was surprised that it fit her perfectly. Another angel placed a golden crown on her head. Beloved bowed and proclaimed, "I'm beautiful 'cuz Life-Giver is beautiful. I don't deserve such a crown."

"Rise up, child, and do not bow your knee to us, for we are merely servants of the Most High King," one of the angels said.

"So am I," she responded, glowing with the glory of both realms.

"The King has sent us to prepare you for life eternal."

"Do I know you?" Beloved asked.

"You have met me before, but I am not the One you seek." The angel held out his hand and said, "Come with me, for your King and Creator awaits your arrival."

As he led Beloved down a street paved with gold, she stopped to look at her reflection in the pavement. "This Or Fan has become a beautiful princess," she whispered, feeling quite giddy. Not one flaw remained on her face.

"You are a princess because your Father is a King."

Beloved had never felt so free or beautiful.

A crystal river ran parallel to the street; its rushing water sang a delightful song. Trees laden with delicious-looking fruit grew along the river bank.

Beloved suddenly realized she could hear and see the tiniest detail from very far away. "I can see with the eyes of my heart," she said. And what she saw next astonished her — the Great King on His throne. "Why's He laughin'?" she asked.

"He is laughing because He is so very happy."

"Why?"

"You may ask Him."

"I think I will."

Beloved waited for the King to stop laughing, but He didn't. She waited for some time — how long she did not know, for there was no way to measure time. There was no sun or moon or stars. There was no need for them, for the place was filled with light, glorious light. How could there be light without a source, *she wondered.*

"He is *the Source of all light," the angel said, answering her unspoken thought and pointing behind her.*

Beloved turned. "Life-Giver!"

Without waiting for an invitation or inquiring as to proper protocol, she raced across the throne room and jumped into His arms. She buried her face in His neck. Every heartache, every pain, every injustice, every unkind word, every loss, every disappointment, every hurt in her life surfaced. Tears, all kinds of tears, ran down her face. Life-Giver captured every one and placed it in a golden bottle.

"You are glorious — like your Father," Life-Giver said.

Beloved took a step back. Life-Giver was dressed in royal garments and wore a golden crown. "You're a King?" she asked.

"I was born the lowly son of a carpenter, but I died the King of kings."

"I thought Your Papa was the King."

"He is the Great King and that makes Me a King."

"Hmm."

"Like Me, you were created to be glorious both on earth and in this realm, and glorious you are!"

"I s'pose this means I won't get to spend a day with the Great King?" she asked, remembering her time on earth.

Chuckling, He responded, "One day is like a thousand years in this realm, Beloved. And a thousand years in this place is forever! You shall spend all eternity in the presence of the Great King! Speaking of which — He has been waiting seven long earth years for your return."

"He's been waitin' for me?"

"Yes."

"Then we shouldn't make Him wait any more," she said, her eyes sparkling with pure life.

With heads held high, the two approached the Great King's throne. "My Father, may I present to You, Our Beloved."

The King descended the crystal stairs. With arms outstretched, He welcomed His daughter. Beloved ran into His arms, and He scooped her up. As He held her close, pure love flooded her being.

Looking up, she asked, "How can You be here and on earth?"

"I am everywhere all of the time and very often I rhyme — like now," He said, chuckling.

"And You're gonna say maybe You should be a poet," Beloved responded, feeling so much joy she did not know if she could contain it.

"That's one reason you must leave your body behind," He said.

"What do You mean?"

"The joy and love you feel here is more than your human body can withstand. Your capacity for both is now endless. My kingdom is a place of eternal, relentless, endless love where joy unspeakable and full of glory resides."

The King of all creation sat down on His throne and cradled her close.

"Papa?"

"Yes, child?"

"You're beautiful," she said, running her hands through His hair that was whiter than snow.

"Do you know why I am beautiful?" He asked.

"Because You're so shiny and perfect?"

"Because I am Perfect Love. Nothing is as beautiful as My Love."

"Nothing's as beautiful as You."

"That is true, and I will love you all My days!" He said.

Laughing, Beloved said, "Your days have no end, so that means Your love for me will last forever!"

"If I were ever to stop loving you I would stop existing," her Papa said.

Beloved sighed deeply, for she was finally home and finally complete.

CHAPTER TWENTY-FIVE

*F*earful not only of what lurked in the darkness but also what tragedy she might find, Hadassah remained curled in a fetal position, praying fervently. *Oh, dear Life-Giver, if You've ever heard my prayers, please hear me now. Please let Beloved and Bethany be safe,* she silently cried while fearing the worst.

Something touched her arm. Terrified, she pulled away. There it was again, but this time she did not draw back. "Who are you?" she asked, daring to touch the hand on her knee. To her relief, it was a girl's hand. Unable to see or hear she searched for the face. Her trembling fingers felt the smooth skin. "Bethany," she said, throwing her arms around her.

The two huddled together in silence for some time, how long was impossible to know.

The ringing in Hadassah's ears finally diminished, but she still could not see clearly. The storm had stopped. Crickets and bullfrogs filled the air with their annoying sounds. "Bethany, can you hear me?" Hadassah asked.

"Yes. Can you hear me?"

"Yes. Are you all right? Are you hurt?"

"I'm not hurt."

"Where's Beloved? She was under that bush and — do you know where she is?"

"Yes, Hadassah, I know where, but —"

"But what? Is she hurt?"

"Oh, Hadassah," Bethany said, her voice cracking, "I'm so sorry, but Beloved is d—"

"Don't you say it! Don't you dare tell me she's dead! This can't be happening — not again! Don't tell me, don't tell me!" Hadassah shouted. Pulling her legs close to her chest, she rocked back and forth, crying her heart out.

"I'm so sorry, Hadassah."

Hadassah wanted to run and never stop. She screamed instead. All Bethany could do was hold Hadassah's trembling body close and pray.

"Human suffering is difficult to watch," Michael said.

"It is indeed," said Life-Giver as tears of pure love ran down His face.

"Why do You cry, my Lord?"

"I weep because the one I love weeps," Life-Giver said as He bore her burden.

"Amazing love."

Bethany stroked Hadassah's hair as tears streamed down both of their faces.

"Is the Great King cruel?" Hadassah asked.

"He's not cruel, just unpredictable."

"He seems cruel to me."

"I know it appears that way, but He did not cause this tragedy, Hadassah."

"Why Beloved? Why her? She suffered her whole life. Terrible people did terrible things to her. No one loved her. Even I turned away — this makes no sense," she sobbed.

"I don't know. I dare say there's no answer that would satisfy your heart right now."

"With every cross there is an unanswered why," the Holy Spirit whispered.

Michael looked over his shoulder at Life-Giver on the cross and heard His cry, "Father, why have You forsaken Me?"

"What happened to Beloved?" Hadassah finally asked.

"I think lightning struck her, but I don't know for sure."

Hadassah sat in silence, unable to process what had happened. She wondered if life would always be filled with so much pain.

She cried herself to sleep. Bethany held her close until she awakened.

"Where were You, Life-Giver? Why did You allow this to happen? Why didn't You stop it? Why this, why her?" Hadassah cried out.

"There are many mysteries in this life, My precious child, mysteries that can only be understood in another time and another realm. Will you trust Me — even when the circumstances of your life do not make sense? Will you believe even then that I am a good?" Life-Giver asked, holding her close, rocking her gently.

Hadassah did not answer, for she did not hear or feel Him. Mind-numbing pain consumed her.

Life-Giver continued to rock her. When the time was right He touched her eyes, and her eyesight gradually returned. When it did, she wished it had not. Lying not far away was Beloved's little body. Trembling violently, Hadassah crawled over and scooped the child up in her arms. Rocking back and forth, she wailed. When her tears were spent, she brushed the curls back from Beloved's face. There were no marks, no sign of a lightning strike. Hadassah cradled the child in her lap and sang her mama's song as sunbeams broke through the trees.

"What's this?" Bethany asked.

"What?"

"These bloody marks on her back — roll her over."

Hadassah turned her over. "They look like claw marks," Bethany said. "She's been clawed by an animal."

"I thought she was struck by lightning?"

"So did I, but these marks were not made by lightning," said Bethany, her brow creased.

"She jumped in front of me," Hadassah said, afraid to believe what she was thinking. The two stared at her wounds. "It seems she died to protect me from something."

Unable to say more, Hadassah backed away. "I just don't understand."

"I don't either," Bethany said, gently folding Beloved's arms across her chest. "She's so beautiful."

"Don't you mean she *was* beautiful," Hadassah replied, a hint of anger present in her voice.

"She's still beautiful. She's more alive now than before, Hadassah. To the King and the hosts of heaven, death is a celebration, for it's the ultimate accomplishment, the promotion, the entering into the fullness of one's destiny. Death is not the end, but merely the beginning . . . and what a glorious beginning it is for those who know their King."

"That may be true, but it sure does hurt those left behind," Hadassah said, her anger growing more evident.

"It does indeed."

Hadassah sat up. "Perhaps the King will resurrect her again. He did that once before — I was there."

"We can always ask."

"That's exactly what we'll do," Hadassah said, returning to the child's body.

Hadassah and Bethany prayed; their tears fell onto Beloved's ashen face. "You did it before, Life-Giver; won't You do it again?" Hadassah pleaded.

The two prayed for hours, maybe days. Hadassah had no idea how long, for her mind had been rendered useless. Bethany finally said, "I don't think He plans to resurrect her."

"We should bury her, but I don't think I have the strength to do so," Hadassah said.

"Then we shall pray for someone who does," Bethany said. Turning her thoughts inward, she petitioned her King.

The two sat in silence for the rest of the day until sleep rescued them from their pain.

The morning sun broke through the forest, casting its golden light on Hadassah's face. Dread filled her. She slowly opened her eyes. Bethany had covered the child's body with leaves and beautiful flowers. For that she was grateful.

"The King is sending someone to help us," Bethany quietly announced.

"How do you know?"

"He told me."

"You saw Him?"

"No, but He spoke to my heart."

"Bethany, do you believe the King can do anything?"

"Yes."

"Then why this?" Hadassah asked, motioning to Beloved. "Why my parents and my sister? Your mother?"

"No one can understand or explain why the King allows ones to die and not another. When faced with tragedy, the only safe place is to fall on your face and proclaim that He is good. It is imperative that we understand and accept the fact that He is not the source of evil. Regardless of what comes our way we must choose to trust Him. He can turn *anything* into good — even tragedy — if we give Him the opportunity and the time that it takes to do so."

Hadassah said, "I've seen little good and way too much bad in my journey so far." The bitterness was obvious in her voice.

"But the bad has been used for your good — you said so yourself. I've learned in my wanderings and shortcomings that He wastes nothing, Hadassah."

"That may be, but right now that brings me little comfort. Right now, I hurt and I hurt badly. And I don't understand why this had to happen."

"Hadassah, be careful, for unresolved disappointment can lead to great resentment which can lead to bitterness," Life-Giver said.

"She has come too far to turn back now," Michael said, looking at Life-Giver for reassurance.

He said, "Michael, remain firm in your stand against the powers of darkness that would seek to take advantage of her during this vulnerable time. Free will is a gift I have given Hadassah. I will not interfere with the choices she makes."

The two girls sat in silence until the not-so-distant sound of snapping twigs caused both to look up. A young man approached dragging a bier behind him. Bethany called out, "Have you come on behalf of the King?"

"I have," he answered, quickening his pace.

"It is well," Bethany whispered, taking Hadassah's hand.

After exchanging introductions, the girls turned away from the child's body while the young man carefully wrapped it in a purple cloth. "The King will see that she receives a royal burial, for He told me she is a princess," the young man announced as he gently laid her body on the bier.

"Thank you," said Bethany.

Bowing, the shepherd said, "Before I go, the Great King gave me a message for you both."

Hadassah barely looked up.

"He said for me to tell you that Beloved is safe in His arms and that He looks forward to your arrival."

"How does He know we're coming?" Hadassah asked.

"The Great King knows everything, my lady. And no one comes to Him without his knowledge," he said with a smile. Nodding, he turned to leave.

"Wait! Young man, you've seen the Great King then? Surely you have, for He has spoken to you," Hadassah inquired.

"I have, my lady."

"What's He like? Is it true that He's kind? Generous? Compassionate? Or is He a frightful tyrant, ruling with His fist rather than His heart? Is He cruel and uncaring? Pray tell me all you know, for I must make some sense out of what has happened here," Hadassah pleaded, falling on her knees, desperate tears running down her face.

"My lady, He's the kindest, most generous and most merciful King alive. He's not only generous and compassionate but He's glorious. As for His rule . . . you will never find One as forgiving and wise as He. And you will never meet another as grand as He, yet His humility exceeds even the most humble on this earth. All who know Him, love Him. And there is not a cruel or uncaring bone in His body — of that you can be certain."

"I hope and pray what you say is the truth, because my circumstances scream otherwise," Hadassah said. "And thank you for your service to my dear friend."

"It is my pleasure to serve both you and the Great King. But I must be on my way, my lady, for the King awaits my return. Good day to you both."

Tears of agony streamed down her face as Hadassah watched him carry Beloved away. Once he was out of sight, Hadassah's knees buckled. Her sobbing filled the forest. Bethany held her close and cried.

Life-Giver wept with them.

Neither spoke nor ate for the rest of the day.

The following morning, before Bethany woke, Hadassah walked a short distance into the forest. Finding a fallen tree she sat down on its broad trunk. Taking a deep breath, she said, "Life-Giver, please tell me You're here."

"I am."

"I guess You know what happened. Of course You do. Like the King, You know everything. I don't want to be angry. I don't want to resent the King or You, but I just don't understand why this happened. I think Beloved was protecting me from something. If that's true, then why didn't You protect her? Can You just tell me why You didn't do something?"

"Hadassah, there are many things that are beyond your ability to comprehend. Unlike you, My Father and I see the end from the beginning. We know everything before it happens, and We do all things well. One day you will understand."

"But what am I to do with my anger?"

"Give it to Me."

"How do I do that?"

"Be honest with Me about how you feel and then ask for My healing power."

"Well, I feel like my heart's been ripped out. I've lost everyone I've ever loved — except Martha, and I kind of lost her. Is there a curse on my life or am I being punished for some sin? I'm confused because the King is supposed to be good and kind and powerful, but His actions lead me to believe otherwise. It appears He doesn't care if innocent children die or people get hurt. I hate it — I hate this! I don't hate You or the King, but I hate injustice!"

"Pain, disease, suffering, death — We do not cause those things. All suffering is a result of a choice that was made thousands of years ago in a garden called Eden.

"Hadassah, do not listen to Satan's lies. He wants to accuse the King and Me for His evil deeds. We never derive any pleasure from suffering. You can trust the King, Hadassah. He is better than anything you can imagine."

"Am I to live in fear of death for those I love for the rest of my life?"

"I have not given you a spirit of fear, but of power and love and a sound mind."

Hadassah sighed deeply. "Will You hold me?"

"I would like nothing better." Life-Giver put His strong arms around her and held her close. He buried His face in her hair and breathed. Her devotion captured His heart. "Hadassah, I call your spirit to attention in the name of the Great King! I invite you, spirit, to take your rightful place, for you were created to have dominion over your soul. So rise up now and step in front of your mind, will and emotions. I bless you with faith, hope and love. And the greatest of these is always love."

Hadassah's spirit did exactly what He asked it to do. His love felt so real that she opened her eyes to see if He was physically with her. She saw nothing with her natural eye, but that did not change the truth. Life-Giver was with her and He loved her. She remained lost in the wonder of His embrace until she heard Bethany calling her.

"I'll be right there," she shouted. "Thank you, Life-Giver."

"Hadassah."

"Yes?"

"If I wanted to change the world, I'd start by loving you."

Hadassah was taken off guard. Not knowing what to say, she said, "Uh. . . thank You, for loving me."

"It is My delight."

"Hadassah," Bethany called again.

"I'm coming," she answered.

"I was afraid you'd left," Bethany said, meeting her on the path.

"I've come too far to turn back now."

"How are you?"

"I just had a great talk with Life-Giver," she said. "I sure hope it's really true that the King is just like Him."

"If you've seen Life-Giver, you've seen the Father; trust me, I know."

"I'm trying to trust," Hadassah said, passing her water-skin to Bethany who eagerly drank. Hadassah continued, "I don't pretend to understand what happened here. I may never know. But I give up my right to have an answer, and neither will I ask the King to defend His actions."

Overcome with emotion, Hadassah fell to her knees. Pressing her hands against her chest, she cried out, "Who am I to require You, the King of all, to give me an explanation? I abandon my rights. I don't need to understand why in order to trust or love You. Instead, I take up my cross and walk in the same manner Life-Giver walked — no complaints, no rights, no accusations and no offenses.

"I can't bring myself to thank You for Beloved's death at this moment, but I will — I surely will in the days ahead. And if not on this earth, then surely in the life to come."

The Holy Spirit poured out His love on her.

Hadassah fell on her face, weeping. Through her sobs she cried out, "Life-Giver, I'll love You in the dark and in the light. I'll love You when I'm weak and when I'm strong. I'll love You when I'm devastated and when my cup overflows with goodness. I'll love You when my world's upside down and when all is good. I'll always love You — through storm, through desert, through tragedy, through it all! I'll never let go of You, for You're the only Hero in my story. And I'll go to my grave shouting that You're good!"

***

Hadassah mourned deeply for three more days. Bethany watched and prayed, for she had never seen such fierce love and pain.

"Hadassah grows more like You, my Lord," Michael said.

"She does indeed."

"How much longer?"

"She is almost there."

On the morning of the fourth day, Hadassah turned to Bethany and said, "I'm ready now. And I'm more determined than ever to find this King. I won't stop until I've seen His face."

***

Bethany led the way through the dark forest with Hadassah driving her on. During the first two days, Hadassah spoke very little and slept even less. On the third day, just as the sun passed overhead, they stepped out of the forest. To Hadassah's great delight, stretched out before them was a beautiful city with white-washed buildings, gardens and countless fountains.

"Surely the King is there," Hadassah said, increasing her pace.

"The King is —"

"I know, I know, the King's everywhere, all of the time. But I want to see His face and ask Him a thousand questions. Do you know where I can find Him, Bethany?"

"I don't. I only passed through the Inner Court when I ran away, and I wasn't looking for Him then."

"I shall draw as near to Him as possible," Hadassah said, hurrying toward the city gate with Bethany barely keeping up.

Upon entering the gate, they saw a small group of elderly women standing on a street corner. Marching right up to them, Hadassah asked, "Have you seen the King?"

One of the women answered, "I'm sorry, child; I haven't seen Him in quite some time. I've been too busy sewing blankets for the poor."

Another woman with beautiful white hair added, "I've only seen Him during times of hardship, and it's been awhile since I've had any troubles."

A third woman spoke up. "I know where He is." Her face was alive, her smile inviting.

"Where did you find Him? How did you find Him?" Hadassah asked, eager to finally find someone who could help her.

"I can't exactly tell you how to find Him, child; it's different for everyone. I do know this — you will find Him when you search for Him with all of your heart."

Another woman nodded energetically and added, "He's here all right. You just have to look for Him."

"But you haven't told me how to find Him," Hadassah said, feeling a twinge of frustration.

"Child, the King's with you even now," the woman said. "He's as close as the air all around you. But rest assured that there's more. Life's a journey into the heart of the King. Every day and every situation is meant to bring you closer to Him."

"Uh, thanks," she said walking away. Turning to Bethany, she said, "Everyone tells me the same thing, but it doesn't really help." Without waiting for a response, she hurried off.

Hadassah stopped everyone she met and asked them if they knew where she could find the King. A few turned away without answering, others said they could not remember where or how to find Him. One really old man said, "If you're desperate to find Him then go to the palace, because that's where the Holy of Holies is located."

"How do I find the palace?"

"Can't say that I remember."

Hadassah went on, fueled by a love that was formed in the furnace of affliction. That kind of love believes all things, bears all things, hopes all things and endures all things. A love like that cannot be quenched, neither is it easily extinguished.

She continued her pursuit well into the night with Bethany close by her side. Finally, Hadassah stopped to rest on a wooden bench.

"Those who search for Him always find Him," said Bethany.

"I'm not discouraged, merely tired."

"And rightfully so."

"Is everyone's life this difficult?" Hadassah asked.

"I don't know. But I believe suffering's a gift."

"I've decided I've had enough suffering."

"The only problem with that is the fact that you live in a flawed world with flawed people. It comes with the territory, I think. But for now, we need to find a place to spend the night," Bethany said, looking around. "What about that shack?" she asked, pointing to a dilapidated building partially hidden behind a new-looking stable.

"It will do," Hadassah said, standing to her feet.

The two walked across the grassy yard arm in arm. Hadassah asked, "Bethany, do you really believe I'll get to spend a day with the King?"

"I'm sure of it. You still have that scroll, don't you?"

"Yes, but it isn't of any value if I can't find Him."

"You *will* find Him."

"How can you be so sure?"

"Because we don't find Him — the Great King finds us."

Her words were like an arrow in Hadassah's heart. "I don't find the King, He finds me," she repeated.

Bethany pushed open the door; the hinges moaned and groaned. Thick cobwebs and stale air greeted them. Peering into the darkness, Hadassah reconsidered. "Maybe this isn't such a good idea after all."

"Just wait," Bethany said. "Give your eyes times to adjust."

"What if a wild animal lives in here?" Hadassah asked.

"I think we'd know that by now. Look over there — we can sleep on those hay bales."

Hadassah followed close, holding on to Bethany's shoulder. Without any fear, Bethany plopped down on the haystack and a cloud of dust enveloped them. Countless mice scattered in every direction; several ran over Hadassah's feet. Squealing, she hopped around desperately trying to avoid the frightened rodents.

Safe on the top of the haystack, Bethany found the scene hilarious. "For someone who's exhausted, you sure move fast!" Bethany said, laughing uncontrollably.

"I don't like mice," she answered, huddled beside her.

"Obviously."

"Did you know that was going to happen?"

"Not exactly."

"You did! You knew it!" Hadassah said, playfully shoving her.

Both girls laughed so hard they cried. "I needed that," Hadassah said, wiping her eyes and nose.

"Yeah, me too," Bethany said. "I'm hungry. Let's ask Life-Giver to send us something to eat."

Bethany and Hadassah made their request known.

"Now, we wait," Bethany said, lying back on the hay with her hands cradling her head.

The two girls fell asleep almost immediately.

CHAPTER TWENTY-SIX

*B*oth girls bolted upright. Hadassah's heart pounded in her chest as she searched for Bethany's hand.

"Who goes there?" Bethany called out.

"Just an old weary traveler who means no harm," the dark figure of a woman answered. "I'm just looking for a place to rest my bones."

Both girls let out a deep sigh as they climbed down.

Bethany said, "Come on in. There's plenty of room." She patted the hay as Hadassah jumped down to help guide the old woman through the dark. Taking her hand, Hadassah introduced herself.

"Good to meet you, Hadassah. I'm Grace."

"Welcome to our humble abode, Grace. The girl on the hay is Bethany. We'd offer you some food, but we don't exactly have any. We do have water. Would you like some?"

"No need. I happen to have more than enough of both. Glad to share what I have with you, if you're hungry that is," she said, plopping down on the hay. Dust filled the air.

Coughing, Hadassah said, "Really? Thank you. I guess you're the answer to our prayers."

"Bless my soul! I always wanted to be the answer to someone's prayers!" she exclaimed as she untied her knapsack. Out tumbled a loaf of bread, a big hunk of cheese, several apples, some carrots, a bunch of grapes and some dried meat.

Hadassah and Bethany's eyes grew big. "Where did you get this? It's not stolen, is it?" Hadassah asked.

"Not a chance! Now, help yourself. Eat all you want."

"Thank you," they said.

They had a grand feast as they shared stories and laughed a little. Hadassah ate until she was miserable. Throwing her apple core in the farthest corner, she stretched out. Her thoughts drifted to Beloved and the apple tree. The memory was bitter-sweet.

Anger and Resentment licked their lips.

"Where are you headed, Grace?" Bethany asked.

"I'm on my way to the King's palace."

"So are we."

"I suspected you might be."

Hadassah asked, "Do you know the Great King?"

"Sure do."

"I'm trying to learn all I can about Him. Please tell me, is He as kind as people say? Is He as rich and powerful? Is He good? Is He forgiving? Is He —"

"Slow down. Give an old woman a chance to gather her thoughts. Now, what was that you asked? Oh yes, that's it. Is He as kind as folks say? I don't know how kind folks say He is. But what I can say is that no matter how kind they say He is He's even kinder, because His kindness exceeds human description. As for His riches, He owns everything that exists, so I'd say He's more than wealthy. As for His power, He's power under control, which is the greatest power there is. As for forgiveness, He doesn't just pardon the guilty — He accepts, encourages and loves them immensely.

"But the best thing about this King is that everything He does is always good, because He's completely unselfish. So, I suppose you can say He's good," she chuckled.

Hadassah said, "Every time anyone describes the King it sounds like they're describing Life-Giver, for that's how I know Him to be."

"That's because they're One and the same," Bethany said.

"I keep forgetting that."

Tying up the food, Grace tucked it close and laid down between the two girls, saying, "This old woman isn't as young as she used to be. Suppose I should get some sleep. Good night, girls."

"Good night. And thank you, Grace, for the food," Hadassah and Bethany said.

"You're most welcome, but the Great King is the One who deserves the thanks. He provided it."

"I'll thank Him when I see Him," Hadassah said.

Hadassah prayed for a moment, but she could not get Beloved's face out of her mind. Rolling onto her side, she fought back her tears while she silently prayed, *Life-Giver, when I find the King, or rather, when the King finds me, will He take away this pain?*

"There is no pain that can remain when in the presence of Life Eternal."

I miss her, Hadassah admitted.

"I know."

How much longer before the King finds me? she silently asked.

"The greater the Treasure, the more difficult the search," Grace replied.

"Did you just read my mind?" Hadassah asked.

"No."

"Then why'd you say that?"

"Because you struggle with fear. But you have nothing to fear, Hadassah, for the King wants to be with you even more than you want to be with Him."

"I'm glad to hear that," Hadassah answered, closing her eyes.

"He is with you, child." Grace silently prayed for her long after she fell asleep.

The three woke early. Grace shared her food with them again. It appeared to Hadassah that the food had multiplied, but she quickly dismissed the thought as ridiculous.

"Grace, where did you come from?" Hadassah asked.

"From here, there and everywhere," she answered with a sparkle in her eye.

"How is it that you travel so much?"

"I am a servant of the Most High King. Where He sends, I go — just like He sent me to you last night."

"What do you mean?" Hadassah asked.

"He told me to bring you food."

"You *saw* Him?"

"No, child, one doesn't have to see the King in order to hear His voice. Life-Giver said those who do not see Him but still believe are blessed. So do not fret. Enough questions for now. We should be on our way, lest I fail in my task."

"What task is that?" Hadassah asked, growing more interested by the moment.

"To bring the two of you to the King."

"What?!" Hadassah exclaimed, jumping to her feet. "The King sent you to bring us to Him?"

"Yes," she said with a smile.

"Then what are we waiting for?"

Hadassah jumped down from the haystack and helped the old woman up while Bethany gathered their few belongings. Throwing her tattered knapsack over her shoulder, Grace led the way out of the shack and into the marvelous light.

Once their eyes adjusted, Hadassah said, "I'm a bit confused. Bethany, why would the King send her to bring us to Him when you know the way?"

"I know the direction to go but don't quite know how to get there," Bethany said.

"Why didn't you say so? You acted as though you knew the way."

"The truth is I wanted to look good. Sorry. I told you I have a problem with pride."

"So were you just going to walk around, hoping to stumble upon the path?"

"I trusted the King to bring me home. After all, none of us can get to Him without His help anyway."

Grace slowed her pace in order to allow the girls to catch up. "Who's the old woman here?" Grace asked, chuckling.

"It appears to be Bethany and me," Hadassah said, coming alongside her.

The three locked arms. Grace said, "Allow this old woman to help you."

"By all means," Bethany said, giggling.

"Hadassah, I dreamed last night that you have something that belongs to the Great King," said Grace.

"What is it?" Hadassah asked.

"I don't know, but I thought you might want to ask Him."

Whatever could it be? Hadassah wondered. "It must be the scrolls. That's the only thing I have that is His. I'll give them to Him as soon as He finds us."

The two maidens followed Grace through the endless maze of streets. They were surprised at the old woman's stamina and friendliness. She smiled and spoke to every person she met. "How do you do it?" Hadassah asked, struggling to keep up.

"Do what?"

"Walk so fast and greet everyone that crosses our path."

"Grace."

"Why are you saying your name?" Hadassah asked.

"I'm not talking about my name, but the grace that comes from the Great King. His grace empowers me and enables me to do what He has asked me to do. Without it I'd be nothing but an old woman with a tired body."

"I need some of that grace."

"Me too," Bethany said.

"The King gives grace to the humble."

Bethany slipped her hand through Grace's elbow and said, "Well, that is certainly something I need."

Hadassah successfully fought off the urge to agree with her.

They walked for hours with Hadassah just behind them. Hot, tired and hungry, Hadassah asked, "I think we're going in circles. Bethany, do you recognize anything?"

"Hadassah, I've never been down this path before."

"It seems to me that we're going in circles. Look — over there! I'm sure we passed that merchant's table already. That butcher's booth looks familiar too."

Bethany said, "I know the Way — His name is Life-giver. But remember how I told you everyone's path to the King looks different?"

"Yes."

"Well, my path back to the King doesn't look the same as the one I took to leave Him. I need grace to get back to the King and so do you," Bethany said.

"What she says is true, Hadassah."

"That may be, but I'm so very anxious to get there."

"I understand that, but don't let fear drive you," Grace said.

"I'm not afraid."

"I beg to differ," Grace said. "Anxiety is a symptom of fear. It's the opposite of trust."

"I'm not afraid," Hadassah said adamantly.

"Why don't you ask Life-Giver if you're afraid and not aware of it?"

It was obvious that Hadassah was offended. Bethany and Grace silently prayed.

The sun was setting when Grace instructed them to stop. Hadassah's nerves were on edge. Gathering palm branches and anything else they could find to sleep on, they camped beneath an old bridge. Once more, Grace shared her food with them. "Your food never ends," Bethany said.

"The King provides our daily bread," said Grace.

"The bread's still soft, the cheese doesn't appear to be diminished, and I know we ate most of it this morning."

"It's multiplied because the Great King has commanded it to do so," Grace answered.

"How do you know that?"

"I know this to be true because I know Him."

"How can He not only multiply food but do so from far away? How is that possible?" Hadassah asked.

Grace answered, "Your King is no ordinary king. He knows you're searching for Him, and He's closer than you think."

Tired, they soon bid each other good night. Hadassah found herself too physically and emotionally tired to sleep and decided to go for a walk. The moon was full and bright. The night air was quite cool. Hadassah wrapped her cloak around her as she climbed up the steep bank. She sat on the bridge, legs hanging over the side, and looked around. Most of the leaves had already fallen from the trees. *Winter will soon be here*, she thought.

Images of Beloved's disfigured face filled her mind. "I don't think I ever told Beloved that I loved her," she whispered to herself as tears spilled over her lashes.

Not too far away an owl hooted. The moon cast its golden light on the dry creek bed below. The various stones glistened in the moonlight causing them to look more like jewels than rocks.

Life-Giver sat beside her.

"I feel Your presence," she whispered. Closing her eyes she focused on the sweetness of the moment. "And I love Your presence."

"And I love your presence," her beloved Companion and Friend responded.

"Please stay with me for a little while."

"I am always with you. It's just that you are not always aware of Me."

"If only I could remember that." She could see herself resting her head against His chest. She sighed deeply and said, "It still hurts."

"I know."

"Is there no end to sorrow and suffering?"

"I saw you when you were shattered and broken into a million pieces. Do you remember?"

"I won't ever forget that dream."

"I didn't leave you broken, did I? I knelt by your side and carefully selected each piece at just the right time and put it in the just the right place, didn't I?"

"You did."

"That is exactly what I am and have been doing for you, Hadassah. And My love will keep you, for it holds all things together."

"I believe that, I think."

"This world is fallen, and much evil is present here. And there is more coming — things that will shake your faith to its foundation. Only those who have gone through the fire of My love will survive, for My fire burns away those things that hinder faith, hope and love. They will not be offended when a thousand fall at their right hand and ten thousand on their left. They will know their King, will rise up with a love that cannot be extinguished and will do great exploits in My name. Hadassah, I must purify your heart now so that you will be able to stand in the midst of what is sure to come."

"Then sorrow and suffering are Your gift to me?"

"They are. I turn what Satan means for evil for your good."

"Is there no other way?"

"It is with great love and mercy that I oversee the events of your life. You can trust Me."

Hadassah's attention was once more drawn to the stones below as she considered His words. "Life-Giver, is what Grace said true? Am I afraid? Is that why I struggle so much?"

"It is true."

"What am I afraid of?"

"You are afraid to believe."

Hadassah paused for a moment before asking, "I'm afraid to believe what?"

"You are afraid to believe that your dream will come true."

Hadassah sat in silence as truth permeated her being.

"Hadassah."

"Yes?"

"Your disappointment and pain have robbed you of hope and faith. If they are not addressed they will turn into anger and resentment."

"I'm not aware of any."

"They are there."

"Show me my heart, Life-Giver."

The Holy Spirit settled over her like an early morning fog.

A lizard-like creature named Resentment crawled out from under her armpit and sat on her shoulder. It lifted its head and looked around. The slimy thing sniffed the air. Smelling Truth, it shrieked and quickly returned to its hiding place. Deep in her belly, Anger squirmed.

Conviction flooded her. She confessed, "Life-Giver, You're right. I'm angry because Beloved died. I was taking such good care of her, and she was beginning to feel happy and loved. I wanted to show her what real love looks like and I resented You for taking her from me. I'm so sorry. I didn't know I felt this way. I just don't understand why," Hadassah sobbed.

Life-Giver held her close. Stroking her hair, He said, "My love, how can you understand when you don't have all the facts, when you can't see the beginning or the end? Did you hang the moon? Did you place the stars in the sky? Do you know all mysteries? My Father is so much bigger than you can imagine. He is beyond your understanding — you will never be able to comprehend Him or His ways with your mortal mind, but you can know Him with your spirit — intimately. And you can choose to trust Him."

"I want to trust Him and You. And I'm trying, but I seem to keep falling back into my old ways. I am sorry."

"You are forgiven. Without My help you are nothing more than a mere mortal, powerless to change yourself or anyone else."

"I know You're right, because I constantly slip back into old behaviors and wrong ways of thinking. I'm as weak as water and as helpless as these rocks."

Resentment and Anger shrieked as they crawled out from their hiding places, falling to the ground. Without Hadassah even knowing what was happening, Michael snatched them both up and flew off.

Life-Giver said, "You are forgiven and loved. But be aware of a subtle tactic of Satan. He wants your weaknesses and failures to be the object of your attention. You may be weak, but if you focus on your weakness you will only become discouraged and grow weaker. Instead, focus on the fact that I am strong. As for feeling worthless — focus on My worth and My endless love for you, not on your self-worth or lack thereof. Fix the eyes of your heart on Me and not your problems."

Hadassah closed her eyes and said, "You created my imagination, and I consecrate it to You. I ask You to come and fill it. Show me what You want me to see."

Hadassah saw herself in a meadow. On the horizon was a Shepherd. Upon seeing her, He ran toward her. As He approached, her heart raced. He knelt before her and said, "You are altogether beautiful, and there is no spot or wrinkle or blemish in you."

"No blemish in me?" she asked.

"None whatsoever."

"But what about those areas of compromise in my life?"

"Washed away in My blood."

"What about my inability to be perfect?"

"You are perfect because I am perfect."

"What about my selfish heart and propensity to sin?"

"All covered by Perfect Love."

"I'm free then?"

"You are not only free, but you are Mine."

Hadassah felt herself relax as her anxious thoughts fled.

"Hadassah, all that I have is yours. My worth is your worth, and My value is your value. The divine exchange has already been made."

For a brief moment, Hadassah dared to look into His eyes. She saw an endless ocean of love. She saw deep longing and perfect peace. Wave after wave of pure love filled her.

"You are a priceless jewel, a treasure, and I love you with an everlasting love," Life-Giver whispered as He kissed her forehead.

"You are most beautiful," she said.

"And you are most beautiful."

He held up the earthenware jar that was in her dream so long ago. It looked even more beautiful than she remembered. *"Because of My love, your greatest tragedies will become your greatest victories. And you will bear much fruit for My glory."* With a nod and a smile, He disappeared.

Hadassah opened her eyes. "He's putting me back together! He's making me beautiful and valuable! I have nothing to fear."

Unable to contain her excitement, she jumped to her feet and danced under the moonlight until her aching feet reminded her of how tired she really was. She returned to her bed under the bridge, saying, "He will make wrong things right. My heart is safe with Him. He says I'm beautiful. He says I'm a jewel. I felt like a worthless rock, but aren't they one and the same? A jewel is merely a stone that someone has attributed value to. And what right do I have to de-value what Life-Giver values? I dare not hate what He loves, and He loves me! He really loves me. And I think I am finally beginning to feel it, not just think it."

CHAPTER TWENTY-SEVEN

$\mathscr{T}$he next morning, the three pilgrims set out again. Hadassah missed Beloved, but to her great relief, the underlying anger and resentment were completely gone.

They soon came to the village marketplace. Both sides of the street were packed with tables displaying everything from blankets to meat. Merchants and their helpers energetically, and at times aggressively, tried to convince all who passed to buy their wares.

Grace said, "These folks work from sun-up to sun-down every day."

Hadassah was about to ask why when Grace called out to a white-haired gentleman.

"Good day, Grace," Isaiah responded as he dropped a heavy crate on the table.

"How are you?" she asked.

"Very well, thank you. I see that you've found two more daughters for the King," he said, nodding and smiling at the two girls.

"I have indeed. With your permission, we'd like to take a shortcut through your booth to fill our water-skins."

"All that I have is yours," he said, bowing slightly.

Grace turned sideways and inched her rather robust frame between his closely placed tables. Isaiah pulled back a heavy curtain behind his tables, and the three stepped through into the village square. Over a dozen women sat around the well eagerly sharing stories. Upon seeing Grace, they ran to her. Hugging and talking all at once, Grace touched their faces and squeezed their hands. Hadassah and Bethany looked at each other. "I wonder how she knows them," Hadassah whispered.

Grace was quick to introduce the girls. Feeling embarrassed by her unkempt appearance, Hadassah excused herself to fetch some water. Bethany followed. The two girls listened as the others shared amazing stories about their encounters with the Great King. Hadassah's heart burned as tears filled her eyes.

Bethany tapped Hadassah on the shoulder. "You can pull the bucket up now."

"Oh, I got distracted," Hadassah said as she turned the handle. "It sounds like Grace led them to the King."

"Yeah," Bethany responded as she grabbed the bucket and steadied it on the edge of the well. While they filled their water-skins, a young woman introduced herself as Sarah. Her black hair was fastened in a tight bun, and her clothes looked like those of a peasant.

"Is Grace taking you to the Great King?" Sarah asked.

"She is," answered Bethany.

"You'll be so glad you pursued Him. Just one day in His presence transformed my life."

"How so?" Bethany asked.

"I came to know Him, which caused me to love Him. And once you love Him, you're never the same. My heart came alive in ways I never dreamed, and now all I want is to be with Him forever."

"I long to know Him," Hadassah said. "May I ask you a question?"

"Of course."

"Grace said that most of the people here work seven days a week. Why is that?"

"I can't say that I know. It's the way it's always been. There's someone who might know the answer. He's the oldest man in our village, and he knows everything. He's sitting over there." She pointed a short distance away to a little old man who appeared to be napping beneath a willow tree.

Leaving the water-skins, Hadassah excused herself, grabbed Bethany's hand and headed for the man.

Hadassah stood for a few minutes waiting for him to look up. When it became obvious that was not going to happen, she cleared her throat and said, "Excuse me, sir, but Sarah told me you might know the answer to my question."

Without opening his eyes, he responded, "I might, but to whom do I have the pleasure of speaking?" He straightened his shoulders and opened his eyes.

"I beg your pardon, sir. My name's Hadassah and this is Bethany — she was born in the palace of the Great King."

"That makes you special, little lady," he said, leaning forward. "But the King gives grace to the humble."

Bethany blushed. The old man smiled. His teeth were perfect. "My name's Jacob. Now what was your question?"

"I was wondering why everyone works all of the time."

"Oh, that's easy to answer. When I was a just a tadpole of a boy," he said, "a traveler on his way to Egypt told us he had read one of the King's personal letters, an ancient letter. He said the letter instructed all who wanted to sit at the King's table to work hard, because performance is the way to gain His approval."

Hadassah's heart sank. "I didn't know that," she mumbled.

"It must be true," the old man answered. "Now, is there anything more I can do for you, little lady?"

"No. And thank you for your help."

Hadassah walked away, stunned. She never considered that pleasing the King meant working hard. *If the old man is right then I have no hope, for I've done nothing for Him. I have no works to present, and neither do I have any skills or crafts to offer. All I have is a longing in my heart to know Him more.*

"And that, My child, is all the King is looking for," Life-Giver whispered.

Hadassah was so busy thinking that she did not hear Him, and neither did she hear Bethany trying to tell her the King was not like that at all.

***

As the day wore on, Hadassah's heart grew heavier. She convinced herself that the old man was right.

"Hadassah, whose voice are you listening to? Ask Me for the truth," Life-Giver whispered.

Stepping onto a street named Straight, Grace shouted, "We're here!"

"Where?" Hadassah asked.

"The most desirable place on earth," said Bethany. "The entrance to the King's Courtyard."

"I don't see anything," Hadassah said.

"Don't fret, Hadassah. Around that corner, there's a curtain separating the Inner Court and the Holy of Holies, which is where you will find the sanctuary of the Great King. No one can step through that veil except those who are sinless. To do so as a sinner means certain death —"

"Why didn't you tell me that before? I didn't come all this way and endure all those difficulties for you to tell me I'm not qualified!"

Before Grace had a chance to respond, Hadassah ran off. She ignored Grace and Bethany as they called after her. Disappearing onto the crowded street, Hadassah looked for a place to be alone. Seeing an alley she eagerly turned into it. As she walked, she asked for Life-Giver's help.

Self-Pity and Despair smelled the scent of her disappointment, offense and frustration. Both creatures sped toward her like flies to fresh dung. "She's mine," Despair screeched.

"No, she's mine — I smelled her first!" said Self-Pity.

"You are both mistaken; this one is Mine," Life-Giver announced, suddenly appearing in front of the drooling, trembling creatures.

With a glance, Life-Giver flung the two demons through the air and back into the hole they crawled out of.

"All is not lost, Hadassah," Life-Giver said, walking beside her.

"Oh, Life-Giver, I don't understand! I have this scroll, but I just discovered that it's useless! It's just as I feared. I'll *never* be good enough! I don't have anything to show the King — no works, no title, no gold or silver. All I have is a flawed me," she said, sobbing uncontrollably.

"Did I ever ask for your silver or your gold? Did I ever ask for the sweat of your brow? Did I ever ask for your performance? Did I ever ask you to be flawless?"

"Grace said one must be perfect in order to enter the Holy of Holies. And Jacob told me hard work is the way to win the King's heart. I'm anything but sinless, and I've done nothing to earn anything!"

"My Father and I do not require and neither do We expect you to be perfect. We created you and are very aware of your limitations. Why are you trying to be something you can never be?"

"But Grace said —"

"I know what Grace said, but you left before she could tell you the rest of the story. She was getting ready to tell you how I died to take away your sins."

"What are You saying?"

"I am saying that I am your perfection. Because I took all your sins as My own, you are sinless. My grace and My love bring you home, Hadassah, not your deeds. Grace is My free gift to you. Grace means that you gain at My expense."

"Grace?"

"Unmerited favor and unrelenting love. You can't earn it, and neither will you ever deserve it. Grace empowers you to be and do what I created you to be and do — nothing more and nothing less."

"The King gives grace to the humble," Hadassah said to herself.

"True humility is knowing that you are nothing without Me and understanding that you are everything with Me."

"What have I ever done to deserve such love?"

"Nothing."

Hadassah had to smile at His answer.

"Life-Giver, why am I so terrified of not measuring up, of not being good enough?"

"Because you don't really know Me."

"I want to know You."

"Then give Me all of you."

"I want to, but I don't really know how. And I do things I don't want to do and leave undone the things that I should do. I am so weak and sinful and I hate it!"

"*This life is not about you, Hadassah. It is all about Me. I am enough. My love covers a multitude of sins and My love never fails to accomplish what it is sent out to do.*"

"That is good news. I just hope and pray that I can remember that." Hadassah sighed deeply. "Life-Giver?"

"Yes?"

"Grace dreamed that I had something that belonged to the King, but she didn't know what it was. What is it? Tell me and it's Yours!"

"*Love.*"

"What? I don't understand."

"*We gave you Our love, and We would like to have it back,*" Life-Giver gently stated.

Hadassah felt confused.

"*Hadassah, before I formed the foundation of the earth, I knew you and loved you. The day you were conceived, I gave you life and poured My love into you. I watched as My Father handcrafted you in your mother's womb. The day you were born I held you in My arms and kissed your face, your tiny fingers and toes. As you grew and learned to walk, My love was right there holding you up and cheering you on. The day you had your first tantrum, I calmed you with My love. As you learned to talk, I delighted in every syllable you uttered. The day you fell into the river, it was My love that rescued you. The day you pushed your sister into that mud puddle, I was right there loving you still. The day your parents left this world for a better one, My love blazed brighter than ever. In the Land of Despair, My love was your constant companion and protector. When Rebekah and Beloved entered into their eternal home, My love kept you and is healing your heart.*

"*You see, My precious one, you have always been in the center of My love and always will be. You have never been alone and never will be. The truth is I love you dearly, Hadassah. And I would like you to give that love back to Me.*"

"I can actually *feel* it," she said, tears filling her eyes. "The love You've deposited in me is bearing fruit."

"*Indeed it is and this fruit shall remain. Now receive My Spirit,*" He said as He breathed on her.

The light breeze swept over her, causing her to feel as if she was slightly intoxicated. "What is this?"

"This is the joy of being loved by Me."

"I don't ever want this feeling to go away," she said, closing her eyes to focus on the joy and love spreading throughout her spirit, soul and body.

She saw herself walking in a hot desert. Life-Giver approached. His shadow fell on her, shading her from the burning rays of the sun. "I am always with you — to the end of your days." With a wave of His hand, the sand before her turned into an endless ocean. The air felt pleasant. Seagulls appeared out of nowhere, calling to the One who gave them life.

On His left, where the beach disappeared into the tall grass, a large, flat rock jutted out from the bank. "Follow Me," Life-Giver said.

On hands and knees, the two climbed up the sandy bank onto the rock platform. With legs swinging, she took in her surroundings. "I think I understand what You brought me here to see — nothing remains the same when I'm with You. Your very presence turns difficulties into opportunities, loneliness into fellowship and death into life. All is well with You by my side."

"Hadassah, always remember this: If you die — you live!"

The vision ended as quickly as it began.

Overwhelming waves of holy desire and delight filled her. Her difficulties, pain and sorrow were washed away. The irresistible undertow of His kindness carried her spirit into the realm of His Spirit once again.

Life-Giver stood before her in all of His glory. She fell at His feet, face to the ground, covered her head with her arms and cried out, "I'm a daughter of unclean lips, and I live among a people of unclean lips!"

With just one glance, His love, delight and mercy flooded her.

Gabriel responded to Life-Giver's unspoken command and brought a coal from the throne and pressed it against her lips.

"Rise, My love," Life-Giver said, His voice like the sound of many waters.

Finding strength from a Source other than herself, she stood, head bowed and knees shaking.

"You have been chosen to be My bride in the age to come."

"How do I rightly respond to such an honor and privilege, my Lord? What shall I do?" Her voice trembled as she stared at the emerald sea of glass.

"Love Me and love others . . . whether friend or foe."

"The more I see, hear and know, the more I love You! I'm now convinced that there is more to my life than meets the eye. And my love is real in Your eyes, and Your love for me is finally real in my heart."

Hadassah tentatively looked up and saw her reflection in Life-Giver's eyes. She was surprised by the beauty she saw reflected there. "I look so beautiful to You."

"What you see is true," He whispered.

He reached out to envelop her. Without any hesitation, she fell against Him and said, "There's nothing in me that You should desire, and yet I can't deny the holy longing that's evident in Your eyes. Therefore, I give back to You what is rightfully Yours — I love You with the love You gave me."

"You are bone of My bone and flesh of My flesh — My longing and My desire."

"And You are my everything."

Life-Giver held her close, tears filling His eyes. He whispered, "All I ever wanted was to love you."

"You are unlike anyone I've ever met."

"That is true."

"Life-Giver?"

"Yes?"

"I feel so safe in Your arms. Why can't You just carry me through this life?"

"If I were to carry you, you would soon become weak and lazy and would never mature. Children are carried for a season, but you have outgrown that season. It is now time for you to step behind me, press your face against My back, wrap your arms around My waist and step where I step."

"But that means I won't be able to see where I'm going."

"That is true, but this is what it looks like to walk by faith and not by sight."

Hadassah opened her eyes. Nothing around her had changed — merchants shouted, dogs barked and children ran through the streets, but Hadassah felt as though everything had changed.

"Thank You, Life-Giver," she said.

"It is My pleasure to give you the kingdom. Now go and possess it."

Hadassah hurried to find Grace and Bethany. They were right where she left them.

"Where'd you go?" Bethany asked. "And what happened to *you*?"

"You might say I'm in love," Hadassah said, grinning from ear to ear.

"In love with whom?" asked Grace.

"With Life-Giver — I found what I've been looking for!"

"What's that?" asked Bethany.

"True love."

"Then you're ready to step through the curtain," Grace said, smiling broadly.

"I am."

"Then what are we waiting for?" Bethany asked.

Grace led the way. When they turned the corner, Hadassah stopped abruptly. Surprise was not what she felt upon seeing the curtain. Shock and dismay were not quite what she felt either. It was a combination of all three. The curtain was nothing more than a thin veil, and someone had ripped it from the top to the bottom. It was wide open.

Hadassah said, "I don't understand. Anyone can walk into the Holy of Holies without any problem. There's no gatekeeper, no guard, no one to disqualify them or ask for their credentials."

"That's true," said Grace.

Hadassah looked beyond the veil, and her breath caught in her throat. She stared open-mouthed at a grand palace. It drew Hadassah like clover draws bees.

"It's finally going to happen," Hadassah said, her knees shaking. "Rebekah, Martha, I wish you could see this! Mama, Papa, how I wish you were here. And my precious Beloved — you would've loved this."

"Your loved ones not only see this place, but they live here," Life-Giver said.

Hearing Him, she laughed. "Of course they do."

Michael turned to Life-Giver. "She hears clearly now."

"That is because she has learned to listen."

"Life-Giver, lead me on to Your Father," Hadassah prayed.

Grace and Bethany looked at each other and smiled.

"What do you say we go spend a day with the King?" Hadassah asked.

The three locked arms. Grace chose an indistinct footpath rather than the wide path leading to the main entrance of the palace. At one point, it appeared as if she was leading them away from the palace. Hadassah felt the familiar fear and wanted to challenge her but fought the urge. She sang instead. The farther away they walked the louder she sang.

As they rounded a sharp bend in the path, Hadassah stopped singing because directly in front of her was the rear entrance of the castle.

"Family always comes to the backdoor," Bethany responded to the questioning look on Hadassah's face.

"But —"

"Haven't you been adopted by the King?" Bethany asked.

Before she could answer, a gatekeeper stepped up to the white picket gate and asked, "Who goes there?"

Grace stepped forward, saying, "This maiden has come from the Land of Despair, where she entered into a covenant with Life-Giver, which makes her a child of the King." Laying her hand on Bethany's shoulder, she continued, "And you already know this child."

Bethany and the gatekeeper exchanged informal greetings. The gatekeeper then turned his attention back to Hadassah. "What proof do you have of this covenant?"

"I have none at all, kind sir, except the love that now fills my heart. But, alas, that is not something I can show you," Hadassah answered, feeling surprisingly peaceful and confident in Life-Giver's ability to complete that which He had begun in her life.

Bethany stepped forward in her defense and said, "No one can prove their relationship with the King in mere outward ways. You know as well as I do that the King's seal on the human heart is the only proof there is regarding eternal life."

Movement in an upper window captured Hadassah's attention. A curtain was being pulled back. A handsome Man looked down at her. When their eyes met, Hadassah was painfully aware of her unkempt appearance. She looked down. Her garments were soiled and torn and nothing more than rags. Her long hair was dirty and straggly. Her face and arms were filthy, for it had been weeks since she had bathed.

Embarrassment and shame filled her. Her eyes fell to the ground. She turned away so quickly that she did not see the holy longing burning in the Man's eyes, neither did she see His welcoming smile.

Suffocating shame rose up from within. She ran away, hiding behind a stone wall. "Life-Giver, are You here?"

"I am always here."

"Your unconditional love has caused me to forget just how wretched I am, how ugly and poor. How will I ever gain entrance to this grand palace looking like this?"

"You are looking at yourself with your natural eyes."

"When You look at me I feel wonderful and beautiful. Why did I feel so ashamed when that stranger looked at me? I don't understand."

"You felt that way because you focused on your outward appearance, which means very little in My Father's kingdom."

"That's so hard to remember."

"What is the truth, Hadassah? Who are you?"

"The truth is . . . I am loved and I move Your heart."

"Who am I, Hadassah?"

"You are the sweetest name I've ever known! You are always the same — yesterday, today and forever. You are faithful! You are beautiful! You are good! You are merciful! You are my Deliverer, my Savior, my Friend, and You love me the most."

"If this is true, and it is, then what is there to be afraid of?"

"I suppose nothing."

"There is no fear in love," said Life-Giver.

"I'm trying hard to remember that," she said, turning to go.

"Hadassah."

"Yes?"

"I can't keep My eyes off of you."

Hadassah let out a deep breath. "I love You, too."

"I love you more."

"I don't know what I'd do without You . . . and I don't want to find out."

"That is one thing you won't ever have to experience."

With a big smile, Hadassah smoothed her skirt. She stepped out of hiding and confidently returned to the gate. As she approached, Grace knowingly smiled. Standing before the gatekeeper, she suddenly remembered the scroll. "I believe I have the proof that you require, sir," she said, placing the scroll in his hand.

Unrolling it, he read it, looked at her and then read it again. "Where did you find this?"

"In a refuse pile."

"Really?"

"Really. The evil prince found it first, but he threw it away. After much searching, I was able to find it with a little help from a deer."

"A deer?"

"It's a long story."

"Well, it appears that you have been chosen. You are free to enter the King's gate to the palace." He lifted the latch and the three walked through.

"But sir, I don't just want to enter the palace. I want to spend an entire day — face to face — with the Great King. How can I make that happen?" Hadassah asked.

"You can't. You aren't that powerful. No one can make the Great King do anything," the gatekeeper said with great intensity. "Everything flows out of His heart to you, not the other way around. He is the Heartbeat of this kingdom. He is the Sun, and you are the moon. He is the Giver of Life, and you are the recipient. He rules and reigns, child, and no one else. You are free to make your petitions known, for the King delights in giving you the desires of your heart. But He alone is King."

"I understand. . . I think."

"And just for the record, my lady, a day is a thousand years to the King and a thousand years is a day."

"What?"

The guard smiled, nodded his head and walked away without explaining.

Hadassah shrugged and then ran after Grace and Bethany who waited at the door.

Hadassah felt as though she had entered another world. She stood immersed in the softest, whitest light she had ever seen. The source was a mystery. There was no flame or lamp to be seen. She stood in an enormous, open courtyard. The floor was made of white marble, the waist-high walls of white stone. Strategically placed around the courtyard were enormous white pots holding a great variety of exotic plants and vibrantly colored flowers. The air she breathed was crisp and clean. Hadassah closed her eyes and allowed herself a moment to just be. It felt so good, so freeing to just be.

"Hadassah, are you coming?" Bethany called out.

"I don't know if I'll ever leave this place," she whispered to herself.

"Hadassah," Bethany called again. Opening her eyes, she hurried after. "I've never experienced such freedom," she said wrapping her arm around Bethany's waist.

"I know what you mean. I didn't realize what I had until I left it."

Men, women and children of all ages walked up and down the golden streets. No one appeared to be in a hurry, and neither did anyone appear to be worried. Laughter and worship filled the air. The combination was quite delightful and like nothing Hadassah had ever experienced.

"Why is everyone so happy?" Hadassah asked.

"Because of the Great King," Grace answered. "Once you've been with Him you'll understand. Now go, child, and explore the beauty of this place."

Elated, Hadassah quietly sang love songs to Life-Giver as she admired the simple yet elegant architecture. Bethany and Grace followed at a distance. Everything — from the gardens to the streets to the furnishings — was so beautiful and pleasing to not only the eye but also the heart. She walked for hours searching every face, hoping and praying for a chance encounter with the Great King.

"Nothing ever happens by chance in My kingdom," Life-Giver whispered.

"I kind of thought that but was hoping there might be an exception," Hadassah said, giggling.

As the sun set, Grace led Hadassah and Bethany to a door tucked just beneath the castle walls. Hadassah's heart was at perfect peace.

"Bethany, aren't you going to the King?" Hadassah asked.

"When He summons me," she said.

Pushing open the wooden door, Grace said, "Welcome to my humble abode."

A beautiful, hand-carved sign hung over the fireplace that read: "Grace will lead you home."

"How true," Hadassah whispered.

The room contained three cots, a table and three chairs.

How odd, Hadassah thought.

"The King has prepared a place for us," Grace responded.

"*He* prepared this room for us?"

"Well, actually, His Son did," Grace said, pulling out a chair.

"I would've thought you'd have a nicer place than this," Hadassah said.

"Why would you think that when this is all I need?"

"I guess because I figured the King would reward you for your faithful service."

"He has, child, but in ways that are so much more important than this. My physical comfort is not the number one priority of the King, and for that, I am thankful."

"I have so much to learn," said Hadassah.

"And you have all eternity to do so."

Sitting at the table, Grace opened her knapsack, and just as Hadassah expected, it was still full. Hadassah laughed. "The never-ending food! I wish I had a heart filled with never-ending faith!"

You have, Hadassah, and it is My gift to you," said Life-Giver.

CHAPTER TWENTY-EIGHT

*H*adassah woke to a strange sound. Rolling over, she listened closely but heard nothing. Rubbing her eyes, she looked around. Bethany and Grace were nowhere to be seen. On the small table was a bowl of fresh fruit and what smelled like freshly baked bread. Her stomach growled loudly. "So you're the strange sound," she said, patting her belly.

I can't remember the last time I slept in a real bed, she thought as she snuggled into the thick mattress. Her stomach growled louder. "I hear you," she said, chuckling. Slipping out from under the warm blankets, she wrapped her cloak around her shoulders and sat at the table. She broke off a piece of bread; it was still warm. Hadassah smothered it with butter and then ate almost half the loaf and more berries and grapes than she wanted to count.

A basin of water sat nearby. Discovering that the water was still warm, she decided to bathe.

"Oh, how good it feels to be clean!" she said to herself. "I only wish my dress was clean." Slipping it over her head, she stepped outside into the bright sunshine.

Hadassah wandered through the King's enormous courtyard taking in the beauty surrounding her. "Life-Giver, I know You're here somewhere. I just want You to know that for the first time in my entire life, I feel peaceful. I don't know how You did it. There's no striving or anxiety in my heart. What's even more amazing is that I no longer feel driven to find the King."

She listened but heard nothing. Even that did not trouble her.

"You've taught me so much on my journey. I've learned how to love and be loved, to sing and to be thankful. My circumstances have been difficult and not something that I'd ever want to repeat, but I'm most grateful for the lessons learned and the peace I now feel. Thank You for all that You've done for me. Thank You for the pain, the suffering, the trials and the victories. Thank You for leading me here."

Hadassah stopped in front of an elaborate iron gate. Expecting it to be locked, she pushed on the handle. To her surprise it opened. Hadassah hesitantly stepped into the most beautiful garden she had ever seen. "The gardener must be the Great King Himself," she whispered.

Numerous angels stepped back, allowing her to enter.

She slowly strolled through the midst of glorious fragrances, stunning colors and pleasing designs. The beauty flooded her senses, and she felt slightly intoxicated.

Seeing a marble bench tucked beneath a dogwood tree in full bloom, she made her way to it. Sitting on the cool stone she shivered. As if understanding her need for warmth, beams of sunlight broke through the branches. "It feels as though I've entered a place beyond tomorrow and my soul feels at home here. No more tears or pain and no more sorrow. Is this eternity?"

A family of sparrows bathed in the nearby birdbath. Their song filled the garden with beautiful music. Hadassah joined their worship.

Her Bridegroom listened, hidden from her sight but drawn closer and closer by her adoration.

She sang,

Your Perfect Love is what I cling to.
Your name is the tower I will run to,
For all others names are powerless to save.
Your strength is what lifts my head.

Your love is like the sun after the rain.

You fill eternity — nothing can contain You!
Oh, my Friend and Giver of Life,
Absolutely nothing is like You!

Death has lost its sting.
It has no power over me.
You've given me beauty for my ashes,
And I will join with the angels singing holy,
For my soul longs for You.

Tears of joy and thankfulness streamed down Hadassah's face. *She did not know that Life-Giver knelt before her. Sighing deeply, He whispered words heard only by His Father. "Look at her, Father. She loves Us! She truly loves Us! Now We can draw her into the very center of Our heart."*

His Father replied, "This is the day of the gladness of My heart."

Unaware of the spiritual activity around her, Hadassah continued her inward pursuit. A deep longing filled Hadassah's soul. "Life-Giver, I know now that all I want is You, for I was made to love You. Your love is what I cling to. You're all I need. Only You can satisfy. I'm content to remain here, in Your presence, for the rest of my life. I need nothing more and want nothing less."

Hadassah was so lost in worship that she did not hear the sound of footsteps until they were almost upon her. She jumped to her feet, wiping her tears. Looking for a way of escape but finding none, she smoothed her wrinkled, soiled dress and ran her fingers through her tangled hair. "Life-Giver, grant me favor with whoever approaches, I pray."

A guard dressed in fine apparel headed toward her. Hadassah was certain she was about to be reprimanded for trespassing. Her mind searched for an explanation but found none. The man stopped in front of her and said, "The Great King has summoned you to the Holy of Holies."

"Me?" she asked. "Are you sure you have the right person? Do you know who I am?"

"The Great King knows you very well," he said ever so kindly.

"But how?"

"The King knows everything there is to know. Shall we go?"

Feeling overwhelmed, Hadassah simply nodded. Following him through the gate, she whispered under her breath, "Life-Giver, I'm about to see Your Father, the King. Please fill me with peace, for my heart's beating so fast that I fear it will burst."

"You have nothing to fear except fear itself."

The guard led Hadassah to a side entrance into the palace. She followed him through a maze of hallways and up several flights of stairs. He stopped before a large set of double doors and said, "You have nothing to fear, my lady."

Hadassah ran her hands through her hair again, reminding herself that outward appearance was of little concern. *I know it's true that the King isn't interested in my outward appearance,* she thought, *but I sure would feel better if I wasn't dressed in rags.*

Taking a deep breath, she followed the guard through the doorway into a room more magnificent than anything she could ever have imagined. The room itself was a circle. In the center was a throne, and sitting on the throne was a kind-looking Gentleman surrounded by countless servants. Over the throne arched an emerald rainbow; its rich colors reflecting on the crystal floor. Hadassah's knees grew weak, and her heart nearly stopped. Immediately, the guard reached out and steadied her.

"Come to Me, child," the King invited.

With the guard holding her steady, Hadassah slowly approached.

"You have nothing to fear except fear itself," the Great King said ever so gently.

"That's what Life-Giver said," said Hadassah weakly.

"You know My Son then?"

"I do," Hadassah answered, wondering why He would ask since Life-Giver said He knows everything.

"My dear child, when I ask you a question it is not because I am looking for information," He said with great tenderness.

Hadassah's longtime companion, Fear, whispered lies in her mind. "Hadassah, you don't belong here. The king doesn't care about someone like you. You should just turn around and run out of here before he has you arrested — or killed. You know you're guilty of so much."

"Come to Me, dear child of Mine, for there is no fear in love. Perfect Love casts out fear. Fear involves punishment, and the one who fears is not perfected in love."

As Hadassah placed her foot on the first step, she collapsed, saying, "Oh, Great King, You're so glorious and I'm so flawed — please don't arrest or kill me!"

"I do not arrest or kill people because they are less than perfect. If that were true then there would be no one alive on the earth." He chuckled softly.

"But I've heard it said that You're too holy to be in the presence of sinful people, of which I'm one," Hadassah said, desperately hoping it was not true.

"Now, who told you that? Oh, do not answer — I know all too well who spreads such lies about Me. Dearest child, the truth is My Son lived on the earth among sinful people for thirty-three years, and He didn't kill one of them. I love sinners, Hadassah. It is sin that I hate, not sinners. And I hate it because it is destructive to those I love."

"You really do love sinners?"

"Of course I do. Now come here, child, come to your Father," He said, arms outstretched.

Hadassah felt as though she was five years old. She scrambled up the steps, ran into His arms and allowed herself to be lifted onto His lap where He wrapped her in His Perfect Love.

Terrified, the spirit of Fear retreated into the dark recesses of her soul.

As she rested her head against the King's magnificent chest, He said, "Sin does not separate Me from you, child. I am not the One who moves when you sin — you step away from Me. And when you do, I pursue you, for I know that I am your only hope."

"I've been told that many times."

"I am so glad you finally believe it, Hadassah."

"I guess I had to experience it," she said, sighing deeply.

Hadassah found herself thinking about Life-Giver's words that there was only One who could tell her who she was. "Great King, will You tell me who I am?"

"Hadassah, you are My beloved child — the one I love and enjoy. You consume My every thought, and I want to share all My love with you."

"You do?"

"I do."

"What do You see when You look at me?" she asked, looking into His eyes.

"I see two hearts that beat as one."

"Life-Giver told me that is my life's pursuit. I want that, but I don't quite know how to make it happen."

"You can't make that happen, but you can allow Me to accomplish it for you. Hadassah, I want to give you all of My love, but I can't unless you believe it and receive it."

"I choose to believe!" she cried out.

"Then receive My love for you," He said, softly blowing on her.

Wave after wave of pure joy washed over her, and she lost her balance, nearly falling over. Had the King not had quick reflexes, she would have certainly sprawled out on the sea of glass.

"Two hearts beating as one," Hadassah said, giggling. She rested against His chest and reveled in the immensity of His love for her.

"Perfect Love has found you," her Father the King said.

"Yes, it has." All of Hadassah's thoughts, fears and concerns disappeared as she was swept away on an ocean of pure love.

Hadassah finally sat up. "Thank You," she said.

"I will always love you, Hadassah."

Emboldened by her time basking in her Father's love, Hadassah finally brought up the deepest desire of her heart. "May I ask You a question?"

"You may ask Me anything."

"I found these two scrolls," she said, placing her treasured possessions in His hand.

"I see," He said, running His fingers over the tattered parchments. Without reading them, He gave them back.

"But . . . You didn't read them."

"There is no need. I wrote them."

"Oh. . . that's right." Hadassah said.

"Hadassah, the invitation you hold in your hand is priceless. Even so, I have made it available to all, but sadly, some reject it altogether. While others are too busy with the cares of the world. There are many who claim to seek Me, but what they really desire is knowledge not true intimacy. Knowing *about* Me is not the same as knowing *Me*."

"I want to know You."

"That is noble and right." The King smiled.

"Well, may I?"

"May you spend a day with Me?"

"Ever since I found these scrolls, I've longed to find You and Your kingdom. I've journeyed far and suffered much. I'd really love to spend an entire day with You that I might come to know You. I understand that I don't deserve it."

"What you desire is difficult to do, for this world fights against the kind of intimate relationship you speak of. How do you intend to accomplish such an impossible feat?"

"I'm not sure. I was kind of hoping You might know how to make that happen?"

The King chuckled. Hadassah realized how ridiculous her question was and said, "You know how to do everything."

"You have grown in wisdom, My precious child. Life-Giver has loved you well, and My Spirit has led you to the Truth. But there is one thing that remains."

"Whatever it is, I'll do it."

"Can you follow My Son for a day and do what He does?"

"Life-Giver? The One I've come to love? Can it really be true? If I follow Him for a day then I can spend a day with You?"

"Yes."

"I can do that!" she exclaimed.

"So be it."

Hadassah could not believe her good fortune. Snuggled in the arms of Perfect Love, she looked around the throne room. "I really like it here."

"I am very glad to hear you say that, since you will be spending eternity with Me."

"Life-Giver told me Your throne and kingdom are inside of me."

"Exactly," said the Great King, the tiniest hint of a smile appearing at the corners of His mouth. "I am everywhere, Hadassah. I am Life. My kingdom is not an earthly kingdom. If it were, My Son would never have suffered at the hands of men."

"I don't quite understand."

"There is much mystery to My kingdom. It is an eternal kingdom with an eternal King who rules and reigns in justice, mercy and truth. Unlike the realm you temporarily reside in, My kingdom has no boundaries. But have no fear, for your destiny is found in My kingdom. You shall be transformed into My image."

"My destiny is to be transformed into Your image?" Hadassah asked, growing more bewildered by the moment.

"That was My original design — a family made in My image."

"Why would Someone as powerful and grand as You care about people who are so flawed, small and weak?"

"I care because I am your Father."

Hadassah thought back to her mama and papa and their love for her. "I can understand that."

"My peace I give to you," He said. "My peace I leave with you."

Hadassah had no idea how long she remained in the arms of her heavenly Father. She only knew that she never wanted to leave. The Great King hummed as He ran His fingers through her hair, happy to be holding His daughter close.

"You're humming Mama's song," Hadassah said, tears spilling over her eyelids.

He smiled deeply and pulled her even closer.

CHAPTER TWENTY-NINE

$\mathcal{A}$s Life-Giver walked into the throne room, every knee bowed. Hadassah was overwhelmed with a flood of emotions. "Greetings, Hadassah," He said.

"You are really real," she whispered.

"I am."

"I knew You were real, but I didn't know that You were *real . . .* uh . . . I mean . . . well, I don't think I know what I mean."

Life-Giver laughed, but not at her. His laugh was that of utter delight, and Hadassah felt it warm her soul. She slid off the Great King's lap only to discover that her legs were a bit shaky.

"Would you like to walk with Me?" He asked.

She nodded.

The sea of glass felt wonderful beneath her bare feet.

"Hadassah, My journey was difficult. I was once poor and without a home."

Astonished, she said, "You, the Son of the Great King, were poor and homeless?"

"Yes."

"How's that even possible?"

"I chose to be."

"But why would You choose that?"

"My Father asked me to do so. I was the only One who could buy you back from Satan. I exchanged My perfect blood for your sin-infested blood. Because of what I did you are free from death," His eyes sparkled like diamonds.

"And I am forever grateful. Your kindness has saved me."

"My kindness is meant to save not only you but the world, Hadassah. If you are going to be My companion for a day, as My Father has informed Me, you will need to love others in the same way I do. Are you able to do that?"

"I'd think it would be easy to do that."

"Easy?" He asked with a smile.

"How hard can it be to go where You go and do what You do for one day?"

"You may find it to be more difficult than you think," said Life-Giver.

"What exactly do You do?"

"I love those who hate Me, share good news, raise the dead, heal the sick, open blind eyes and deaf ears, feed the poor, care for widows and orphans, set people free from prison, and confront every form of evil."

"You do all that in just one day?"

"I do all that and much more."

"Oh my! Maybe it won't be as easy as I thought."

"You will find it to be impossible."

"What? I don't understand. You're asking me to do something I can't do?"

"Yes."

"Why?"

"So you will realize that I am all you need."

"I thought I already knew that."

Life-Giver stopped. He looked deep into her eyes. Hadassah knew the truth. "I guess I have much to learn," she said, lowering her eyes.

Nodding slightly, He smiled and then resumed walking.

"Hadassah, everyone who leaves house or family for My sake will receive a hundred times as much in this present age, along with persecutions. And in the age to come, they will inherit eternal life."

"Did You just say persecution? Does that mean if I follow You, I'll be persecuted?"

"Yes."

"That doesn't seem fair," she said.

"Who told you life was fair? There is nothing fair about Satan and his kingdom — he is completely void of mercy as he creates havoc for those who love Me." Life-Giver paused to give Hadassah time to process. "Knowing this, do you still want to follow Me?"

"Of course I do. No one else loves me like You do!"

"That is true." He kissed the back of her hand. "Hadassah, as you follow, remember that you are in a battle both within yourself and without. You will not have ease or comfort. You will have all you need, but not all you want. You will experience momentary, light affliction because it produces in you a glory far beyond anything this world can give you. Be careful not to focus on the things which you can see, for they are temporal. But set your gaze on the things which are eternal, for those are the only things worth your time and attention. And be aware that your enemy, Satan, will try to deceive you on every turn. But have no fear, for those who love the truth will not be deceived.

"Count the cost, Hadassah, for once a soldier enlists he is not fit for battle if he looks back."

"I can't go back."

"You can, but it would not be wise. The battle will purge and purify those things in your heart that are in need of healing and deliverance. Count it all joy, Hadassah, when you encounter various trials, knowing the testing of your faith produces endurance. Will you allow endurance to have its perfect result, so that you will be complete, lacking nothing?"

Hadassah pondered His words. "What You say sounds impossible. But if I don't follow You, then I can't spend a day with my Father, the King. And if I can't spend time with Him, how will I ever come to know Him?"

"If you have seen Me you have seen the Father. My Father and I are One. And Our desire is for you to be one with Us."

"You are the only One who can give me life, so I shall pay whatever price necessary. Behold, I am Your bondservant and I will follow You for a day, for a thousand years, forever."

"Then meet Me by the sheep gate at first light."

"I'll be there," she said bowing. Life-Giver squeezed her hand, bidding her farewell. Crossing the room, He left through a rather small door to her right.

The same servant that escorted her to the throne room was now by her side. Taking her arm, he whispered, "You are dearly loved, my lady."

"I am beginning to believe that."

As they left the throne room, the doorkeeper proclaimed, "See what great love the King has bestowed upon Hadassah that she would be called His child!"

***

Hadassah was so excited that she barely slept. Rising well before daylight, she packed her few belongings, ate some bread and then bid Bethany and Grace farewell, saying, "I shall return tomorrow."

"To spend a day following Life-Giver is better than a thousand elsewhere," Grace said, holding her tightly.

"To follow Life-Giver for a day is a dream come true — and to think that I not only get to be with Him but also the Great King is more than I ever hoped for," she said as she hugged Bethany.

Walking down the dark street, Hadassah shivered. The air was quite cool. She pulled her cloak tighter. *Unbeknownst to her, the Holy Spirit and a mighty army of angels escorted her to the One who eagerly awaited her arrival.*

The Holy Spirit announced, "This one has been found worthy to join the fellowship of the sufferings of the One who gave His life to set her free. She will be asked to walk into the furnace of true love, which will consume those things that are not holy and refine those things that are not yet complete."

"May I ask what will be the outcome?" Michael asked. "Will she love to the end?"

"Love is stronger than the grave, Michael; many waters cannot quench this love. And Perfect Love never fails to accomplish what it is sent out to do."

Hadassah turned the corner. The sheep gate was now in sight. Her heart leapt, for Life-Giver, dressed in glorious apparel, seated on a beautiful white stallion, awaited her arrival. Seeing her, His heart leapt. He smiled broadly and nodded. Hadassah, heart in her throat, nodded in return.

Hadassah bowed low and said, "Behold your handmaiden." Lifting her head but not her eyes, she said, "I will go where You go. As You love, I will love. Not my will, but Your will be done."

Life-Giver turned His eyes to the King and announced, "Father, there is none so lovely. There is none so fair. I cannot escape her beauty."

"Behold Your bride," His Father responded.

Turning His eyes back to Hadassah, He asked, "Are you ready?"

She looked away, her heart beating wildly. "I find myself feeling afraid," she said.

"Come anyway," He said.

"She has yet to understand the fullness of who she really is," said Michael.

"The discovery of one's true identity is a journey that takes a lifetime," the Great King said.

"Allow Me to help you. Will you take My hand?" asked Life-Giver.

"Am I to ride with You?' she asked, feeling smaller than she ever thought possible.

"If you so choose," He answered, smiling.

"I so choose." Hadassah put her small hand in His big one. With the greatest of ease, He lifted her behind Him.

"I don't trust my ability to stay on," she said, gripping His garment as fear gripped her heart.

"You are right to doubt your ability to keep yourself, for I am the only true security there is. This journey is not about what *you* can do, but what *I* can do."

With an almost imperceptible nudge, Life-Giver turned His magnificent steed toward the gate. They cantered out of the palace grounds, and headed toward the sun.

"Where are we going and what shall we do?" she asked.

"We are going to the weak, to the lonely, to those who have lost their way. We will give water to the thirsty, food to the hungry, hope to the hopeless and freedom to the prisoners."

"But wouldn't it be better to stay in the Holy Place?"

"That depends on why you want to stay there."

"Because it's easier and because the King is there?" she said, hoping it was the right answer.

"Easier isn't always better. Taking the easy path often produces immaturity, laziness and apathy. Difficulties, on the other hand, bring about perseverance, which develops proven character. And proven character produces hope. As for the King being in the Holy Place — He is everywhere, Hadassah, all of the time."

"Are You trying to warn me that we're going to have a difficult day?"

Life-Giver paused before answering. "I died for you, Hadassah."

"I don't understand."

"The question isn't whether or not you're going to suffer — the real question is will you die for Me since I died for you?"

"I'm going to die — *today!*?"

"If I had chosen not to die, then you would be without hope."

"You want me to *choose* to die?"

"I put before you life and death — choose life."

"Now I'm really confused. Do I live or die?"

"They are one in the same. Except a kernel of wheat fall into the ground and die it cannot live. If you die, you live."

Hadassah suddenly remembered her papa's words, *"The King's love for people was so strong and powerful that it killed His Son."*

He continued, "While you were lost in your sins, I gave My life that I might offer you freedom, thus demonstrating My unselfish love toward you. I once was dead, but now I am alive. Not only am I alive, but I now have the power to impart that life."

"Is that how you got Your name?"

"I am the highest Life and the only Giver of Life. And there is only one way to the Father, and that is through Me."

"Is that why I must spend a day with You first?"

"Spending a day with Me is to prepare you for an eternal life of complete abandonment and trust, for it is the only way to know true love," He said, reining in His horse. "This is where you get off."

Hadassah hesitated. "I don't understand."

"Will you trust Me?" His fiery eyes pierced her soul. How is it possible to possess such love and power? Hadassah thought.

"I want to trust You," she answered, taking His hand.

He helped her down. She waited for Him to dismount, but instead He said, "I must continue on."

"But I'm supposed to spend the day with You. Where are You going?"

"Where I am going, you cannot follow," He said, turning His horse to the west. "Blessed is the one who perseveres under trial; for once you have been approved, you will receive the crown of life which the King has promised to those who love Him."

"But I don't want a crown; I just want to spend a day with You and the King!" she shouted, running after Him.

"Every season has a purpose, Hadassah," He called back over His shoulder. "And nothing is ever wasted in My kingdom. I will never leave you or forsake you!"

Hadassah shouted, "Please wait for me! I must follow You!"

Without another word, He rode off.

Thankfully, He did not travel very fast, and Hadassah was able to keep Him in sight. She ran after Him as fast as she could, praying for help. She quickly grew tired. *I don't know how I will ever keep up with Him,* she thought. *But I must not allow fear or doubt control me.*

"Life-Giver, help me," she cried out.

She prayed harder. She no longer had the strength to run. Plodding along, she said to herself, "I don't understand why He left me."

"He hasn't left you, Hadassah," the Holy Spirit whispered.

"Is that You, Life-Giver?" she asked without stopping.

"I am the Holy Spirit. I am with you, Hadassah."

"You sound just like Life-Giver. Did I do something wrong? Is that why He left me?"

"You have done nothing wrong."

"Then why did He leave without me?"

"He left to prepare a place for you."

"Holy Spirit, I don't understand any of this."

"Hadassah, it is not for you to understand. It is for you to simply trust."

"Is He coming back for me?"

"Of that you can be certain. There is no power strong enough to keep Him from you. Until then, I will remain with you and will lead you into all truth."

CHAPTER THIRTY

*H*adassah kept her eyes fixed on the distant image of Life-Giver. When it became obvious He was heading into the desert, she cringed. Not again, she thought.

"Just one day," she reminded herself. "I can do anything for one day."

Plodding through the white, hot sand, she heard a familiar voice in her mind. *"Life-Giver doesn't love you. If he did, he wouldn't have left you. You mean nothing to him. You should return to your comfortable life with David and Naomi, with your sister. Life was easy there — unlike this godforsaken place."*

Hadassah tried desperately to ignore the voice, but it only grew louder and more aggressive. *"Why are you subjecting yourself to such humiliation? On the rare chance that you do succeed and are permitted to spend a day with the king, then what? I'll tell you what — after one day you'll be thrown away like an old, worn-out shoe. You're wasting your life, Hadassah."*

"Stop it!" Hadassah shouted, clamping her hands over her ears.

"If this king's so good, then why did he let everyone you love die? He didn't care about them, and he doesn't care about you. He's a liar and a thief."

"Just keep walking," she said to herself, trying desperately to ignore the voice.

"My Lord, shall I silence her Accuser?" Michael asked, his hand resting on the hilt of his sword.

Life-Giver answered, "No, Michael. Maturity never comes without a struggle. Her love is being tested, purified and strengthened. She has been well prepared for this day. Have no fear, for I am more than able to keep her."

The Great King stood up and all of heaven took notice. A holy hush filled the throne room. His voice, like a waterfall, echoed throughout heaven. "Do you not know? Have you not heard? The Everlasting God, the Lord, the Creator of the ends of the earth does not become weary or tired. My understanding is unfathomable. I give strength to the weary and to those who lack might I increase power. Though youths grow weary and tired, and vigorous young men stumble badly, yet those who wait for Me will gain new strength. They will mount up with wings like eagles, they will run and not get tired, they will walk and not become weary."

Gabriel, Michael and every angel trembled in awe of the One they served. Life-Giver joined His Father. Every angel fell on its face and sang, "His name is Prince of Peace, the everlasting Son of God, Redeemer, Lamb of God, Beautiful One and the Bridegroom King!"

"You alone are worthy," Michael added, bowing before his Creator.

"My angelic friends," Life-Giver announced, *"Hadassah must now walk out what she has learned."*

"And what is that, my Lord?" asked Michael.

"That she does not have the power within herself to successfully follow Me . . . not even for a day."

Hadassah trudged through the hot sand, draping her cloak over her head in an effort to shade her face from the burning rays. Lifting her eyes to the ever-shrinking dust cloud on the horizon she said, "Giver of Life, please strengthen me. Fill me with Your truth, grace and resolve, for I can't do this without You!"

"And so I shall," the Spirit of God responded.

"Life-Giver, I know You're with me even though I can't perceive Your presence."

The mocking voice returned with a vengeance. "You can't see him because he's not here. He's not here because you aren't important to him. He doesn't care —"

"I refuse to listen," she shouted.

"Then you're a fool, for I am the voice of wisdom. You have no future here, none at all. You'll die a fool's death in this godforsaken desert, and for what? For the sake of one day with the king? It's not worth it! You can have pleasure, comfort and ease right now. Just turn around and go back. I'll make sure you have a life filled with whatever your little heart desires."

"Why would you offer me such things? You don't know me."

"I know you better than you think. I existed long before you were born and know well the ways and desires of mankind. I was in the garden where it all began. . ."

"Then you are an even greater fool than what you accuse me of being. I heard the story of your fall."

"My fall? I didn't fall! It was man that fell, and I was the one who accomplished that admirable feat," the voice said with great arrogance.

"You did fall, for that was the beginning of the end for you. You may rule this earth right now, but there's a day coming when the Great King and His Son will take back this earth and all that it contains. And you, Accuser, will be cast into outer darkness along with all of your minions."

"You are but a child, a foolish child at that! If you want to keep believing Life-Giver is worth pursuing, then so be it. But don't come crawling back to me when you discover that I'm really the one worthy of worship, for I am the prince of this earth."

"You may be the prince of the air, but I know the Lord of the heavens and the earth. Now be gone from me in the name of Life-Giver!"

Hadassah, surprised by her sudden burst of confidence, held her breath. To her great relief, the voice in her head was silent. "Good," she sighed, quickening her pace.

"She did it, my Lord!" Michael exclaimed.

"No, we did it," said the Holy Spirit, a twinkle in His eye and a big smile on His face. "Now go, Michael, and shade her from the burning rays of the sun."

"It is my pleasure to do so."

To Hadassah's surprise, a cloud suddenly appeared directly overhead. "Little cloud, I know you. You've been sent to me again, and I thank my King for you."

Seeing that Life-Giver's horse had stopped, Hadassah was overjoyed. *This gives me an opportunity to catch up with Him,* she thought. She quickened her pace.

She had not gone far when a movement on her left caught her attention. Approaching was a horse and rider. Hadassah turned her focus back to the Object of her affection.

To her surprise, the horse and rider suddenly blocked her path. Hadassah looked up into the eyes of a very old woman. Without any formal greeting, the woman coughed and said, "I haven't had a drop of water to drink in nearly two days and neither has my horse. Please share your water with an old woman."

"I have very little," Hadassah answered, not knowing what to do. To give the woman what little water she had left would most likely have devastating consequences for herself.

"Perhaps you could share just a little?" the woman asked, sliding off her horse.

Hadassah felt the battle within.

The woman was tiny, not more than five feet tall. Her salt and pepper hair was twisted tightly in a bun on top of her head. Her skin was dark and tough from years spent in the sun, but her eyes were soft and gentle. And her smile was irresistible.

What should I do, Life-Giver, Hadassah silently asked. No sooner had she asked than she knew the answer.

"I've freely received, so I shall freely give," Hadassah said, pulling the water-skin from her shoulder. "Here, drink what you need."

"May the King bless you for your kindness to an old woman."

The Holy Spirit whispered, "When you give a cup of water to the least in the kingdom you have actually given it to Life-Giver."

Hadassah did not hear, because she was watching her precious water being consumed. Smelling the water, the horse nuzzled the woman's cheek.

"May I?" the woman asked.

Before Hadassah could object, the woman poured the remaining water into a large tortoise shell, which she held up to her horse.

Hadassah nearly cried as she watched the last of her water being consumed by a horse. She collapsed on the hot sand, her heart sick.

To Hadassah's amazement, the woman filled the shell numerous times. *That's impossible. That water-skin has to be empty,* she thought. The horse finally had his fill and turned away. The woman chuckled, put the shell to her lips and said, "Waste not, want not," and drank the remaining water.

Hadassah's throat was parched. Her lips were cracked and peeling. She needed that water.

The Spirit laid His hand on her belly and said, "Out of your belly will flow rivers of living water."

Hadassah reminded herself that Life-Giver's kingdom was built on sacrificial love. *"I will trust Him,"* she said to herself. Rising to her feet, she faced the woman and said, "I don't mean to rush you, but I need to be on my way. May I have my water-skin back?"

"Forgive me. Of course. As for water, there's a pool a day's journey east. That's where I'm going. I'd be glad to give you a ride."

"East? I'm headed west. Would you ride west, for I could certainly use the speed of a good horse?" Hadassah asked, hoping she would be agreeable.

"I'm sorry. But I must go east, for I have business to tend to. Thank you for the water. You saved the life of this old woman and her horse."

"May the Great King bless your travels," Hadassah said, putting the water-skin to her mouth, hoping to find water. All she found were a few precious drops.

Flinging the empty bag over her shoulder, Hadassah faced west and scanned the horizon. "Life-Giver has resumed His journey," she said to herself.

The blessed cloud moved with her. "Life-Giver, I won't give up — I won't quit. I'll press on to the end because I am loved. I'll set my mind on things above not on my suffering. I'll give You everything, even if it's difficult."

"Her love runs deep," said Michael.

"She has grown from being merely a bondservant, to a disciple, to a friend, to a daughter. And now she is learning to be a bride," the Spirit said.

Unaware of her heavenly escort, Hadassah encouraged herself by proclaiming, "Your ways are higher than mine, and I bend my knee to Your will for my life. You alone hold the script of my life in Your hands. Not my will, but Your will be done, I pray."

"So be it," said the Spirit.

Hadassah felt strangely comforted and even hopeful as she continued to follow the speck on the horizon. She had traveled quite a distance when she heard someone calling out. Turning she saw a child running toward her, waving wildly. For a brief moment, she thought about ignoring her — she dared not lose sight of Life-Giver. But she could not help calling out, "Are you in need, child?"

The girl, no more than ten years old, answered, "I've lost my way!"

Hadassah ran to her. "Where's your family?"

"I wandered off while they were sleeping. When I realized how far I'd gone, I couldn't find my way back. I've been looking for them most of the day," she said, her voice breaking as tears ran down her dirty face.

Hadassah looked over her shoulder. Life-Giver was just a tiny dot on the horizon. She looked back at the small child. Images of Beloved flashed through her mind. *I can't turn my back on this child . . . regardless of what it costs me,* she thought.

"Whatever you do to the least of these, you do unto Me," the Holy Spirit whispered.

Life-Giver, should I take her with me or try to find her parents? she silently prayed.

"Look with the eyes of your heart, Hadassah," said the Spirit.

Looking down at the child's sunburned face, she saw the pain and fear. "Let's go find your parents," she said, turning east. "What's your name, sweet child?"

"Rebekah," she answered.

Hadassah felt as if someone had punched her in the stomach. Her sister's face flashed before her.

"What's *your* name?" the child asked.

She took a deep breath and said, "Hadassah."

"You okay?"

"Yeah. It's just that I had a sister named Rebekah; she was so dear to me."

"What happened to her?"

"She died," Hadassah said, spreading her cloak over her and the child. The cloud had remained behind.

"I'm sorry."

"I miss her, but she lives with the Great King now. Enough of that. You must be hungry."

"I sure am."

Hadassah handed her a piece of bread and some cheese and asked, "Is there anything you can tell me that will help me figure out which way your family might be traveling?"

"Well, we were heading northwest — I know that much. And I've been walking since this morning. But I'm a daydreamer, so I don't really notice where I'm going."

"Do you believe in Life-Giver?" Hadassah asked.

"Can't say that I ever heard of him."

"Well, He's the Son of the Great King. You've heard of the Great King, right?"

"Of course. Everybody's heard of Him."

"Good. Let's ask for His help, because finding your parents is going to be like looking for a needle in a haystack."

"How do we ask someone for help that we can't see?"

"We pray. Praying is easy. It's just talking to Life-Giver. Like this: Life-Giver, please tell us which way to go."

"Turn right."

"I think we should walk this way," she said, turning to the right.

"How do you know?" Rebekah asked.

"Life-Giver told me."

"Who is this Life-Giver?"

"Oh, He's the most wonderful Person I know!" As they walked, Hadassah told her all she knew. Sharing about Life-Giver and her journey took her mind off her troubles and fueled the furnace of devotion in her heart even more.

"I want to know him, too!" said Rebekah.

"Now that's good news indeed! Why don't you tell Him that?"

"Right now?"

"Sure. He's always with us; we just can't always see or feel Him."

Rebekah silently talked to Life-Giver as Hadassah prayed for supernatural help in locating her family. When Rebekah looked up, her face was beaming.

"Well?" Hadassah asked.

"Well . . . I told Life-Giver that I wanted to trust Him with my life. I said I needed His love. I think He heard me, because I suddenly felt so much love that it made me want to laugh and cry at the same time. That's when I asked Him to help us find my family. Did I do it right?"

"That was perfect," Hadassah said, stopping. "What's that?"

"What?"

"Rebekah, please tell me your parents are traveling in a caravan."

"Yes . . ." Looking in the direction Hadassah pointed, Rebekah screamed, "That's my papa!" She took off running with Hadassah following close behind.

Rebekah squealed and waved at the man running out to meet them. Hadassah watched as Rebekah's papa scooped her up in his arms.

After Rebekah told her parents how Hadassah helped her, they thanked her profusely. Uncomfortable with the praise and eager to resume her journey, Hadassah bid them goodbye. Rebekah grabbed her hand and said, "Hadassah, don't go! There's room in our wagon. Papa, please tell her to come with us!"

"Hadassah, you're certainly welcome to join us," he said.

"Thank you, but I'm heading west in pursuit of Life-Giver. I really must be on my way," Hadassah said.

"At least take our horse; we have an extra one. It will make your journey much easier."

"But how would I return it?"

"There's no need, for you have already returned to us what is most precious. It's settled then — you'll take our horse. Come!"

While Rebekah's papa prepared the horse, her mother filled Hadassah's water-skin. When Hadassah refused to take the time to eat, she filled her pouch with some dried meat, a loaf of bread and goat cheese.

Rebekah hugged Hadassah long and hard as she whispered, "I'll tell everyone Life-Giver's story, so they can follow Him, too."

"That's wonderful, Rebekah. And, remember, He laid down His life for you, so you should lay down your life for Him."

"That's what you did for me today," Rebekah said.

"Well, I wouldn't say I did something as heroic as laying my life down. I simply did what I thought Life-Giver would do," she said as she settled herself on the back of a beautiful white stallion.

"You laid down more than just your life. You laid down your dream of spending one day with the King. Once again, you have chosen to love another more than yourself."

But Hadassah did not hear His words of affirmation, for she was trying to figure out how to get her horse to move. Seeing her dilemma, Rebekah's papa gave Hadassah a quick riding lesson.

After several tries, Hadassah finally rode off with Rebekah running by her side, waving wildly. "Stay close to Life-Giver and your family, Rebekah. And no more wandering off."

Rebekah blushed. "Bye," she said.

"Bye, Rebekah."

Hadassah headed west. "Now I have a chance to catch up," she said, feeling overjoyed.

Hadassah scanned the horizon, but there was no sign of Life-Giver. No footprints, no dust cloud, nothing except an endless sea of hot, white sand. Her horse neighed loudly. "I wish you could speak," she said, stroking the mare's long, sleek neck, "maybe then you could tell me what to do.

"Life-Giver, what do I do now? I want to follow You with all of my heart, but I don't know which way to go."

"Look up, child, for that is where your help comes from," said the Spirit.

CHAPTER THIRTY-ONE

*H*adassah looked up and saw smoke in the distance. "Life-Giver must've stopped. Now's our chance to catch up," she said to the stallion, spurring him on. The horse bolted in response, causing Hadassah to nearly fall off. "That was a bit rough," she said, holding tightly to a handful of mane. "For a moment, I thought you were going to leave me behind."

Taking a deep breath, she said, "If we're going to be partners, I suppose I should give you a name. I wonder what I should call you."

She had ridden for quite some time when the smoke was no longer visible. Not knowing what to do, Hadassah continued on hoping she was right. "I'll call you Faithful Friend," she suddenly announced. Running her fingers through his white mane, she said, "Faithful Friend, if I don't spend a day following Life-Giver, then I can't spend a day with the King. And if I can't spend a day with the King, then —" Hadassah could not bear to finish her sentence.

The sun was directly overhead when Hadassah spotted a small dust cloud on her far right. *Perhaps that's Life-Giver*, she thought as she pulled on the reins, but the horse refused her command. "You're not being very faithful," she said as she pulled harder. The horse neighed loudly and fought to continue on.

When she looked up again, her heart sank. The horse was now close enough to see that the rider was not Life-Giver.

"Now I'm glad you didn't obey me," she said, stroking Faithful's sleek neck. "I'm sorry."

Hadassah hoped and prayed that the rider would simply pass her by, but that was not to be.

"Hello," the stranger said, turning his horse to come alongside hers.

"Good day, sir," Hadassah said without making eye contact.

"I'm so happy to find another soul in this desolate place. My name's Issachar, and I wondered if you might like some company."

"My name's Hadassah. And thank you, sir, but I'm fine."

"Where are you headed, Hadassah?"

"I'm following Life-Giver."

"How wonderfully perfect! That's where I'm going. Two are always better than one . . . especially out here."

Hadassah looked closely at the young man. He was quite handsome and appeared to be about her age. His eyes seemed kind, and his smile was definitely contagious.

"You can trust him," a voice whispered.

"I don't want to put you out," she said, ignoring the uneasiness in the pit of her stomach.

"On the contrary, I'd love the company of a beautiful lady."

Hadassah blushed.

As they rode, Issachar talked non-stop about his grand adventures in life. Hadassah found herself relaxing more and more. She was so enthralled that she soon forgot about Life-Giver. It was not until the sun was low in the sky that her thoughts returned to Him. Scanning the horizon, she saw neither Life-Giver, the dust cloud or His campfire. What she did see was an oasis a short distance away on her right.

"We should take advantage of this gift from heaven and allow the horses to drink and graze," Issachar said.

"But I don't see Life-Giver."

"Don't worry. I know exactly where Life-Giver is. I've followed him for years. As soon as our horses have rested, I'll lead you to him." Without waiting for a response, he turned his horse toward the oasis, motioning for her to follow.

Faithful Friend resisted Hadassah's leading. "My horse doesn't seem interested in following, which makes no sense. He should be dying of thirst."

"Don't let him tell you what to do," he shouted over his shoulder.

No matter how much Hadassah pulled on the reins Faithful Friend refused to turn. "This isn't working," she said.

Tying his horse to a tree, Issachar hurried back and took her horse's reins. Faithful snorted and pawed the sand, refusing to obey. "We'd better get you off this horse before he hurts you," he said, offering Hadassah his hand. She hesitated.

"I don't bite," he said.

"Faithful would never hurt me," she said, placing her hand in his. As she slid off her horse, Issachar wrapped his hands around her waist and pulled her closer than she was comfortable with. Hadassah quickly stepped out of his grasp. Taking Faithful's reins, she led him toward the oasis, her heart and mind racing.

"Pardon me," Issachar said, running up beside her, "but you descended quicker than I expected. I didn't mean to upset you. I was just trying to keep you from falling."

Hadassah said nothing. She led Faithful to the water's edge. Careful to keep her distance from Issachar, who had brought his horse to drink, Hadassah filled her almost empty water-skin.

Issachar removed his shirt and tossed it on a nearby bush. Hadassah felt herself blush as she looked away. He walked into the water. "This feels great. You should join me," he said, swimming across the small pond.

Certain that Issachar was sufficiently occupied, she pulled her skirt up to her knees and waded in. The water did feel great. Faithful followed, nuzzling her back and snorting. "What are you doing?" Hadassah asked, laughing at the persistent animal.

Faithful neighed loudly. "Are you trying to get my attention?" she asked, running her hand along the animal's sleek neck. Faithful snorted. Hadassah scooped up handfuls of water and offered him a drink. The horse refused. "What's wrong?" she asked. Faithful nudged her again. "Are you hot?" she asked, splashing water on her horse's belly. Before she realized it she was soaked from head to toe. Faithful finally took a long drink.

She was enjoying herself so much that she did not notice Issachar come up behind her. He laid his hand on her shoulder. Startled, she spun around. The two stood face to face. Her pulse quickened. *Why does his presence have such a profound effect on me?* she wondered.

Mumbling something about her horse needing to graze, she tore herself away. Grabbing the reins, she quickly led Faithful out of the water.

Issachar followed. "I'm sorry. I didn't mean to startle you."

Hadassah kept walking. Tying Faithful to a bush, she spread her cloak under a nearby tree and sat in its shade.

"I hope I haven't offended you," Issachar said as he secured his horse.

"No, you've done nothing wrong. It's just that I —"

"It's just that you have feelings for me," he said, spreading his blanket beside hers.

"That's not what I was going to say," she said, her face turning bright red.

"What were you going to say then?"

"I was just going to say that I feel a bit nervous around you."

"Why?"

"I don't know."

"Well, allow me to remedy that. Perhaps knowing my intentions might help ease your fears."

"Perhaps."

"Hadassah, I don't believe our meeting was a coincidence. I believe the king meant for us to meet."

"Why would you say that?"

"Because I saw you in a dream."

"You saw *me* . . . in a *dream*?"

"Yes, I saw you," he said leaning close.

She leaned back. Faithful Friend neighed loudly.

Issachar retreated, smiled his gorgeous smile and then said, "Hadassah, a fortnight ago, I had a dream and you were in it. You looked stunning. It was love at first sight. When I awoke I knew that one day I'd find you and make you my wife."

"I don't understand." Hadassah's mind raced to make sense of what she was hearing.

"I can't say that I understand it either. How can anyone understand the ways of the king?"

"Why didn't He tell me? I just talked with Him, and He told me if I followed Life-Giver for one day I could spend a day with Him. The King never mentioned meeting you or me being your wife."

"Didn't he tell you that you would know true love?" Issachar asked, offering her some grapes.

"How'd you know that?" she asked, refusing his offer.

Ignoring her question, he said, "The king told me that I'm your true love, so nothing else matters."

"That can't be the truth! Life-Giver's my true love."

"A person can have more than one true love, Hadassah. If that wasn't true, then how would anyone ever get married and serve the king?"

Hadassah looked long and hard at the handsome young man. *What he says makes sense,* she thought. *Issachar appears to be harmless. As a matter of fact, he appears to be wonderful. He certainly knows a lot about the King, much more than I know.*

"*Hadassah, why are you reasoning in your heart?*" the Holy Spirit asked. "*Perceive with your spirit, Hadassah.*"

She did not hear Him.

"Hadassah, I understand this must be a shock to you. Please don't fret. We can talk more of this later. I imagine you're quite hungry. I have more than enough food. Grapes, pomegranates, figs, cheese and venison," Issachar said as he opened his pouch and spread a feast before her. He offered her a fig. As he did, his foot rested against her ankle. Strong emotions surged through her being as Hadassah nervously twirled a strand of her hair.

"Aren't you going to eat?" he asked.

"Uh, sure."

"It's all good, I promise."

"I'm sure it is," she said, biting into the fig. "Figs are my favorite."

"That's wonderful — I have a whole orchard of fig trees."

"You own an orchard and so young?"

"Sure do and so much more. No one gave them to me either. I worked hard to achieve the success I have."

"Where do you live? What's your family like?"

"I grew up in a little village about two days' journey from here. My parents died when I was just a boy. Having no one to help me, I had to grow up quickly. I learned how to steal, swindle and talk people into almost anything. That's how I survived, and I was really good at it. It wasn't until I was seventeen that I learned about the king. That's when I changed my ways."

"But you talk as if you've followed Him for years."

"That's because I've experienced much in a short time." He popped a grape into his mouth and then took a bite of cheese. "Mmm, it's good, isn't it?"

"Very," she said, blushing again.

"The grapes came from my vineyard and the cheese from my goats. I baked the bread. Try it, it's very good."

Breaking off a piece, she bit into it. "It's delicious. Who taught you how to bake?"

"I figured it out myself. It's not hard, you know."

"No, it's not," she said. "I'm sorry to hear about your parents. My parents died of the fever when I was just a child."

"So how'd you survive?" he asked, setting his bread aside.

"An uncle took my sisters and me in."

"I wasn't so lucky. I didn't have any relatives willing to help me."

Hadassah thought she detected bitterness in his voice but quickly dismissed it as her imagination.

The Spirit of God called her name, but Hadassah chose to dismiss that as well.

Issachar turned his body toward her and leaned close. "Hadassah, I'm so sorry your parents died." His eyes were filled with compassion.

Hadassah looked away, her heart pounding.

"Has anyone ever told you how beautiful you are?"

She blushed dreadfully. "Uh . . . thank you, but I don't feel very beautiful."

"Well, you are. And I'm overjoyed to know that you'll be my wife," he said, kissing the back of her hand. She felt as though she might faint. "Hadassah, I love you."

"How can you love me, since we've only just met?"

"I fell in love with you in my dream." He leaned closer. She could feel his breath on her cheek. Everything in her wanted to run, but she was powerless to move. His lips brushed her cheek and then her mouth.

Her head spun and her heart raced.

"I love you," he whispered.

"I don't know . . . you," she said, turning her face away.

"You can know me. Let me show you who I am and how much I love you," he said, running his hand through her hair and pulling her close.

"I don't want this! It's not right! I love Life-Giver," she said, pushing him away.

"You know you want me," he said, kissing her again.

Hadassah's head spun as a variety of emotions, thoughts and desires filled her.

A variety of hideous creatures quickly crawled out of the ground and surrounded the pair. They chanted and drooled and clapped.

Life-Giver knelt before His Father's throne and prayed, "Father, I pray that You will keep her, for You have given her to Me. She is My beloved and I am hers."

Countless angels instantly responded to the unspoken command from the Great King. They encircled the pair. The angels waited, ready to intervene, should Hadassah cry out for help.

Paralyzing fear swept over Hadassah as she responded to Issachar's touch. Within moments, her world went dark.

CHAPTER THIRTY-TWO

*H*adassah shoved Issachar off and jumped up. "We shouldn't have done that!" she sobbed.

"And why not?" he asked, smirking.

"Because you're not my husband and never will be!"

"You're right, I'm not your husband. But I take what I want when I want it. And you just happened to be what I wanted."

"You lied to me!"

"You wanted me as much as I wanted you, and we both know it."

"No, I didn't!"

"Yes, you did."

"What you did was evil! You exposed me to lust, but I was made for love. You made me fear, but I was made for faith. You thrust me into darkness, but I was made for light. You came to me as a sheep, but you're really a wolf. I rebuke you and reject what you've done to me this day. And I pray I won't hate you!"

Without looking back, Hadassah grabbed her belongings and ran to her horse. As she swung her leg over the stallion's back, Faithful raced off; it was all Hadassah could do to stay on. "Life-Giver, I'm so sorry!" she sobbed.

"I know, dear one. I am here with you," Life-Giver said, *pouring love and comfort into her.*

Hadassah felt His unconditional love, and it broke her heart. *"I don't deserve to be loved,* she thought.

"Your actions do not change the way I feel about you — nothing is ever strong enough or powerful enough to make Me stop loving you."

"That's so difficult to believe."

"One day you will know the truth and that truth will set you free."

Consumed by her guilt and pain, she allowed Faithful to go wherever he wanted. *She was unaware that an angel led the way.*

"Michael, cover her."

Michael immediately obeyed.

The angelic cloud followed her until the sun began to set, but she did not notice. Hadassah's heart sank further. "Not only do I feel disqualified, but now I have no hope of being with the King — I've failed horribly in my quest to follow Life-Giver. I've strayed so far that I don't even know which way to go."

Faithful stopped. When the horse didn't move, Hadassah slid off. Not bothering to secure him, she spread her cloak on the hot sand and sat down. Faithful remained by her side. "I sure did choose the right name for you. It seems you're way more faithful than I am." She poured some water into the tortoise shell she used for drinking and held it to Faithful's mouth. While he drank, she absentmindedly stroked the stallion's face as her tears washed the dirt from her face.

Emotionally exhausted, Hadassah laid back. Even though it was not yet dark the moon, bright and full, had already appeared. "Life-Giver, I allowed myself to be distracted, deceived and seduced. I'm so sorry. Please forgive me. If only I'd kept my eyes on You this wouldn't have happened. I know I'm guilty, but only partially. I didn't want what he did. Actually, part of me wanted it, but the other part didn't. If only I'd listened," she said, sobbing loudly.

"I am faithful to forgive and cleanse you, My beloved. And I will heal your heart, for I love you dearly. You are My beloved and I am yours."

"Thank You, for loving me still," Hadassah said crying deeply, for her pain and regret were great.

Hadassah cried herself to sleep. When she woke it was morning, and Faithful Friend slept by her side. She sat up and looked around at the endless ocean of white sand. Her heart was very heavy.

Discouragement whispered in her ear, *"Your quest is hopeless. Just give up. I told you before that you don't deserve to be with the king and now you've proven it. You are worthless."*

Hadassah listened to the creature's lies.

Faithful Friend lifted his head and then stood. He buried his nose in her hair and gently nudged. Hadassah ignored him. He nudged harder. "If you're trying to tell me to get up, you're wasting your time," Hadassah said. "I don't think I'll ever get up again. I have no reason and nowhere to go."

"You have two choices, Hadassah. You can allow this painful event to defeat you, or you can accept My mercy and get up. It is your choice and your choice alone," said the Holy Spirit.

"I don't understand Your mercy toward me."

"I don't expect you to. I only hope you receive it."

"Even if I don't deserve it?"

"No one deserves My love or mercy, Hadassah. It is a gift based solely on the extravagant nature of the Giver, not on the goodness of the recipient."

"But what about my weak heart?"

"I understand your pain, even more than you do, but you do not have to allow it to keep you from following Me."

"But it's so hard and I'm so tired."

"Now that you know the truth, what are you going to do about it?"

"I guess I'm going to get up."

"Before you do, will you do Me a favor?"

"What is it?"

"Would you give Issachar a gift he doesn't deserve and could never earn?"

"What gift?"

"The gift of forgiveness."

Hadassah was silent for a moment. "Like You did for me?" she asked.

"Yes."

Hadassah wrestled with the unfairness of what He asked her to do.

"My kingdom is not built on fairness, Hadassah, but on unconditional love. How can you withhold what was freely given to you?"

"Help me, please."

"With pleasure. Receive My grace, Hadassah," the Spirit said as He breathed on her.

Hadassah felt strength and compassion flow into her. Her heart still hurt, but the anger was subsiding. "I choose to forgive you, Issachar," she said. "I forgive you for seducing me, for taking advantage of me. And I don't hate you, because Life-Giver doesn't hate me. I pray that the King will find you and heal you."

"Thank you, Hadassah. Now will you forgive yourself?"

"The way I feel right now makes that impossible."

"Nothing is impossible with Me."

"But I don't deserve it."

"Why should you be punished for something that has already been forgiven and redeemed?"

Hadassah thought about His words. "As usual, You are right. I choose to forgive myself based on what You have done for me."

"Now you are truly free. Will you take My hand and follow Me? As we journey together, I will heal your pain and restore you to wholeness."

"Thank You, Holy Spirit. Thank You very much."

Hadassah swung her leg over Faithful's back. As they plodded along, Hadassah rejected the guilt and condemnation assaulting her mind. "I am loved and forgiven," she told herself over and over. Preoccupied with the battle raging in her head, she barely held on to the reins. *She did not know that the horse could see what she could not — Life-Giver and His angelic army waiting for her on the horizon.*

It was not long before Faithful stopped before the unseen army and neighed loudly.

Countless angels welcomed the horse and its rider. The angels then bowed before Life-Giver and sang, "Blessing, glory, wisdom, thanksgiving, honor, power and might be to our God forever and ever! Amen."

Unaware of the spiritual activity before her, Hadassah ran her fingers through Faithful Friend's silky mane, saying, "What's wrong? Why did you stop?"

The stallion slung his head back and forth, snorting and pawing the ground. *As Life-Giver's army charged ahead, Faithful bolted.*

Gripping his mane and reins, Hadassah prayed for help to stay on. She suddenly became aware of danger. The hair on the back of her neck bristled as chills ran up and down her spine. Hadassah repeatedly tried to stop her horse but was unsuccessful. *The stallion saw what she could not — Life-Giver leading His army toward a horde of dark beings.*

The spirit of Fear pressed against her with all its strength.

With her horse out of control and fear breathing down her neck, Hadassah cried out, "Life-Giver, I need You!"

He reminded her of her papa's words. *"Should the King see fit to lead you through the valley of the shadow of death you will have nothing to fear, for He will be with you."*

Fearing the worst, yet desperately trying to believe the best, she cried out, "No matter what happens in this desert, I will still love You!"

Life-Giver, with banner held high, responded, "You are beautiful and you are dearly loved!"

The Spirit shouted, "Clear the way for the Lord; make smooth in the desert a highway for our God! Let every valley be lifted up and every mountain be made low! Let the rough ground be a plain and the rugged terrain a broad valley!"

In response, the unruly terrain in the unseen realm obeyed the word of the Lord and became a smooth plain. When that happened every demon hiding behind every tree, hill and boulder was instantly exposed. Like mice chased by hungry cats they scattered in every direction.

The Holy Spirit touched Hadassah's eyes. For a brief moment, she saw into the unseen realm and what she saw terrified her. Her horse was racing straight toward the most hideous-looking army of dark beings she could ever imagine. She did not see Life-Giver, the Holy Spirit or the Great King riding beside her.

Hadassah tried once more to rein Faithful in, but the horse would not respond. "Life-Giver, help me!" she repeated. "Why can't I hear You?" she asked, frantically looking around.

With all her might, she pulled on the reins. This time Faithful stopped abruptly. Hadassah lurched forward, nearly falling off. Choking on the dust, she called out, "I'm so afraid. Please help me."

Her spiritual eyes were opened once more, for just a moment, and she saw a glorious Light. She nearly fainted as the beautiful Light enveloped her. Comfort and strength poured into her body, soul and spirit.

"You really *are* with me."

"Hadassah, your fear blinded you. That allowed the things you are afraid of to overwhelm you. With Me by your side, what do you have to fear?"

"I don't mean to be afraid."

"Be bold and very courageous, Hadassah, because I am with you and always will be. Trust Me."

"I want to trust You, but I don't feel very courageous at the moment."

"Lean on Me, Hadassah, for I am your courage. Remember I live to intercede for you. The kingdom of heaven suffers violence, but the violent take it by force."

"I couldn't even do something as simple as follow You for a day. How do You expect *me* to take anything by force?"

"Hadassah, the issue that is in front of you, demanding your attention, is not the real issue. That is the issue your enemy wants you to focus on. Every difficulty, persecution and hardship is always about one thing and one thing only. It is always about your relationship with Me. As long as you do not quit pursuing Me, you will win."

"I can't quit."

"My dear one, you must understand that you have a very real enemy who wants to destroy you. Hadassah, you have grown in wisdom and statute. It is now time for you to stand up and take back what is rightfully yours. What are you going to choose — faith or fear?"

"Nothing can conquer an army like I just saw."

"Oh, but that is where you are wrong! There is nothing either created or uncreated strong enough to defeat Perfect Love."

Hadassah desperately hoped it was true. Taking a deep breath, she said, "My life belongs to the One who gave me life. I will choose faith."

The Holy Spirit wrapped His arms around her and said, "It is because of the blood of Life-Giver and the word of your testimony that you will overcome."

"I don't understand any of this, but this I do know — Life-Giver is good and He loves me. I will not be offended. I will not deny Him, and I will not be distracted or deceived again. I will be faithful unto death and will love Him forever!"

The demonic creatures screamed and shrieked as they tried desperately to protect themselves from her declaration of sacrificial love.

Hadassah looked up and could not believe what she saw — the evil prince from the Land of Despair rode toward her. Her stomach felt sick as dread and fear filled her heart. *This can't be happening,* she thought. Images of the massacred soldiers flooded her mind, followed by memories of her nobleman master and then of her recent encounter with Issachar. A myriad of emotions washed over her — fear, worthlessness, apathy, hopelessness and the most crushing of all, shame.

A host of demons pulled and clawed at her, desperately trying to find an entrance into her soul.

"Life-Giver, I need to know my enemy. Is the evil prince a demon or a man?" she cried out as Faithful Friend raced away from their pursuer.

"The prince is merely a man possessed by Satan."

The evil prince soon cut her horse off and shouted, "I've come to take you back to where you belong."

Biting her bottom lip, Hadassah cried out for Life-Giver's help.

"No one can help you," the prince said as he drew his sword. Faithful Friend bolted. The prince and his horse bore down on them.

"Be still, child, and know that I am good," the Holy Spirit said.

Her soul was so fearful that she did not hear Him, but her spirit heard. Hadassah took a deep breath. From deep within her being she heard words long forgotten, *"I no longer live, but Life-Giver lives in me; and the life which I now live, I live by faith in the One who loved me and gave Himself up for me."*

"Hadassah, keep your eyes fixed on the One who loves you the most," the Spirit encouraged.

"I'm about to die," she whispered, trembling from head to toe.

"If you die, you live. My word resides within you," reminded the Spirit, bringing her papa's words to her mind, *"The only power evil has over you is what you give it."*

"I will give him no power. I will fear no evil, for You are with me!"

As she turned her horse around and raced headlong toward what she feared from her past, Fear's long-held control over her was severed.

Shrieking, the evil creature fell to the ground and Faithful Friend trampled it.

Hadassah and the powers of darkness collided. The evil prince shouted, "You are defeated!" He rammed her horse, knocking both horse and rider to the ground. Faithful Friend struggled to his feet. Laughing, the prince thrust his blade into Faithful's hindquarters. Faithful collapsed.

Hadassah could not move. Blood trickled down her forehead and into her right eye. As she wiped it away with her sleeve, she heard the Holy Spirit say, *"You are not defeated and you are not alone. You are at war with a relentless, merciless enemy. Look up, Hadassah."*

Still reeling from the blow, Hadassah looked up. *All around her were countless angels of light.*

"Trust Me," the Spirit said.

Seeing Faithful lying in a pool of blood, Hadassah whispered a prayer for him while pressing her hand against the gaping wound just over her ear. "Please give me the strength I need. I will die for You, if that's what it takes to live!"

Hearing Hadassah's willingness to die for love, Satan howled like a crazed wolf. Furious, he turned toward the King and demanded, "Give her to me for just one moment — I don't need a day! Just give me one minute, and she will deny you and your pitiful, revolting, endless love. I demand permission to sift her like wheat!"

"Bow before Me, Satan!" the Great King commanded.

Like a whimpering dog, tail tucked between his legs, Satan fell at His feet.

"Make no mistake about it, Satan, you have no right to demand anything from Me. I am the King, and I alone determine your actions and boundaries. It is My will for you to sift her, but you cannot take

her life. That deed has been reserved for Perfect Love, not for you. Do you understand Me?"

With a great deal of spitting and sputtering, Satan nodded.

"You, Satan, are a liar and a thief, and your days are numbered — you are already a defeated foe! Now go."

Not daring to lift his eyes, Satan mounted his horse. With a sick, evil laugh, he hurried to rejoin his demonic army.

Michael bowed low and said, "My Lord and my God, I do not understand Your ways. Why subject this child to one so evil?"

"There are times when I use Satan to sift and purify My chosen ones. I turn his evil into their good — every time. You see, Michael, pain and suffering are a natural enemy to the dark part of humanity where Self is worshipped. Adversity crucifies the worship of Self like nothing else can."

"The end result is worth the suffering then?"

"Indeed it is, for she will live forever in whatever measure of light she attains on the earth. Therefore, it is to her advantage to go through the purging fire now."

Hadassah silently prayed. *The Holy Spirit remained in and around her while pouring the oil of grace over her.*

I need You more than I need to breath, she said in her heart.

"That's right, lean on Me. Remember the truth, Hadassah."

"What's the truth?"

"The truth is this: Who can separate you from My love? Shall tribulation or distress or persecution or famine or nakedness or peril or sword separate you from Perfect Love?"

"No. Nothing can separate me from You."

"That is truth."

The Spirit touched her eyes and handed her a sword. And when He did, Hadassah could see in the spirit realm. Standing, she swung the sword high and cut off the head of a lying spirit that held fast to her ankle.

She cried, "I'm convinced that neither death, nor life, nor angels, nor principalities, nor things present, nor things to come, nor powers, nor height, nor depth, nor any other created thing, can separate me from the love of Life-Giver and my Father!"

"Is that so?" Satan shouted, knocking her to the ground.

Hadassah opened her eyes. Satan had disappeared from her sight. It was now the evil prince who towered over her. He shouted, "I can and shall separate you from the one you follow! I've done so already!"

Faithful Friend raised his head and snorted weakly. He fought to stand but was unable. Hadassah prayed for him again.

"The truth is that it only *feels* like my Beloved has forsaken me. I've chosen to walk by faith and not by sight!" Hadassah said.

"We'll see how far you walk with a hole in your belly." Plunging his knife into her gut, he screamed, "You'll never be good enough! Your heart's wicked, you're a sinner and always will be. I know all about Issachar." He mocked her with his laugh.

The prince slowly removed the knife and then retreated to a nearby rock, wiping the blade on his sleeve. Hadassah clutched her stomach as his deadly words spread like poison throughout her being. "I'm a sinner. I'll *never* be good enough," she repeated.

Instantly, Michael and Gabriel stood by her side looking at their Commander. The King answered their questioning gaze, "I have granted permission for her to be sifted, My angelic friends."

"Can she count it joy when she suffers the loss of all things?" asked Michael.

"If she does, she will reflect the glory of Sin-Bearer, for He endured the cross for the joy set before Him," said Gabriel.

"Trust in My love for you. Do not lean on your own understanding or your own strength," Life-Giver whispered.

The evil prince continued his verbal assault, "You have no future with your so-called king. Just look around you — the one who said he'd never leave you has done exactly that! He promised to love you. He said his love was endless, but it sure looks like it has run out to me. Why are you following someone who is unfaithful? Why are you pursuing someone who offers you no comfort or pleasure or power or riches? Tell me, little girl, why are you being so foolish, so stupid? Why not curse him and die? You do not deserve his attention."

Hadassah did not answer. Instead she turned her eyes heavenward and silently prayed, *"Life-Giver, it's not about me. My life is all about You! And I want to be so in love with You that nothing else matters — not even my own life."*

"And so you shall," the Holy Spirit said.

CHAPTER THIRTY-THREE

𝒯he prince continued his barrage of tormenting accusations, but Hadassah refused to take her spiritual eyes off of the Joy set before her.

"You don't understand who I serve, do you?" the prince asked, leaning toward her.

"I understand you're a man possessed by great evil."

"I have power that you know not of, little girl, power that could transform your pitiful life."

Satan placed his rough hand in Hadassah's, and she suddenly found herself standing on the top of a high mountain. Her wounds were gone and a cool breeze swept over her blistered skin causing her to shiver uncontrollably.

"Since Life-Giver couldn't heal you, I did it for you," Satan said.

"Where am I, and how did I get here?"

"You are in my kingdom, and I brought you here. I have the power to do whatever I choose to do."

"Just who are you?"

"You insult me with your unbelief! I am the Prince of this world. And I not only have the power to heal you, but I also have the power to make you great. This kingdom, as far as you can see, can be yours. Claim it and you can have it. Look upon it, ask me for it, and I'll give it to you."

"All I have to do is look and ask?" Hadassah asked, growing more confused.

"Unlike your unfaithful king who asks you to give him everything, I merely want a niche in your life. It doesn't have to be a big place — just a small corner of your affections, a secret closet in the recesses of your soul. No one need know; it can be our secret. Give me access to that place, and I'll grant you pleasures and comforts that you have never known and adventures that exceed your wildest imagination. Come now, child, and trust me, for unlike Life-Giver, I keep my promises."

Unbeknownst to her, a large dragon named Witchcraft stood behind her casting its evil spell. Hadassah felt dizzy as tempting images raced through her mind. Looking at the green, lush valley filled with fruit trees, streams of water and bountiful life, she said, "It is beautiful here, and I suddenly feel very tired."

"What do you want, Hadassah?" Satan asked.

"I don't know. I'm not sure."

"I know you well, so let me tell you. You want what every human wants — comfort, ease and pleasure. In order to have that you need to be rich and powerful."

"How does a peasant become rich and powerful?"

"Take my hand and follow me for just one day, and I'll make you richer and more powerful than you could ever imagine."

"Just one day . . . that reminds me of something . . . or someone. What is it?" She closed her eyes, trying desperately to sort through the massive confusion bombarding her mind.

The dragon leaned closer, blowing its toxic breath over her. And all the while, Life-Giver knelt before His Father interceding for the one He loved.

With her eyes shut tight, Hadassah suddenly saw a tiny glimmer of light hovering over her. She reached up. As she did, the light exploded showering her with unexplainable joy, strength and love. Opening her eyes, she shouted, "Now I remember — you're not the one I want!" Hadassah took a deep breath and said, "Please help me, Life-Giver."

Hadassah looked at the Prince of the world and said, "You asked me what I wanted? I'll tell you. I want life, and that you can't give me. There's only One who can give me —"

In the blink of an eye, she found herself back in the desert, lying on the hot sand, her body racked with pain. The evil prince glared down at her and said, "My master showed you what he could give you. Now look around and see what your master offers you."

As far as she could see was nothing but white, hot sand. Vultures circled overhead. The sun, like a blazing inferno, beat down on her already blistered skin. A sudden gust of wind blew dust in her mouth and eyes.

Ever so weakly she said, "Life-Giver, I know You are good and Your love for me has no end. I trust You."

Blinded by jealous rage, the evil prince ran to Faithful Friend's side. "Let me show you how powerless your so-called Life-Giver is." He thrust his knife into the horse's throat and shouted, "Life-Giver is powerless against me!"

Hadassah covered her face.

"You are a fool!" the prince screamed as he knelt beside her. He slowly ran his razor-sharp knife down her arm from shoulder to wrist. Arrows of fiery pain shot through Hadassah's body and mind as tears coursed down her face. "I don't understand why this is happening!" She gasped for air. "Life-Giver, why have You forsaken me?"

Life-Giver knelt beside her, praying fervently as tears streamed down His face. The Prince of the world hovered over both of them, drooling and rubbing his hands together.

"I thought I could do it," she whispered, "but that was merely pride speaking. I'm so much weaker than I thought. Without You, I can do nothing. As much as I hate to admit it . . . I can't save myself. Even if You slay me, I will love You to the end!"

Her confession and whole-hearted surrender filled the spiritual atmosphere with sweet-smelling perfume. Satan's high-pitched shriek caused hundreds of demons to run for cover. But Life-Giver, the Great King and the Holy Spirit drank deeply of her sacrificial love.

"She is broken, my Lord," said Michael.

"A broken and a contrite heart I will not despise. A bruised reed I will not break. Brokenness is to be desired more than any success or fortune. She has come to the end of herself, which is a good thing, for that is the only place one can find life. There can be no true

humility or compassion or meekness without loss — just as there can be no true love until selfishness and pride are mortally wounded."

"You could shield her from this, yet You do not," Michael observed.

"I love her too much to rescue her. Some of life's greatest treasures come out of life's greatest tragedies."

"Like Job," said Michael. "He suffered the loss of everything . . . except his wife who encouraged him to curse You and die."

"In the midst of his suffering Job's flesh collided with Divine Life. That collision resulted in the revelation that life is all about Me. You see, Michael, the moment most humans experience suffering and discomfort, they tend to complain and worry and do everything possible to escape. But not so with Divine Life . . . just look at My cross."

Michael turned and saw His Maker — innocent, falsely accused, beaten beyond recognition and alone, painfully alone. He did not complain and neither was He worried. He accused neither God nor man. He endured the suffering while staying true to His heart, to His character and to Who He is and was and always will be.

"It always goes back to the cross, does it not?" Michael asked.

"That is because the cross is where it all begins. Tribulation and suffering are among some of the greatest blessings in life. If you doubt it, just look at the fruit of My suffering," He said, pointing to Hadassah.

"You reproduced after Your own kind."

"I did. I was not a victim and neither is she."

"Will this one die a martyr?"

"There are some necessary repairs in the human heart that martyrdom cannot accomplish. Some things require a measure of sorrow and suffering in order to bring about the necessary transformation. Martyrdom is not the goal; living for and loving Me is the goal."

Sighing deeply, still unable to perceive the presence of Life-Giver, Hadassah pushed herself up with what little strength she had left. Trembling, she looked around at the endless nothingness surrounding her. "I did my best with what little I had," she whispered. "I place my future into Your hands."

The evil prince stood over her, gloating. "You stupid girl, you can't escape my grasp."

"I'll love Life-Giver until my final breath. And when I stand before Him with nothing, should He find me worthy, I will, at least, have Him. And He's always enough."

"If you continue to follow him, you'll have nothing!" the evil prince shouted.

"I've been destitute for most of my life, so that doesn't frighten me. There's only one thing I fear and that is to be separated from the One who is Eternal Life. I will not, by the grace of God, sin against Perfect Love."

"The thing you fear has come upon you! Look around you — he's not here, is he? He hasn't come in answer to your pitiful cries, has he? He hasn't rescued you or bothered to explain his actions. And your loving Life-Giver has given me permission to destroy you!" the evil prince laughed, thrusting his blade through her stomach again. "You didn't know that he is the one who told me to torture you?"

Mind-numbing pain gripped her; her head swam. *It can't be true. He loves me,* she thought.

The Holy Spirit whispered, "There are many seasons in this life, Hadassah. There is a time when the trees are green and a time when the trees are barren, a time when the north winds blow and a time when the south winds blow. All seasons come from My hand, and all have a purpose. It is both the season of prosperity and the season of suffering that bring spiritual growth and maturity."

Hadassah could not hear Him, for she had fainted. But her spirit heard every word.

***

The sun was low in the sky when Hadassah forced open her eyes. The vultures still circled overhead. Her mouth and throat were so dry that she could not swallow. There was no sign of Life-Giver; her heart sank. *I had hoped You'd come for me,* she said silently.

Her unwelcome tormentor glared at her from the rock. "I'm happy to see that you're still with me. How delightful, for I would not want my pleasure to end too soon."

If I die, I live, Hadassah thought.

The prince stood and looked behind him. With a wave of his hand, in just a matter of minutes, a dust storm rose up from the earth.

Satan and the dragon were in the midst of the storm.

Hadassah pulled her cloak over her head. It did little to keep the sand out of her mouth, nose and throat. She coughed and sputtered, trying desperately to breathe. Pain wracked her body. Mentally, she said over and over, "I may be afflicted, but I'm not crushed. Perplexed, but not despairing; persecuted, but not forsaken; struck down, but not destroyed. I *will* love You to the end!"

Michael turned to Life-Giver and said, "Hadassah possesses an uncommon love."

"Indeed she does," He said, praying fervently for her.

When the storm calmed, Hadassah used every bit of strength she had to push her way out from under the sand that threatened to bury her. She brushed the sand from her eyes and mouth but was unable to sit up. "I will love You to the end," she whispered.

"What! How dare you! Deny him!" the evil prince shouted.

"How can I deny the One who gave me life?" she said, her voice quite hoarse and weak.

"Deny him or die! He doesn't love you — if he did he wouldn't allow you to suffer," the evil prince screamed.

"Life-Giver suffered immensely for me. . . I'm honored to suffer a little for Him! He died for me, so how can I do any less for Him?"

"You're a fool! You could've had so much, and now you have nothing."

"I have everything that matters."

"Deny him!" he said, kicking her bleeding belly.

Hadassah gasped. Once she got her breath, she responded, "I will not deny Him. I'll go to my grave proclaiming that He's good." Lifting her eyes heavenward, she said, "Life-Giver, You mean everything to me, for I've found in You true love."

Life-Giver stepped through the veil. One glance from Him sent the evil prince running for cover.

Endless, Perfect Love cradled Hadassah in His arms. Brushing the hair from her face, He said, "Even in the face of death, your love for Me remains true and constant! Oh, how beautiful you are to Me!"

"You came for me," she whispered.

"I've been with you all along."

"I couldn't see or feel You."

"I know."

"I can see love in Your eyes," she whispered, the pain evident on her face.

"My love for you is stronger than the grave, and it will never end."

"I didn't believe You were with me. I'm sorry," she said, placing her trembling hand on His cheek. Her blood stained His face.

"But you remained faithful even though you believed I had abandoned you," He said, kissing the back of her hand as He stared in adoration at the bleeding life before Him.

"I'm not lonely anymore," she whispered. Her chin quivered as tears pooled in her eyes.

"Neither am I."

"You? Lonely?"

"Before I laid the foundation of the world, I longed for the day when you would become My bride — two hearts beating as One."

"I long for that, too. May I go with You now?" she asked, desperately trying to grasp His hand but lacking the strength.

"Not just yet, but it won't be long, My love. There is more. Remember, I am always with you — even when it does not seem like it."

"I won't forget this time, I promise," she said, her hand slipping out of His.

No sooner had His presence left than the evil prince returned, shouting, "Deny him or die!"

Ignoring his command, Hadassah looked for those things that cannot be seen with the natural eye.

"Then suffer the consequences." The evil prince put his foot on her belly and shouted, "I will not give up until you deny him!"

Hadassah remained silent. He pushed with all his might, but she felt nothing — she had fainted.

Hadassah lapsed in and out of consciousness for hours as the vultures kept watch. Each time she woke, the prince tormented her without mercy, but Hadassah remained faithful, crying out to the One whose love sustained her.

"Deny him!" the prince shouted for the hundredth time.

"I will die before I'll deny Perfect Love," she said, her words barely perceivable.

"Then let me help you!" he shouted, thrusting his blade into her chest. His evil laughter filled the air. The vultures screeched in response. *Countless demons danced wildly around the girl.*

Hadassah looked up into the pool-like eyes of her beloved Life-Giver. Purity and passion erupted from His heart like a volcano. She saw the earth reflected in His eyes and then she saw her face. Overwhelmed, she looked away, but only for a moment. "I did not know the depth or purity of Your love for me," she said silently.

"It is endless."

"Please let me die that I might live," her spirit prayed. With arms spread wide and heart exposed, Hadassah drew her last breath.

CHAPTER THIRTY-FOUR

Michael looked on with horror. "Life-Giver, the evil one has killed her."

"On the contrary, Michael, love has killed her in much the same way that it killed Me."

Life-Giver cradled Hadassah's bloody body, kissed the back of her hand and said, "Arise, My love, My fair one, and come away with Me!"

Hadassah's spirit stepped out of its fleshly confinement. She found herself fully alive and fully in love as she stood before Life-Giver. As He gazed into the depths of her being, she was keenly aware that He knew every thought and every deed she had ever done — and yet she saw nothing but acceptance and love in His eyes.

"I am loved in spite of my weakness!" she exclaimed.

He nodded, smiling broadly.

"And You are Life-Giver, Endless Love and the Lord Jesus Christ! You are Star-Breather, Perfect Love, the Beginning and the End! You are the Lamb of God, Lion of Judah, Prince of Peace, and Lord of all Hope! You are the great High Priest, the only way to the Father, the Bright and Morning Star! You are the Perfect Sacrifice, my Redeemer and my Advocate! You are the Bridegroom King, my Deliverer, my Healer and my Comforter! You are my Beloved, and You are my Friend!"

"I am all that and so much more."

"You loved me when I was nothing more than a worthless earthenware jar."

"No one is ever worthless, Hadassah. And before you knew Me, I said to My Father, 'I want her. I love her — she's Mine! Dress her in a bridal gown of fine linen, put a ring on her finger, place a crown on her head and capture her tears in a bottle.' Then I engraved your name on the palm of My hand."

Hadassah traced the letters and whispered, *"I'm finally home."*

"Indeed you are."

"You rescued me out of a deep, dark pit and carried me through this life. You took my shame as Your own. You were naked so I never would be — even now I stand dressed in Your righteousness. You have loved me so well."

"My love is powerful enough to save an entire world."

"I believe that."

The two stared into each other's eyes. Hadassah felt more alive and at peace than she ever had.

Life-Giver lifted His eyes. Hadassah followed His gaze and saw a staircase leading to a Door standing open in the midst of the clouds. A voice like the sound of a trumpet said, "Come up here!"

She looked at Life-Giver. Before she could ask, He answered, *"I am the Door, and no one comes to the Father except through Me."*

"It is only by Your grace that I stand before You."

"My grace is, was and always will be sufficient. It is now time for you to enter the rest that I prepared for you."

Immediately, she found herself running up the stairs. Standing in the Doorway, with one final look over her shoulder, she stepped through the Door onto thin air. To her amazement, a golden staircase appeared beneath her feet. Joy flooded her being as she raced to the top of the stairs.

Standing on the landing, she stared in disbelief at the scene before her. An endless, green pasture filled with a multitude of vibrant wildflowers awaited her arrival. The flowers swayed back and forth in the gentle breeze like dancers on a ballroom floor. Hundreds of gloriously colored butterflies fluttered here, there and everywhere. Various trees, tall and stately, greener than green, waved a thousand welcomes to her. Soft, billowy clouds floated carelessly across the bluer than blue sky. Hadassah was perplexed by the fact that there was no sun, yet glorious light flooded the place, leaving no room for shadows.

A snow-white Dove appeared in the distance, capturing her attention. Watching Him approach, Hadassah thought of the Dove who spoke to Beloved. The memory filled her with indescribable joy. The Bird glided effortlessly to a nearby olive tree and landed on a branch.

Hadassah walked through a world more glorious than anything she had ever seen or imagined. The grass was softer than a baby's bottom, the air cleaner than a mountain stream. She skipped and danced and sang her way through the pasture as countless butterflies fluttered all around her. A great variety of colorful birds filled the air with their delightful melodies. Hadassah could understand what they were singing — they were all singing about Life-Giver and the King.

The Dove flew over her head with an olive twig in its beak. Delighted, she followed Him to a babbling brook. Hadassah splashed into the ankle-deep water without any hesitation. She laughed and twirled her way to the middle of the stream. Taking a deep breath, she stopped to enjoy the awesome beauty surrounding her.

As the crystal clear water danced around her ankles, she heard its water song. It, too, sang praises to Life-Giver and the King. She began to tune into the sounds around her and discovered that she could also understand the grass song and the flower song and the butterfly song and the wind song. "Everything in this place appears to have a voice," she whispered to herself.

"It is as it should be," said the Dove, the leafy twig falling from His beak.

"Are You the Dove who spoke to Beloved?" she asked, catching the twig.

"I am," He answered, coming to rest on her shoulder.

"That was very kind of You; it changed her life."

"That is why her Father sent Me to the child."

"Why do You carry this twig in Your beak?" she asked, twirling it between her fingers.

"It is a reminder to heaven and earth that a time like the days of Noah is nigh at hand."

"What do You mean?"

"In the days of Noah, the people lived for selfish pleasure. They took no thought concerning their eternal destiny. They decided for themselves what was good and what was evil while mocking the truth. But there was one man who loved righteousness, therefore We saved him and his family. And so it shall be again. The earth is about to be thrust into deep darkness because of the gross injustice and evil that has saturated it. The darkness will seem to prevail, but it will only seem so for a moment."

"Is the earth going to be destroyed by a flood again?"

"Not by water, but by fire," said the Dove.

"How will anyone survive?"

"Nothing is impossible for the Great King."

As Hadassah thought about His words, a doe and her fawn stepped out of the trees. The doe greeted Hadassah before taking a drink. Unaccustomed to talking animals, Hadassah stuttered a response.

"Is this heaven?" she asked the Dove.

"It is what people on earth call heaven," He answered.

"It isn't anything like I thought it would be."

"And what did you think heaven would be like?"

"Clouds and harps and angels singing, I guess."

The Dove chuckled. *"There is so much more to this realm than that."*

"The trees, flowers, animals — all have life in a way they don't possess on earth," Hadassah said.

"As you can see, earth pales in comparison to the glory of this place."

He took flight once more, saying, *"Follow Me."*

Hadassah did just that. She followed the Dove toward a glorious temple set on a hilltop. She was awestruck by its beauty — the colors, the architecture, the sky and the surroundings — absolutely divine.

What is it about this temple? *she wondered.* It seems so familiar.

"You were born here," the Dove said.

"I was born here?"

"The day you accepted Life-Giver's gift of salvation you were born from above, from this place in the very heart of the King."

"I was born here," Hadassah repeated, feeling a sense of awe.

"Welcome home."

"I had no idea."

"Would you like to see the Great King?"

"Oh yes."

Hadassah followed the Dove up a steep and narrow pathway. Everyone they encountered was filled with perfect peace and love.

How different from most of the people I met on earth, *she thought.*

"You have entered a place of Sabbath rest, which means that all striving and works have ceased," the Dove said.

"A place where one doesn't focus on doing but on being?"

"Exactly."

"Amazing."

As they continued on, people greeted Hadassah as if they knew her intimately and accepted her completely.

"It feels like family, does it not?" the Dove asked.

"What I feel here is better and greater than anything I've ever known."

"It is as it should be."

The Dove led her on. Hadassah asked, *"How does one enter the courts of the Great King?"*

"You enter His gates with thanksgiving and His courts with praise," the Dove said as He landed on a golden lamppost just outside the temple.

"Is this the temple of the Great King?"

"There is no temple here, for the King and Life-Giver are its temple."

"I don't understand. What am I seeing?"

The Dove did not answer.

"Am I to enter in then?" she asked.

"You are already in," He answered, spreading His wings and taking flight.

To her amazement, when she turned around she stood before a glorious throne, but the One sitting on it was even more glorious. An emerald-colored rainbow was above the throne. Encircling the throne were twenty-four thrones where twenty-four elders sat clothed in white garments with golden crowns on their heads.

Coming out of the throne were flashes of lightning and sounds and peals of thunder. Burning before the throne were seven lamps of fire, which were the seven Spirits of God. In front of the throne was something like a sea of glass, like crystal. In the center and around the throne were four living creatures full of eyes in front and behind. The first creature was like a lion, and the second creature like a calf, and the third creature had a face like that of a man, and the fourth creature was like a flying eagle.

And the four living creatures, each one of them having six wings, were full of eyes around and within; and day and night they did not cease to say, "Holy, holy, holy is the Lord God, the Almighty, who was and who is and who is to come."

As the living creatures gave glory and honor and thanks to Him who sat on the throne, to the One who lives forever, the twenty-four elders fell down before Him. They worshiped Him who lives forever and cast their crowns before the throne, saying, "Worthy are You, our Lord and our God, to receive glory and honor and power; for You created all things, and because of Your will they existed, and were created."

Hadassah fell on her face, saying, "The angels, elders and saints bow before You and so do I! You are the eternal King, and You are my Father. I will worship You forever."

Hearing a sound like that of many waters behind her, she turned. Standing in the middle of the lampstands was One like a Son of Man, clothed in a white robe reaching to His feet. Girded across His chest was a golden sash. His head and hair were like white wool, like snow. His eyes were like a furnace. In His right hand, He held seven stars. His face was like the sun shining in its strength.

She fell at His feet like a dead person. He said, "Do not fear; I am the first and the last, and the living One. I was dead, and behold, I am alive forevermore! I possess the keys of death and of Hades."

Hadassah trembled at His words.

Life-Giver reached down with His right hand and lifted her to her feet, saying, "Two hearts now beat as one."

"My Beloved and my Friend," she said bowing low.

"Rise up, My love, My fair one, and come away with Me." He took her hand and led her down a long hallway. Angels bowed low as they passed.

Hadassah was acutely aware that the concept of being in a hurry or having to be somewhere at a certain time did not exist. Everything was present tense — everything was now — even the past and the future.

Life-Giver stopped before a wall of fire and said, "Your life is saved because of My blood sacrifice, but every word, every deed, every event, every thought must pass through this purifying fire. Those things that proceeded from the tree of life will remain. Those things that came from the tree of the knowledge of good and evil will be consumed."

"Will it hurt?" Hadassah asked.

"There is no fear in love," He reminded her. "And yes, there will be some aspects of your life and choices that you made that will cause you pain and regret. But have no fear, for I have overcome the world."

"I will do anything for You," Hadassah said as she stepped into the fire. Life-Giver followed close, picking up the jewels that fell around her feet. Hadassah felt great remorse as various events from her life flashed across her mind. Tears ran down her face. Life-Giver caught each tear and placed them in a bottle marked Tears of Regret. She watched as the wood, hay and stubble that fell from her was instantly consumed by the fire of His love.

I wish I had chosen to love more, *thought Hadassah.*

"It is redeemed — all of it. And I will use those things in your life that proceeded from My Father to make you a glorious crown."

As she stepped out of the fire, unspeakable joy flooded her being.

"In My presence is fullness of joy," Life-Giver said.

"I understand so clearly now that You, Life-Giver, were the Joy that was ever before me as I ran the race called life."

"As it shall always be," He said. Taking her hand, He continued, "Come, I am to lead you to the Judgment Seat."

"The judgment seat?" she asked, not liking what that implied.

"There is no fear in love, Hadassah."

Everything I think and feel is known here, *she thought.*

"You are right, all is known. And you will know as you are known."

Hadassah told herself to be careful what she thought. Life-Giver turned and looked at her, chuckling. Hadassah could not help but laugh.

As they entered the Judge's chambers, a Judge with snow-white hair said, "My child, approach the bench."

Trembling, Hadassah glanced at Life-Giver, who nodded. She cautiously approached and bowed low. When she looked up, an angel shrouded in a dim light stood on her left. The moment the angel spoke, she recognized its voice. "You're the one who tormented me in the desert," she said.

The hooded angel looked down at her. Hadassah gasped, for it was not the face of a man or an angel but the face of a serpent. The evil one turned his attention back to the Judge and presented his first accusation.

Hadassah had never felt so powerless or scared. She knew her life on earth was filled with many things of which she was guilty. She also knew her only hope was Life-Giver. Where is He, *she wondered as she looked around.*

At that moment, a Man appeared at her right. She looked at Him and gasped, for His face was horribly marred. "Life-Giver, is that You?" she whispered.

He smiled.

She heard an angel say, "Sin-Bearer has chosen to be her Advocate!"

"You are Sin-Bearer?"

"I am."

The Judge motioned for Sin-Bearer to speak. "The Accuser has no legal grounds for his indictment against this one. Every accusation belongs to Me; it is My sin the Accuser speaks of. I am the guilty One. Look closely, Your Majesty. Your child has been blood-bought and blood-cleansed — she stands here before You perfect and sinless. I am the One who stands before You accused and condemned."

The Judge said, "It is as it should be. Satan, you have no case against this one. She is not only not guilty, but I pronounce her innocent. She is free from judgment and condemnation."

A defeated Satan slithered out of the room. Hadassah recalled her papa's words, "If any one sins, he has an Advocate with the Father."

She sighed deeply. Turning to Sin-Bearer, she said, "May I ask who wounded You?"

"I was wounded in the house of My friends."

"Your friends did this to You, and You still call them Your friends?"

"Oh, but they are so much more than friends to Me now! Many are destined to rule and reign with Me as My bride. And you are one of them. I am even now preparing to return to the earth that I might bring justice to My bride and judge the evil found there."

Looking over Sin-Bearer's shoulder, Hadassah saw in the distance what appeared to be an endless army of angels gathering from the north, south, east and west. Without a word being spoken, Hadassah knew they were being commissioned for war.

"For such a time as this," Sin-Bearer announced, turning toward the angels.

They responded in unison, "The Deliverer has come."

Sin-Bearer's appearance changed before her eyes. His scars were gone and He was tall, strong and mighty in form. He took His place before the army. With arm raised high, He led them through the Door into the second heaven where Satan had established his throne. The battle had begun, and the cries coming from the earth caused Hadassah to shiver.

Hadassah was amazed that she could see the earth so clearly. Light, unlike anything she had ever seen, invaded the tiny planet, yet the earth grew darker than darkness itself. "How is that possible?" she asked.

"You are looking at Armageddon, the Battle of the Beginning," the Holy Spirit answered, now appearing before her as beautiful, blue Light.

"The beginning? I would think it would be the end."

"A thing must end if it is to begin again. This battle will bring an end to the reign of the evil prince and Satan. It will usher in the Age of all ages. In this new, glorious age, the Bridegroom-King will rule over the new earth and the new heaven, and His bride will reign with Him. And the masterpiece that she became will be revealed to angels, principalities, powers and the entire human race."

Hearing the cries of those being slaughtered by the great evil spreading across the face of the earth, Hadassah said, "So much pain, so much suffering."

"We do not view suffering in the same way humans view it," the Holy Spirit said.

"How so?"

"Suffering is meant to produce glory. Everything a human experiences on earth is meant to draw them closer to the King. Life is meant to be lived like an intoxicated lover — no fear, no inhibitions and no withholding of affections toward the One who loves you the most," the Spirit of God responded.

"That is what I desired."

"And that is exactly what We accomplished for and through you. Life-Giver did not go to earth to just save you, console you or make your life comfortable. His mission was to completely transform you.

"We have two highly effective methods to transform the human heart. One is through My residence within you; I continually work to expand and mature your spirit, which causes transformation to happen from the inside out. The other method is the cross and its sufferings, which consume and crucify those things that hinder Me from being able to fully possess you."

"Holy Spirit," Hadassah asked, "is it permitted for me to ask why I was orphaned and sold into slavery? Why did I lose my dear sister and friend?"

Drawing her close, He said, "While living on the earth, it is impossible to understand what a privilege and honor it is to be chosen to have fellowship in the sufferings of your Lord. You were born from above, and being born always involves pain and suffering for both the one giving birth and the one being born. But know this, the greater the pain, the nearer your King."

"I am most grateful now, but it's a bit harder to feel that way while on earth. I don't think I've ever thanked You for Your help, Holy Spirit. You were with me during my darkest times."

"It was and is My pleasure to serve you."

Hadassah marveled at the love and adoration she saw in His eyes. "This love I see in Your eyes, who is it for?"

"I am in love with both the Lion and the Lamb."

"Is Life-Giver the Lion and His bride the lamb?"

"*Life-Giver is both the Lion and the Lamb. He lived on the earth the first time as a sacrificial Lamb and the second time as a roaring Lion ushering in justice. His bride has been chosen to walk in His footsteps and live as He lived. Like Him, she is both a lion and a lamb.*"

"*So many mysteries.*"

"*Unconditional, sacrificial love will always be a mystery.*"

Hadassah suddenly perceived that Someone had walked up behind her. Turning, she found herself face to face with the Giver of all Life.

CHAPTER THIRTY-FIVE

Life-Giver smiled.

"I thought You were on earth leading the battle," said Hadassah.

"I am."

She giggled. "I forgot — again."

Taking her hand He said, "Come walk with Me."

"I will follow You anywhere."

As they walked, she somehow knew He was taking her to the King's chambers. "I just keep going from glory to glory," she said, feeling quite exhilarated.

"Eye has not seen, ear has not heard and heart has not conceived all that My Father has prepared for those who love Him."

Hadassah reveled in her newfound existence. Free from the myriad confinements, limitations and fears that permeated her life on earth, Hadassah's heart soared. This is what I was made for, she thought.

"That is true. You were created for My love, and there is absolutely no fear in love."

"I never knew I could feel so free. I now understand in a way I never thought possible that there really isn't any fear in true love."

"None at all," Life-Giver said, stopping before a beautiful, ornate Door that was at least twenty feet tall. The ancient Door hung on enormous gold hinges. As she ran her hand over the smooth wood,

she realized the story of creation was carved on its surface. What mysteries await me on the other side? *she wondered.*

"Why don't you look and see?"

She smiled and He nodded. Turning the golden handle, her heart raced. The Door opened on its own volition.

Glorious beams of light beckoned her to enter. As she stepped over the threshold, the Great King stood from His emerald throne. Every angel and human spirit bowed low, including Hadassah. It felt as though the universe itself fled from His holy gaze. Silence filled the heavens.

"Gather My godly one to Me," the King said as He took a step toward Hadassah.

Trembling, she pressed her face against the glassy sea, happy that Life-Giver stood in front of her.

"He's talking about you,' Life-Giver said, kneeling beside her.

"Me?"

"Yes, you. Why don't you run to the One who loves you the most?"

Hadassah slowly sat up. And when she did, the King opened His arms and smiled a thousand smiles. Feeling like a small child, she jumped up and ran into His embrace. He scooped her up and spun her around. Nestled against His heart, Hadassah's spirit reveled in the immensity of His love for her. "You really do love me," she whispered.

"I really do," He said as He carried her back to His throne. Placing her on His knee, He continued, "Hadassah, you loved not your life unto death and you learned to love — even your enemies."

"Only because You first loved me."

"Indeed I did."

According to time on earth, Hadassah remained snuggled in His arms for twelve months. The King thoroughly enjoyed having His daughter so close. He delighted in answering her many questions. At the end of that time the Great King said, "Hadassah, being seated with Me in heavenly places gives you a clear view of your former residence."

"It does?" she asked, looking in the direction of His gaze.

On the earth, blinding Light clashed against gross darkness, pushing it back and subduing it.

The King said, "Light-Bearer will usher in My glory, which will cover the earth like the water covers the sea."

"I thought Deliverer was leading the fight."

"Life-Giver, Deliverer and Light-Bearer are One and the Same."

"I never knew Life-Giver to be a warrior. He always came to me as a gentle, loving Friend — fierce against sin but kind toward sinners."

"Sin was defeated on the cross. It is evil that He fights now," He said. "And woe to His enemies, for He is a fierce Defender and devoted Lover."

Watching the bloody scene, Hadassah shuddered, feeling quite thankful that she was not His enemy. "I pray that Light wins."

"My dear child, there is no doubt that I win. The victory has been secured, but the battle must be fought."

For the first time, Hadassah noticed something flowing from beneath the throne. She looked closer. "There's a crystal clear river flowing beneath this sea of glass," she said.

"It is the River of Life," the King said.

"What purpose does it serve?"

"Those who live here wash in it."

"May I wash in it?" Hadassah asked with an excitement that far surpassed anything she ever felt on earth.

"You may," He answered, extending His arm toward the river and smiling.

Hadassah slid from His lap and followed the river as it flowed beneath the glassy floor. The life-giving water flowed through the throne room, out the east door and into a grassy meadow. On either side of the river was a tree, heavy laden with fruit. Fascinated, Hadassah stopped and counted twelve different kinds. "It is the tree of life," her Father said.

Turning her attention back to the river, she sailed through the air making a big splash. Sinking, she saw that the water had turned blood-red. She felt no fear, only peace. Surrendering to the blood-bath, she continued to sink. As she did, she discovered she was able to breathe under water. "How is this possible?" she asked aloud.

The Holy Spirit answered, "Nothing here is as it was on earth and that includes you. You no longer have a human body, Hadassah."

"Oh, I forgot," she said, giggling. "Holy Spirit, I hear You but I can't see You."

"I am everywhere, all of the time."

"I knew that," she said, laughing.

The water felt as though it permeated her being. Again the Spirit spoke, "Life instead of death, blessing instead of curses, freedom instead of punishment — the gift of unconditional love and eternal life instead of death and the grave."

"What a glorious gift!" Hadassah exclaimed as she stepped out of the water. "So strange that a red river can make me whiter than snow."

"Nothing is more powerful than the blood of the Lamb," He responded. "You may now eat from the tree of life."

As she approached the tree, Hadassah felt a tremendous sense of wonder. "Which one should I eat?" she asked, nearly overcome with joy.

"You may have your heart's desire, for they all contain eternal life," said the Great King.

Hadassah chose a large orange and red striped fruit. Biting into its juicy flesh, she closed her eyes and moaned deeply.

The Spirit chuckled and said, "Blessed are those who wash their robes, so that they may have the right to the tree of life and may enter by the gates into the city."

"It is as it should be," her Father said.

Hadassah eagerly devoured the truly satisfying fruit.

"I am blessed beyond the curse!" said Hadassah. "I don't believe I've ever tasted anything so good."

"That is what they all say," the Spirit and the King said in unison.

"Come, My precious daughter," said her Father. Taking her hand, He led her into a beautiful, sunny courtyard. On the far side of the yard was a walled city.

Hadassah stared in awe of the amazing structure before her. The foundation was made of precious stones.

"This is the new Jerusalem," the King said. "There are four walls, each having three gates. The gates of this city are pearls and will never be closed. And you, Hadassah, are to live there."

"*Really?*" she asked. *Without waiting for a response, Hadassah ran to the gate. An angel stopped her.* "*Is your name written in the Lamb's Book of Life?*" *he asked.*

"*I don't know,*" *Hadassah said, surprised again that she felt no fear or anxiety.*

"*Perfect Love casts out all fear,*" *the angel said as he opened an ancient book and turned the whiter-than-snow pages. Looking up, he smiled and said,* "*Your name is indeed written here. You may enter the eternal city.*"

"*What else is written there?*" *she asked, standing on her toes.*

"*Just your name. The story of your life is written in that book,*" *he answered, pointing to the book on the other side of the gate.*

"*May I?*" *she asked as she hurried to the rather large book.*

"*You may.*"

Hadassah ran her hand over the leather cover. "*The Book of Remembrances,*" *she read. Her name was written on the title page. The first three chapters recorded every detail of her conception, birth and childhood. The fourth chapter began with her acceptance of Life-Giver as her Savior.*

"*Why are so many pages blood-stained?*" *she asked as she flipped through the remaining pages.*

"*The blood stains are all that remain of your sin,*" *the angel answered.*

"*My sins are not recorded in heaven! They're truly gone. It's as if they never happened!*"

"*In heaven's eyes, because of the blood of the Lamb, they did not happen.*"

"*Amazing love,*" *Hadassah said, as she looked over her shoulder at the King.* "*Thank You,*" *she called out.*

The King nodded and then responded, "*It is My pleasure to give you the kingdom. Now enter into the place prepared for you.*"

Closing the book, Hadassah approached the beautiful gate. As she stepped through, she stopped abruptly. Waiting for her, shining bright and clear, was her dear sister, Rebekah.

The two sisters squealed and embraced. "*I missed you so much,*" *Hadassah said repeatedly.*

"*I can't say that I missed you, dear sister, because I have been well aware of your life. It is as if I was with you. I did intercede for you every step of the way. I am so very proud of you, for you loved not your life unto death."*

"You saw me?"

"Yes. And not just me, but you had a whole crowd of witnesses watching and praying."

She's even more beautiful now, *Hadassah thought.*

"Everyone here is beautiful. Haven't you noticed?"

"I thought only the King and Life-Giver knew my thoughts."

"Everybody knows everybody's thoughts," Rebekah explained.

"It's going to take me some time to grow accustomed to this," Hadassah said, laughing freely.

"Time exists on the other side of the veil, Dassah. You now live free from the restrictions of time."

"Bekah, it's so different here. Nothing at all like I thought."

"That is true, dear sister. And the glories awaiting you make the difficulties of your earth-life so insignificant in comparison."

"I am already aware of that and I've only been here a short time. There I go again talking about time. Perhaps I should say that I've only just begun to experience this realm. Rebekah, I'm so very glad I found that scroll."

"Finding the truth was not enough; you had to believe and pursue it — and that you did."

Arm in arm, Rebekah escorted Hadassah on a tour of the eternal city. The street was pure gold, like transparent glass. The city had no need of the sun or of the moon because the glory of the King illuminated it.

Engrossed in conversation, Hadassah did not notice the small child running toward her until the girl was upon her. "Hadassah!" the girl exclaimed as she threw her arms around Hadassah.

Hadassah looked down and her heart soared. "My dear, dear Beloved! Oh, glorious day!"

Beloved said, "Life-Giver told me you were here, but I was givin' the young ones piggy back rides. They kept beggin' me for just one more. And I couldn't bear to leave them, for they're so delightful."

"I'm so very happy to see you, dear one."

"And I'm so happy you're here. Hadassah, there's so much for you to see and experience. You'll be so glad you're here and not down there." She pointed through the open Door to the dark earth.

"I'm already glad."

Beloved looked absolutely beautiful. There was no darkness, no pain, nothing impure, no flaws or any evidence that there ever were any.

I wonder if I look different. *Hadassah was just about to ask when she heard familiar voices calling her name. She turned to see her mama and papa hurrying toward her. If Hadassah had had a physical heart, it surely would have burst.*

"Oh, happy, happy, happy day!" she exclaimed as they ran into each other's arms.

"My beautiful treasure," her papa said. "Welcome to your eternal home." His bright countenance reflected his immeasurable joy.

"My dear one, how glorious you are," her mama added as she kissed Hadassah's face, the love evident in her eyes.

"How young and strong and healthy you both look!" said Hadassah, taking a step back.

"The King makes all things new and beautiful," her mama said.

Her papa said, "Your journey was difficult. But Life-Giver proved faithful, and you held fast to Life."

"I missed you both terribly," Hadassah said. "Did you know that Martha is married?"

"Yes, dear, we can see everything that happens on earth. Did you know that she has given birth to a beautiful baby girl? She named her Hadassah Rebekah. Little Dassah is almost a year old now, according to earth time, and what a precious child she is. Martha and Caleb no longer live in Jerusalem. Life-Giver led them to another land far from the battle," her mama answered.

"I am so full of joy that I'm afraid I might burst."

"You need not fear that," her papa said, chuckling. "Your capacity for pure emotions is now endless. You live in a place where there are no limits to faith, hope, love, joy or peace."

Just like the Great King, Life-Giver and the Holy Spirit, *Hadassah thought.*

"Come now," her papa said, "let us join together and intercede with our Lord for those still living on the earth."

"You always were a praying man," she said, laughing. Her laughter actually contained life as it echoed endlessly throughout the heavenly city.

***

All of heaven prayed fervently as the battle on earth escalated. Blood ran like water through the streets of Jerusalem as countless vultures blocked the light of the sun over the holy city.

The final blow came when Light-Bearer stormed the gates of Jerusalem and threw the anti-Christ and his prophet, the evil prince, into the bottomless pit. Having cleansed the city of all evil, Light-Bearer sat on the throne. And when He did, great joy flooded heaven and earth.

Hadassah was dancing with King David on the streets of gold when she noticed a horribly marred Man walking toward her. She thought it was Sin-Bearer but quickly dismissed that idea, because this Man was dressed in royal garments unlike anything she had ever seen or imagined. Even though He was terrible to look at, she was strangely drawn to Him.

"Do I know you?" she asked, trying not to stare at His hideous wounds.

"I am the One who purchased you."

"Life-Giver?"

"I Am."

"I'm sorry, but I didn't recognize You. I've never seen You like this."

"I come to you as the Bridegroom God."

"Where are You going?"

"To My wedding."

"I don't quite understand — are You a Man or God?"

"I am fully God and fully Man. I laid aside My glory, forever, that I might bear My bride's sin, shame, flaws, mistakes and humanity. This is the price I paid to purchase mankind from slavery."

"I am forever grateful to You, and I love You for it," Hadassah said as she bowed low, her forehead touching the sea of glass. She smiled, for her reflection looked just like Life-Giver.

"Arise, My love, My fair one, and come with Me," He said, offering her His hand. She placed her hand in His as she stood before Him.

The hideous scars were gone. He now stood before her perfect in every way.

"You are the Lover of my soul, are You not?"

"I AM that I AM," He responded, smiling broadly.

Hadassah looked deep within His Being. She saw her Father and the Holy Spirit resident within Him. "You really are One and the same," she whispered.

"Three hearts beating as One," the Bridegroom God said in unison, their voices like the sound of many waters.

Hadassah heard what sounded like a multitude of people singing in the distance. Looking behind her she saw a sea of people — men, women, children and infants singing praises to the King. Every tongue, tribe and nation was represented. As the glorious throng approached, Hadassah excitedly joined them, and they became one bride with one voice and one heart. "You are Faithful and True. You are the One and Only," they sang.

The Bridegroom God took His bride's hand and said, "There were many who did great things for Me, but you, made Me great, instead of yourself."

"Faith, hope and love — and the greatest of these is eternal Love," said the bride.

"And love never fails," Hadassah added.

"It is as it should be," said the bride and the Bridegroom in perfect unison.

As innumerable angels escorted the heavenly Jerusalem and the Bridegroom God to the earth, the Father called His Son's name.

"Yes, Father?"

"My Beloved Son, she won't reject You this time."

The End and the Beginning

Then I saw a new heaven and a new earth;
for the first heaven and the first earth passed away,
and there is no longer *any* sea.

And I saw the holy city, new Jerusalem,
coming down out of heaven from God,
made ready as a bride adorned for her husband.

And I heard a loud voice from the throne, saying,
"Behold, the tabernacle of God is among men,
and He will dwell among them,
and they shall be His people,
and God Himself will be among them,
and He will wipe away every tear from their eyes;
and there will no longer be *any* death;
there will no longer be *any* mourning,
or crying, or pain;
the first things have passed away."

And He who sits on the throne said,
"Behold, I am making all things new."

Rev 21:1-5a

A Personal Invitation from the Author

One of many amazing facts about God is that He does not want anyone to spend eternity without Him. He loves and desires even the vilest of sinners to become part of His family. He loves the weak, the lost and the least – no one is too broken to be loved.

His invitation offers something that money cannot buy. That something is an eternal existence spent with your Creator. An existence that is so much more than eternal. By accepting His invitation, you will find yourself fully enveloped by perfect Love. No more tears, no more sorrows. No more struggles or striving. You will be free from all fleshly confines – fully alive and fully *in* Love.

His invitation is free for everyone, but it must be received. Like a wedding, if both parties don't say yes the marriage never happens.

Our Father sent His Son to the earth to purchase us back from Satan's rule. He paid the price, but we must accept His ransom in order to be free from eternal death. Accepting it is easy, but like marriage, it takes a lifetime of walking with Him to experience the full measure of His gift.

The invitation is here. What are you going to do about it? Will you ignore the invitation, set it aside, reject it or embrace it? Be very careful, for your answer determines your eternal future.

Will you put your hand in His and accept His gift of eternal life? He has made it so simple, but it does require trust and surrender. If you find yourself wavering, ask Him to give you what you need to take this life-changing step. You will be so glad you did – especially on the day you stand before His throne.

If you would like to respond, the following is an example of what your prayer might be.

Rhonda Calhoun

God,

I acknowledge that I need a Savior. I believe that Jesus (Yeshua) is the Son of God and that He died to set me free from sin and death. I have sinned and I know that Jesus (Yeshua) is my only hope. I can't save myself. Therefore, I accept Your gift of salvation and Your gift of eternal life with You. I offer You my life in return.

Thank You for forgiving me of all of my sins and accepting me into Your family. Now fill me with your Holy Spirit, lead me on the narrow path and live Your life through me. In the name of Jesus (Yeshua), I pray. Amen.

***

Once you've accepted His invitation, it is important for you to find a community of believers who will walk with you as you continue your personal journey to the palace of the Great King. You've just begun a glorious life that has no end. Welcome to the family of God!

For My Beloved King and Savior,

Rhonda

Announcing:

TREE OF LIFE
Gifts of Encouragement

Go to www.TreeOfLifeGifts.com to find all of the **books** and **teachings** by **Rhonda Calhoun**. There's also a newly-designed t-shirt. We have some wonderful, new items in the works and will be updating the site as these become available, so be sure to visit the website often!

*❧ **Tree of Life Gifts** was created with a dual purpose:*

1. To provide you with products that teach, inspire, and encourage.
2. To help support the various projects of Harvest Home, Inc., which hosts summer camps for kids and also provides a place and a process for women and young girls who've suffered abuse to find healing. To learn more about this ministry, please visit www.harvesthome.org.

❧

*For more information or to order items by phone please call Danny at **816 522-9011**.*

www.TreeOfLifeGifts.com

MORE BOOKS
by Rhonda Calhoun:

Great Gift Ideas!

❧ **The Bride** ~ *The Bride* is a fascinating and life-changing allegory based on the Song of Solomon. You will enjoy the journey with a young shepherdess as the King of kings wins her heart and reveals his glorious character. This book will delight your heart and create a greater desire to know and be known by your Bridegroom King!

❧ **The Simon Peter Trilogy** ~ (*Simon Peter and the Master, Simon Peter and the King, and Simon Peter and the Savior*) ~ This story portrays the relationship between Simon Peter and Jesus through Peter's perspective. Rhonda artistically presents a fictional portrayal of Peter's account by using the real events portrayed in the four gospels. This story reveals the beauty of God's grace, the endless nature of His unconditional love, the power of His extravagant forgiveness, and the tremendous mark all of these left on Simon Peter.

❧ **The Great I AM** ~ *"Come on a journey with Me,"* God is inviting to all who will listen. Experience in vivid color the nature and personality of The Great I AM through Rhonda Calhoun's personal interactions with the Lover of our souls. You will encounter His passion and depth in ways rarely discussed, and may even find yourself caught up with Him in your own personal visions and experiences. We believe this book will greatly impact all who read it.

❧ **Beautiful!** ~ A children's story about God celebrating the birth of a baby girl. While praying for her newborn granddaughter and soon-to-be-born grandson, Rhonda whispered, *"Father, what happens in heaven when a baby is born?"* Images and words suddenly flashed through her mind. Grabbing a pen and paper, she captured the story, and *Beautiful* and *Valiant* (about the birth of a son) were born.

All of these books, *and so much more*, can be found at
www.TreeOfLifeGifts.com